# WANTED
# FUGITIVE

*a novel*

## MIGUEL OLMEDO

Visit our website at
**www.StillwaterPress.com**
for more information.

First Stillwater River Publications Edition

ISBN: 978-1-965733-99-8 (paperback) 978-1-968548-00-1 (hardcover)

Library of Congress Control Number: 2025918188

1 2 3 4 5 6 7 8 9 10

Publisher's Cataloging-in-Publication
*Provided by Cassidy Cataloguing Services, Inc.*

Names: Olmedo, Miguel, author.
Title: Wanted fugitive : a novel / Miguel Olmedo.
Description: First Stillwater River Publications edition. | West Warwick, RI,
    USA : Stillwater River Publications, [2025]
Identifiers: LCCN: 2025918188 | ISBN: 9781965733998 (paperback) |
    9781968548001 (hardcover)
Subjects: LCSH: Murder--Fiction. | Multiple personality--Fiction. |
    Psychotropic drugs--Fiction. | Antidotes--Fiction. | Confession of
    judgment--Fiction. | LCGFT: Thrillers (Fiction) | Medical fiction. |
    Detective and mystery fiction.
Classification: LCC: PS3615.L5893 W36 2025 | DDC: 813/.6--dc23

Written by Miguel Olmedo.
Published by Stillwater River Publications,
West Warwick, RI, USA.

*Wanted Fugitive*

# TABLE OF CONTENTS

# PROLOGUE

I was then thrown back into solitary. It was the lowest thing in my life since I ran away ten years ago. I knew my life as a runaway was going to be bad, but I didn't expect that it was going to be this bad. For ten years, I'd failed to keep my anger under control. I'd failed to find peace, and finally, I failed to succeed. I realized if I wanted peace, I would have sought it years ago. If I could start all over again, I would have found a way and still be who I was.

It was nice to have memories before my dark side was unleashed. That life was the only thing that was close to my heart, and it became nothing but a memory. For about one month, I had been in solitary with crummy old food that the guards gave me. My heart became hardened, and I'd become unfeeling. I grew a small beard and had a lot of hatred and distrust toward others. I wanted to die so badly, and I didn't care if it was quick or slow because I had already experienced all the pain this world had to offer.

I began to hear voices again, saying, "You weakling."

I began to yell with a loud voice, "Shut up! This is your fault!"

"No, it's his, remember?" Then I understood that he was referring to someone—not the man in black but instead Dr. Patrick Barton.

I then replied, "Go to hell!" Then I felt a slap on my face, and D appeared out of nowhere, yelling, "This is hell, and I'm the devil."

Then the voices began to laugh over and over. I thought I was going to crack when suddenly, to my shock, a guard opened the door and said, "You're free."

Then he escorted me to the lunchroom, with my hands shaking. I then went to receive my lunch, with my hands still shaking.

About eight seconds later, it was slapped down by none other than Henri Lombardi, who was, for most patients and guards, a king. But to me, he was a bully.

After he slammed my food on the floor, he looked at me and sarcastically said, "Oops."

He saw me shaking and thought I was afraid, but I was only shaking because I was pissed. I saw Brendan Johnson at his table, eating while laughing at what Lombardi did—not just Johnson, but everyone else. This started to fuel me up, but not as much as what Lombardi said.

"I heard that Mexican slut left you. Maybe some of my boys could pick up her curvy ass and show her what a real man—or men—can do for her, huh, James?"

"There's only one problem," I said.

"What problem?"

"I'm not James."

Then I blacked out.

At that moment, I knew that it was too late for me to be redeemed. My life didn't matter. My history in the resistance was irrelevant. Now James David Truman was sentenced to death by my fellow rebels at the resistance. Blackstone let it happen because of the deformity of Blackstone patient Henri Lombardi, who suffered multiple physical traumas and nearly death by—you guessed it—me, or in reality, my other half.

After I blacked out, I realized D turned Henri Lombardi's face and body into a physically scarred, toothless, and hideous freak. According to those who saw me doing it, they said that I beat him so badly he began screaming, with blood splattering everywhere and on the guards' uniforms, who were yelling, "Get off him!"

One of them was that jackass who body-slammed me. He stabbed me with a syringe in my neck, and then I grabbed it and stabbed him in the eye with it, leaving him in agony, while some of the guards came to his aid and others still tried to stop me from killing Lombardi. According to Brendan Johnson, he saw me turn Lombardi backward and grab the lower part of his back by squeezing through his skin, and everyone heard a horrible crack so loud it sounded like I was twisting his spinal cord, and Lombardi began to cry.

Then the guards began punching me over and over in the head, hoping to knock me out. Another kicked me in the cheek, and I bit his leg like an animal and nearly chewed off another guard's finger.

While all this happened, they saw me getting up while grabbing Lombardi by the neck as if I was going to break it, but then I began to feel weak, and I fell to the floor.

While I realized what happened, I asked myself, why did this happen to me? Who would care to answer that question? I did the crime, and somewhere around 12:41 a.m., I would have my brain cut, leaving me brain-dead. Everyone, even my lover Celia, considered me a lost cause. Before, Celia gave me a quote from Psalm 23.

After she had given it to me, she left to go back to her old life. I knew in that moment I wouldn't see her again.

I was then told by the guards, the Bartons, and even McNally and Talbot, who looked at me in my room, "It's time, kid." I was escorted to a van with other lost causes. I thought a lot about Celia and wished the best for her.

About two hours later, the driver drove us to the resistance hideout, which had now become a base since I left. The city became cleaner and brighter and had people for the first time without green jumpsuits. Now they wore average clothing that I heard was later found from the state of an extinct race. Everybody seemed to see the light in this world, but to me, all I saw was darkness. The van stopped, and I was led with the others to be executed.

And lo and behold, I was the first one. When I went inside, a rebel gave me a sedative so I wouldn't fight back. My hair was shaved, and I was escorted to be sedated.

When I lay down, they put restraints on me. I saw in a window all the faces of everyone that were my friends and partners. I felt destroyed, but not as much as when I saw a lady looking at me—and only me. It was Henri Lombardi's mother, looking at me with disgust, and in that moment, I felt broken.

Then I heard a voice saying, "You have anything to say?"

I then turned with a sad voice, "I—" Then suddenly, to my horror, in the window, I saw him. I saw the man in black, with the crowd of people looking at me. I yelled, "Oh my God! It's him! Get him!" Then I saw Dr. Barton, and I yelled, "Doctor, he's there! It's the guy that did this to me! Get him!" I yelled even louder, "He's right there! He's right there next to you!"

Then I saw the man in black leaving the building, but before that, Dr. Barton turned and saw the back of his body for the first time. He then looked at me and yelled, "James!" Then in a blink of an eye, out of nowhere, just as the man in black was leaving, I was in a fiery explosion!

All I could remember before the explosion went off was a huge, bright light that came from the glass. I was so terrified I believed I was going to die. When I woke up, I was on the floor, and blood was coming through my nose.

A lot of things happened during that night. I was surrounded by smoke, fire, and electricity. I tried to get up, but I realized I was still in restraints. But at the same time, because of the shock of the explosion, the sedative burned out of my system, and I could feel more active. But I knew it still didn't matter because I was going to burn unless I did something!

I tried to get out of the restraints, but one of my arms was too connected to the ropes, which made it impossible to break out the easy way. So, I made a brutal choice. I broke my arm so the ropes could loosen a bit. I got out and started to find my way through to save my friends and partners. But sadly, because of my arm being damaged, I only managed to save three people: Dr. Barton, Sarah, and McNally. The rest of them—the rebels, Talbot, even Lombardi's mom—wouldn't make it.

I then ran to the woods when suddenly I was pushed to the ground, and the rest of my friends fell like rag dolls. I turned and saw the man in black. I then got up and tried to tackle him, but he punched me on the cheek, and I fell to the ground. Then he started kicking my face over and over again to the point when my nose started to get bloody.

I then tried to reach the others, but he pulled me away by the leg and said, to my surprise, "You know, I'm the only one who can fix you. Too bad you won't live for that to happen. I'll be going to Hong Kong."

Then he picked up a rock and threw it at my head, and I fell unconscious. About eleven minutes later, I woke up, and I saw everyone still on the ground and in their same position—except Dr. Barton.

I came over and saw something on his head. I realized it was a knife. "Barton!" I yelled.

Then, while feeling like my head was squeezing from the inside as if a machine was putting pressure on it, I crawled to him and tried to pull out the knife. Blood poured out from his head.

I yelled out in horror, "Don't bleed, please!"

Then I heard a voice from one of the people I saved. I turned and saw it was Sarah. She turned and saw me with the knife next to Dr. Barton, and I foolishly thought she was going to ask, "Who did this?" But my heart sank when she said, "What have you done to my husband?"

I turned to the knife and Dr. Barton's remains and realized what she meant.

"It wasn't me, Sarah."

I explained to Sarah, but she refused to believe me, then tried to shoot me, saying, "I should have after I told you the truth about who I was."

I was stunned and heartbroken that our friendship had come to this.

"Get the hell away from my husband!"

"Sarah, I didn't do this."

"Screw you!" Then she shot me where my arm was broken. I was in a hell of a lot of pain. The bullet felt like metal going through my bones. I then tried to escape from the woods while she was shooting at me.

I was almost to the streets, but I fell to the ground, with my damaged arm next to a log. At that moment, I decided to give in and let her kill me. I realized it was impossible for me to go on, so I waited for her to find me and shoot me. I sat down with my arm and my head swelling, with a bloody nose dripping onto the dirt.

I then began to close my eyes and said, "It's over."

Five seconds later, I saw Sarah coming closer. I just didn't care anymore. So, I waited.

While waiting, I heard a voice, but this time it wasn't an evil voice but something else. The voice sounded like someone I knew, but I had no idea who it was. It said, "Don't give up."

I replied to whoever it was, "There's no hope for me."

"Maybe for me, but there's always hope for the living. If you die here, then my killer wins."

Then the voice stopped, and I realized that voice. I decided to say to myself, You're right, Dr. Barton. I won't give up! Then I got up on my two legs and ran to freedom.

Behind me, I heard Sarah yelling, "James!"

I turned and said, "Goodbye, Sarah." I then lowered my head for about five seconds and ran off and never looked back.

ONE YEAR LATER

Now my journey began. I wrote this while visiting the graves of thirty innocent civilians who were killed by the explosion. While twenty of them survived, they suffered third-degree burns in many parts of their bodies. Four people had perished in that explosion, including Mark Talbot, Henri Lombardi, Nicole Lombardi, and yes, even Patrick Barton—the husband of an old friend who was now searching for me so I would be lobotomized.

As the new leader of Smart City, Sarah had made me public enemy number one. She mistook me for killing her husband and for planning the explosion that harmed fifty innocent civilians. To this day, I was haunted by that reality.

I hoped that someday, somehow, society would know the truth.

I would always wish to live a normal life, have kids, and die old, but now I saw that was impossible after what happened. Even if I would find the man in black, how was I going to pick up the threads of an old life? How could I go on when I knew there was no turning back and that all I saw was darkness? The best I could do was find the real killer and make him confess for killing Dr. Barton, along with others, and force him to heal me.

I never asked for this life. But just as I was running away from my family, I was also running away from my friends and even Celia. But no matter how bad it might seem, I would find a way out because even though it was a long shot, it was all that was keeping me going—not just to survive but also to prove that everybody who hated me to this day was wrong about me and that I was not a mistake. I would seek justice for the death of Dr. Patrick Barton.

This was January 1, 2024.

I was leaving the gravesite of fifty poor souls, some of whom I once knew, before I took a boat out of Smart City with the alias of Robert Dent. I had already grown a goatee and cut my hair short, with a few new clothes that were previously from another lifetime that I had inside my backpack. I decided to use these to cover my identity.

I would hope when I escaped, there was not going to be a storm, and I prayed it wouldn't interfere with my quest to find Dr. Patrick Barton's murderer. But now, to this day, what mattered was to run and to keep on running until I made that bastard responsible for destroying my life. I would make him confess for what he'd done, and I refused to go back and get my brain cut open, especially when my own friend thought I killed her husband.

I would never give up, and I would never forget until I found the man in black—and I knew where the bastard was going. I hoped to find him there, to unmask him, make him confess, and cure me of this evil.

I'd be going to Hong Kong, hoping to find him. He was probably working for another crook similar to Linda Smith, but whatever it took, I would find him—hopefully sooner than later.

My name is James David Truman, and I'm a wanted fugitive.

I

# THE BUM SHIP

It was a very stormy night. I was alone for the first time since I ran away from home. I dressed in a black jacket, a yellow polo shirt, brown boots, and khaki pants. My head was shaved. I also have a goatee instead of a beard. I was traveling around with my brown backpack and planning to go on a boat far away, but it wasn't a boat for citizens, but an illegal boat for undocumented immigrants. So instead of me asking for my ID or my name,

I was led downstairs to a room that smelled like something took a crap. The bed was filled with pornographic magazines that had somebody's sperm covering all of them. The floor looked like someone vomited, and when I dared to sit on that filthy couch, it easily snapped. I almost became furious, but I knew if I did lose my mind, who knows what my other half might cause.

I then said to myself that I can't stand living in this filth, so I decided to go outside and smell the ocean. I happened to think a lot about Celia, McNally, and Sarah. I felt like I had failed them. I also started to feel that I'm failing to find The Man in Black.

It has been a year, and I slowly began to doubt not just being able to find him, but if he even existed since I was the only person with the knife when I woke besides Dr. Barton. I was afraid that what if The Man in Black wasn't real, and I really did kill Sarah's husband. While this was happening, I saw a man being pushed around by some thugs, so I ran at them and started punching them to the ground. While they were on the floor, I yelled at them to leave the man alone. I tried to give that man a hand, but he slapped my wrist and yelled, "I don't need your help."

"Okay, just tell me why these thugs pushed you around?" and he said, "I don't have to tell you a damn thing, so just go!" I decided to walk away and told the captain on the boat that a man was being beaten up. He looked at me, and then suddenly I felt as if I was hit by a hammer. Then I fell to the floor unconscious.

Then about either twenty or thirty minutes later, I was awake, but I couldn't see and could barely breathe. I was trying to move, but my hands and feet were tied, and so was my mouth. I thought to myself, what is this? Then I realized I was in a bag with three bricks next to me. I later heard someone saying these words, "Are you sure he is unconscious along with the other one?" And the voice was somewhat familiar, but I couldn't tell for sure because of the bag making it hard for me to understand.

But about a few seconds later, I was able to recognize the voice, and it was the captain. I yelled for help with my mouth gagged. Suddenly, I heard another voice, and that person said to him, "Here's one, twenty thousand dollars." I realized that the captain just sold me. I was so mad that I thought I was going to explode. Then the bastard said to the other one, "Throw him in the river." Then I got scared and was trying to break out, but I couldn't move. I was starting to freak out so much that I could hear D's voice in my head screaming, "Let me out!" Then about ten seconds later, I was thrown into the water. I then realized that the person who gave the worker a hundred dollars was The Man in Black, but at the same time, I felt I was going to die drowning. Until suddenly, the ropes from my hands were broken, and I blacked out.

I then woke up to realize that I was suddenly on the ship again. I then realized that something was very different about the ship, so much so that I said, "Is it just me, or has this place become a lot dirtier than it was before?" Next to my hand was the same man who slapped my wrist, but this time he was unconscious. I realized that somehow, in some way, D saved his life... but why?

Before I could continue thinking that, I began to hear footsteps coming. I believed it was the worker and The Man in Black, so I grabbed this guy on my back and began to save ourselves while hiding. I ran while holding him, but it just made it slower. I realized I couldn't just leave him, so I went along with it. I went downstairs running when the guy I was holding began to wake up. He yelled, "Hey!" I told him to be quiet. I then realized that the footsteps were coming downstairs. So, I then realized that there was no way I could get out easily, so I let him down and tried to break the window in my room. About three seconds later, I realized it was starting to get hard to break. I thought to myself, "We're screwed!"

Yet suddenly, I realized that the person who I was about to confront turned out to be not one of the workers but instead another man. And this time it turned out to be just one of the homeless men. He looked at me and said, "Could you keep it down while I'm sleeping?!" Then I said to myself, "Really?!" About a few seconds later, I went to the man I was carrying and was trying to wake him up. He looked at me with these large blue eyes and said, "Get off me, slug ass."

"Hey, I just saved your life."

I said, "By what?"

"By that psycho worker!" And the man who came downstairs said to me, "There's nobody here, dude. This boat is abandoned."

"But I thought someone was here?" I spoke.

Then the man I saved said, "Don't tell me you're homeless and crazy."

I got a little pissed off and yelled, "I'm not crazy!" After I yelled, they both were in shock and stayed silent for a while. Then I went up the stairs only to, to my horror, realize I'm really in an abandoned ship. I thought to myself, "Am I going crazy?"

I felt horrified, so much so that two men went to me and said, "Are you okay?"

I then shrugged them off by saying to them, "Yeah, whatever."

Then I decided to go upstairs, but before I did, I asked the men their names. They replied to me by saying, "My name is Mike De Veny," and the other said, "My name is John Doe. I was in a hospital, and I woke up with no memory of before."

And I said, "Oh."

"What's yours?" said De Veny.

"Robert Dent."

"You can stay now."

Doe replied, "I can't." Then I went upstairs to leave the boat and began to think about what's going on with me.

While I was leaving, I began to wonder if I'm losing it or if Flakka is making me delusional. I then began to walk to the streets to get a ride, but nobody would lend me a hand. So, I became tired by saying to myself, "This is insane. I don't know how long I can keep this promise."

Suddenly, out of nowhere, I was approached by the same two men whom I'd left. I got a bit nervous and, at the same time, frustrated that I yelled at them by saying, "What are you two doing following me? Can't you take a hint?"

"Sorry, man, we were just wondering if you're okay."

I answered them, saying, "I'm fine. Now go."

"Jeez, we were only asking," said De Veny.

"And now I'm asking you to go!" Then about three seconds later, they walked away, and I began to walk alone once more.

While I was walking away, my feet began to get tired, and I fell on the road. I decided not to get up and was hoping for someone not to notice me and run me over. About three or four minutes later, I was still on the floor waiting to be killed, yet I never did get run over, and the road seemed to have no cars for whatever reason. I then closed my eyes and started waiting and waiting until I heard laughter around me, and it started to remind me, and I noticed that it was the same laugh that had been breaking me for two years. It was D.

# II

# BLACK AND WHITE

A t that moment I began to wonder if I had made a huge mistake by running away from everybody, including my father, sister, and Celia. I feel as if my own mother, wherever she may be, would feel incredibly disappointed in me if she saw me right now.

Her name was Wanda; she was born in a Jewish family named the Meyers. She met my father, whose name was George, when she immigrated to America in 1959. She was working in a hardware store called Hogan's Hardware, owned by a man named Terry Hogan, who was a man in his 40s with big thick glasses and a very unattractive face. At least that's how my parents saw him. My dad was buying a shotgun for his dad, whose name was Frederick, but he couldn't go in because, in those days, my dad was living in a time where segregation was legal. My dad was an African American man, and my mother was Caucasian, but she hid the fact that she was Jewish, especially from her boss.

While trying to get a shotgun, the sign said "Whites Only." My mother saw this and felt bad for him. So, while working, she said to my father that she would secretly give him the shotgun at night when the store was closed. Afterwards she gave it to him, and instead of paying for it, my mother used her own money in order to create the illusion that someone else paid for it. But later on, Hogan would find out about it and eventually fired my mother for not only giving a gun to a customer without paying, but more outrageous, giving it to a black man.

While being unemployed, my dad and my mother would later become friends and soon became lovers. Time had shown them later that they could be together, but it would take a civil rights bill signed by President Lyndon B. Johnson to make that happen. My father was very happy because now he and my mother could finally get married after a series of persecutions and torment these two had experienced. When both were married, they decided to not have any kids, but it was not until they saw a single parent on the street with a kid that it convinced my mother and father to have one.

Then about two years later my mother gave birth to me at Saint Luke's Hospital in Texas, and she told me when they both saw me, she started to cry, and my father started jumping in excitement. Then about a few minutes later both my mother and my father saw that I wasn't moving. For a second the doctors thought I was stillborn until they slapped me on the bottom, and I started crying. I was a very large baby, around 20 pounds, and everybody thought I was going to be a big kid until about three years later when my sister Karla was born. I became a very scrawny kid.

When I first found out that I was having a baby sister, I was happy, but then I realized my mother had to stay in the hospital. I became upset for two days, but when I came to the hospital to see my mother and Karla, the first thing my father said was to watch my hands, and I did what I was told. About ten seconds later I went inside and saw my mother holding the baby. I went close to Karla so I could hold her, but my dad said no because he was afraid I might drop her. But my mother said that it was okay.

So, she gave the baby to me, and I held her and thought about a lot of things, even when I was three years of age, that made me realize that I needed to take responsibility for taking care of her, even if I didn't like to.

After all that I had just said, you may have presumed that my life was the average American dream or whatever, so much so that it later became a terrible thing to waste. We all know what happens next for me, but God knows what happened to my family.

And to this day I can now convince myself, besides seeing Celia again and losing her, I know for a fact that I will never see my family again.

And besides my family, it has been two years after The Man in Black came and affected my life. I have failed many people in my life, and now I wonder if I am going to fail to honor Dr. Patrick Barton's memory.

Before, it was somewhat easy to make this promise come true, but now I feel as if Flakka is destroying me—not just my life—but slowly turning me more into D. I'm slowly falling into a pit of pure darkness with no escape. I know I've done a lot of mistakes, and now I just don't care anymore.

While all of this was happening, I've begun to hear D. mocking me inside my head. I can hear his voice screaming, "You're going to die like a dog on the streets in the middle of nowhere? Go ahead and die, fool! Die! Die!! DIE!!!"

I've been on the floor for quite some time and still hoping that someone would not notice me and kill me immediately, yet no one had come. I then looked around, and I started seeing around the bushes. At that moment I saw a lake. I decided to crawl through the bushes, hoping to drown myself.

Yet sadly, I didn't have the strength to go all the way to the lake and managed to put my legs in the streets while my waist was on the grass. Then I said to myself, "I'm sorry, Mom."

Then suddenly, after about a few minutes on the floor, I saw a van coming toward me. I thought to myself that this was my end, but instead of running over me, it stopped, and I saw a man come out of his car and yell, "Oh my God!"

He rushed toward me, saying, "Sir, are you okay?"

I looked up and said nothing. The driver was a bald Asian man with a white sweater, jeans, and black boots. He was about to go for his phone and call the ambulance. I was scared because while I was still weak, I tried to snatch the phone from him, but I couldn't gain the strength to do so. My words were, "No, no hospital."

"But sir—"

"But nothing! Just let me die!" He wouldn't listen, and I began to feel sick. Then my whole body was shivering. In that moment I wanted to die. About a few minutes later the ambulance came. I yelled, "No!" only to feel myself cold and voiceless. I began to shake as if I was experiencing a seizure. I thought to myself, "What is wrong with me?"

Then the paramedics carried me up and into the ambulance. My body was on a bed, and they thought I was having a seizure. But little did they know that I could hear every word they were saying. The doctor said, "Hold him tight!" They held me so tightly that I thought I was going to pass out.

About thirty or fifty seconds later they drove all the way to the hospital. While near the hospital I began to slump down as if I was dead. The man who called the ambulance saw my face looking very drowsy. The paramedics yelled at him, saying, "Get out there and call somebody!" and he did just that.

They laid me down and restrained me with belts all over my body. Doctors and nurses came to me, seeing my body shaking and jumping. The paramedics said, "He's seizing!" but one of the doctors looked at me and saw something else wrong with me.

"He's not having a seizure," he said.

"What?"

"That's not a seizure—it's some sort of psychosis."

The paramedics looked very confused, and another doctor yelled, "Nurse, give me a tranquilizer!" The nurse gave him a big syringe and put it inside my neck and pressed a liquid that was so strong I wanted to scream. After that I saw nothing but darkness.

Then after all that, I opened my eyes and saw a bright light. My eyes were blurry, and I thought I was dead and went to heaven. But my thought of being in heaven turned out to be a living hell. I gasped over and over, my heart started beating, and I realized that I couldn't breathe. I was going into a panic while slamming everything around me. I started throwing cups and pills everywhere.

Then a doctor came and said, "Sir, what's wrong!" Then they saw me with my eyes wide open and breathing only out of my body. The doctor realized I couldn't breathe. He then looked around and found a syringe in his cabinet. He tried to hold me, but he began to struggle, and I smacked him in the face and knocked him down. Afterwards a group of doctors saw what happened and started holding me. The doctor got up and said, "I'm sorry, but this is going to hurt!" He put it inside me, and I yelled as if I was that little kid from the movie *The Grudge*.

About ten seconds later I began to breathe while my heart was beating like hell. I asked the doctor, "What just happened?"

He smiled at me and said, "You're at the hospital, mister."

"Robert, uh... Dent." They began to look at me strangely, and I thought to myself, "Stupid, why did you go up for?" But they managed to shrug it off, and the doctor asked the other doctors to leave so I could breathe more.

While they were leaving, I began to get up, but the doctor said to me, "Just lie down."

I asked him, "Who brought me here and who are you?"

"My name is Dr. Julian Griffith, and the man who brought you here is outside waiting to meet you."

"Who?" I said.

"The man who saved your life."

I waited for a few seconds until I said with a surprised voice, "Oh, the guy who called the ambulance. You're going to let him in?"

"Of course, we just need him to sign some legal papers, if that's alright with you."

"Sure, doc."

While all of this was happening, I realized I was dressed in a hospital gown. I thought I looked ridiculous, but I said to myself, "Hey, at least it's not a green jumpsuit." I began to think about a lot of the people that I may never see again. I especially thought of The Man in Black, because I don't know what's real anymore, and I'm not as confident as I was two years ago of his own existence. You can convince yourself of many things, but when you have doubt, it's like everything you believed before was a bitter lie!

About one minute later the man who saved me came in and looked at me with a nice smile, but I was still not trusting him or even my own mind at this point.

I said, "Hey, so you're the one who saved my life."

"Yeah, man," said the stranger. "What have you been doing, falling in the streets?"

Then I had to make a lie because I was afraid if I said I was trying to get run over, they'd point me to a mental hospital, or worse, they would report me to Sarah Barton.

"I was walking to a homeless shelter, but I was sick."

"Yeah, I know, you were fighting with the doctors. Are you sick physically or mentally?"

"Just physically. A little tired and dazed."

I felt like he wouldn't believe what I said, and he looked skeptical, but he looked at me and said, "Okay, sir. I will sign some papers, and I hope you feel better."

He was about to leave until I said, "Wait, what's your name, and did you really pay for me?"

"It's Lee Chen, and yeah, I did help you a little bit with some cash."

"Thanks, dude."

"No problem. See you soon."

About twenty minutes later I was out of the hospital and still didn't know what else to do but to find The Man in Black. I decided that I needed a car, so I was walking as a drifter. But before I was going to look for a car, I saw Lee looking at me, and he said, "You're okay, man?" I was surprised that he would even ask that question.

I knew he helped me, but I never thought he would get a stranger some help, and I said, "You're really going to help a complete stranger?"

"I'm a former Buddhist monk."

"And?"

"Well, the Buddha said, 'Consider others as yourself.' So I think you need to go back to your family."

"I have no family."

"You have a home?"

I then smiled and said, "I live wherever I go."

"That's the same as living nowhere."

"I'm homeless."

"Sorry, man, but do you know where a shelter is?"

"I think I need that."

"Then come on!" said Lee.

"Okay, okay." About nineteen minutes later we traveled the town looking for a shelter, and what we saw was this big building called the Bradley Home. Lee brought me there, and I said, "Thanks a lot," and I waved goodbye while walking toward the shelter.

# III

# THE SHELTER

Around Everett Ave. I was looking around to see if there's a tree with fruits on it because I hadn't eaten all day, and I was starving while walking around at midnight. While looking around, I saw a tree that had small grapes. I took some without caring if it was healthy or poisonous.

About three seconds after eating the fruit, I went inside this big building. While walking, I bumped into someone by accident. It was a young Black lady who was about 5.0 in height, and I said, "Sorry, ma'am."

She looked at me and said, "It's okay, sir."

"Uh, I was looking to sleep over. I'm homeless."

"Sure, I'll call one of the workers to come get you."

"You're the manager?"

"Director."

"What's your name?"

"Frankie Dolomba."

I shook her hand and said, "Robert Dent."

About twelve minutes later, one of the workers came. I was told to sign my name and was told to pay twenty dollars, but I didn't have a wallet, so I asked her if I could pay tomorrow morning, and the worker said, "Okay, sir." I was told to go to a room filled with people sleeping with blankets on the floors and another blanket on them, with pillows

19

that looked old. But I had no choice but to sleep there. I thought to myself, "This is even more of a shithole than the boat."

So I laid down my head and decided to sleep, and I knew I couldn't pay money for the shelter, so I was planning on doing something I hadn't done since I was a kid—to steal money from one of the homeless people. Just like I did when I stole money from a young girl who was trying to pay for her medicine so I could give my dad beer. I never saw that kid again. She had pale skin, red hair, and braces. I can't remember her name, but I'll never know if she died or whatever. That was the first time I felt really bad about stealing because I saw her face looking really sad. But now, looking back, I decided that I'll find a better way. So my plan was to wake up and sneak outside and leave.

About twenty-three minutes later, I was resting in this horrific excuse for a bed but was able to rest. Then I started sweating for some reason, and I looked up and saw The Man in Black.

"Hello, you miserable wretch!"

Then I got up screaming—a scream that could be heard around the room—and everyone in the room yelled, "Shut up!" That was when I realized it was just a nightmare. So I went back to sleep and started believing that The Man in Black really is a figment of my own imagination. I thought about it so hard that I really believed I should just go back to Smart City and turn myself in completely to Sarah.

In that moment, I said to myself, "What's the point? I'm sick. I miss my family, my friends, and Celia. I need to give up this bullshit!"

So I decided to go, not tomorrow but now. I left the building without paying a dime while all the workers upstairs were doing whatever— maybe smoking pot or something. Who gives a shit?

While leaving, I decided to find some coins on the streets, and I used them to see if there was still a payphone. Surprisingly, there was. I checked the payphone to see if it still worked to make a call, and surprisingly, it did. But I was not trying to turn myself in. I was trying to call anyone I knew.

I looked at a phone book and began looking at names A through Z, and I saw a handful of names from Barton to Mendoza. But to my shock, I saw a name that I never thought that I would ever see again, and it was someone very special for me—and her last name was Truman.

When I saw my own sister's name, at first I didn't want to answer, but after a few seconds, I realized I had nothing to lose. To make sure that I'm coming back for my execution, I wanted to tell her that I love her and I'm so sorry that I never came back home. While the phone was ringing, I said, "K... Karla."

But about three seconds later, I thought nobody would come. Finally, I heard her voice. She said, "Hello. Hello?"

Wow. I wanted to cry so bad, so much so that I nearly broke down in tears. I then thought to myself, "What could I say? Karla, I love you? Or I missed you and I'm okay?" The more I waited, the more I heard her voice getting annoyed. "Hello, isn't anyone there?"

I didn't have the courage to answer, so I slammed the payphone over and over until the whole phone broke, and I yelled, "I'M OKAY, YOU DUMB BITCH!!!"

Realizing what I said and having the phone destroyed, I slumped down with my hands over my face for hours. I then fell asleep with these two words coming from my lips: "I'm sorry."

About four or five hours later, I think I woke up on the floor. I would have stayed longer, but I would have been seen as suspicious or recognized. But in that matter, I just didn't care anymore. I thought to myself, what's the point?

In that single moment, a woman came to me and said, "Sir, are you okay?"

"Go away!" I said. "What's your problem?"

"Nothing, just mind your own business!"

After I chewed on her, she wouldn't leave, so I threatened to snap her neck. The lady ran away, and while I thought she was gone, the next thing that happened—I saw her on the floor. I thought she was faking until I saw blood coming out of her head.

"Oh my god!" I said to myself. Then I ran out of the phone booth and went to her. I yelled for help, and many people started coming to me. I said, "What are you morons gawking at? Call the damn ambulance!"

"What did you do to her?!"

"What are you talking about?"

"She ran away from you!"

I began to stutter and tried to explain to them what happened, but none of them listened. One of them called 911, and at first, I thought she was going to call the police, so I grabbed the phone from that punk and said, "Don't you dare!"

"What are you talking about? I'm calling for help, you maniac!"

"I'm not a maniac!" I said.

"Well, prove it! Get off me!"

So I let him go, and the people started accusing me—saying I'm bloodthirsty or a murderer. I kept saying I didn't do it, and about thirteen seconds later, I saw the lady coughing, and I knew she was alive. I said to her, "Ms., did I knock you down?"

She did a tiny smile and said, "No." Then the mob stopped attacking me, and about nine minutes later, the ambulance came. They asked a few of the witnesses, including myself, to drive to the hospital.

I froze, and the paramedic said, "Move your black ass and drive!"

"Well, my black ass doesn't have a car, moron!" I said.

"Oh, so come with us!"

So I did and was in the van with the lady. She had black short hair with a ponytail and a nice-looking face. When I saw her with the bandages on her head, I thought to myself that I have no choice but to say sorry. For the first time since last year, I really felt bad for something I did. Maybe I have a soft spot—or actually, maybe this is my soft spot.

IV

# THE WOMAN IN BANDAGES

We rushed up to the hospital with the paramedic. I began to shake like hell, so much that I began to sweat when I saw her on a stretcher. I said to her, "Lady, do you have any family that I can call?" She looked at me and said, "Daughter! I have a daughter!" Then they moved her all into the hospital room, and one of the nurses said, "You can't come in yet, sir."

I was stunned and told her to get out of my way, but she refused and said, "No, I'm sorry, sir, but I can't do that."

"Why not?"

"Because they are about to do surgery on her." And in that moment, I thought I was going to vomit because now I really felt bad.

"You can wait here while they are finished," said the nurse, and I did so accordingly. I sat down and waited for about two to three hours, slowly falling asleep while they were doing surgery on her skull. I began to shake and move around as if I had some kind of seizure because, for one, I didn't want to be blamed if she died, or I didn't want to be exposed as a fugitive.

And when hours came, I was about to leave the building until the nurse yelled, "Sir! Mrs. Ty Shen wants to see you!"

I looked at her and said, "Who?"

"Mrs. Ty Shen, the lady who had a skull fracture. She wants to thank you." Then I began to feel relieved, and I followed the nurse into her room, where she was talking to the doctor. I went to her room and knocked on the door while they were both talking. I saw the doctor—he was very skinny with light gray hair and looked somewhere between forty-nine or fifty-two years of age. I saw the lady with bandages all over her head. I also noticed she may have had very little hair after the surgery, and that one side of her face looked very strange compared to the other side, as if she had a stroke or something.

While I entered the room, I said, "Hello."

"May I help you?" said the doctor.

"Yes, I've heard that Mrs. Shen wanted to see me?"

The doctor smiled, saying, "Are you the man who brought her here?"

"Y-Yes."

"Well, good work, sir."

"May I talk with her?"

"Of course. Excuse me."

Then I went inside and shook hands, saying, "I am so sorry for what happened."

"Don't blame yourself, mister."

"Uh... Dent. Robert Dent."

"Well, I would like to thank you, Mr. Dent."

"So, how's your daughter, Mrs.?"

"Shen... Ty Shen. And she'll be here soon. A friend of mine is going to bring her to visit me."

Then I said to her, "Well, nice to hear that, Ty Shen." Then I began to be curious about how this happened to her, so I asked her, "How did this happen?" Her entire face went from thankful to regretful, as if she had done something wrong. So I asked her again, "Miss, how did this happen?"

She said to me, "I'm sorry, Mr. Dent, but I can't talk about it right now."

And in that moment, I knew something was wrong.

"Did someone attack you?" I said. Then she began to touch her head and looked like she was in pain. I was a little worried in that moment and decided to stop asking too many questions, yet I didn't know at the time whether she was really in pain or she was just faking to dodge my questions.

Then I said, "You're okay, miss?" Then the doctor came and said, "Sir, I believe it's best you should leave. She needs to rest."

Then I looked at both him and her, saying, "Alright, I hope you feel better, Ty Shen."

"Good luck, Mr. Dent."

"You too," I said. So I left the building, but I couldn't let go of the possibility that she may have been attacked by someone dangerous, and my suspicion of others began to grow in this place—so much so that even though I couldn't get answers from the victim, I decided to wait and see what happened when the police or the rebels came to talk to her. Because I sure couldn't do it myself as a wanted fugitive—they would just put me back in the electric chair again.

So I decided to wait until the next day and then come back to the hospital to see what was going on. I waited all day outside the hospital to make sure what happened. About the next day, around 12:40 p.m., I saw a few rebels inside the building. I knew I couldn't let them see my face, so I decided to just hear what they were saying to make sure what happened to Ty Shen, because I felt responsible for what happened and didn't want another burden on my conscience.

While they were at the hospital, I could hear words, but none made sense. Then one of the rebels began to pat one of their own on the back and said, "Dude, look at that guy—do we know him?" Then I began to slowly walk away and refused to turn my head back for him to see me. But I then realized that it didn't work, and to my shock, I saw the man the rebel was talking to—it was someone I hadn't seen in a while. He was Wilfred McNally, who happened to be Sarah Barton's right-hand man and a former friend and team member of mine. McNally began to sprint toward me, and I began to run for my life.

He began yelling, "Go! Go!! Go!!!" Then I began to run while they began chasing me. One of the rebels, who began to get tired, started shooting at me, but the man stopped chasing me after he realized that his own partner was shooting like a maniac. So he slapped him on the wrist and yelled, "Don't shoot, ya idiot! I'll call Barton!"

And in that moment, I lost them. But I knew it wouldn't be for long until they tried again to find me so they could put me in the electric chair. But I knew if I had any chance of surviving, I needed to get out of Smart City, because it would be too dangerous. And I knew that would mean I probably would never see Celia again, but I also knew it would be better this way than to have something bad happen to her by one of those jack-booted thugs.

So I decided to leave Smart City and never come back until I finally found the one man responsible for turning me into having this darkness inside of me—and turning me into a fugitive.

The Man in Black

V

# Uncle Walter

I t's been a while since I escaped, but I've finally got my chance to find The Man in Black. I am living in Hong Kong.

I have hope that escaping here, in a place that doesn't know the name James Truman, would help calm down the manhunt for me, even if my own manhunt will be harder to find.

I've got a job as a dishwasher at a place called Guohua. It's a nursing home for people with Alzheimer's, and the man who was the manager, his name was Dai Sheng. He was balding with a stubble, way taller than me, and had a strong voice that could convince you of anything.

Even though I came to Hong Kong without papers, I expected things to be quite difficult for me, especially in a country where it nearly took me a year to learn the language. Things have been going pretty well for me. I've rented a home there and made some money. The minimum wage here was way higher than it was in Smart City or even America.

Even so, I missed the people back in America. I've begun to have a good time with my fellow coworkers Kang Chu Tien and Li Mai. They gave me a nickname that made sense for a majority-Asian facility: "That Yankee Dishwasher." At first, I thought it was an insult, but soon I began to see it as a badge of honor.

27

So yeah, everything was doing fine until one day I knocked on my boss's door and said, "Dai Sheng?" And I saw him with some dude wearing a muscle shirt, black pants, black shoes, and a fedora. He had these long nails that were dripping with a dark red liquid.

When I saw this, I nervously asked again, "Dai Sheng?"

"What do you want, Dent?"

"Nothing, it's just..." Then he stopped me and said, "Then go!"

"Ok, but who's this?" I said.

"Don't you understand me, Yankee? I said scram!"

I had never seen Dai Sheng snap at me the way he did, and I nearly got sick to my stomach. But I knew if I stayed, I would probably turn into D. again, so I decided to take a deep breath and went back to work.

One day, Li Mai came and saw me looking pretty miserable and said, "Are you okay, Robert?"

"Yeah, sure."

Then I went back to work, cleaning some of the silverware that the residents were using. I almost wanted to snap while doing the dishes because I couldn't get Dai Sheng's outburst out of my head, as if D. was taunting me by putting memories in my mind.

When I was finished, I decided to go to the break room. I sat thinking about Celia a lot, wondering what must have happened to her without me. I wanted to find a way to see her again, but I didn't want to endanger her as an accomplice. I sat there until about 7:30 PM. I decided to leave, grabbed my backpack, and clocked out.

Then suddenly, a flash of light came through. I turned and saw nothing, but then out of nowhere, I saw that light again. I turned even faster and saw some jackass taking pictures of me.

Out of fear of being exposed, I yelled, "Hey! What are you doing?" I went through the back door, and the little weasel took another picture and started to run away. I chased him for about 20 or 22 seconds, but then he jumped on a motorcycle and escaped.

After that, I noticed that he had dropped something. It turned out to be a badge. I grabbed it, and it read "Pàn jūn," which is Chinese for "Rebels."

After I found out who they were, I was both confused and frightened at the idea of them being in some way connected to Sarah Barton.

I tried to close my eyes and take a deep breath so that I wouldn't keep freaking out. I went back to work and started cleaning a bunch of dishes. While minding my own business, I felt something touching my back. I turned and saw Li Mai.

"Robert?"

"Uh... yes?" I said.

"I got something to tell you, but don't tell the boss, okay?"

"Why? What's wrong?"

"I... uh... I may have lied to him about something important."

"Okay, what is it?"

She then asked me to come closer and said something that nearly made me pale. She told me she stole some of Dai Sheng's money while he was not looking.

"Why, Li Mai?!" I said.

"Because I needed it to feed my child. She was starving."

In that moment, I wanted to quit my job because I always thought my boss was a jerk, but I didn't know he was that cruel. I looked at her and said, "Okay, I won't tell anybody. If you need any help, I'll give you some money from my savings, okay?"

She hugged me and said, "Thank you, Robert."

So I went back to work and kept working. I never thought that I would have two big events from what happened outside to what just happened inside. While I was cleaning all the dishes and the floors and taking out the trash, I talked to Li Mai again before I left and asked her where she lived so I could give her some of my money. She wrote her address down for me, and I called a taxi.

I was driven back to my apartment and thanked the cab driver while giving a few Hong Kong dollars. I went walking, but while I was doing so, I saw a handful of people looking at me strangely. Some stood there looking, while others were walking closer to me. I began to freak out and started walking faster, but not too fast, hoping they wouldn't chase me.

I went into my apartment and tried to open the door, but the keys fell to the floor because I was shaking too much and feared I would flip back into D. again.

Then I opened the door and rushed in, locking the whole house to make sure nobody could get inside. While this was happening, I sat in my chair reading two books: *The Strange Case of Dr. Jekyll and Mr. Hyde* as well as *The Hobbit*.

Suddenly, I heard someone knocking at my door, and I began to hide behind my chair like a child. The more I stood in fear, the more the tapping got louder and louder, to the point that I just had enough.

I grabbed a lamp and yelled, "You better be careful, pal, because if I hear any more tapping, I'm going to put you in the hospital eating a straw!"

Then the tapping stopped. I unlocked the door and opened it, but to my surprise, nobody was there. I thought to myself that it was the drug in my system playing tricks on me again.

I went back, and suddenly I felt a pain in my head, so agonizing it was like my bones were being crushed. I fell to the floor and turned to see a man with a large heavy log. My eyes were so blurry I couldn't see his face well, but in my heart, I knew who it was. My last words before passing out were, "You?!"

I saw something that I thought I would never see. It was the face of someone I know, but I was afraid and confused about why and how that person found me after all this time. I had left Smart City a year ago, only to find him...

However, the person I saw was NOT Sarah nor Celia or even the Man in Black, but it appeared to be an old familiar family member from my past. His name is Dr. Walter Myers, my uncle.

Ever since I was knocked out, I awoke in agony, tied to a chair in my own apartment. I saw him; he was half bald with jet black hair, big round glasses, and a very wrinkled face. I said to myself, "How?"

Then Uncle Walter slapped me in the face and said, "You do realize we looked everywhere for you."

"I didn't want to be found. And how the heck did you find me, Uncle Walter?"

"Don't you dare call me uncle, and you know how I found you."

"No, I... Oh yeah, you're a billionaire... for a psychologist, I'm shocked that you can't control your temper."

"I'm not a psychologist anymore. NOT since I spent my years trying to help your father and sister find you."

"Really? Huh, I thought they told you why I abandoned them."

"And I never thought that you were a murderer."

Then I smiled and said, "You really believe all that crap about me killing those people? Newsflash, Doc, I never killed anybody."

Then he slapped me again and said, "Don't lie to me."

"I'm not."

Then he punched me in the nose.

"Christ, what is wrong with you, man?"

"Wrong with me? What about you?"

"I swear to God, if you don't let me, I'm going to..."

"Do what? Kill me like you killed that lady's husband?"

"I DIDN'T KILL HIM!"

My heart started to pound. I began trembling, my whole body began to lash out with anger. I couldn't breathe, so much so that my own uncle began to walk back on me. But then I realized, even though I was furious with him, I closed my eyes and began begging him to get away from me. He looked at me with terror in his eyes.

I begged him over and over to go, but he wouldn't.

"FOR CHRIST AND ALL THAT IS HOLY, GO AWAY!"

Then I saw through my uncle's eyes that he slowly began to understand what was going on with me. He looked at me with fear, as if I were a serial killer. He then walked back slowly and ran to the door where I was knocked out.

I began screaming like a wild man, and then suddenly... nothing.

I awoke in my own apartment on the floor next to the sofa. I looked around and said to myself, "What a nightmare."

But then I realized my apartment was nearly demolished, with the wall broken, holes, dust coming out, and stains of blood all over the floor. I saw the door I opened split in two, and then I realized it wasn't a nightmare. In shock, I realized I had forgotten someone.

"Uncle Walter!" I yelled. I went through the broken door and began to search for him. I was afraid that D. may have killed him. I began running everywhere to find him, and to my shock, I saw his glasses on the floor.

In that moment, I realized something had happened to him. I tightened my fist and screamed in a loud voice. Then, out of nowhere, I saw a man reaching his hand toward me, and he said, "Help... me."

It was Uncle Walter. I could tell he didn't notice me because he was without his glasses. He then fainted in my lap, and I wanted to call for help. But if I did, I would probably be exposed as a wanted fugitive, so I brought him into my broken apartment and tried to clean him up.

I checked to see if he had any damages, but to my surprise, not a single blow had been inflicted on him. I thought to myself, how could he be knocked out if nobody touched him?

Then I realized he was old and may have had a heart attack or a stroke, or something close to it. I began to think about what to do because I had no medical experience, so I was very fearful for his life. I tried to find anything in my broken, bloody apartment that could help him, but I couldn't find anything useful. I began to panic, but I looked at my uncle and tried to calm down for his sake.

Even though he hit me, it was my fault that I left my family after all these years. I thought to myself while he was breathing in a strange way that I swear, in my mother's name, that I did not and cannot be a murderer, or I could even murder my own flesh and blood.

I began to see his eyes open and close many times, and I began to beg him to fight because I couldn't do anything to help him except tell him to fight on.

I began saying to him, "I'm sorry. I'm so sorry."

He then looked at me with open eyes and smiled.

"Is that true, nephew?"

And I smiled back and said, "Yes... yes, Uncle."

He then said to me, "How did you get here?"

I smiled and said, "I was about to say the same thing."

"You know I have resources, Jimmy, my boy."

"Yeah, I know."

"So, ask me how you got here."

I explained to him everything that had happened to me in the past twelve years, from past to present. He slowly began asking questions: why, how, when, and who. But the greatest question he asked was *who*...

"In who was this Man in Black?"

I explained, "I don't know. Maybe I'll know eventually. All I know is that he's the key to my freedom."

Then Uncle Walter wept, and I, for the first time, hugged him. He apologized for being so cruel to me because he thought I was a terrible savage bent on destroying innocent lives.

I explained that it wasn't me. On the contrary, it's what's inside of me. I then told him I could never go home until I found the Man in Black. But Uncle Walter refused to accept that. I tried very hard to help him understand and said, "Uncle Walter, the Man in Black turned me into this and framed me for killing my best friend's husband. I can't go home with you until I find him. If I go with you, the rest of my family would all be protecting a criminal."

"I don't care!" he said.

"I do."

He then put his head down and said, "So what can I do?"

I took a breather and said, "Go back home and tell my father and sister that you found nothing."

"I can't do that."

"You have to, for me and for our family."

"No, I don't want to lie to your father and sister."

"Uncle, please, there's no going back to what we had before."

"I can't accept that," he said, crying.

"It's okay."

"It's...it's not okay... It's... I... not o... kay!"

I began to close my eyes and put my head on his, while saying, "You have to be strong, Uncle. Things will never fully go back to normal, but it can be okay if you go back and tell them until I find him."

"Do you really think you can find the creep in black? Do you really believe that, Jimmy?"

"It's a long shot, but it's all I have... unless—"

"Unless what?"

Then I had an idea that could help, not just my uncle but myself. In order to find the Man in Black, I realized that if he had the resources to find me, then he could have the resources to find the Man in Black.

"You found me, right, Uncle?"

"What are you up to, nephew?"

I explained to him, "If you have the money and people to find me, then you can find the Man in Black."

"I... I don't..."

"What's wrong, Uncle? You and those people were able to find me."

"Yeah, but..."

"Uncle, I need to know if you can find him. Only then can I go home, and I promise I will."

"But you never did, James. You never came back when we needed you. Why now?"

"I... um..." Then I closed my eyes and said, "I don't want to be alone."

"But you were alone for twelve years, right?"

"No, I wasn't... I had friends and Celia. I spent years with them when I was with the rebels. And now, I've begun to realize how much I missed them and how much leaving my family alone was a big mistake. I just hope you understand."

"I understand, James."

I asked him, "Now that you understand, would you find him for me?"

"But how would I be able to call you?"

I smiled and said, "You still live in New York?"

"I do."

"Well, I suggest you write me your phone number so you can call me when you have any clues."

Then he took his time thinking and said, "Okay, I will do it." He asked for a pen and a piece of paper and wrote down his phone number.

"Thanks, Uncle Walter, for understanding."

"Remember, nephew, I don't like to lie, but I hate to lose you."

"You won't lose me, Uncle Walter. You were always in my heart."

Then we went outside together, and he hugged me one last time. He asked if I was going to live somewhere else because of the damages to my apartment. I said, "There are always new places to sleep."

He smiled and said to me, "Shalom, nephew."

"And I said, 'Shalom, Uncle Walter.'"

Then he walked away. I saw a few men in suits next to his limo, and I assumed they were his bodyguards or the people who had found me. He went inside, and he was gone.

# VI

# PÀN JŪN

After my first-time encounter with Uncle Walter, I began to try and clean up the mess of my apartment, hoping that it would look good enough for myself and perhaps for someone who would like to visit.

After a long day of cleaning, I went on the couch trying to sleep, but my thoughts of my uncle were too strong for me to rest, so I spent hours struggling to sleep until I got up and began to drink a couple of beers from the refrigerator so I could relax little by little. I then went back to sleep.

The next day, I woke up and began to get ready for work. I dressed up in my uniform and walked ten minutes from my apartment to Guohua. When I saw that building, I yawned and said, "Well, here we go again." I went inside with my key fob and signed in my name.

I then went upstairs and began to hear something that sounded like an argument, so I rushed up, thinking it was one of the elders. But then I realized it was Dai Sheng and Li Mai arguing, and I thought to myself, "What the hell?" Before I got to work, I began to hide next to the door to see what was going on. I heard them arguing in Cantonese, and at the time, I only understood a little bit of Chinese, but I was terrible at speaking the language.

I heard things like "Please" over and over again, and Dai Sheng yelling "Get out," all in Cantonese. I then saw Li Mai walking towards the door where I was hiding, with her mouth covered and crying. I jumped out of the way and saw her with a terrible look on her face.

I thought to myself, "What happened?" Then I realized that Dai Sheng may have found out about Li Mai stealing money to help her daughter, but I didn't want to prejudge, so I confronted Dai Sheng and said, "What happened, boss?"

"Oh, it's you again."

"Boss," I said, "what happened?"

"It's none of your concern." Then I saw Kang Chu Tien smiling, and I began to get very upset and yelled, "You got something to say to me, bitch!?"

"Yeah, asshole. She stole money!"

"What do you mean?"

Then Dai Sheng said to me, "She stole money to feed her miserable daughter!"

"Hey, don't call her daughter that."

"I could say whatever I want. After all, she's fired now. Get back to work, Yankee boy!"

After realizing what happened, he turned his back on me, and Kang Chu Tien left with a smirk. In shock, I stood there for a minute and then ran outside to find Li Mai.

I searched everywhere outside until I saw her car and tried to talk to her. When we both saw each other, she blamed me for what happened, as if I was responsible for her losing her job, and she began to cry and yell.

"Now I can't feed my child, I have no job, nobody to help me because of you!"

"That's not true, Li Mai," I said.

"Then how did Kang Chu Tien know?"

I stood confused and asked, "Kang Chu Tien?"

"Yes, he told me that you told him about me stealing money from Dai Sheng."

Then I began to feel a rush of anger. I was burning hot because I just realized what really happened, and I yelled, "That stupid—!" My hands started shaking, and I began to feel D. coming out. I rushed back into the building and ran with the speed of a jaguar, starting to curse and slur my words. I was so hot and burning up with anger that I was spewing coals.

Then my eyes started to drip with water as if they were on fire. I saw Kang Chu Tien's terrified look for the first time ever, from a cocky little piece of trash to a scared creature, and then I blacked out.

While all of this was happening, I got up and saw my hands and shirt covered in blood, along with the whole kitchen. I thought to myself, "What could have happened?" After about fifteen minutes, I realized the blood was Kang Chu Tien's, and I saw him on the floor, still breathing heavily but covered in blood. I looked closer to realize his rib was broken, his fingers were cut off, and his tongue was gone.

I then looked for Dai Sheng to see if he was still alive, but out of nowhere I felt a crack feeling on my back. I fell to the ground and turned to realize it was Dai Sheng, who had a cut on his lip with a broken wrist. He then yelled, "Pàn jūn is coming for your miserable ass!"

I thought about what he meant, only to realize it was Chinese for "rebels." I wasn't sure if it was Sarah Barton's rebels or some kind of copycats in Hong Kong, but either way, I was in terror. I tried to get out of the building, but Dai Sheng grabbed me by the leg, and I started kicking him with the other.

I ran outside and heard him yelling, "You're fired! Do you hear me? You're fired!"

I realized I couldn't stay in Hong Kong anymore if the rebels were after me. I realized my only option was to disappear far away from here, and I did. I left Hong Kong and everything behind. I ran so long I thought I couldn't run anymore, but then I felt another crack and fell to the floor. I would later find out it was a tranquilizer dart.

I looked everywhere to see what hit me but then I realized who they were, and that I was too late. I never thought I would have so much crap in my life, but I shouldn't be surprised because, after all, I left home many years ago when I was 20, but I never dreamed it would get this crazy.

I was dragged out with my body paralyzed and put in the trunk of a car. My heart started beating rapidly like a drug addict. I was afraid if I didn't move I would die, but I was also afraid that if I did move, I would die. All I knew in that moment was that I was screwed.

While this was happening, I was thinking about what was going to happen to Celia and wondering how the Man in Black might react to seeing me in the back of a car. He might as well be laughing his way to the bank, knowing that he may have just won.

About nineteen minutes later, I began to feel a sudden sensation in my fingers. Out of instinct, I punched the wall of the trunk. My knuckles were cut. I still couldn't move my whole body, but I could still punch and suddenly I was able to scream.

I began screaming for help over and over until I hoped someone would notice. Then I felt the car stop, and I heard the door open and shut with a loud noise. Footsteps came speeding toward me, and then I saw a bright light. The trunk door was opened, and I saw a man with a gun pointing at me yelling, "Shut up!" Then he hit me with the gun, and I was knocked out.

Later, I awakened to see myself tied up on a chair with duct tape on my mouth and my eyes covered. I was looking everywhere, confused, only to see nothing but darkness.

Then I heard footsteps again, and I heard about three or four guys talking. It looked like they were screaming at each other. Suddenly, I realized I was kidnapped and began to freak out, with memories of what happened to me the last time I was tied up. I began screaming over and over again until I heard these guys coming closer, yelling, "Shut up, damn you, shut up!" I screamed even harder and slowly began to black out, until I heard a voice I recognized. It was Uncle Walter.

"James!" he said.

"Uncle Walter."

"Yes, yes, it's me. Nephew."

Then he told the men in Chinese to let me go and wondered who the hell put me in here.

"What are you doing here? I thought you returned to New York?" I said.

Then he sighed and said, "I lied, nephew. I went to them for help."

"Help from the freaking rebels, Uncle?!"

"No. These people are NOT the same rebels," he explained to me. Pàn jūn are not the rebels I knew. Apparently, there are more rebels globally than just in Smart City or North America, but they have different techniques and different goals. Ever since the world blew itself up and created the rise of tyrants like Linda Smith, I was shocked to find out there are more rebels in the world with national goals.

I then got up and said, "Are you connected to these guys, Uncle?"

He smiled and said, "A billionaire is connected to many people, James."

"So why are you here with them, and why did you let that jerk hit me with his gun?"

"Don't worry, nephew. Me and Pàn jūn took care of him."

I stood frozen and said, "Uncle, you're a doctor, NOT some gangster."

Then he looked at me with a smirk and said, "Nephew, a lot of things changed since you were 20 years old."

"What? Killing people?"

"It's strictly business."

I thought to myself, "Who am I talking to?" But he told me to go upstairs and sit down. I went up shaking until I saw a big room with gold and silver everywhere, as if I were in the house of the king of England.

He then sat down with me and ordered a cup of coffee, but I said no. So he asked his men to give him one just for him. He then saw me still shaking and said, "Nephew, it's okay. Breathe in, nephew."

"What have you become?" I said.

Then he closed his eyes and opened them with a sigh, saying, "What have you become, nephew?"

"I didn't ask for this!"

"Neither did I, nephew, but you have to believe me, I didn't want you to see me like this."

"Then why do it?"

He explained to me that it was to find the Man in Black.

"You know what, Uncle? Sometimes I just don't care anymore about that man if my own family are turning into creeps because they needed me and I was there for you guys."

"James, you can't blame yourself."

"Of course I can!" I then started to freak out to the point where my uncle yelled for me to calm down.

Then he said, "I know you felt responsible, but it's not your fault. You did what you had to do, James, and I love you either way. We still love you."

Then I saw his eyes looking into mine, and I began to see him as the uncle I knew since I was a kid. I slowly calmed down and said, "Yeah... yeah, I know."

"Now you're going to be okay?" he asked.

"Yeah... so why the kidnapping?"

"What?" Uncle Walter said.

"You know why you kidnapped me and freaked me out."

"Well... heh... sorry about that, nephew, but I did that to prevent one of the jackasses from getting to you."

I looked confused and said, "They just did, Uncle."

"I know."

"So, what are you trying to say?"

"What I'm trying to say is that these people—I bribed them before the other members of those jackasses got to you."

"You bribed them?!" I screamed. "How much power do you possibly have?!"

Then he began to laugh, and I said, "I'm serious, Uncle!"

"Okay, okay, nephew." I then asked him if he found the Man in Black, but he explained that he has yet to find out who it might be. He did say, however, that he is getting closer.

He then said something in Chinese to one of the corrupted members of Pàn jūn, and they both explained to me that both Uncle Walter and Pàn jūn are looking for someone like me to help. I thought it was some kind of joke, but then I realized they were serious.

I said to them that I was a liability, and my uncle pulled something out of his hand and said, "Here!"

"What's this?" I said.

"Tranquilizers. They will keep you calm, but only take them when you begin to feel something wrong."

"How did you get this? Did you steal it from a psychiatrist's office?"

He smiled and said, "I got it because I was a doctor, nothing corrupt."

I smiled and sighed in relief and said, "So, what now?"

"These men will get you ready for the job with Pàn jūn so you can keep busy and NOT get caught while I try to find out who the Man in Black is."

"So, what am I supposed to do?"

"Well... remember when you and the rebels took down Linda Smith?"

"Yes."

"Then we need to do the same thing again for another tyrant here in Hong Kong."

"You're serious?"

"Very serious, James, and this guy is pretty serious too, but I only want you to do small-time work, nothing dangerous."

I smirked and spoke, "Come on, Uncle Walter, I can take these clowns easy as pie."

"Perhaps, but I won't risk my nephew getting hurt."

I rolled my eyes and spoke, "Fine."

"Do we have a deal?" Then I stood up and raised my hands for him to shake, but he looked at my hand, then looked right at me, got up, and hugged me. He said, "We do." I almost wept, but then I asked Uncle Walter, "Who is the dictator of Hong Kong?"

In that moment, he said his name was "Snake Eyes." He then explained how he looked, only for me to be in shock. I said, "Oh my God."

"What, nephew?"

"I think Snake Eyes went to my job at Guohua, Shinji."

My uncle looked surprised. I turned and pointed to one of the members of Pàn jūn next to him and said, "You looked familiar too." The guy said, "Of course, Mr. Truman. You chased me through the window after I took photos of you."

"Wait a minute, that was you?!" I said in shock.

"Yes, your Uncle Walter paid me to do so."

I laughed at how stupid this whole thing was, then asked my uncle, "Can I have that coffee now?"

# VII

# SNAKE EYES

It was like old times; in fact, it felt like my days as a fugitive never happened. It took me a while to take it all in, but I slowly began to remember many things about being a rebel again.

When I first joined Pàn jūn, they almost kicked me out of the building because they said I was not one of them. But Joseph, the man who worked with Uncle Walter by taking photos of me, convinced them to let me stay as a janitor, and slowly they began to agree. I was accepted.

My days as a janitor were no different than my days as a dishwasher. It was painful at first, but I slowly got used to it. The only thing I was concerned about was cleaning other people's urine and feces in their base.

While this was happening, another janitor patted me on the back and said, "The boss wants to talk to you." I went in and saw a balding, big-boned man with thick eyebrows wearing a muscle shirt and a long purple robe. His name was Wei Guó, and he wasn't just the boss—he was the biggest badass I had ever seen. He was able to knock out a brick twice its size just by slamming the side of his fist. At first, I laughed at the idea and thought he was some kind of faker, but seeing what he was capable of, and the way he fights and shoots, it was almost hard to believe.

I once asked him, "What was that?!"

He said in a calm, friendly voice, "Dim Mak."

I asked him, "Can you teach me?"

But he refused, saying he didn't want others to abuse it, especially someone he didn't fully trust.

Later, I went to meet Wei Guó. He asked me to sit down, but there was no chair available, and he was on the floor with a rug covered in Chinese letters.

"Where should I sit?" I asked.

"On the floor," he told me. I sat as he instructed, and he began to speak.

"I want to apologize."

"For what?" I asked.

"That I seem like someone who lacks the ability to trust others. It's just… twice, Snake Eyes' own spies came as new members only for us to have our base invaded and moved."

I thought, *If he only knew who I was, I could tell him about the Rebels.*

"Wow, I didn't know, boss."

"Yeah, so I hope you can understand why I wasn't teaching you."

"That's alright. I can defend myself just fine," I said. Wei Guó smiled.

"Perhaps," he replied.

"So, that's it?"

"Not exactly," he said.

"Then what?" I asked.

"I have a meeting for peace talks with somebody, and I would like you to be a driver."

"You want me to be a driver?" I said.

"Yes."

"And who are you going to make peace with?"

He said something that surprised me: "Snake Eyes."

"What?!" I said in shock.

"Shhh… I know it may be surprising to you, but we have come to an agreement for peace. Hong Kong would no longer be invaded—neither by Snake Eyes nor by China."

I looked at him with confusion and doubt. "Boss, you do realize these people can't be trusted. They have to be taken out."

"I know you seem skeptical, Mr. Dent, but we do things differently with Pàn jūn than our Western friends."

"The Rebels?"

"Yes. Unlike them, we don't use violence or betrayal to get things done."

I almost got upset—*who are you, and you're a pathetic excuse for rebels, giving up so easily and calling people like me violent traitors?*—but I locked in my emotions, knowing it could do more harm to myself than him.

"But we can learn many things from them," he added. Wei Guó laughed and asked, "What's so funny?"

"Oh, nothing, Mr. Dent. I can clearly understand your willingness to learn from them, but to have the Geilo lecture me on how to defend Hong Kong after they almost lobotomized one of their own while getting betrayed at the same time is absurd."

Oh boy, did I want D. to come out and eat this guy apart—so much so that I could hear him in my head screaming, *If you don't kill this son of a bitch, then I will!*

But then Wei Guó looked at me with a concerned expression and said, "Mr. Dent?"

"Yeah?"

"You're... okay?"

"Yeah, I just need some water."

"Well... I got some tea." He gave me a cup and asked if I wanted some. I accepted it, drank it, and shockingly felt D. gone from me as if he had never been there.

"Wow!" I said.

"What's wrong now?"

"Nothing, boss. It's just... I... What did you put in this tea?"

He looked confused. "Why are you asking?"

I lied. "It's just... incredible."

Then he smiled and said, "I'll only tell you if you accept my offer."

It took me a few minutes to think, and I eventually said yes. In my thirty-two years on this earth, I knew what tea tasted like, but this was no ordinary tea. I didn't think it was tea at all—it felt like some kind of medicine, something that could get rid of my inner demon forever.

This wasn't necessarily the smartest move, and it could be dangerously gullible, but it was either leave and not be free of this poison inside me or take a visit to one of the most dangerous thugs in the world since Linda Smith.

I drove Wei Guó to the headquarters of Snake Eyes. He gave me directions to find the man while I asked a few questions—how he joined Pàn jūn and why he wasn't reluctant to speak with Snake Eyes, an enemy of Pàn jūn. He replied, "I volunteered to join Pàn jūn with a friend who brought me there many years ago since the great war happened."

"Who was this guy?" I asked.

"He was a good man who made some wrong choices."

"What made him change?"

Wei Guó got agitated. "Can you just shut up and drive?"

"Okay, no need to be personal."

After a few long minutes, we found a building that looked a lot like a Chinese restaurant I used to go to as a teenager. It was red and looked very similar to the headquarters of The State, with a few differences here and there.

I parked about thirty-nine steps away from the headquarters because it was heavily armed. Only Snake Eyes and a few of his men knew we were coming; the meeting was nearly under complete secrecy.

We walked to meet Snake Eyes. Along the way, a few of his armed men stopped us.

"What do you want?!" they yelled.

We both raised our hands and tried to explain that we came to negotiate with Snake Eyes. They dismissed us and began to laugh—until Wei Guó explained the deal in detail while calling them fools. They pointed their guns at his cheek in anger and yelled, "I swear, call me a fool again and I'll blow your cheek off!"

Out of nowhere, a bullet was fired—but not by one of those fools. Snake Eyes had a golden magnum, similar to the one Linda Smith had, and he yelled, "Hold back, boys. They're with me!"

"You could have come earlier! I almost got killed!" Wei Guó said.

"Well, you always know I'll be there to help, right?" Snake Eyes replied. Suddenly, these two men hugged each other, and my jaw nearly dropped. Now I finally knew who the "friend" from Wei Guó's past was.

"What the hell was that?!" I yelled.

"Oh, don't act surprised. You knew damn well I had a friend who helped me join Pàn jūn."

"Yeah, but never mention Snake Eyes?" I asked.

"I was trying to surprise you, Dent."

"Screw surprises! One of his thugs tried to shoot you?"

Suddenly, Snake Eyes shot the same guy who had pointed a gun at Wei Guó and blew his brains out.

"Jesus!" I yelled.

"Oh, quit being a bitch and let's get inside," said Snake Eyes.

"Who are you calling a bitch!" I yelled.

"Hey, hey, let's just get inside, Robert."

"Yeah, let's get inside, bitch!"

We almost ran after them until Snake Eyes, in anger, and his men pointed guns at me. I started shaking and felt like I was going to black out again.

"Alright, enough! Arnold, tell your men to knock it off!" Snake Eyes yelled.

I snapped out of it and looked around, thinking, *Wait, his name is Arnold?*

"Okay, you think this is the time?" Wei Guó said. I started laughing, and he tried to tell me to shut up because he didn't want Snake Eyes to kill me.

"What's so funny, you little runt?" Snake Eyes yelled.

"You're named after an 1980s action hero?"

Snake Eyes ran towards me while pointing a gun. "I'll kill your black ass!"

"Arnold! Stop!" Wei Guó yelled.

Then Snake Eyes turned to him and said, "You're only alive because of my friend here, okay?" I nodded, and we both went inside for the meeting. Wei Guó told me to wait outside because he didn't have any more blood to spare, and I understood. I waited outside.

VIII

# FIRE OF DESTINY

W

ow, I couldn't believe how boring this was, just waiting in the car over and over like a moron. I was doubting that I was ever going to see Wei Guó, and to be honest, even though Snake Eyes, or Arnold, or whatever his name happens to be, was friends with Wei Guó, I still didn't trust him. Sure, people can say I'm just holding onto a grudge about how he treated me like dirt, but after all this, that guy was dirt.

It started to take about two hours of waiting, and I nearly had a panic attack because I didn't trust these people who lived in this cesspool. I was afraid that I would freak out enough to flip back to becoming D. again, but I couldn't help myself. It felt like the car was squeezing me, as if it was some kind of claustrophobic nightmare coming to attack me.

In that moment, I decided that it was enough because I felt like I was going to explode. I lost my patience once before, and I wasn't going through that nightmare again. I got out of the car with the keys in my hand and slammed the door, leaving the keys in it. While walking back to the meeting to see what was going on, my temper started to get out of control.

I smelled a strange odor, as if someone was cooking hot dogs, and I thought, "Are these clowns seriously cooking food while I stay in the car starving?!" At that moment, I began to flip out until that same smell started to turn like burning coal mixed with meat, and my anger slowly turned into curiosity. I was seriously wondering what was going on the closer I got, and I was starting to feel nervous.

Then my curiosity became terror when I saw what was going on. It was as if my life was going through a repeat of the one thing I could never overcome, and now it was happening again. Snake Eyes and Wei Guó were still inside, but worse than that, the headquarters was on fire.

As this was happening, I began to panic, and flashbacks of what happened back home sunk my heart. I yelled, "My God, not again!" I began to shake, and instead of running toward the fire like some kind of hero, I walked backward and was about to let it go out because I didn't care anymore whether I lived or not. Then suddenly, I saw a man coming through the flames yelling, "Help me!"

He looked very familiar. I thought it was Wei Guó, but after three or five seconds, I realized who it was, and I couldn't believe it. I screamed at the top of my lungs, "You!" It was The Man in Black, running with flames behind him as if he was the Devil himself. I ran to get him, but the man who was yelling "help" started yelling, "What are you doing? Help us?!"

In that moment, I realized I had to make a choice, and I was totally conflicted. In an act of instinct, I started to run after him. He turned toward me with a surprised look on his face, and I yelled, "That's right, jackass!"

But then I saw the fire and realized that I couldn't just let him go, but I couldn't just let people die either. At first, I didn't care, so I still ran after him, but I couldn't stop thinking about those people and how similar it was to the fire back home. I began to sweat, wondering what was real and what was not, because this wasn't the first time I was hallucinating. Either out of complete stupidity or just nobility, I decided to go back and save the men who were trapped.

While all of this was happening, I saw that man who came out of the fire, and I said to him, "Don't worry, I'll be back." But when I saw the fire, I almost freaked out and started shaking. I tried to keep myself together, but I began having flashbacks about the last time I tried to save people while The Man in Black was there. I almost left, but in that moment, I decided that if I died, then at least I'd die with some redemption because I felt it should have been me burning to death.

I rushed into the fire screaming to find survivors while pieces of the building were collapsing. I heard a voice screaming and yelled, "Where are you?!" Then I heard that same voice get louder, and I yelled even harder, "Where are you!!!" I looked around, trying to find where the voice was. Smoke started filling my lungs, and I began to cough. I almost freaked out in that moment, but I tried to calm myself. I grabbed my jacket and put it over my face so the smoke wouldn't go inside me.

Then I heard the voice coming through a wooden door. I saw a bit of light and tried to open it, but the knob burned my hand because there were too many flames inside that room. I started kicking the door over and over until it flattened on the floor. The smoke, fire, and screams started piling up. I saw the flames face to face—it was like something out of hell. In that moment, I truly believed that I was going to die in that building.

I looked around while coughing. "Is anyone there!" Then I noticed a huge wooden bat on the wall. Afraid it might burn my hands, I used my jacket to wrap around them and grab it. It almost looked as if I was holding an umbrella. I searched everywhere in that room while the screams continued. Then, out of nowhere, the person screaming sounded very close. I turned and saw who it was—it was Snake Eyes.

I rushed to him, trying to grab him out with all my strength, and started yelling, "Where's everybody?!" To my shock, he yelled back, "Dead! They were burned alive!"

In that moment, I was paralyzed with shock and guilt. It was déjà vu all over again. I wanted to just die and let the fire take me away, but Snake Eyes screamed, "What are you waiting for? Let's go?!" So we rushed out of the fire, and we managed to get out. An explosion threw us through the air until we fell, with Snake Eyes breaking his leg and me getting my skull cracked.

I saw so much blood on me that it went into my eyes, and I thought I was blind. I wiped it off with my hands and felt moisture and stickiness, so I wiped them on my pants. I saw Snake Eyes lying on the floor, and I felt I should just leave him. But because I still had a conscience and didn't want to feel guilty that he would die alone, I decided to scream for help, hoping someone would call the hospital.

No one came, so I started to search for his phone and called for help. "Hello?!"

"Who's this?"

"It's me, Uncle Walter."

# IX

# THE TEA

Look, I knew this guy is a piece of trash and I hate him, but even so he's still or was Wei Guó's friend, but he sure as heck isn't mine. But that didn't stop me from trying to help this sucker.

I grabbed Snake Eyes and put him on my back. I managed to go to my car and put him on the seat next to me. He was bleeding profusely, so I began to check his body for injuries, and it was revealed that he didn't just have a broken leg but a piece of his leg was missing.

I knew I couldn't go to the hospital out of fear that somebody would recognize Snake Eyes and try to kill him because who knows how many enemies this guy has if not The Man in Black himself.

While I was finished checking with him, I used a piece of my shirt and tied it up to his leg, hoping that it would stop the bleeding, and I drove off. But suddenly I began to question why The Man In Black would be in Hong Kong, why he would attack Snake Eyes, and does he know the identity of The Man In Black.

When I reached closer to Uncle Walter's home, I just couldn't take it anymore. I felt a rush to my body and started shaking so much that I nearly had a car accident, so I parked and began to try and wake up Snake Eyes. I checked his leg and his pulse to see if he stopped bleeding and if he was still alive. I began slapping him in order to try and wake him up.

I slapped him repeatedly and then suddenly he yelled in shock, "Wei Guó! Wei Guó!"

"It's me, you idiot!"

"Oh, you...where am I?"

"Trying to help you see a doctor." Then he started laughing and said, "Back off, I don't go to some freaking doctor. I have my boys!"

"Ha! Sure you do." Then he began to look confused and asked what I am talking about, and I explained to him that his men, along with Wei Guó, had been burned alive.

"What?!" he yelled. "I tried to save them. They didn't make it. Both Pàn jūn and your thugs are gone. It's over!"

"How can this have happened?!"

"You tell me. Did you see somebody?"

"No!"

"Are you sure?"

"Yes, I'm sure, you hard-headed Yankee!" And I began to be skeptical and I yelled, "ARE. YOU. SURE?!"

"What do you want me to say?"

"Did you see him?!" Then Snake Eyes looked confused and said, "Who?"

"A man!"

"What man?!"

"A Man in Black." Then his face started to look serious and almost like he saw a ghost.

"A Man in Black?" Snake Eyes began to feel puzzled and looked at me as if he saw a stranger. "Wait a minute..." Then Snake Eyes gasped as if he sensed something horrible.

"What...what is it? You're him!"

"What?" I said in confusion.

"You're James Truman!" Then I grabbed him by the collar and yelled, "Who is he!"

"Get off me, you freaking maniac!"

Then I got upset and started squeezing his leg and I heard him screaming, "WHO. IS. HE!"

"I can't tell you!" Then I squeezed his leg even harder and he yelled, "I can't! I can't!" Then my fingers started scratching pieces of his flesh with blood on them and he began begging, to the point he finally gave in and yelled, "Okay!"

"Talk while you still can!"

"Okay, the name is..." And like that, he couldn't answer because he was shot seven times in the back by The Man in Black.

"No! No!! No!!!" I yelled in agony and I turned and saw The Man in Black laughing. I rushed to the other side of the car to confront him, but he hit me with his gun and ran off while I was unconscious.

Then suddenly, I found myself awake in a sunny morning, realizing that I had been unconscious for hours. I turned to my right side and noticed the cold dead body of Snake Eyes. I rushed towards him, but I did not touch him because I didn't want to make the same mistake that led Sarah into believing I killed her husband. But I did get closer enough to realize a giant letter written in blood in front of the window, and it was a letter M, which made me believe that Snake Eyes attempted to reveal The Man in Black's identity, but all he was able to do was write a single letter, with me having no idea if it was his first or last name. But it gave me an idea of who he could be.

I heard a phone ringing and I looked everywhere and noticed it was on the floor. I picked it up and realized it was Uncle Walter.

"Hey, um...Uncle Walter."

"Nephew, you called me since midnight. Where are you?"

Then I looked at Snake Eyes and I was having flashbacks of when Sarah believed I killed her husband and started to get nervous, so I lied to him saying, "Oh nothing, I just had a bad dream. Nothing else!"

"Well, okay, nephew. You sounded like something bad happened."

"No, Uncle Walter. Everything is okay."

"Okay, I'll see you soon when I find that man in black."

Then I gave him an idea. I told him, "Uncle."

"Yes, nephew?"

"If you are still looking for him, try to find a man with the letter M, either on his first or last name."

"What, you found a clue?"

"I...I think so."

"That's great, nephew! How did you find it?" Then I began shaking the phone while looking at Snake Eyes and I told Uncle Walter, "I'll tell you later. Goodbye, Uncle."

Then I hung up and fell on my knees, wondering how this happened and why this happened. Then suddenly I realized something that Wei Guó told me, and it was the tea. I thought that maybe, just maybe, this could be my way out of getting rid of D. once and for all without the help of The Man in Black. But I knew if I drove there, people would get suspicious of me driving with a dead buddy, so I realized I would have no choice but to get rid of the corpse of Snake Eyes by myself.

I drove the car a few blocks away from Uncle Walter's house and went to the garbage and threw his body there. I thought to myself, "What in the world am I doing?" Then I threw his body in the garbage and covered it with other pieces of trash on top of it just so no one would notice there was a corpse inside a pile of trash.

And I drove off the headquarters of Pàn jūn while giving myself hope for the first time in a long time since I left Smart City. I almost drove like a maniac, so much so that I almost crashed a car, and the jerk honked at me, so I gave a middle finger at that dude and he began yelling, "Yeah, screw you! Screw you!" I knew that I was driving so fast, but I was afraid at the possibility someone may have gotten there because if he knew where I was, then he may have known about the tea, so I was nervous about that while driving all the way to where the headquarters of Pàn jūn is.

I drove about nearly ten minutes, hoping that I wouldn't be too late. But sadly, I would realize that the headquarters was still there, but only just, because I realized to my horror that it may have been too late, because Pàn jūn is not only gone, but so is their headquarters. It had been demolished.

I got out and started screaming, "Oh God, no!" I started rushing towards what's left of the building to try and pull out pieces of the building to find if the tea was there. I was so sure that it was. I searched over and over with false hope, but it was destroyed, only to find a note behind the mess, taped to a broken tea cup. It read:

*"Sorry to rain on your parade, you miserable wretch. I just wanted to make sure that you will never get back to what you were before. And by the way, I tipped off Mrs. Barton to pay your uncle a little visit."*

When I read those words, I had a mix of fury and worry boiling up in me. At that moment, I was seriously considering killing myself while wondering why I was even born. Yet I started thinking about my uncle even more and the good times I had with him, and they outweighed the bad, so I rushed back to my car and drove to save Uncle Walter before Sarah got to him for helping me.

I began driving like a wild man, trying to speed as far as I could. I didn't care what I hit or what would happen to the car. All I cared about was trying to just get there and save my uncle while hoping to reason with Sarah about how she is wrong and could never kill her own husband.

Then I finally saw Uncle Walter's house, and I parked the car in the wrong position while freaking out. I raced to get to his home while my heart was beating harder and harder. I knew if I don't take a breath and relax, I would snap right back as The Demon, so I began to slow my breathing. In that moment, I felt hopeless and helpless because I screamed, "Oh, what's the point? How can I save my own uncle when I can't even save myself!"

Then I heard them screaming, and that got me even more in shock. I began to race toward the door, only to find Uncle Walter outside, but he wasn't alone. To my horror, I saw Sarah and McNally outside too, with Uncle Walter in handcuffs.

"Get your hands off me, you animals!" said Uncle Walter.

"Quiet, old man!" said Sarah.

When I heard her say that, I got so pissed, and I wanted to strangle these two for touching my uncle and telling him to be quiet. I began shaking while making a fist, but I knew if I let all my stress out, it would be too late for not just Uncle Walter, but for myself as well if I let D. try to attack them, because I felt like I wanted to kill them for this.

Then suddenly I saw Sarah look at me face to face from far away, and she yelled, "Truman!"

When she saw me, I stood frozen and didn't know whether to explain to her and save my uncle or run for my life. I saw her chasing me, and in that moment, I decided to let D. come out. I just didn't care anymore. Then I heard Uncle Walter scream through the top of his lungs, "Stay away from him!" Then McNally kicked Uncle Walter in the ribs, and then I started blacking out because I was really angry. I closed my eyes, and then I heard Uncle Walter yell, "Run, James! Don't worry about me!" Then I opened them up, and Sarah was gaining on me, and I began to run, and ran, and ran again.

I knew that Uncle Walter would be going to jail for aiding and abetting a wanted fugitive, and I knew if I stayed I would have joined him. But my fate would be to get the lobotomy. After all that, I knew there was no way my uncle would help me find The Man in Black, and all I had was an initial that could lead me to his identity, and that wasn't enough. After the arrest, Uncle Walter disappeared from my life.

Three Years Later

When I was a kid, I used to read the Bible most of the time. I had been to church with my folks when I was still happy. Believe it or not, I sometimes wondered if I would ever be happy again, then I realized maybe that would never happen.

After three years since I left Hong Kong, I traveled to Tibet, where I climbed the mountains to find my peace. I nearly slipped a couple of times, but I never fell. Sometimes I wish, for my sake and everyone else who came close to me, that I did, because I knew that I wouldn't be free until I finally found my peace.

I managed to keep climbing up the mountains with snow coming through my skin, even though I had goggles, along with a coat and some gloves, but it still didn't matter. The pain inside of me was way worse than anything the world could give.

While all this was happening, I managed to get to the top of the mountain. With me was a knife. I looked up at the sky and was thinking about Celia and how much I felt like I failed her—not just as a lover but as a man. I took the knife from my pocket, aimed it at my throat, started shaking, and began to feel D. coming out. Out of fear of blacking out again, I stabbed the knife inside my throat twice and fell to the floor, bleeding. I thought to myself, "This is it. It's all over now," and I closed my eyes as if I were dead. Everything faded to black.

Suddenly, I woke up. I was in a country-like farm where I could see animals outside the window. My bed was made mostly out of rags, and the house had plenty of wooden walls, as if I were living in a log cabin. I got up out of the bed, only to fall from my feet after stepping on a toy car. I yelled, "Crap, that hurts!" and noticed that my voice was different, almost feminine. I got up and looked around and saw posters that I hadn't seen since I was a kid, like Star Wars and E.T. I thought to myself, "What the hell?!"

I got up and started looking around, saying, "Hello?" I was looking for anyone that could help me know what was going on. I looked through the window and noticed an American flag and that the place I lived was a rural area in the United States. "How long have I been gone?" I looked at my hands and noticed that they were soft. I touched my neck to see the cut on my throat, but I realized there was nothing there.

I began to keep looking, and I heard a voice saying, "James?" I turned and realized who it was, someone I hadn't seen or heard from since Smart City. To my surprise, I knew who it was—it was Karla Truman, my sister.

"James, are you okay?"

"Karla?"

"No, it's the queen of England. Of course it's me, James." I started to get emotional, knowing that she's back with me. Somehow, I began to feel bad as if I failed her, but then a smile came through me. She asked, "You're okay?"

"Yeah."

"You're sure?"

"Yeah, yeah, I'm okay." My eyes almost started to water. I began to feel confused but also something I hadn't felt before, and that was happiness. I then asked her how she found me.

"How did I get here?"

"I didn't find you." Then I heard footsteps coming closer to me, and I saw a woman. She said, "You guys found me, remember?" To my horror, I realized what was going on. My eyes became wide with a look of terror. Then I heard two others calling for me, "Son, you're okay?"

"Are you okay, dear?"

I realized this was not the present but the past. I was not a man but a child, and I was in complete shock.

"James, what's wrong?" I began to feel lightheaded and began slowly lose balanced "help somebody help!" yelled Karla then I fell to the floor in shock and in a split second I was awake.

X

# THE MYSTIC

I gasped for air in fear when I snapped out of that nightmare. I kept on gasping, but I still couldn't breathe well, only to realize that I had cut myself. But now I am in a place that looked like a giant tent. I tried to get up and cry for help. I tried to scream "Help!" but then I noticed something strange about my throat. I touched it, and yet somehow my skin had no cuts like I didn't just try to kill myself and wondered what happened, only to remember that I almost tried to kill myself. When all this was happening, I realized I was alive and started to feel even more bitter, knowing that my quote on quote death was nothing more than a failure.

I got up asking with a voice that sounded like I was smoking a million times, but then I got up and saw an elderly man with no shoes and dressed in yak skin cooking a bowl of stew. I started asking him who he was in different languages, thanks to years traveling around the world, but he wouldn't answer as if he was deaf. I then decided to give up and said to the man, "Well, this is pointless. Thanks for saving me...I guess." Then I turned away to get out of the tent, only to realize my clothes were missing and all that was left was my pants and boots.

"Oh, for God's sake, where are my damn clothes anyway?!?!" I said, and I started searching around. Then I got even more pissed off to the point that I said, "Why does the world hit me every single time? Why can't I just die already, for God's sake!"

Then I heard someone speak, saying, "Don't let the world get to you!"

"Who said that? Hey, old man, did you hear something? Oh, what am I talking about, he can't even understand me."

"No? Because I just said something." And to my shock I replied, "You can talk?" and he said, "Yes." Then I got annoyed and asked, "Then why the hell didn't you answer me when I asked you?"

"I guess I only answer when I hear your true self."

"What?" I asked. Then he began to explain to me that if I said, "Why does the world hit me every single time," and I asked him, "Go to hell," but the man smiled and said, "Which one?"

"You know, if you weren't an old man, I would throw you out of this tent and beat the hell out of you!"

"Why so angry?" the man said.

"Because I am angry, duh!" and I decided that I just wanted to leave and try and kill myself again, but this time by throwing myself off the cliff of the mountain. "Look, old man, you don't know me, so why don't you mind your own damn business!" Then I opened the tent and he spoke.

"I know who you are, James Truman." Then I stopped myself and turned my head and asked, "How do you know who I am?"

"Because a few of my students met you before," he said.

"What are you talking about, old man? Who are you, and why isn't my throat cut open?"

"First of all, I'm not just an old man, and second of all, I think the real question is who are you?"

"What's that, a joke?" and he looked at me with a very kind look on his face and asked for me to see my hands. I asked him why, but he smiled and said that I would see. At first I thought he would do something harmful, but the way he looked had a very peaceful side to him, so I reluctantly showed my hand. He stopped me and with his fingertips started to squeeze them like he was doing acupuncture, but instead of hurting my skin I began to feel like I had something going on inside myself, that my heart felt like it was melting all the pain and anger I had, as if I didn't feel like dying. In fact, I couldn't feel him at all. "What did you do to me?"

"I relieved you of your inner pain the same way I relieved you of your physical pain."

"What do you want from me?"

"Just to help you."

"Why?" Then I heard another voice saying, a more familiar voice, "Because you helped me, and we helped you."

"Who's there?!" I yelled. Then I saw a man hiding outside the tent, and I looked around and saw someone I haven't seen—three people I haven't seen—since I began to run as a fugitive, and they were here. "How?"

"That's a good question that you should ask yourself," one of them said, and I know who he and the others were. They are Mike De Veny, John Doe, and Lee Chen, who I haven't seen in years.

Then I felt a touch on my shoulder, and I turned and said, "I helped them find their peace. Mike was a U.S. Marine with a traumatic past, John was a man with amnesia, and Lee was a former Buddhist monk. He lost his family...I was myself. I had a tragic past too, so I understand what you've been going through, just like they understand as well."

Then I was confused and asked, "Who's Ivan?" Then I saw John come up and said, "It's me, James. I remember who I was and how." And I smiled and said, "That's nice, man, but how did you all know who I was when I didn't even tell you?"

The man said, "Because they all said that a lady with red hair came and started interrogating."

"Red hair?" I said.

"Yeah, James, she was very bitter and angry," Mike said.

"Oh my God, Sarah."

"That's her, Sarah Barton. The lady tortured us for days," said Lee. And when he said that Sarah tortured them to get to me, I almost fell to the floor in shock, because if this could happen to them, what could have happened to Uncle three years ago? I could never have believed that she could become this cruel. I couldn't believe my own partner and friend would become such an obsessive, vengeful bitch and would torture people just to get to me.

When they saw that I wasn't doing great, they asked, "You're okay, James?"

"No...no, I'm not okay!" Then the old man came and said, "I think you need to relax, my son."

"How can I relax if people I know are suffering because of me?"

Then the old man touched my shoulder and had a very empathic look in his eyes and said, "I also had people I loved suffer because of someone trying to get to me."

"Yeah, who?" I said.

"He was the President of the United States...or at least he was before the bombing blew him up." And I looked at him in the eyes and said, "President Walker?"

"Yes."

"Are you a fugitive?"

"I am." Then I started to smirk and said, "Yeah right, what did you do wrong to get into trouble?"

"Nothing," he said.

"Then why are you a fugitive?" Then he explained to me that he was an assassin that came to kill a monk, but the monk saved both himself and him. He explained everything about his life, like being separated from his family to become a child assassin to becoming a monk and to not let vengeance consume him. He explained in every single detail.

"I'm sorry," I said.

"I know. I just want you to know I can help you, just like my master helped me."

"How can you help me? I've been struggling for years trying to get rid of the demon inside me."

"By searching for a mysterious man in black." Then I was shocked and said, "How did you know?"

"So, it's true." Then I breathed a sigh and said, "Yeah, but nobody will believe me."

"We believe you."

"Thanks, but they won't, and I've tried to get rid of the demon for years, and nothing worked."

"Because you wanted that man to help you?"

"Yes."

"Perhaps I can help you." Then I looked at Mike, Ivan, and Lee, started to think, what do I have to lose? Because if he can help me find some peace like these three, and if he can have peace within himself, then what can I lose to help control what's inside me? So I responded, "Perhaps I should."

"Good. We will begin shortly." Then he turned with Mike, Ivan, and Lee following him, and I asked the old man, "Wait, what's your name?" and he turned with a smile on his face and said, "Wan Po."

And Wan Po taught me many things when I accepted to be his student. He once said that man can be weak; it is only a matter of time when his strength is no longer useful. The idea of losing the will to live is a very destructive thought, especially when you fear to lose your life by reasons of either family, religion, or even death—yes, even for myself.

I fear to die, but not in those three reasons. I fear death because a part of me wants to die. But I know if I die there won't be a second chance of finding redemption. My life has been one destructive year after another, and the fear of dying is miraculously stronger than wanting to die.

A year ago, I overcame death just to envy it afterward. I was forcibly injected by a drug called Flakka, but it was forced on me far more than most victims of the drug. What came out of that drug was the shadow that followed me for the past ten years of my life, something that not even a demon would want to destroy, because the thing that came out of that drug was The Demon.

My name is James David Truman. The people who were once my friends are now my enemies. I travel alone and try to keep myself away from people to protect them as a homeless drifter who's traveling from the west to the east.

Whoever is reading this, I hope that you would have a better life than I had, because being abandoned and alone isn't worth spit. I've also wanted you to know that whatever life may hold, running away from it will only find you in the end. A long time ago, I ran away from the people that I loved until I saw one of them again, only to lose her all over again.

I've abandoned everyone that I came in contact with, and I've abandoned them because I fear that being with someone would soon bring more damage, and I was right. For when you say no but your heart wants to say yes, and you let it while realizing the danger you just put yourself and others through, and then the bad things happen, you have no one to blame but yourself.

While writing these words, I've recently lost two people who were killed by someone I put my trust in. Yes, I got revenge on my betrayer, but only to lose more people in the end. While writing this, I am in tears for the first time in many long years. I never thought the idea of escape would turn out to be a delusion.

I am beyond redemption of any hope of having a normal life, but I give my hopes and dreams to anyone who is reading this to enjoy his or her life and to never have to go through the same nightmare that this life had to offer me. This is not a story of hope but a story of will. This is how it all started, and it began with one man who gave me the will to live. His name was Wan Po, a sage from Tibet, dressed in hairy clothes made from a yak and without any sandals or shoes or socks.

Not a lot of people heard of him, and most people thought such a man could never exist. There were myths that he lived in the Himalayas as a hairy wild man like the Abominable Snowman, and as a man who witnessed a lot of crap, I never saw such a man, but when I did, he gave me strength in my lowest moment. He was there for me in the bottom, and how did I repay him but by doing nothing more than disappointing him.

Before meeting Wan Po, he was born on October 31st, 1942, in China. His father, Chen Wan Po, and his mother, Ling Lee Po, gave birth to Wan Po during a terrible war between the United States and China. When Wan Po was two years old, their beloved son was kidnapped by a rogue U.S. General named Richard Alexander Walker, who put children in cages. They took Wan Po away from his parents. His father fought back, and so did his mother, but they were outnumbered by U.S. soldiers. He was then sent to a U.S. cage with aluminum blankets, never to see his parents again.

In 1950, six years later, Wan Po was released and was sent to the U.S. as a child assassin. He grew angry and fearful. He was as callous as the men who destroyed his life and used him to kill people who they considered a threat to the U.S. government.

It wasn't until 1965 when he was sent to kill an old monk in Tibet named Wong Le, who somehow knocked out Wan Po, and instead of killing him, he tied him up with a rope and began to teach him how to let go of his hate. After about three months, Wan Po was healthy enough to let go of listening to the men who destroyed his life and spent the rest of his days in Tibet.

While this was happening, Walker, now the President of the United States, was wondering about Wan Po and why he hadn't heard of him. When he found out what happened, he ordered soldiers to kill Wong Le and Wan Po. When Wong Le heard rumors of U.S. soldiers coming to Tibet, he was suspicious and told Wan Po to go to the mountains and meet his sister named Tang Chu. But Wan Po begged to stay because he saw a father figure in Wong Le that he hadn't had in a long time, but for his sake, then Wong Le pointed a blade next to Wan Po's neck and yelled, "Run!" and out of fear Wan Po did. He then slammed the door to Wong Le, and he started crying. Wan Po tried to break the door, but then he heard the U.S. soldiers break through the back door, and they riddled Wong Le with bullets. While realizing that Wong Le was dead, he slumped down crying for the first time since he was a child, leaving any darkness out of his system forever. Wan Po traveled to the mountains.

About three days later, Wan Po managed to hide and live in Tibet there, and he met Tang Chu. She accepted him in when he explained that he was a student of Wong Le, but he was scared to say that Wong Le was killed. When he did, she wept for the loss of her beloved brother. Tang Chu wanted revenge, but Wan Po didn't.

"How could you not want to get back at the people who destroyed your family?" said Tang Chu.

And Wan Po said, "Because I don't want to be any better than them."

Then Wan Po finally understood that revenge wouldn't bring any of the people he loved back, and maybe he'd never see them again, but he knows that if there is life on this earth, there is hope.

# XI

# KU SOO

Wow, I used to think that living in a small world was only a metaphor. To think that the strangers that helped me when I was alone are back after all these years and in the same place where I am is too good to be true.

All three of them with me—Mike De Veny, John Doe, whose real name is Ivan Kovelenko, and Lee Chen—all together to help me find peace. A bum who was suffering so much he attempted to kill himself but was saved by the same people who saved me.

And even though they were so kind to me, of them aiding a fugitive, and yet I stayed because Wan Po was also a fugitive with a more tragic past than me and was able to overcome that. I wanted to know how he did it and hopefully control my inner demon once and for all.

I've spent the last seven months with my gang meditating, and I had problems focusing, and the more I meditated the more I struggled—sometimes in anger and other times in sadness—and while all of this was happening, I felt Wan Po coming closer to me, and he said, "You're okay, James?"

"Not really."

"You're struggling, aren't you?"

70

I lied to him by saying, "No, why would you say that?" because I didn't want to fail, and I wanted to keep on trying on my own, in which he replied, "James, I can see it in your eyes. It has the same look that I had when I was lost." And instead of feeling better, I got a little bit tense.

I didn't want to be too destructive, so I said to him with one word, "Yeah."

"So tell me, what's wrong, my son?" And I got nearly upset and got up from my meditation and said, "I think this was a terrible mistake." I got up and was about to walk out, and Wan Po yelled, "Wait!" I turned, and he said, "Don't give up... Follow me." I looked both at Wan Po and outside and decided to stay because I truly believed he could find a way to help me.

While I followed him in the same place, he was cooking his food, and he said to me, "I got something for you."

"What?" I replied, and I looked and noticed something in his hand. It looked like some sort of cup. I realized that it was a tea cup, and I said to Wan Po, "You're giving me tea?"

"Not just any tea, my son, but something that can control your darker urges." At first, I thought he was just joking with me until I realized something was familiar about the way he said it. To my shock, I realized what he was talking about could be the same tea that I tried to get three years ago before the Man in Black destroyed it.

"Oh my God!" I yelled in shock. "You know this tea?"

"You're talking about the tea I tried to use three years ago, right?!"

Wan Po smiled and said to me, "You do know that this tea is violently strong, but it can help man's inner darkness from destroying him. It was one of the best things my former master gave me to help me overcome my inner demons."

"Can I have it?"

"Of course... but..."

"But what?" I asked.

"I don't have the tea itself. It is hidden in a Shaolin temple high in the Himalayas. It is owned by a Shaolin monk. His name is Master Ku Soo. He can help you have it."

"Alright, let's go."

"I'm afraid I can't do that, my son. I'm too old to join you, but don't worry. He'll give you the tea if only you do something for him in exchange."

"And what's that?"

"You must try to fight him."

I began to laugh and thought, "Yeah, right." But then Wan Po had a very serious look on his face, and I said, "You're serious?" I looked at Wan Po and asked him in the eye, "I'm not going to fight that guy. If I do, I would lose myself again."

"Sometimes, James, you must fight for your freedom."

"No, I'm not doing that. Why can't one of your students fight him?"

Wan Po smiled and said, "It's not their place or mine, James. We have already done our part. Now it's up to you to do yours."

"You don't understand," I said.

"Oh, I understand, my son. You're afraid of turning into some type of maniac."

"I'm not a maniac!" I yelled. Then I saw Mike, Ivan, and Lee run towards behind me and ask, "Master?!"

Wan Po yelled while raising his hand, "Peace!" and they stood still, confused, and about five seconds later, they went back to meditate. "Look, I'm sorry, my son, but don't let your anger and pain define you, because you must define yourself. Do you understand?"

"I guess."

"Good, and when you come back and face him, he will give you a chance of freedom when you get back."

Wan Po told me to climb up to the top of the highest point of the mountain, and he asked me to change my yak robe and replace it back to my hiking gear. After I was finished dressing up, I was about to leave until he explained, "Before you go, remember, once you drink this tea it could heal you, my son, but it could also do more harm than good." I nodded to him and went off the mountain, and boy, was it the worst day of my life getting up there. It was even more cold than last time.

I was freezing so much that I thought I was going to give up completely and fall down the hill, because even with my coat and gloves I felt like I was having frostbite—so much so that at times I nearly slipped to death—but I managed to hold on. In about nine hard minutes freezing my ass off, I somehow managed to go up to the Shaolin temple and began to breathe heavily. When I was finished, I began knocking on the door, but no one answered. I tried even harder, but no one came, so I decided to scream, "You know what, screw your ass!" I was ready to walk down the mountain until I heard the door start to open.

I ran back and noticed a small elderly man, and I said, "Are you Ku Soo?"

He smiled and said, "No."

Then I asked, "Is he inside?"

"No."

Then I started to get agitated and replied, "Then where is he?"

The elderly man came to me and said, "Come." So I entered the temple, and the man closed the door. I began asking him many questions about who Ku Soo is and what he looks like. He explained to me that Ku Soo is like a spirit, a man with deep spiritual abilities, like a ghost. I looked confused, not understanding what he meant, because he's just a wise old man with a robe who knows kung fu, that's it. But little did I know back then how complicated things were.

When I walked with the old man, he started asking me a few questions—like who I am, how someone like me got to Tibet, and does anyone I know know where I was. I tried to be nice to the old fella while thinking he was harmless.

Then suddenly I heard a crack sound on the floor, and there was smoke coming, but it had a strange green-like color. I looked down and realized the smoke was coming from a broken vase. At first, I thought I broke it, but then I turned to my side and tried to say sorry to the old man, but then I noticed that he was gone, as if he vanished out of thin air.

When all of this was happening, I heard a voice calling me. I turned around and saw nothing, and I began to try and clean up the mess and started wondering what happened to the old man. So I began saying, "Hello?" but nobody answered. I asked again, a little louder, "Hello?!"

but nobody was answering, and I was getting a bit nervous that something might have happened. "HELLO?!?!" I yelled, and yet nobody came.

Out of nowhere, I heard that voice again calling me, and I thought, who was there? Then I noticed a door that came out of nowhere, and I began to hear the voice getting louder and louder, but at the same time very calm and decent sounding. At first, I thought, where did that door come from? But I became more focused on what was happening. Then I heard the voice again, and it called my name over and over again. "James... James."

"I'm here," I said.

"Come. I will help you find peace."

"Who are you?" I asked.

"I am Ku Soo."

Then I thought to myself, what is going on here? And then I asked him, "What is this place anyway?"

The man who claimed to be Ku Soo answered in only one word: "Nirvana."

He then asked me if I wanted peace, and I replied sarcastically, "A piece of what?"

He replied, "You have been struggling for years now, and all your life you have been seeking this journey of freedom." I got a little annoyed because it was as if the guy knew me, and I asked him, "Okay, Mr. Psychic, if you know me so much, then you must know that I am a wanted criminal, right?"

He said, "Of course, but I also know that you're innocent."

I was in shock and said, "How do you know that?"

"Because I know you better than you know yourself, James." Then I felt confused as to what was going on, as if I was either hallucinating or just dreaming. But then I said to him, "Look, I just came here because my mentor told me about a tea that you have that can help me."

"To control that devil inside of you, right?"

"How do you know all this?"

"Let's say I've seen bad things too, James." Then he said to me that if

I want the tea, I can have it, but it was to come through me. So I said to myself, what do I have to lose? I opened the door, but to my surprise, I felt a large pain out of nowhere. I screamed through the top of my lungs and closed the door. "What the hell was that?!?!"

"You wanted to come in."

"Shut up! You snapped my nose!!!"

"I didn't say it would be easy."

"Screw this, I'm out!!!" I was about to walk away until Ku Soo said, "Then how are you going to be free if you give up so easily?" I stopped myself and turned to the door and said, "You think I would quit easily? I lost everything! I never freaking quit! I lost my family, I lost my friends, and I lost my freedom, and I still kept on going! So don't you ever accuse me of quitting!!!"

"But why?"

Then I thought to myself that I don't need to listen to any of this and was about to punch him after opening the door again, but then he punched me through the nose again, and it felt like hot water mixed with oil and fire, and I screamed in such a way that I thought I was about to lose my mind. I felt my nose so broken up that at first I thought a piece of bone was missing, and then I began cursing at Ku Soo and yelled, "Why are you doing this?!?!"

"I am not doing anything, James. But if you want that tea, you have to face the truth."

"What freaking truth, you stupid asshole?!?!" I yelled.

"That it wasn't your fault."

"What are you talking about?"

"That it wasn't your fault that you didn't have the life you wanted when you were a child." Then my fist began to clench, and I began to punch the door over and over again, but the door was shut so hard that all I was doing was hurting my hands, and I began to feel the cuts and the blood coming through both of them, and I yelled to Ku Soo, "Is this what you want from me?! Do you have pleasure in seeing me like this?!?!"

"Of course not. But do you have pleasure in hurting other people before blacking out?"

"What do you know about me, huh? You don't even know me, you stupid freaking piece of shit."

"I know you are upset, James."

"Okay, dickhead, act like you know me again, and I don't care how many bones I have to break, I will ruin you!!!"

"Like you ruined Celia Mendoza's life?"

I got very angry and yelled, "You keep her out of this!!!"

"You miss her, don't you?"

"Shut up!!!"

"I can understand why you're so angry."

"SHUT UP!!!" I screamed through the top of my lungs and began to bang the door even more like a maniac and began to scream, kick, and spit on the door, but nothing worked. I fell to the floor and broke down in tears. For the first time, I could feel my eyes beginning to water, and all that rage became sadness and a feeling of defeat.

Then I saw a small piece of the door open, and I saw a piece of Ku Soo's robe, and I jumped up and yelled, "YOU!!!"

Then he began to grab me by the shoulder, and I grabbed him by the neck and said, "James, stop!"

"I won't stop until you're dead!!!"

"I didn't mean to hurt you but to help you. Now let me go!"

"Not until I get rid of you, you hear me?! Not until you're dead! Dead!! DEAD!!!"

Then Ku Soo pushed me to the floor and asked, "Who are you?"

"JAMES!!!"

"Just James???"

Then I was about to answer until I realized something strange happened. I felt very confused because if I was snapping like a kook, then how am I staying here and D. isn't? And to my shock, I realized that I wasn't blacking out and that I was still myself. I was so much in shock I didn't say another word after all this, but Ku Soo said to me, "I see... you are James and only James now, because you were trying to help yourself from struggling to control your inner demon, and you have prevailed."

Then, out of nowhere, my eyes began to see things clearly, and I saw Ku Soo's face for the first time, and it was my own. And I finally understood what he was trying to do, and it worked. I could now control D., and I realized that the "tea" that Wan Po told me about wasn't an actual tea but something more spiritual. I was so surprised that I closed my eyes and fell to the floor as if I were dead.

In about some seconds later, I awakened to realize that I felt something I never felt before, and it was almost like I could have full control of my life for the first time in years. I got up and noticed that my cuts and bruises were gone, as if nothing had happened. Then the old man who vanished came back to me and said, "Hello, James."

"What happened to me, and how did you know my name?"

"I didn't at first, but I did know what happened to you." Then he turned to his side, and I noticed that the vase was still there, and I replied, "You drugged me?"

"No, I gave you what you always wanted—at least something like it."

"And what's that?" I asked.

"Control over your life."

"Who are you, and why did Ku Soo look like me?"

To my shock, the old man said, "There is no Ku Soo."

"Then what was all that?"

"Your conscience."

I laughed because I thought he was joking, like he was somehow comparing me to Pinocchio, but then I realized, even with that small smile, that he was serious.

"So the tea didn't exist?"

"It does now, child. It does now."

"So am I free from D.?"

"No... but you are free to have a choice. When you get upset, either you let him consume you, or you can be yourself and learn to live with him."

Then I started to think about how this could happen, but then I slowly changed from wondering how to instead being happy that it happened. I felt a weight was somehow lifted from my shoulders, and even though I'm not cured, I finally can live without fear of being a destroyer of life.

I asked the old man for his name, and he said, "Why do you ask for my name?"

"So I can thank you."

"You already thanked me by seeing you happy, James."

We both smiled, and I left not knowing who that man was or where he came from, but it didn't matter. I knew he was a kind, sweet old man, and that's all I needed to know. I left down the mountains to meet up with Wan Po and the others.

# XII

# SAVING MIKE DE VENY

When I went down to meet up with Wan Po and the others, I saw them while they were finished meditating. While all of this was happening, I asked him if Ku Soo was even real. He looked at me as if he knew what I had just seen and told me, "I see you've had some control of the burden you're trying to heal."

"You knew?" I said.

"Of course, James."

"And what about the tea?" Then Wan Po smiled and explained that he had told a little white lie about having some type of special tea, but he wanted to help me because I was experiencing a very severe depression.

"How did you know all this?" I asked.

"It's simple. I learned it from my own master."

"You mean Guangping did the same thing to you?"

"In a manner of speaking, yes, but at the same time he also helped me through mindfulness."

"Was Ku Soo ever a real person? And who was that old monk?"

Wan Po smiled and said to me, "Ku Soo is real, but he's also a part of all of us that stands for one thing."

"And what's that?" I asked.

"Peace."

I then smiled and asked him also about the old monk, and he said,

"His name is unknown to many of us, but he is referred to as The Guardian." Then Wan Po explained that he wants to help me the same way Guangping helped me—by now finding a way out of my demon's influence.

"Like how?" I asked.

"By getting rid of him once and for all."

I thought to myself, is this finally happening? I couldn't believe that I could both be free from D. without finding the man in black. At first, I was ecstatic knowing that this could be the first time I would be free from having to wrestle with that devil. I told Wan Po, "You can do that?"

"If you do your part, James, I promise you that you will be cured."

I started to have some doubts about the whole thing and even got a bit nervous because the last time I tried to get rid of D., it was with Dr. Patrick Barton, and both he and I failed. That led to the complete and utter destruction of my life and the lives around me. I told Wan Po about my doubts and said, "I don't know, Master."

He reassured me and said, "But I know, James, as long as you do your part."

"You think I can finally find peace?" I asked him.

Wan Po said to me, with his hand on my shoulder, "Of course."

While all of this was happening, we did a few things before my meditation. We began with yoga as well as breathing. He then told me that it was time, and we both went down and crossed our legs while meditating. At first, I was a bit nervous, but I slowly calmed down step by step and managed to relax.

While all of this was happening, I began to feel numb and tired. About nine minutes of slowly breathing and focusing, I began to feel the stress leaving me, along with the hate and anger, as well as the need for blood and revenge. A smile came across my face, and I felt for the first time D. leaving me.

I was in so much peace that I felt like sleeping, and then I heard Wan Po tell me to open my eyes. I did, opening them with a long, happy smile on my face, and I asked Wan Po, "Thank you." Then I turned and saw, to my surprise, that he wasn't there.

At first, I was very confused. I got up, looking around, and asked, "Master?" Then I looked around and asked, "Mike?" and nobody was there. I kept looking around inside and outside, "Ivan?" Yet the same result kept going. "Lee?" I really believed that something was strange, but I started to get curious. I went outside and noticed a strange light in the sky. I thought, "Huh, now that's a hell of a thing."

I was walking back inside until I tripped on something. I thought, "Who put logs on the floor?" Out of curiosity, I noticed something strange underneath the snow. I started to dig out what it was. At first, it looked like nothing of interest, but I kept digging, and it started to look familiar. I saw a white-looking color inside of it and managed to touch it.

At first, it looked like a stack of yarn, but I felt something like fur. I kept on pulling it slowly, and while all of this was happening, I finally knew what it was. I yanked it out and, to my horror, discovered that it was the head of a human being. Worse, it was the head of someone I recognized: Wan Po. At first, I started to freak out and ran out, only to realize that the rest of the group—Mike, Ivan, and Lee—were all decapitated. I was so angry and in shock and wondered who was responsible for this. I heard a voice behind me, and it sounded very familiar.

I turned and realized who it was, and the bastard hit me in the face. I fell to the floor, and at the same time he turned his back on me and ran away. I was so mad that I got up and ran to him like a wild animal capturing prey, but in this case, it was me capturing The Man in Black.

Despite feeling the cold and having the sensation of frostbite in my flesh, it was my anger that kept me going. I ran and climbed down, jumping snow to snow to catch this guy. I was seeing red, and the anger kept me from dying in the mountains.

I yelled at the man in black, "I'll break your face, you son of a bitch!" and I heard him laugh all the way. The echoes of his laughter made me angrier. I didn't even care if there was an avalanche; all I could think about was trying to get revenge for what he did to them. "I'll kill you!" I yelled. The more I yelled, the more I could hear the echoes starting to create an avalanche.

After a few minutes, I was able to jump off the hill where The Man in Black was closest. I grabbed him and threw him down. I yelled while he was laughing and giggling like a maniac. I yelled, "Stop laughing!" but he wouldn't. I then noticed that this could be my time to know who he really was. I yelled, "Who are you?!?!" but he wouldn't answer. I screamed even harder, "Why did you kill them?" Still no answer; he kept going with that stupid laughing.

I got so mad that, out of fury, I began to choke him slowly to death. I felt his pulse getting high at first, but then it slowly began to get fainter and fainter until there was nothing. I knew I had made a terrible mistake and began to be in shock for what I just did. Now nobody was going to believe me that The Man in Black existed or that he killed all of those people. I knew I was done for, knowing there was no hope for me and no way out.

While this was happening, I decided to say screw it and grabbed his hat and mask off his corpse. The answer to who he was and why he did what he did came, and I stood there in shock. My skin began to have goosebumps, knowing what I saw would change my life forever. I stood there, knowing that the avalanche was going to consume me and The Man in Black at the same time, and I finally realized who he was. He was me.

Then I closed my eyes, knowing I was going to die. I heard a voice screaming, "James! James!! JAMES!!!" I opened my eyes to realize my hand was grabbing Mike's throat. I heard the others screaming my name, trying to stop me from choking him to death. At that moment, I realized it was all a nightmare and I let him go, my heart still beating.

I saw him losing a lot of blood all over him. I started to walk back in shame and stuttered, "I...I...didn't mean...I didn't know!" Mike and the others started looking at me as if I was dangerous.

Then I saw Wan Po looking at me, and he yelled, "What did you do?!?!" That was the first time I ever heard him yell like that to me. I began to get scared and begged him, "I'm sorry, I didn't know." He yelled at me, "Get out of my face!" At that moment, I slowly began to feel D. again and realized that maybe I couldn't control or get rid of him that easily without hurting those closest to me. I put my head down and went outside.

Wan Po was yelling, "What is wrong with you?" I thought the same thing. While all of this happened, Wan Po and the others took Mike outside. Wan Po started to treat him with a few ancient Tibetan medicines to help ease the pain and relax him. I tried to see exactly what Wan Po was doing, but Ivan and Lee blocked me from seeing.

Ivan looked at me and said, "He doesn't want to see you."

"But it was an accident! I didn't know what I was doing."

Lee turned to me and said, "Sorry."

I was told to wait outside with a hideous yak robe. I nearly sobbed, feeling bad for what happened, but also not knowing what was real anymore. Sometimes I wished that I had died years ago and forgotten. For the first time since I became a fugitive, I looked up and saw only darkness.

At that moment, it was one of the most brutal days of my life. I was about to walk away, knowing I had screwed up another life, when I was stopped by Ivan.

He noticed me leaving and rushed towards me, blocking my way.

"Get out of my way!" I yelled.

"You're not leaving," said Ivan.

"Why? So you could punish me? Newsflash: I've been punished for years."

Ivan explained that wasn't his goal; he wanted me to see Wan Po.

"Oh, so he could chew on me again?!" I asked.

"No, just please go talk to him."

"Why should I?"

"Because he's not going to get mad at you, James. He just wants to talk before..."

"Before what?"

Ivan looked at me sincerely. I knew he was telling the truth. Even though something strange was going on, I knew that if I didn't meet Wan Po, I would regret it. I decided to go inside.

While I was inside, Ivan and Lee reassured me that Wan Po wouldn't snap at me. They both went outside, and I asked, "Why?" They said, "You'll see," and "Good luck."

I saw Wan Po. He looked calm while Mike was on the floor, resting with some strange-looking thing on his arm. Wan Po came and said, "Hello, James," in his calm and kind voice. I had to hold my emotions because I didn't want him to see me get emotional.

"Come, I want to talk to you, my son." I did, but I slowly walked forward because I still believed I had become a disappointment to him. He never showed hate or anger towards me, only love and sadness.

"It's okay, my son."

"How can you say that, Wan Po? I nearly killed Mike." I put my head down. He asked me to look at him and said that he now understood what happened. He had been thinking about what was going on with me and knew that I had a sickness in me, but he wanted to let me know that he had forgiven me because he didn't want me to feel like I failed him.

"Sit, James. Sit." I did, and we began to talk. I explained that I had multiple nightmares since I became a fugitive and sometimes didn't know what was real and what was not anymore.

"James, we all have our darker side, and it doesn't dominate you if you have people you love with you. Once you realize this, that devil inside of you will never win."

"How do you know?"

"Because if somebody like me can suffer and become somebody who helps others, you can too, James."

I nearly laughed and thought, *yeah, right,* but I slowly began to realize he might be right. Then Wan Po said something I would never forget:

"Remember, James, I want you to take good care of yourself because when you are good to yourself, you can be kind to everybody else. I would seriously like to see that before I go."

I looked confused and asked, "Go where?"

"I will be going away soon to save Mike."

"You mean you're going to get more medicine?" Wan Po smiled and said, "I'm going to die."

"What?!"

"I'm going to use every drop of blood I have to save him, and that includes my life."

"I don't understand."

"Mike has lost a lot of blood, James. He's dying, and I'm going to use everything I have as a mystic to save him."

"No!" I yelled.

"James, please!"

"But you healed me when you found me. Why can't you do the same thing to him?"

"That's because your injury wasn't fatal. Yes, you tried to slice your throat, but the force wasn't enough to kill you." I looked down in shame, feeling guilty. For the first time since the death of Dr. Patrick Barton, I never thought I would have to go through this again.

"Why can't I do it?" I asked.

"Because I'm older while you're younger. Besides, you don't have the type of blood he needs, my son."

"What about Ivan and Lee?"

"I refused to sacrifice those I take in."

I put my head down again and tried not to break down. "No, I can't believe this. This is my fault."

"No, it's not. It's that demon's fault, and you're not him."

"Don't do this, Wan Po." He put his hand on my shoulder and said, "Be strong, my son, and take good care of yourself."

"Please don't do this." I kept putting my head down until Wan Po said, "Look at me, James." I did and looked straight into his eyes. He said, "You are the best student of mine that I have ever had in so many years. Many people went to see me, and some quit or were banished, but you never gave up on me, and I never gave up on you."

While he said that, I was silent. Wan Po looked straight into my eyes and also said, "No matter what, just remember: you are not a murdering maniac. You are a good man."

We looked at each other and just sat together. He asked me, "It's time." I said to him, "But there has to be another way."

"There isn't."

"I can't accept that." I looked at Wan Po's face. He had a very sad look in his eyes and said, "Then I'm truly sorry."

I felt a pinch in my shoulder. I turned and saw Lee and Ivan. I noticed that Lee had put a dart through my shoulder. I began to feel numb all over. The last thing I said was, "You sons of bitches!" and everything went black.

Wow, what a bunch of idiots. I couldn't believe they actually knocked me out while trying to save Wan Po. It was very hard for me to believe, but as soon as I was able to get up, I noticed I was lying on the floor with a stitched-up blanket and a log on my head.

When I got up, I nearly forgot about Wan Po and asked what the heck just happened, but to my surprise, nothing came to mind, as if everything went blank. I slowly realized what had happened before I was shot with a dart: Wan Po was going to save Mike by taking his own life. I rushed up and started running everywhere like a maniac, trying to find Wan Po.

I rushed outside and realized I might have been too late because I heard people crying but didn't know where. I began to run around in the snow, hoping to find the source of the cries. The more I tried, the more lost I became.

Finally, I found where the cries came from. At first, I saw only Ivan and Lee, but then I realized more people had come to visit Wan Po. To my surprise, it wasn't just a few people in yak clothing, but some in Shaolin monk robes and other Tibetan-style clothing. They had fire and trumpets with them.

I realized Wan Po wasn't just some parish priest; he was like a god to so many people in Tibet. At that moment, I understood who Wan Po was. What I couldn't understand was how they managed to calm everyone and how long I had been gone for them to organize a memorial for him.

I saw Lee and Ivan. They saw me, and one of them said, "James."

"I...Ivan...I...Lee?" Both rushed towards me. At first, I tried to block them from touching me because I thought they were going to attack me, but instead they hugged me. I almost broke down in tears, knowing it was true. I even blamed myself for not saving Wan Po.

"It's okay, James. You can't blame yourself for this."

"Yeah, right."

"No, you can't."

I asked how long I had been gone. They told me the dart was strong, and to my surprise, I had been knocked out for about a week.

"A week?"

They told me to be quiet because of the funeral. I asked who the people were, and they explained that they were former students of Wan Po. Then I realized Wan Po hadn't just helped a few people over the years, but many in Tibet. I thought, *wow, he must have been some type of Dalai Lama.*

"Can I see him?" I asked. They smiled and said, "Of course." I walked toward the group and was getting closer to see Wan Po's body. Suddenly, it all came crashing down when I heard a loud voice:

"WHAT IS THIS SON OF A BITCH DOING HERE?!?!"

I looked around and realized it was Mike.

"What is he doing here?!"

"Mike, please!" said Lee.

"No, I will not."

"Mike, this isn't James's fault!" said Ivan.

"Yes, it is! This is his fault! It is all his fault!!!!"

I began to freak out, started to breathe heavily, and panic. That guilt began to grow inside me. I looked at Mike, and he had a very angry look in his eyes. I was about to black out and could hear the voice of D. trying to let him out. I shook my head in fear, remembering what Ku Soo and the Shaolin monk told me: I'm in control. I closed my eyes, but then when I opened them, I was punched in the nose by Mike and fell to the floor in pain.

"You broke my nose!" I yelled.

"Yeah, and I'm going to break more than just your nose, you murdering bastard!"

A bunch of people tried to hold Mike down, but he managed to break loose, biting one person's hand and slapping another.

Then Mike looked at me and yelled, "Now I'm going to kill you!" Lee and Ivan held onto Mike. They yelled, "James, you have to get out of Tibet! He's going to kill you!"

"No, not like this."

"James, please go!" yelled Ivan.

"No."

"GO!!!" they yelled.

Then Mike managed to break out when Ivan was spat on and Lee was punched in the groin. I was able to see the others try to stop him. I begged Mike to stop and that I was sorry, but all he could yell was, "Shut up!" I tried to reason with him, but he just kept beating them one by one. I saw Lee yelling, "Go, James, go!" and all I saw in the funeral were the bodies of so many people on the floor. I saw Mike acting like a wild animal, and after he beat the crap out of these people, I was so shocked and stunned. I yelled to him, "My God, what have you become, bro?!?!" I didn't get an answer, but I did see a raging, bloodthirsty look in his eyes. Mike came slowly like a zombie and yelled, "Now I'm going to kill you!" I began to shake, and at that moment I was very much willing to let D. come out, but I refused—even when the last thing I saw from Lee and Ivan was them on the floor with sad and painful looks in their eyes, begging me. I never forgot the tears that came from them.

At that moment I saw so many people injured or unconscious and heard their haunting shrieks. I ran for my life down the mountain, crawling and jumping my way from Mike. The more he chased me, the more we both nearly screamed for our lives. I could hear the avalanche that looked very much like the one from the nightmare that started it.

I managed to keep running for my life. After I heard a large sound as if the earth was shaking and the noise began to rumble so much that I nearly sprained my foot while trying to run, somehow I kept going. I managed to keep running until I realized I was alone again and, worse, that Mike was no longer chasing me. In that moment I knew that something awful might have happened.

"Mike!" I turned back and looked everywhere in that fat, awful snow that swarmed nearly everything. My legs disappeared to my waist. I realized that Mike may have been devoured by the avalanche, but I kept digging with my hands while on me and managed to handle it thanks to my gloves.

I looked everywhere and nearly lost my mind because even though Mike went too far, he was my friend and my brother. While this was happening it took me about nineteen minutes of looking around like a moron. When I really believed that Mike was dead, I walked away while struggling to get out of the snow. Suddenly I tripped and fell to the floor as if I had hit a log. I got up with snow all over me, and for a moment I thought, what if the thing that made me fall was Mike? I went down again with the burning snow on me; the only thing that kept me alive was the yak robe.

I kept looking over and over again to see if there was Mike. It took a few more seconds before I decided to just give up and go up, but to my shock I saw a human arm. I had to go back, dig closer to what I saw, and grabbed it. It was Mike's; miraculously he was alive. I managed to pick him up on my back and started slowly getting the hell out. Each time I nearly hurt my back and my feet because Mike was a big guy, and I nearly got frostbite each time I had to take a break.

We managed to travel many places day and night trying to get back down. Even though it had been somewhat easy for me to go alone to the Himalayas, it was a nightmare trying to do it while saving Mike.

I realized this would take days to survive, eating snow to satisfy my hunger. Each day I worried Mike would wake up. I realized he wasn't just unconscious but in a coma due to a terrible head injury—I later figured out he was hit with a rock covered in snow. About three days into struggling to save him, I realized it was nighttime. I looked up at the moon and stars and wondered what I'd gotten myself into. I started to shake and began to have a terrible fever; my skin felt like it was being cut open with knives.

When I closed my eyes, I felt someone's hand on me. I opened up and, to my absolute terror, it was Mike. He yelled, "I'm going to kill you and everyone you love!" I awoke to realize it was just another nightmare. I turned my head left and right to see Mike's body cold and unconscious. I wondered if I should leave him to die, but I knew that if I did, I would never be able to live with myself.

On the fourth day, I managed to climb down a few more times while holding Mike, and then I fell to the floor. To my surprise and joy, I noticed a couple of people who looked like foreigners climbing the Himalayas. I got up and raised my hands, trying to have them see me. Thank God they did. The two men had traveled from Hong Kong. They took both me and Mike to meet up with another group they had with them. I kept walking; they asked me to stop and rest, but I replied, "No, I need to keep going."

"No, you need a doctor," said one of the men.

"You have one?" I asked.

"Yes." I still pushed forward, but then I saw a group below. They managed to put a harness on both me and Mike, and all of us went down together.

They took me to a doctor. He looked at me and at Mike's unconscious body and shouted, "Call for a pilot ASAP!" In that moment I smiled and finally fell asleep, knowing that both me and Mike were saved.

A few minutes later we were put on a stretcher inside a helicopter and managed to escape from Tibet. I looked at Mike and tried to reach him. The last thing I said before I slept was, "Mike, I'm so sorry."

And just like that I let myself fall asleep.

What a nightmare it had been to see my own friend blame me for the death of someone he needed for peace. Sometimes I wondered if he was right about me. Even though it was the demon that attacked Wan Po, he was still a part of me, born from the deep rot that existed inside me. I wondered if I could overcome this. Sometimes I got confused about who I was.

While I was questioning my own identity, I awoke in a white room. At first I thought it was a mental asylum, but then I realized it was a Hong Kong hospital. When I got up I said, "Hello?" and nobody responded. I realized I had a hospital gown on and started to walk.

Then I suddenly bumped into another person. I was shocked to realize it was Mike. He was unconscious, and I breathed a sigh of relief. I wanted so badly to say how sorry I was for him; even though he chased me and blamed me, I still understood and believed he had a reason.

When I opened the door, I noticed two doctors who were stunned to see I was awake. They had a strong Chinese accent that I couldn't fully understand—like many others from Hong Kong who speak English.

One of them tried to explain something to me, as if asking who I was, but I couldn't quite respond because I had difficulty understanding. I tried to talk and understand, but I decided to yell, "Screw this!" and tried to walk away. I was stopped by a man who looked familiar; I realized he was the doctor who rescued me and Mike. I was surprised.

"You!" he said.

"Me," I answered.

"You're awake."

"Of course I am. Why wouldn't I be?"

He looked me straight in the eye and was about to say something, but the other two doctors began talking Chinese with the doctor who saved me. They argued about me, but it looked like the doctor who saved me got them to back off and they left.

"Now I see you're okay."

"Why wouldn't I be, doc?" I said.

"How long do you think you've been out?"

"I don't know, doc. You tell me."

"Sir, you were in a coma and we couldn't identify the man who was with you."

"I was in what?!?!" I yelled in shock. The doctor tried to calm me. He explained I had been unconscious for nearly a month. I was so shocked I nearly fainted and wondered how long Mike would be asleep.

I tried to rush out of the building because I didn't want Mike to come and try to kill me—then I let D. save me from him. I thanked the doctor for saving me and tried to walk out, but he explained I couldn't without answering some questions and putting on clothes.

"I don't know, that's a good idea, doc?" I muttered.

"Why not?"

"It's a long story, doc, but I seriously need to go." He blocked me with his hand on my chest and said, "You're not going anywhere until you're dressed and we ask some questions."

I got very pissed off and yelled in a dark, vicious voice, "DON'T TOUCH ME!!!" I pushed him to the side and he fell to the floor. I realized what I'd done and noticed I almost let D. slaughter that guy just for doing his job. The doctor looked at me in shock. I said, "I'm sorry...I...I didn't mean to," and I tried to reach for his hand, but he looked terrified and didn't want me to touch him. I saw people and other doctors looking at me. Guards were coming straight for me. I ran for my life before things got worse and managed to outrun the guards. I never saw the doctor who saved me again.

# XIII

# THE BROTHEL

While living back in Hong Kong I was so tired and needed time to take a break from running. I couldn't stop thinking about the man in black, but at the same time I couldn't stop thinking about how much I missed Karla. After all this time I attempted to go to a phone booth again and say the same words—that I loved her, that I missed her, and that I was okay—but again I couldn't even say those things. I couldn't even pay for the phone booth because I didn't have enough money. In fact, I didn't have any money. So I gave up and walked away, sleeping on the street cold and alone, just wanting to be left alone so I wouldn't have to hurt anybody.

While all of this was happening I spent many days as a panhandler, begging for somebody to give me money or food either to make a phone call to Karla—hoping I would have the courage to do what was right—or to satisfy my hunger and move on trying to find the man in black. Even though sometimes I doubted he might be real or that I had made him up because flakka was in my system, whatever was true or not, I still felt destined to be alone in an endless loop, trying to find a man I didn't even know or even whether he existed.

After a few days of trying to get money as a panhandler, I managed to have enough to call Karla a third time. When I did, I went to make the call and I managed to reach her. This time I heard her voice, a very sad tone, as if she still missed me after all these years. Her voice said only one word: "Hello."

I sighed with a deep breath and heard her voice again, "Hello, this is Dr. Karla Truman. Please leave a message after the beep." In that moment I was surprised to realize that my little sister had become a doctor, and instead of feeling worried about what might have happened to her I felt a sigh of relief that my sister was going places.

In that moment I decided I had enough and that I wasn't going to waste my time not talking anymore. I did something I never thought I'd have the courage to do—I opened my mouth to leave a message. I said, "Karla?" I closed my eyes and tears came out, and I almost felt at peace letting that thing out of my chest. I was going to say more, but I stopped myself from saying everything else, including who I was, because while all of this was happening I noticed someone I thought I would never see again. She was unrecognizable at first because she had become a prostitute in skimpy, revealing clothes. She wasn't the kind dishwasher and mother I'd met three years ago anymore. I realized who she was: Li Mai.

At first I didn't know what to do. Hearing Karla's voice and seeing Li Mai for the first time took me about five minutes to process. I looked back at the phone and hung up. I nearly let my emotions out, believing I would never see Karla again, and I really believed I may have just made the wrong choice.

Regardless of what happened or what could have been, I went up to see Li Mai, but each time I stopped myself because I was afraid of how she would react. I knew that if I didn't speak to her I would be haunted, not knowing what had happened to her and her daughter. I kept stalking her. She came out of nowhere and asked, "Hey honey, want to have a good time?"

At first I stood in shock that Li Mai would say that to me, but I was more shocked that she didn't even recognize me. I knew she blamed me for losing her job. I lacked the courage in that moment to tell her who I was, so I responded, "No thanks. I'm married," because I didn't want her to think I wanted to have sex with her.

"Okay." In that moment I knew if I said nothing I would lose her forever. "Li Mai?" I called, and she turned and looked at me for a couple of seconds. Then she finally recognized me.

She came to me and yelled, "You!" She spat on me, began hitting me, and blamed me for ruining her life.

"Li Mai, stop."

"No. My life is ruined because of you."

"Li Mai, please."

"Screw you!"

Then a man with a muscle shirt and black glasses came at me. He had a golden cane and started rushing toward both me and Li Mai. He said to her, "Baby, what's wrong? Why are you beating the loser?" Li Mai lied to him and said, "He tried to rape me and steal your money, Daddy."

"This guy?"

"Yes, Daddy." He looked at me with his cane and started beating the crap out of me. At that moment I nearly snapped and almost let D. out, but I looked at Li Mai and she had nothing but contempt on her face, even a tear running down her cheek.

When her pimp stopped beating me, they left me bleeding on the floor and went inside a brothel a few blocks away. In that moment I wished I had just called Karla and forgotten about Li Mai. I almost did, but while I was bleeding I slowly began to think about what Li Mai was going through and that she didn't know it wasn't me who had ruined her life. Even so, there were times when, bruised and bloody, I just didn't care anymore. But in my heart I knew letting her stay with that piece of shit wouldn't be fair to her or to myself in the long term.

When I got up, all bloody, I wobbled around trying to see Li Mai again. A few prostitutes looked at me—some were in shock, others were laughing. The more I saw, the more I almost let D. out. There was this one bitch laughing at me; I went straight to her face. She freaked out and ran away because she thought I was going to kill her. When she ran away, her laughing turned to crying. When I noticed what I'd done I almost felt bad and wanted to apologize, even though she was the one who pissed me off. I decided instead to focus on seeing Li Mai so I could make her understand.

Bleeding with a broken nose and bruised body, I went to the brothel. A man in a gimp suit stood in front of me and asked, "Are you okay, sir?"

I disregarded what he said and asked if he had a napkin. He gave me one and asked, "Are you a client?" I lied and said, "Yes."

"Name?"

"Robert Dent." I gave him a few dollars that people had given me. He asked who the lucky girl was, and I told him, "Li Mai." He looked at me and said, "Oh... she's speaking with her Big Daddy," and told me to wait a few minutes.

While I stood waiting I asked if there was a bathroom. He said, "Yes. It's upstairs to the right." I went to the bathroom and cleaned the blood off me. When I finished, I was going to go to the bar, but I stopped myself. The manager's office was a few steps away and I could hear arguments coming from inside. It sounded like a fight between two people. I felt in my heart it was Li Mai arguing with her pimp. I went to the door and put my ear to it. I heard a man yelling, and the more he yelled, the more I could hear a big slap. The person getting slapped was crying and screaming as if begging for their life. I realized the voice was a woman's—worse, it was Li Mai's voice. I heard the pimp yelling, "Where's my money, bitch?!" and Li Mai was struggling to speak as if she was being choked.

At that moment I used all my strength to break the door through, and I did. I saw Li Mai being strangled by the pimp who had beaten me. Li Mai was cut and bleeding on the floor just like I was. The pimp turned to me and yelled, "You!" He rushed toward me, stomping his boots on the floor. I stood my ground. He was going to punch me in the nose, but I dodged and used all my strength to knock him out. I did.

When I saw her pimp on the floor, I went to Li Mai and asked, "Are you okay?"

"Don't touch me!" she snapped, and she slapped my hand. I told her that it wasn't me who told her former boss years ago about her stealing money, yet she still wouldn't believe me. I asked, "Okay, if you don't believe me and I'm a scumbag who destroyed your life, why would I even help you?!" She stared at me with an angry look, and the more she looked at me, the more her face slowly morphed into confusion. She said, "You're serious... Y... you didn't do it."

"I. I think so."

"Okay, now let's get out of here before this asshole wakes up," I said.

"Wait. We can't go like this."

"What do you mean?"

She explained that if we left right now, downstairs they would notice something happened and the police would come. I looked for a way out and noticed a window with stairs that went both up and down. I told Li Mai, "I think I got an idea." We opened the door, climbed out the window, and managed to get out of the brothel.

I asked Li Mai if there was a car. She said, "Robert, we are both injured badly. Neither of us can drive like this." I smiled and said, "Okay. Let's see who is injured the most and then we'll go."

"Yeah—how are we going to do that?" she asked.

I suggested we stretch our arms as best we could and whoever dropped theirs first wouldn't drive. We did, and after a few seconds I dropped my hands. She laughed and I laughed too. "Okay, let's go before he wakes up and call the police," I said, and we did.

She got in the car and drove to her home while I began to rest. I felt tired, and even though I hadn't called Karla, I knew one day we would meet again. If I could see Li Mai again, then I could do the same with Karla. I smiled and closed my eyes.

## XIV

# WELCOME MR. DENT

When Li Mai drove me to her home, I was glad that she believed what happened three years ago wasn't my fault. But in my heart, I wasn't glad that I didn't have the courage to call Celia. While I was resting in the chair, I wondered if that would ever happen.

Sometimes I wondered how I was still alive after all these years. I wondered even more how Sarah hadn't caught me yet. After what happened to Uncle Walter, I decided that I wouldn't let anyone get close to me, not even Li Mai. If I had the chance, I wouldn't get close to Celia either, even if I wanted to. I guess that's why I never called her back—I didn't want her to get involved.

But whatever the reason, it didn't matter because I was in the here and now. While I was resting, I saw Li Mai looking weak and hurt as she drove. I asked her, "Are you okay?"

She smiled and said, "Yeah... I think so." I noticed her arms trembling and asked if I could drive. She told me, "You don't know where I live, Robert."

"So, let's go to the hospital," I asked.

"Why?"

I explained to her that her hands were shaking. She didn't say anything, as if I wasn't even there. While I begged her to go to the hospital, she began to get annoyed. The more I begged, the more agitated she became, until she pressed her foot hard on the brakes.

I nearly had my chest ripped open, and my head snapped. "Jesus, Li Mai, what the hell is wrong with you?"

"Listen, Robert. You just came back to Hong Kong, and you have no idea how dangerous this place is since you've been gone."

"What the hell are you even talking about?" I asked, anger rising.

"Robert, if we go to the hospital, my pimp is going to find me and kill me."

"I'm sorry, what?"

She explained that things had gotten darker since Hong Kong was overtaken by someone even more brutal. After the tyrannical dictator Smith was taken down three years ago, a foreign leader from the United States was taking control of Hong Kong—and that new leader was even more brutal than the last.

"Who?" I asked.

She said something that froze me in shock. The new leader was, of all people, Sarah Barton. My body started to tremble.

"Robert, are you okay?"

I closed my eyes, put my head down, and said, "Li Mai, there's something I need to tell you."

"What?"

Before I could speak, her cell phone rang. She picked it up and began speaking in Cantonese. I stood there, trying to figure out who she was talking to, waiting for the right moment to tell her the truth about who I really am.

After a few minutes, she hung up. I asked, "Who was that?"

She explained it was her daughter and that there was something important she needed to know. I smiled. She said, "You wanted to tell me something."

"Yeah."

"Then tell me," she said.

Instead of telling her the truth about who I really am, I told her something else. "Remember Dai Sheng and Kang Chu Tien?"

"The two assholes who got me fired back at Guohua Shinji?"

"Yeah."

"What about them?"

"After you got fired, I got fired too."

"Oh," she said.

"But I kicked their ass before I left."

She looked at me in shock. "No way."

"Oh yes, I made them my bitches."

She started laughing, and so did I. For a minute, we forgot all the bad things that had happened to us because we were glad some good moments existed. Then we drove back to Li Mai's apartment.

When we arrived, I saw Li Mai's daughter for the first time. I still remembered the times Li Mai felt so helpless and powerless to feed herself and her daughter after getting fired by Dai Sheng. I nearly choked up because I felt so bad for Li Mai for years, almost as much as I felt for Celia.

When she entered, Li Mai started speaking to her. I couldn't completely understand what she was saying, but I believed she was saying, "Mom, there's something you need to see." I saw her daughter trying to convince her of something. Li Mai looked at me and smiled. "Stay here, Robert. I'll prepare a med kit for both of us."

"Sure, Li Mai," I said.

Before she opened the door, I asked, "Is everything okay in there?"

Li Mai told me, "Oh, I think some visitors came to ask some questions."

"Okay, I'll see you," I said.

While waiting inside, I nearly fell asleep. I could tell something was going on, and I started getting bored. I didn't want to sleep in her car like I was disrespecting her, so I looked around. Something in my gut told me something interesting was happening. About nine minutes later, I saw Li Mai going outside with a big shirt to cover herself, wearing the skimpy clothes underneath. I also saw her daughter coming outside. I finally understood what was happening—I was horrified to see Sarah and McNally with them. I began to panic inside.

When I saw Sarah and McNally with Li Mai and her daughter, I hid behind the wheel, hoping nobody noticed me. About three minutes later, the door opened, and I started freaking out.

"It's me, Robert."

"Li Mai?" I asked.

"Yes. Why did you freak out like that?"

I looked around and noticed nobody was there except Li Mai and her daughter. Li Mai told me her daughter's name was Mai Ming and introduced her: "Mai Ming, this is Mr. Robert Dent." She looked a little nervous and began hiding behind her mother.

I smiled. "Hey, it's okay." I did a little magic trick with a penny I had in my pocket while begging in the streets, making it look like it was coming from her ear. She smiled and giggled. I was surprised she could speak English and asked Li Mai why she hadn't told me.

Li Mai smiled. "Why didn't you ask?"

We all smiled. I looked at Li Mai's face and saw a bunch of bandages. I smiled and asked if I could come inside.

"Of course. That's why I brought you here, remember?" Mai Ming giggled again.

I looked at both of them and said, smiling, "Okay," and we went inside. Li Mai began patching my wounds. While she worked, Mai Ming played with her dolls. We asked each other questions about what had happened over the past three years. We laughed and smiled. At one point she asked, "Hey Robert, do you still live around here?"

I had a sad look on my face while trying to smile. "I live wherever I am."

"That's the same as living nowhere?" she asked.

"Yeah."

She realized I was homeless and needed a place to stay. Mai Ming turned to Li Mai. "Mom, can Mr. Dent sleep here?"

Li Mai looked at me. "I think he can, sweetheart," and began speaking to her in Cantonese. Mai Ming giggled again.

"What's so funny?" I asked.

"I told her yes, but I need to sleep on the couch." I laughed.

"And Robert?"

"Yes?"

"Did you hear about James Truman?"

I froze. Li Mai looked at me, concerned.

"Robert, are you okay?"

"Yes... um, just a little tired... um, you mean the wanted fugitive?" I asked.

"Yeah. Sarah Barton and Wilfred McNally told me about a dangerous man living in Hong Kong. His name is James Truman. Did you ever hear of him?"

"Well... um, I heard of him, but I never really knew him. I mean, I knew people that may have known him, but I didn't."

"Okay," she said.

"Do you mind if I sleep here?"

"Sure, but before you do, I think you should take a shower first."

"Of course."

Li Mai showed me the bathroom. I took off my clothes and showered. When I was done, I asked if she had any clothes I could wear. She gave me pajamas and a white shirt, explaining that the clothes I was wearing belonged to her late husband many years ago.

After my shower, I grabbed a towel, dressed, and was ready to sleep. Li Mai asked, "Do you have any family members I can call?"

I thought of my father and sister and told her a lie—that they had passed away long ago.

"Oh, I'm sorry, Robert."

"Yeah, but that was another lifetime ago."

She turned off the lights and said, "Good night, Robert."

I smiled. "Thank you, Li Mai."

I went to sleep, tired, and promised myself I would never get close to people again. But I would soon break that promise and later regret everything that happened. This was the moment that started it all.

## XV

# THE TRUTH

When I stayed at Li Mai's house, I began to think about Sarah and thought to myself what if she finds me here in Hong Kong. I knew if I stayed here, it could endanger Li Mai and Mai Ming.

However, I knew they questioned Li Mai and left, but I know Sarah enough to suspect that she would try again if she even suspected me being here, and now that Hong Kong is being occupied, it would be very hard for me to keep hiding from her.

While I was thinking about this on the couch, I noticed footsteps coming towards me, and out of paranoia, I got up and covered myself, hoping that somebody wouldn't come again and attack me. Then I heard a voice, and it was Li Mai's daughter, Mai Ming. She came to me and said, "Mr. Dent."

"Yes," I spoke.

"Where are you from?"

"From Hong Kong."

Mai Ming looked at me like I was playing stupid and spoke, "No, I mean where are you really from?"

"America."

"Really?"

"Yep."

Then Mai Ming asked me if I had family there, and I smiled and told her that she asked a lot of questions.

"Sorry," Mai Ming said.

"No need to be sorry, I'm just a little tired today."

"Okay, Mr. Dent. Good night."

"Good night, Mai Ming."

I went back to rest for about a few minutes, but then I heard a voice.

"You think this is going to end well for us, you fool!"

I knew exactly who it was, and I began to shake to my bones because in that moment I knew it was D.

"No, not you again!"

He began to lecture me about how I'm nothing and that he's going to kill every single person in this house and take over my body forever.

"You think you can have a normal life and escape me? You cannot escape me!"

I got very angry and yelled straight at him, "Shut up!"

The voice began to laugh, and the more I spoke, his laugh grew louder and louder.

"Shut the hell up, you freaking demonic elf!"

"NEVER!!!"

Then I saw my left hand shaking, and I slowly began to become numb. I couldn't feel anything at all. I began to call for help, but nobody answered. Then I realized that my hand was getting possessed by D.

"Help! Somebody help!" I yelled, but nobody answered.

Then I noticed that my right hand grabbed me by the throat and started choking me, squeezing away what little strength I had.

I tried to escape by punching with my right hand, but I lost so much oxygen, and his grip on me was completely stronger than mine. I couldn't let go, and after a few more seconds of terror, I could feel my heart fainter and even fainter until nothing, and everything went dark.

Even though I was choked into darkness, I heard another voice, and it was someone I knew, but I wasn't sure. It was like my senses were blocked, and somehow they slowly came back. When they did, I noticed a tear on my cheek when I realized who the voice was.

"Celia?"

I nearly broke down and wept because I really believed that I would never see her again.

"How did you find me?" I asked.

"Wake up," she said.

"Wake up?" I stood there looking confused.

Then she said it again, "Wake up."

"Wake up what?!"

"Wake up, Robert!"

Then Celia's face slowly morphed into Li Mai, and I woke up.

"You're okay, Robert?" said Li Mai.

I looked around and saw both my hands. I touched my throat and noticed that everything was okay. I breathed a sigh of relief and said to Li Mai, "Yeah."

Li Mai looked at me sadly and spoke, "You had a bad dream, didn't you?"

"Yes."

"Well, I think it's over."

I nodded and smiled at Li Mai. She told me that the reason she woke me up was because she was going to work for another pimp at a brothel and was afraid that her old pimp would try to kill her. She wanted someone like me to make sure she was okay.

I worried about her and told her, "There are other jobs, Li Mai."

She scoffed at the idea, and I asked her, "Why, of all jobs, did you pick to become a—"

She stopped me mid-sentence and spoke, "What, a whore?"

I put my head down, and she looked at me and spoke, "You think I didn't try to get a job?"

Then she told me not to move and wait until she came back.

After a few minutes, she came back with a pile of job applications that she said she'd been trying to find for a year, but no one would hire her because she stole money from Dai Sheng.

"What about your daughter?" I asked.

"She can take good care of herself."

"She's just a kid, Li Mai."

"And she's my daughter," she rebutted.

I was shocked by what she said and the way she said it because it was almost like I was talking to a complete stranger. While we argued about all this, I kept trying to convince her that what she was doing was wrong and that there's always a way to get a better job, but she said she already tried and failed.

"Li Mai, what would other kids say to Mai Ming? Do you even care?"

"I care, and I always will care about Mai Ming, but she shouldn't care about what other kids think of me, and neither should you."

At that moment, I knew I was losing the argument and that I would never convince her, so I felt ashamed for her.

"Robert, it's okay," said Li Mai.

I looked her straight in the eye and shook my head. I got up off the couch and told Li Mai that I wasn't going to play this perverted game because I just saved her life, and now she's endangering her own and the life of her daughter because of her twisted idea of a job.

"I'm sorry, Li Mai, but I can't do this."

"What do you mean?"

She looked at me with a sad look on her face, but deep down, I knew she understood what I was trying to say.

"Oh... well, so am I," said Li Mai.

I got up, and Mai Ming came to Li Mai and said to me, "Mr. Dent, are you leaving?"

Li Mai looked at me and her daughter and consoled her. Seeing Li Mai and Mai Ming looking at me while I stood in front of the door reminded me a lot about my father and sister when I left them many years ago. I began to open the door.

When I opened the door and took one step out, I noticed, to my shock, that something was wrong because I knew who the people were a few steps away from me. They had come back to find me, and to my surprise, they were Sarah Barton and Wilfred McNally again.

I went back and shut the door with a loud sound, and Li Mai yelled, "What the hell is wrong with you, Robert!"

I rushed back into the house. While running into the bathroom, I put my whole body into the empty tub and covered myself.

While all of this was happening, I could hear Sarah and McNally's voices coming closer. While hiding for my life, I could also hear the voice of D. in my head, laughing and calling me a fool.

"I told you that you can never escape, Truman!"

I covered my eyes with my hands while staying in the tub for about five minutes. The longer I stayed, the more I could hear that demon's insults in my head. At that moment, I wanted to die.

While I couldn't understand everything they were saying, I heard a few things. One of them was, "Have you seen this man?" I knew exactly who that was, and in that moment, I was scared to death.

While I was freaking out, I heard Li Mai's voice, and I closed my eyes. I thought to myself, this is it, but to my surprise, I heard her voice again, and she said to them, "No, I've never seen that man."

I opened my eyes and heard a few other things—footsteps, and then the door being closed.

I got up out of the tub and opened the curtains. I asked if Li Mai was there, and she yelled loudly, "ROBERT!"

In that moment, I knew she knew who I really was and that she had become an accomplice.

I got out of the tub and went to her, and I noticed that she was the only one standing in front of me.

"Where's Mai Ming?" I said.

"She's upstairs in her room."

In that moment, I knew I was screwed.

"Listen, I know what you're thinking."

"What! That you're a criminal?" Li Mai said.

"Look, I'm not what you think I am."

"Oh, I know exactly who you are, Mr. Dent."

At that moment, I confessed to her something I hadn't told anyone in a very long time—that my name wasn't Robert Dent.

"What?" she said in shock.

"My name is James Truman. Dent is just an alias."

In that moment, she was freaking out because now she knew that Robert Dent wasn't a real person but instead James David Truman, the wanted fugitive.

"I'm calling!"

"No, wait!" I begged her.

"If you're Truman, why should I trust you? Everything else you have to say is more lies."

"Because you're wrong!" I yelled.

Then she slapped me and said, "Wrong about what?!"

I replied, "That I'm guilty."

"If you're not guilty, then who is?!"

I remained silent, and she ran to get Mai Ming, yelling, "Me and my daughter are going to Barton and McNally!"

As she said that, I held her, and she yelled, "Get off me, psycho!"

"Listen!" I begged her.

Then we looked at each other in the eye, and she said, "Who do you think you are?!"

"I don't know, but I know that I'm not guilty. They got it wrong."

"If you're not guilty, then who is?" she asked.

"I'm looking for someone who really is."

Li Mai looked very serious and said, "Get off me."

"But—"

"Get off me!"

I did, and she looked into my eyes like she was looking into my soul and asked, "Is your name Robert Dent?"

I said, "No."

"Are you a criminal?"

"No."

"Then who is?"

I told her, "Someone that ruined my life."

I explained to her everything that happened. Sometimes she almost stopped listening and was about to call for help, but deep down she knew who I was. She knew that an evil man wouldn't care about people like her or Mai Ming.

While all of this was happening, I told her about my whole life—from Smart City, Hong Kong, and Tibet—every single detail. Her eyes began to water, and I knew in that moment she gave me her sympathy, but I wasn't sure she gave me her trust.

"Now do you believe me?" I asked.

"I believe you, James."

I told her that I needed to go.

Then Mai Ming came and yelled with her little voice, "No, Mr. Dent, no!"

I saw Mai Ming and said, "I'm sorry, little one, but I need to go."

"But why?"

I bent my knee down and told her, "It won't be the end. I will see you soon someday, okay?"

She looked at me sadly, and I felt sad too for her because the whole experience reminded me of myself and my sister Karla a long time ago. I struggled not to stay because I didn't want to be haunted by a repeat of my old life.

"Mai Ming, Mr. Dent needs to go."

"No!" yelled Mai Ming.

"Mai Ming!"

I looked at Li Mai, and it really reminded me of my father and sister. Because of my big heart and stupid mind, I told Li Mai that I would stay but only for three days.

"But you can't," said Li Mai.

"It's okay, Li Mai. It's only going to be three days so I can meet up with that man, help you find a better job, and say a better goodbye."

Li Mai said to me, "Are you sure about this?"

I smiled at her, and she looked at me seriously, but then she looked at Mai Ming, and after a few seconds, she smiled at her and said to both of us, "Okay."

Mai Ming was so happy she even jumped into my arms like I was her father. I stood in shock for about five seconds. I hugged her, and in that moment, I almost felt for the first time that I was like a father to her—and I knew she needed one.

"So, what are we going to do?"

I told her that we were going to see her pimp and that I was going to be her bodyguard, and that was the beginning of our relationship—but it would soon be the beginning of a tragedy.

XVI

# THE PIMP AND I

It was kind of strange and a little nerve-wracking—the idea of having myself be a bodyguard, especially in a place with many thugs and perverts trying to get a piece of someone who has the type of life Li Mai has. And sometimes I wondered, what am I doing, and should I even be with someone when I'm a fugitive?

But even so, I couldn't handle living a life not knowing, just like with Celia and my family back home. In this part of life as a wanted fugitive, I felt weak and questioned what's the point of running, and even if The Man in Black exists or is a figment of imagination, it's hard to keep running for years trying to find one man in a city like Hong Kong.

And I guess I kept running because I couldn't stomach the idea of losing him, and even though I would regret it, I also couldn't stomach the idea of being alone. So that's why I decided to be a bodyguard for Li Mai in order to meet her new pimp. Even though I objected to her going to meet that man, I wanted to help her find a better life because I believed she would soon regret the whole thing.

When myself and Li Mai drove to meet her new pimp, the more I asked her if she was sure about this, she always smiled at me like I was an innocent child. Even though she never answered, I felt somehow this would end up badly.

Later, in about thirty minutes, we managed to park the car, and we saw a giant old warehouse that looked very rusty. I thought to myself that it must be an abandoned building, and Li Mai told me that her pimp is on top of the warehouse. I really got worried for Li Mai's safety. When we both got out and walked to meet up with him, we began talking to each other. Before we took one step inside the warehouse, I asked Li Mai again if she was sure about meeting this guy, and she said, "James, it's okay." Because she called me James, I was in shock and said, "Keep your voice down!"

"Why?! It's y..., oh," she said.

"Yeah!"

"I'm sorry."

She looked at me with the smile of someone embarrassed, and I said to her, "It's okay."

We went inside the abandoned warehouse, and boy, did we get tired because the whole warehouse was filled with all types of urine, feces, alcohol, and drugs. It looked like a place where homeless people lived, and I was one of them, but I never felt like puking while trying to get up to an abandoned warehouse.

"I feel like I want to vomit!"

"Just hold it, we're almost there."

"How can you handle this garbage?" I asked.

"I worked in dishwashing and sex. What's more disgusting than that?"

I shook my head while laughing and spoke, "Boy, you're really something else, Li Mai."

After about a few more minutes, we managed to go up to the top of the building, and to my shock, we both saw something that surprised me because nothing was there.

"Hello?" said Li Mai.

Nobody answered, so Li Mai looked around and noticed nothing except the sky and the people below looking like ants. I kept looking around, and so did Li Mai, but nothing was there, and we began to question if we had gone to the wrong place.

Then Li Mai asked me to go down while she stayed up looking around, and I was stunned when she asked me to do that.

"What about me being your bodyguard?" I spoke.

"Just do it."

"Li Mai."

"Don't worry about me. I can take care of myself. I've been doing this for years."

I looked nervous and said, "You're sure?"

"Yes, I'm sure!"

"Okay, Li Mai."

I did go down and looked around for about a few minutes, but nothing came of it. While all of this was happening, I tripped and yelled, "Oh, come on!"

When I got up, I thought to myself, what kind of idiot put junk on the floor? Then I looked down and noticed that I didn't just trip on junk but on a gun, and I picked it up.

"Whose gun is this?" I wondered.

When I picked up the gun, I noticed it was loaded, but that wasn't the most disturbing thing I noticed, because the gun had a name on it, and it was the name of someone I hadn't seen in a long time.

"No, it can't be!"

After I realized who it belonged to, I could hear screaming coming from upstairs.

It was Li Mai's screams. "Help! Help!" she yelled.

I ran to go up the warehouse to see what was going on, and I was stopped in the middle when I saw Li Mai taken hostage as a human shield by a man with a pistol on him, and the guy yelled, "Remember me?"

"You're the same pimp at the brothel!"

The man began to laugh and said, "Damn right, asshole—or do you prefer Truman?"

Then I tightened my fist and yelled, "LET HER GO!"

"Or what?" said the man.

"Or I'll kill you!"

He began to laugh even harder, and the more he laughed, the more I felt D. coming out inside of me, and I was going to let him. However, my blacking out didn't come from D. but from something else. When I realized what it was, I noticed that I was bleeding in the stomach—then I realized that he shot me.

"I'm going to tie you up and have fun with this bitch while I cut you with my knife. I want you to feel what I felt!" Then he knocked me out.

## Two Hours Later

When I woke up, I was tied up on a chair, and I saw two men in front of me. One of them slapped me in the face and yelled, "Wake up, Truman!"

I opened my eyes and yelled, "How the hell do you know who I am?"

"I heard that red-haired skank looking for you, as well as that blonde clown!" said the man.

"Sarah Barton and Wilfred McNally?"

"Yeah, that's them!"

I was in shock and told him, "When I get out of here, I'm going to break your face."

The man laughed, then he grabbed his knife and cut a piece of my shirt off—as well as my skin. "Shut your freaking ass up!"

I felt blood coming out. It was like a burning feeling from my own skin.

"What do you want from me?!" I spoke.

"I said shut up!" and he cut me again on my stomach.

"Please stop!"

I began to bleed even more from my body. While all of this was happening, I noticed Li Mai also being tied up on a chair, and the jerk who knocked me out was there next to her.

"Li Mai."

"Oh, she's just warming up, buddy."

I got very angry at the man and yelled, "If you lay one finger on her, I'll cut it off!"

"Oh really?"

Then he turned me, and I could see Li Mai without her clothes, with a ball gag in her mouth. I was in shock.

When the man who did all of those things to Li Mai stood there, I was furious. I was going to scream in his face, but instead, he grabbed me by the mouth and yelled, "You beat the crap out of me, and now I'll beat the crap out of you!"

In that moment, I knew Li Mai's former pimp was going to torture us both and then kill us, all for payback for getting his ass kicked. While this was happening, the pimp grabbed my arm and looked at me with an evil look in his eyes. Then he grabbed his knife, saw my finger on my right hand, and yelled, "The only finger that's getting cut off is yours, boy!"

I begged him over and over, yelling, "No! Please don't!" The more I begged, the more they laughed. Then they cut a piece of my finger off, and I screamed and screamed and screamed.

I knew from the very start that it would be a trap, but I had no idea it would be something I couldn't handle—especially being held hostage by Li Mai's ex-pimp and knowing that the new pimp never existed. Worse, I was now tied up without a finger, which was just the first step in torturing me.

While Li Mai was being knocked out, I kept begging that psycho to stop, but he wouldn't listen. In fact, he told me that Li Mai was going to be sold into sex slavery. He laughed in my face, and the more he did, the more I could hear the voice of D. yelling over and over, "KILL HIM!"

I struggled to get out, and the more I did, the more they began making fun of me. "What are you going to do, Truman—kill me like you killed that doctor?" When he said that, I knew what he meant.

"I DIDN'T KILL HIM!"

"Oh, like I didn't trick you and force your bitch to drink beer and smoke weed over and over while raping her?"

I was in shock when he said that. I could even feel the strength and hatred from D. coming through me, and he wanted me to let him out to slaughter that bastard.

"What did you say?"

That freaking pimp told me with a grin, "That's right, I made her suck my cock!"

And like that, I snapped into a fury of anger and yelled with the voice of D., "YOU DIE!!!" Then I began to try to break out of the ropes that tied me. The more I did, I felt my flesh burning and the pressure from my whole body growing stronger. The more I struggled, the more he laughed again, and the more they laughed, the more I found the strength to get out. Slowly they noticed the ropes ripping apart, and he stood there frozen in shock. I even saw sweat coming from that pimp.

"IF YOU TAKE ONE MORE STEP, I'LL KILL YOU!" yelled the pimp.

"NOT SO FUN WHEN SOMEONE ISN'T TIED TO A CHAIR, IS IT, YA BASTARD?!?!"

Then the pimp came at me, but to his surprise, as well as mine, I was freed from the chair and the ropes. When I was freed, I grabbed him by his throat and began to choke the life out of him.

I saw his tongue coming out and his face turning red as an apple. As for me, I slowly began to black out and let D. take over. Then I was stabbed again with his knife. I grabbed the pimp by the wrist and broke it. Then I rushed to the window and said to him, "YOU'RE NOT LAUGHING NOW, ARE YOU!"

The last thing I saw before the blackout was the eyes of a frightened man who really believed he was going to die. Then I noticed my hands shaking toward his throat as if D. was controlling me again, and my hands were on his throat. Before I blacked out, I yelled with the voice of D., "LAUGH NOW, ASSHOLE!!!" and I began to laugh and laugh and laugh.

Then suddenly, after I came back from my anger, I noticed that I was still standing and my hands were still in the air like I was still choking the piece of crap. I turned left and right wondering what happened, and instead of being thrown out the window, he was on the floor with a terrified look in his eyes. He wouldn't move, as if he were in a catatonic state, and in that moment, I knew he was gone.

It was dark outside, and I didn't know what to do. After about ten seconds, I kept looking at the pimp and said, "Good riddance."

I was about to walk away downstairs, but then I noticed I forgot someone and told myself, "Li Mai?" Then I turned and saw her unconscious, still tied up naked with a ball gag in her mouth. I grabbed the pimp's own knife off the floor and used it to cut the ropes off Li Mai. I took out the ball gag, threw it out the window, and put my jacket on her so she wouldn't be cold.

I picked her up and carried her with both my arms while my body was in pain from all the cuts that had been inflicted on me. At first, I struggled to go down while carrying Li Mai, but I managed to go outside and put her inside the car, and we drove back to her house.

While I was driving, I was thinking to myself how people could be so disgusting, and I wished the life I had never happened. In fact, I would rather have a normal life than to ever leave my home to go to Smart City and become a rebel. I wondered if there was any hope for me to get out of the life that was put on me. But at the same time, I knew that could never happen. When I drove back to Li Mai's house, I wondered, what am I even doing, and is this really my life?

Then after about thirty more minutes, I managed to get to Li Mai's house. I carried her out of the car and grabbed her keys to get inside her house. While all of this was happening, I noticed that the room was very quiet and filled with many lights. I could hear Mai Ming's footsteps coming toward us, and when she saw what happened, she looked at us with a sad face and said, "Mr. Dent?"

"Mai Ming, call the ambulance, please!" I said. She looked terrified when she saw Li Mai on the couch half naked.

"Mai Ming, please!"

She looked at me and her mom, and after about four seconds, she grabbed the phone and called the ambulance for help.

## XVII

# THE HOSPITAL

After Mai Ming called for the ambulance, they put Li Mai on a stretcher and gave bandages to my finger while we rushed to the hospital with the paramedics. I began shaking in fear when I saw Mai Ming crying and asking for her mother to wake up. I said to her, "It's going to be alright."

She looked at me and said, "Is Mommy going to die?"

I looked at her straight in the eye and told her, "No, Mommy is going to be okay."

"Promise?" she asked.

"Yeah, I promise."

After a few minutes or more, we managed to get to the hospital, and they moved Li Mai into the emergency room. I tried to hold Mai Ming in my arms while the paramedics rushed her mother to her room.

While we rushed with the paramedics, I saw Li Mai's eyes barely opening. When I saw her eyes opening and closing, Mai Ming got scared and yelled for her mother. I patted Mai Ming on the back, trying to calm her down.

When I saw Li Mai's face and her eyes opening and closing, I said to her, hoping she could hear me, "Li Mai, you're going to be fine."

As Mai Ming and I followed the paramedics, one of the nurses told us that this was as far as we could go. I was stunned and told her to get out of my way, but she refused and said, "I'm sorry, sir, but I can't do that."

"But this girl is her daughter!" I yelled.

"I understand that, sir, but you have to wait until she recovers."

I stood there shaking with both fear and anger and almost felt D. coming out again because of the whole crisis. I told Mai Ming that we had to stay for a while until we could come and visit her mother. She asked, "Why?" and I explained to her that the doctors would need to focus on helping her.

In that moment, I thought I was going to vomit because I just couldn't handle the stress. So much so that I had to bring Mai Ming with me to the bathroom, but I left her outside the door while I vomited. I must have vomited about three or five times. I flushed the toilet, washed my face with water, and went back out.

When I went to see Mai Ming, I saw her waiting the whole time. We sat down in two chairs, and a bunch of other people were sitting nearby. We talked about Li Mai's health. She wondered what had happened to her and me, and I couldn't exactly say in detail because I didn't want to make her feel too bad. I explained that some people did something bad to us, and that's why my finger was cut and why her mother was sent here. She began to cry and asked me, "Why?"

When she asked that, I nearly cried because I felt a certain amount of responsibility for what happened. If I hadn't gotten involved, none of this would have happened, and Li Mai and Mai Ming would still be okay. The moment Mai Ming asked, "Why?" was the moment I felt guilty. But I didn't want to give her false hopes, so I gave advice that I knew she would never forget.

"Don't ask why, ask how."

She looked confused, so I explained: don't ask why this is happening, but instead, ask how you can fix what is happening. After a few seconds, Mai Ming looked up at me and asked, "Did your mommy have something like this happen to her, Mr. Dent?"

In that moment, I couldn't take it anymore. A tear came down my cheek, and I told her, "Yes."

She then wiped the tear from my cheek. I told her, "This was a mistake."

"What?" she said.

"I shouldn't have been with you two. I shouldn't have been with anyone."

Mai Ming felt sad for me and said, "That's not true!"

"It's true, Mai Ming!" I spoke.

"No, it's not!" She slapped me on the face to make me snap out of it and said, "What happened to Mommy wasn't your fault. It was them and them alone. Do you understand?"

Then she saw me with my head down and asked, "You want a hug?"

I smiled. She gave me a hug, and I began to cry. We waited for Li Mai to recover.

## THE NEXT DAY

Wow, I couldn't believe we had sat down and waited for almost 24 hours. The longer I stayed waiting, the more nervous I got about Sarah and McNally coming after me. In fact, I nearly had daydreams about them being right in front of me at times and nearly freaked out. One of those times was when the nurse came to me and said, "Sir?"

I started shaking as if I had a seizure, but then she told me, "Sir, it's okay. It's okay!" My vision went back to normal, and so did my senses.

"Sir, Misses Li Mai wants to see you!"

I looked at her and said, "She's awake?"

"Yes, you can come visit her."

I began to feel relieved and told Mai Ming to wake up. We both followed the nurse into her room. I knocked on the door, and I heard Li Mai's voice say, "Come in."

All three of us saw her. Mai Ming rushed toward her mother, and they hugged and wept. The nurse told us she would let us be alone for a while. I entered the room and said, "Hey, Li Mai."

"Hey."

She was on the bed with Mai Ming in her arms. I told Li Mai, "I'm so sorry."

"What for?"

"This was all my fault."

She smiled and asked, "How can this be your fault? You saved me."

"But for how long?"

"Don't blame yourself. You did the right thing. If you weren't there, I would have died or been sold." I nodded my head.

"You may be right."

Then the doctor came and told Li Mai that she had been discharged. I thought to myself, wow, how fast.

Then the doctor said, "You'll be right?"

She told him that she would, then told both Mai Ming and me to turn around.

I asked, "Why?"

Then I looked at her clothes and finally noticed that it was a hospital gown. I said, "Oh," and we all laughed.

She then got dressed, and we walked down the hall to the exit, hoping to get a taxi. Before we did, she told me something I would never forget until the last time I saw Li Mai and Mai Ming:

"My friend, don't ever blame yourself for another's crimes. No matter how dark, scary, and hopeless life gets, there will always be light at the end of the tunnel for you."

I smiled at her, we hugged, and Mai Ming hugged us as well. Then we went to get a taxi to take us to Li Mai's house.

# XVIII

# DEATH AND REVENGE

Li Mai managed to pay the taxi driver a few bucks to get us to her home. When I asked to take us where she lived, the driver ignored me as if I wasn't even there. I tried again, but he still wouldn't answer. When I was about to ask a third time, he interrupted me and said something to Li Mai in Cantonese with a very agitated look in his eyes. Li Mai responded, and we drove.

"What did the guy say, Li Mai?" I asked.

Li Mai almost had an embarrassed look on her face and responded, "He asked me to shut you up and then he'll take us wherever I want."

I was pissed off and wanted to jump on him, but Li Mai held me back. I turned to Mai Ming, and she asked me, "He's not worth it."

So, I sat back with my arms crossed, and the driver began to drive. But little did we know, he began to drive like a damn lunatic for some reason. That psycho began speeding and nearly bumping into other cars as well as not stopping at stop signs.

I thought we were all going to die, and I wanted so badly to punch this piece of crap. But the car kept bumping everywhere, and everybody, including me, nearly panicked. I even saw Mai Ming crying while Li Mai was trying to comfort her, and because of that, I wanted to punch that sucker so hard.

After about thirty seconds of his driving, I began yelling at the driver

122

to stop the car and cursed at him. "Stop the damn car, you freaking psycho!" I yelled, and all he did was turn and smile at me. I really wanted to break his neck, and I tried many times, but I couldn't reach him.

It wasn't until Li Mai grabbed Mai Ming into my arms and she opened the door outside that we managed to stop the freaking car. When he did, I was in such a rage that I gave Mai Ming to her mother and got out. I slammed the door while going to the driver and yelled, "What the hell is wrong with you? Are you freaking crazy!"

He started talking Cantonese in a very smart-ass way, and he even started laughing.

Then, out of nowhere, I felt the hand of D. coming out, but only with my whole arm out of my control when the driver had my—or his—hand on his neck. I began choking and saw him with fear in his eyes. Li Mai and Mai Ming looked at me with terror and begged me to stop. While all of this was happening, I was in such a rage that I couldn't hear them. But when Li Mai's voice kept yelling for me to stop and grew louder, I looked at them. Only then did I see her. Li Mai looked at me with fear.

When I saw their faces as well as my arm on that jerk's neck, I began to feel less numb and was able to let him go. The driver looked at me with fear and drove off with tears in his eyes.

I then turned to Li Mai and Mai Ming and said, "I'm sorry you had to see that."

Mai Ming started crying and began hiding behind her mother. I never felt so bad in my life, as if I had some glimmer of hope and now both of them feared me. I began to beg them to forgive me. I even kneeled down in tears after Li Mai told me not to touch her.

"Li Mai, please, I'm sorry!"

"Just... just take us home and don't get near my daughter!"

I began to feel in shock, like this was becoming how it was when Sarah blamed me for what happened to Patrick four years ago. I kept begging her to forgive me, and Mai Ming kept hiding behind her.

She then picked up her phone, and I wondered what she was trying to do. When I realized what she was doing, I begged her again.

"Li Mai, please don't call Sarah and McNally!"

"Take us home, or I'll call them!"

"Okay, okay."

"Remember, this is your third day with us, so you need to leave after we go home!"

When she said that, I was devastated and felt like my life was really repeating what happened a long time ago.

While all of this was happening, we began to wait for another taxi to get us there. While waiting about eight minutes in the streets, I put my head down in shame and didn't even look at them because I didn't want them to be afraid of me.

When we managed to find a taxi, we got in, and Li Mai put Mai Ming in the side door so she wouldn't be afraid of me. I was heartbroken. The girl and her mother had given me hope, and now they just blew it up in my face.

I knew that things wouldn't be the same, and besides, this was the third day before I had to leave anyway, so there was no chance of them not being afraid of me. About eleven minutes later, we managed to get to Li Mai's house.

When we came home, I didn't know what to do with myself. Inside the house, Li Mai told Mai Ming to go to her room and let her and me talk. At first, Mai Ming didn't want to because she was afraid I would do something bad to her mother, but Li Mai promised that nothing was going to happen. She gave her a kiss, and Mai Ming went to her room.

Li Mai then sat down with me, face to face, while looking at me with a very serious look on her face for about a minute or two. The more she stared at me, the more I thought she was going to scream at me and kick me out. But instead, she said words I would never forget.

"James... I know you think that I hated you when you grabbed that man, and I know what you did was defending us against that man. But you didn't want to beat him—you wanted to kill him, and I saw it in your eyes."

"Li Mai... I..."

"No, James. Listen to me," she interrupted.

"I am grateful you helped me and Mai Ming, and I still believe that what happened four years ago was not your fault, and I'm sorry you had to go through these things."

I nodded my head and asked, "What's your point?"

"My point is that we both know you have to leave before Sarah Barton and Wilfred McNally suspect you of being with us."

"So, I have to leave?" I asked.

"Yes... But I will give you some money to help you."

"But not enough for me to find The Man in Black?" I asked.

"No, but it's enough to survive."

Li Mai then got up and started searching around her house. She gave me a handful of money to help sustain me. She then asked me, "What would you do now?"

"You know, sometimes I really don't know."

Li Mai looked at me with a sad look, and I asked her, "What would you do?"

"Get a better job," she said.

We both smiled for about three seconds until I began to think about Mai Ming and asked Li Mai, "What about Mai Ming?"

"She'll be okay, I promise." I smiled and put the money in my backpack and went next to the door.

"Goodbye, Li Mai."

She smiled with a tear in her eye and said, "Goodbye, James."

I then had a huge sigh and touched the doorknob, but about a second or two later, the door opened itself. To my shock, two people were outside, and I knew who they were: Sarah Barton and Wilfred McNally.

At that moment, I shut the door on their faces and tried to run out the back entrance while yelling at Li Mai, "Go, Li Mai, get out of here!"

She blocked me and yelled, "Why?"

"They're here!"

Her face turned pale. I was trying to escape, only to realize the only place left was a glass window in the bathroom. While all of this was happening, I could hear Sarah and McNally banging on the door over and over again. I tried to find a way through without cutting myself, wrapping a small towel around my hand to prevent injury.

At that moment, I was afraid Li Mai was going to get jumped on by them. While getting worried about her, Li Mai started yelling at me to hurry. I broke through the glass by punching it with all my strength. I could see cracks at first and then a huge explosion the second time, and I knew I could finally escape. I jumped out of the window, hoping they wouldn't catch me.

When I got out, I landed next to Li Mai's neighbor's fence and almost broke my leg, but I managed to get up and hide. When I turned back, I worried about Li Mai and Mai Ming and didn't want to sacrifice them to save myself. I ran back to take them with me, but to my shock, I was caught—not by Sarah or McNally, but by an old friend turned enemy, Mike De Veny.

When I saw Mike De Veny for the first time in a while, I noticed he had a gun. I raised my hands and started begging, "Why are you scared, James?"

"Mike, please!" Then, out of nowhere, Mike shot me in the leg, and I yelled in agony. While all of this was happening, I could hear Sarah's voice yell, "Who the hell opened fire?!" She began rushing outside to see what was going on. Mike grabbed me by the neck and pointed the gun at my temple.

"Don't be afraid. It's going to be quick, unlike Wan Po's."

"That wasn't my fault!" I yelled.

"You say one more word and I'll shut you up!"

Then, out of nowhere, I saw Sarah and McNally a few steps away from me. Sarah yelled at Mike, "De Veny, stop! I want him alive!"

"Why?"

"So he can rot, that's why!"

"Nice idea...but no." Then I heard Barton's gun firing on the floor next to De Veny. Sarah yelled, "I'm warning you, De Veny! Let him go!"

Mike looked at Sarah, then turned and looked at me. He let go of his gun and gave it to Sarah, but she told him to give it to McNally because she would be arresting Li Mai and Mai Ming for aiding and abetting a wanted fugitive.

"No, you can't do this, Sarah!" I yelled.

"It was when you said that, bitch, who you are—and she did nothing!" Sarah shouted.

"Sarah, I beg you!"

"Oh, like how my husband begged when you killed them and the rest of the thirty civilians?!"

"That wasn't my fault!" I yelled.

Then she rushed to me and yelled, "Then who was it?!"

I told her it was The Man in Black, who was drugged with Flakka, but she started laughing and yelled, "There is no Man in Black!"

While in the car, Sarah went inside and grabbed both Li Mai and Mai Ming by the hair. Li Mai tried to fight Sarah, but she was much tougher and more skilled.

Sarah then turned to McNally and yelled, "McNally, we'll take the girl to foster care and put this bitch on a plane to Smart City, okay?!"

In that moment, I felt déjà vu all over again with Wan Po and his parents. I became enraged to see how awful Sarah had become and yelled at her, "You family-separating bitch!"

Sarah came to me and told me, "They separated themselves!" Then she turned to McNally to give Mai Ming to him, but McNally disappeared as if he wasn't even there.

"McNally?" said Sarah. Her voice got a little louder, "McNally? McNally?!" There was no response. "MCNALLY?! MCNALLY?!?! MCNALLY?!?!?!"

About nineteen seconds later, Sarah finally found him, but to her horror, she realized he was being held hostage as a human shield by Mike De Veny. He had a gun on him, pointing at McNally's temple.

"You!"

"Yes, me!"

Then came the worst day of my life: the worst day since my mother died, the worst day since I left my family after attacking my best friend Kyle Jadiel and my girlfriend Celia Mendoza, the worst day since I was drugged and sent to Blackstone, the worst day since I was framed for multiple murders by The Man in Black, and the worst day since Wan Po died while saving Mike De Veny.

Out of all the days, this must have been one of the worst combined. It was completely unthinkable and unforgivable, done by a former friend who blamed me for ruining his life. In some ways, I believed every word he said, but deep down, I always knew it would come to this.

When Sarah grabbed Li Mai and Mai Ming by their hair, instead of Mike shooting Wilfred McNally, or Sarah Barton, or even myself, he instead shot and killed two of the best people I had met in a long time. The first was Li Mai, and the second was Mai Ming, who was just a little girl.

I felt so powerless to stop it while handcuffed and in the car. The last thing I saw were the eyes of a mother who failed to protect her daughter and the eyes of a frightened girl. When I saw them shot to death and lying on the floor, my body went numb for about ten seconds.

When I saw Sarah's clothes in blood and Mike using McNally as a human shield with a gun in his hand, I didn't know what to feel.

While all of this was happening, Sarah pointed the gun at Mike and yelled, "You asshole! Why did you kill them?!"

"To prove a point, you red-headed bitch."

Then, out of nowhere, McNally broke free from Mike's grasp and began twisting Mike's arm.

"You better keep your mouth shut because you have the right to remain silent!"

In that moment, I was in so much denial and despair that this was happening, and I couldn't believe it was even possible. I kept telling myself, "No! It can't end like this! They're not dead! They can't be dead!" I kept repeating it like a broken record, my voice growing louder and louder while my mind was stuck in complete despair and anger.

Then Sarah and McNally began to call an ambulance for Li Mai and Mai Ming. She called the rest of her men who traveled from America to Hong Kong to arrest both myself and Mike and put us on trial back in America.

When I found out they were getting an ambulance, I had false hope that Li Mai and Mai Ming would survive. But when I saw their bodies for about thirty seconds, I knew they were gone. They were only getting the bodies for the morgue. When I realized they were really gone, I started to shake in anger while my heart beat over and over again. I began to scream in a loud and ugly voice, with tears in my eyes and my face turning red with so much anger.

While all of this was happening, Sarah and McNally noticed my suffering and didn't want Mike to sit next to me, so they held onto him until one of Sarah's men came with a car to get him. About twelve minutes later, her men arrived, many of them former colleagues from the resistance.

They put Mike in a separate car. The ambulance came and took Li Mai and Mai Ming's bodies. When I saw their faces with their eyes open and pieces of their heads showing, my eyes began to cry, and I felt a pain I had never felt before. The only word I could scream was "No!"

That was all I ever said until they took me to the airport to return to Smart City to face "justice." I knew my life would never be the same again because of this. My life would be just as scarred as it was four years ago when Dr. Patrick Barton was killed by The Man in Black.

At the airport, I was forced to be cuffed everywhere—from my ankles to my hands, and even my neck—as if I were a slave. It took thirty minutes to rush to the airport with Sarah, McNally, and a bunch of rebels, who were basically agents working for them, dragging me to the plane.

While all of this was happening, I saw many people looking at me, either laughing or afraid. The one that made me feel horrible was a little boy hiding behind his mother. It reminded me of Mai Ming hiding, and Li Mai and I began to put our heads down in shame.

We were taken inside, which looked more like a private jet than an airplane. Mike De Veny was already there before me, and we were seated next to each other while also being cuffed. In that moment, I knew this was the end for me. All I could think was, why did this happen to me? Deep in my heart, the answer was silence.

We were on a private jet back to America for me to get lobotomized while Sarah, McNally, and the rest of my former team members watched me. I couldn't believe this. I wondered about my whole life, asking myself how a young man, half white and half black, could start with such a happy life beyond anyone's imagination and end up in the exact opposite.

I began asking myself: what's the point of living just to find The Man in Black? What if he doesn't even exist? Worse, what's the point of having a wonderful life in the first place if it's going to end like this? Why was I even born just to end up losing a piece of my brain for three decades of my own life?

I saw the chains on me and felt like one of those slaves taken from Africa to America—except this time my "slavery" would be getting a lobotomy while traveling from Hong Kong to America.

I didn't care about anything. I didn't even try to escape this time because I accepted my fate. I was ready to see my last days pass with no antidote, no justice, and no peace. I was ready to go, seated next to the man who sold me, who would also suffer consequences.

I laid my head down and looked through the window, thinking about my family back home and Celia. Mostly, I thought about failing Sarah and her late husband, Dr. Patrick Barton. The more I thought about him, I even questioned if The Man in Black existed or if I had made him up because of the Flakka in my system.

The first words I spoke inside the jet were, "Forgive me, Dr. Barton. I've failed." I bowed my head and thought about the many people in my life who had died and how much I wanted to be with them.

Suddenly, Sarah came to me. She saw me with a sad look, but instead of mocking me, she asked, "James, look, I'm really sorry about what happened. They didn't deserve that."

I didn't answer.

"James?" she asked again. I still didn't answer. I kept bowing my head.

"Hey, Truman, it's not my fault that they did, okay? It was that ass-hole that shot them. Me and McNally tried to stop him!"

I still didn't answer.

"Oh, what's the point? At least now you know how it is to lose someone." And in that moment, I didn't bow my head anymore, but instead I put my head up in anger and asked,

"What did you say?!"

"I said karma's a bitch." Then I got up and tried to jump on her, but I couldn't get out because of those damn chains, and the more I tried, it looked like slapstick because I kept struggling over and over again, but I couldn't get out.

"What, moron? Are you feeling angry and sad? Is that it?!" yelled Sarah. Then I could hear Sarah coming towards me in anger, and I could tell she wanted a fight, and so did I, so much so that I even spat on her face and yelled, "Screw you, bitch!"

In that moment, Sarah touched her face with her left hand and slapped me in the face with her right hand and kept on attacking me over and over again.

But then McNally and many of my former friends turned enemies came to Sarah and restrained her by her neck while trying to calm her down, while McNally held onto her, yelling, "Relax!" Sarah turned to them and looked at me while pointing her finger, screaming, "YOU'RE LUCKY ASSHOLE!!!" Then she left with McNally and her team, and they sat back down to their seats.

When that whole incident happened, I went back to sitting down with the cuffs and everything on, and I kept my face with a very angry look towards everyone, especially towards Mike, so much so that I wanted to jump on the bastard and freaking squeeze his eyes. When I turned to Mike, he turned to me and said, "That could have gone better."

In that moment, I got up again while trying to attack him. Mike began laughing at me, and the more I struggled to attack him, the more I was pissed, with a shit-eating grin as well as his face, especially the way his eyebrows moved in laughter. The more he laughed, the more the voice of D. came out, and I began yelling at Mike while he was laughing at me, "I'LL KILL YOU MIKE, YOU HEAR ME? I'LL SLAUGHTER YOU FOR WHAT YOU DID TO THEM!!"

But instead of getting afraid, he kept laughing, and the more he laughed, the more my anger began to sweat through my whole body, to the point I was going to say screw it all and let D. take all control that I was taught by Wan Po and Ku Soo. In that moment, with his laughter and my anger, I began to slowly lose what little control I had before and was ready to let D. consume me with all the anger and hatred that I had, thanks to Flakka, without a sliver of control this time.

In that moment, I finally snapped and lost everything I had to let D. take over. While all of this was happening, I realized that my whole life was cracking open like glass until it fell apart. The more Mike was laughing, the more I was losing any self-control left with D., and I knew that that rotten devil inside of me was one hundred percent free to get out without even struggling. Despite all the wisdom that Wan Po and Ku Soo taught me to gain control over D., I realized for the first time in a while that it wasn't there anymore and I'd lost complete control again.

Then suddenly I heard another voice, and it was also laughter, but it was the voice of that evil maniac. He began to laugh at me while mocking me by calling me a fool, and in that moment, a tear came to my eye because I realized how low I had sunk.

"What? You're going to cry now?" said Mike.

"SHUT UP!"

"Come on, cry, bitch, cry!"

"I SAID SHUT UP!!!"

The more Mike and D. mocked me, the more it was like they were merging into one evil creature. The more they laughed and mocked me, the more I struggled to get out while losing my freaking mind in despair and anger.

Then suddenly my terrible crisis of being subjected to laughter and mockery took on another crisis, but this time it was so unexpected. To my horror, I realized why Mike was laughing and mocking me, and he wasn't just doing it to get a rise out of me, but to escape from his chains.

Little did I know, Mike found a way to escape with a key that was taken by one of the men who worked for Sarah. How he got it was a complete mystery to me—either someone helped him, or he took it behind their backs. But whatever the case, Mike got out, and he did.

Mike began to jump on me like a wild man and started grabbing me by the throat. While all of this was happening, Sarah, McNally, and the rest of her men saw what happened, and they rushed to get Mike off me. The more they struggled to get him off me, the harder Mike's hands squeezed, and my eyes started to close with my heart beating over and over again. Suddenly, I could hear D. yelling at me to let him out.

They managed to get him off while he started cursing and spitting on people. I was completely broken and humiliated to the point I decided to say, "Screw it," and I let D. out and blacked out to the point that I felt all the anger and pain flushing out of me. However, to my surprise, I was still conscious and didn't even black out.

While realizing what had happened, I thought I could get up and see Mike being taken away on the private jet somewhere, probably to get beaten to a pulp. I didn't want to miss seeing that, but my body wasn't responding. In fact, D. was still in control of me physically. Instead of my hand, he controlled my body to try and break out of the chains.

I couldn't feel a thing, and I knew that D. would use that numb feeling to get me out. At first, I wondered what was going on and how he could get me out with all this crap, but I would later see that D. would do what he did the last time he was chained—to break out with all his strength.

I couldn't believe how the human body was capable of something so strong. The more D. used my body to get free, the struggle of the chains slowly became a huge fight—one that I was able to win. I wondered something I should have realized about D.—that I should have learned a long time ago. He wasn't just a maniac that came out of nowhere; actually, he was motivated to handle whatever pissed me off. The more he fought back against the chains and pieces of it came out, the more I realized perhaps D. wasn't a destroyer but a protector of mine.

After about three minutes of fighting, D. did something that I never thought any human body could do—he finally did it, and I was freed.

When I managed to escape, I could feel D. coming back inside me. I asked him inside my head, "Why did you save me?" and D. then said something that surprised me.

"Because I'm not a demon, I am you!"

In that moment, I didn't know what to feel, but I knew what I felt when Mike was getting manhandled by Sarah's goons. I wanted to throttle him so much that I chased after him and grabbed Mike by his neck. When I did, Sarah, McNally, and the rest of my ex-friends and colleagues looked at me in shock.

"You too!" yelled Sarah. Then she got up and pointed the gun at me, but I managed to punch before she even pulled the trigger. She fell to the ground with a bloody nose. McNally went to Sarah's aid, as well as some of her men, but most of them had their guns pointed at me and yelled for me to back off.

Noticing that there were a lot of guns ready to shoot me, I let Mike go and walked three steps away. They then told me to turn around and place my head above my head, and so I did.

One of them grabbed my right hand and even tried to grab my left hand, but little did he know, D. was also ready to grab someone. I felt my left arm getting numb again, and it grabbed the guy's gun, knocked him out, and started shooting all over the place, including at Sarah's men.

While the shooting was happening, nearly every single one of these clowns either ran to hide or got shot so badly they couldn't do anything but scream in agony. McNally was using his body to cover for Sarah.

While the shooting was happening, out of nowhere the plane began spinning out of control. We all fell to the floor and realized the pilot may have been shot. The plane was going nuts, and I knew we were going to crash. I used all my strength to crawl and fight back, my arm slowly recovering from D. I then tried to grab Mike, but Sarah started yelling at me,

"Get back here!" she yelled.

I didn't listen. I then noticed an emergency exit on the plane. I wanted to grab Mike, so I took him down with me while jumping off the plane. When Mike saw me crawling after him, he started kicking me over and over again, and I got angry and started biting his ankle for him to stop kicking me.

Then, out of nowhere, the plane started moving side to side, hitting my head left and right while I was in between both seats. When things started to get somewhat in control, Mike managed to slowly get up, and he and I wrestled our way while the plane was going down.

Mike then hit me on the head over and over until I fell to the floor.

He grabbed a gun from one of Sarah's men and pointed it at me, saying, "Say hi to them for me!" Then he had a smirk on his face and was ready to shoot.

But the plane started to spiral out of control, and Mike fell to the floor along with the gun. I then crawled again to get the gun and started to hit Mike with it over and over again until he started to bleed. I then grabbed him by the collar while crawling. The more I crawled, the more he struggled to fight me off, but he could not because the plane was completely out of control.

I then saw the emergency exit and slowly began opening the damn thing. Sarah had a gun pointed at me and said, "Put him down now!" But instead of listening to her, I looked at Sarah and told her something that I knew she wouldn't forget. I looked straight in her eyes so she could know in her heart that I was telling the truth.

"I didn't kill your husband."

She looked at me and told me, "I know what I saw, and killing him won't change that!" I looked at Sarah with a serious look on my face. Then I turned to Mike. He had nothing but contempt on his face, and in that moment, I knew I had to make a choice. I chose to throw the bum out.

We both were screaming while out of the plane. We both hated each other and couldn't believe we were friends in the first place. It was like something out of a nightmare that we couldn't wake up from, and nobody could do anything to get us out of it.

We felt the clouds and the sound of the wind coming from all our bodies before we splashed down into the ocean. We were freezing from the water, which was very strong, but our hatred towards each other was much stronger. So much so that we began to punch each other while water splashed our faces.

I grabbed Mike by his neck, and he looked me straight in the eye and yelled,

"Why don't you kill me? You killed before, haven't you James? Aww, what's the matter, are you scared, you pussy? I've killed your woman and her daughter, so come on, kill me!"

Then my hands began to shake with anger so much that I didn't know what to do. I foamed at the mouth like an animal.

"If you don't kill me, I'll kill you and everyone you love, you stupid bitch! Come on, murder me!"

Then Mike started laughing at me, and I felt D. coming. I looked at Mike's eyes, and he looked at mine with all my hatred. I grabbed him down into the water with me with my fingers on his eyes, and then I slowly began to black out. The last thing I remembered was him screaming and screaming and screaming.

## One Year Later

My last days in Hong Kong didn't really go as planned from beginning to end. In fact, all I wanted to do was to find the Man in Black, make him confess to his crimes, and force him to give me an antidote to get rid of D. once and for all.

But little did I know that not everything goes to plan, and I accepted that because not only did I lose my peace, but I also lost Wan Po, Mai Ming, Li Mai, and even Mike De Veny. All I have left is D.

While all of this was happening, I had visited the graves of Li Mai and Mai Ming, and in that moment, I couldn't help but feel like I'd failed—not just in finding the Man in Black, but as a friend and especially a human being. So much so that I brought a gun with me to kill myself, but I couldn't find the will to pull the trigger.

When I realized that I lacked the will to take my own life, even after everything I'd been through, I came to the conclusion that my miserable life would have to keep going. I began to cry uncontrollably, feeling that it was my fault for what happened to Li Mai and Mai Ming.

For the first time in five years, I came to the conclusion that there can be no redemption for myself and no chance for future happiness or atonement. Instead, I have to be cursed to find the Man in Black forever, and I didn't want to live that life anymore.

So instead of killing myself, I curled up into a fetal position and broke down in tears, rotting in my own self-pity for nearly an hour of pure suffering.

Afterward, when I was finished in that pathetic state, I said to myself, "I can't spend another year alone. I can't let this happen anymore!"

In that moment, I really felt sorry for everything that had happened to me—my mistakes over the years—and I knew what I had to do now. What I had to do was go back to America and go back home. But not to Smart City—instead, back to somewhere I never thought I would return to.

Somewhere that, if someone told me I would come back to, I would think they were either stupid or crazy. I decided to go back to the people I once called family—back to my father and my sister—for the first time in fifteen years.

It was like I was blind for so long, and now I can see. For the first time, I realized how much I missed them and decided to see them again, hoping to regain some happiness.

If somehow Sarah and McNally survived that plane crash and wanted to arrest me, I would not hesitate to surrender—but instead, go to them first before they came to me, because I didn't want anyone else to get hurt.

I've lost two people who were friends, and now they are nothing but a memory. I don't want my family to become another memory. So when the time comes and Sarah is looking for me, I'll be there waiting.

Because right now, I am no longer in Hong Kong. Far from it—I am back in America, hoping to face some of the ghosts of my past back home. Not in Smart City, but in Kansas—back to the farm where I once grew up with my family.

It wasn't easy to come back. In fact, I hesitated at first and thought killing myself would be a better option. I nearly tried multiple times over the years, but none of them were successful because I was afraid of the unknown side of death.

I was also afraid of not knowing what happened to the people who loved me and yet I'd abandoned. It may be a cowardly way of trying to live a life with nothing but suffering and death all around me, but not knowing what happened to them was much worse.

I refused to take my life in exchange for not knowing what happened to those I once loved more than anything, so I refused to take my life and instead kept on living to find the Man in Black, even if it was simply a long shot.

While all of this was happening, I began to walk my way through town to town until I found the farm I grew up on and the people I once called family.

While I was walking along the road, I tried to ask for a lift from cars, but none came, and I gave up and kept on walking, hoping I would find the farm.

While walking, I had been thinking a lot about Li Mai and Mai Ming. I couldn't let go of the way they died and how I felt guilty, like I was the one who killed them, because I should have left when I knew Sarah and McNally were in Hong Kong on day one.

But I stayed because I couldn't spend another day abandoning people I cared about—especially if they reminded me of my father and sister.

I guess that's why I shouldn't have expected too much of a normal life, because in my world everyone I love suffers when I'm a fugitive. The moment I see someone like Sarah or McNally again, it would be the last time I'd see people I love.

While all of this was happening, I decided to try one more time to ask for a ride, so I reached my arm out so someone could give me a lift. But instead of a car, my arm was bumped by a mailbox.

"Ow!" I screamed.

I said to myself, "Who's the dimwit that put a mailbox there?!" Then I turned, and to my shock, I found out who—and it had my last name on it. I knew in that moment where I was.

"My God... I'm home!"

Then I looked to the side and saw the farm, and it looked exactly how I left it fifteen years ago. In that moment, I was at a loss for words because I sincerely believed I would never return home.

Every emotion I had bottled up for those years somehow came back, and for the first time ever, I felt like smiling.

"I've found you!" I said while looking straight at the farm. In that moment, I didn't know what to do next—it was a mix of wanting to go and not wanting to go. I turned to the road that would probably lead me to endless pain, and I turned to the farm, which could give me some peace.

When I decided, I didn't even hesitate. I chose to go back to the farm, even if it was for a short time, or even if I was rejected by my own family. I decided to walk toward the farm, and I did.

It took me a while to walk all the way from the road to the farm, but I managed to get there. I noticed the house where Karla and I grew up, and in that moment, I really felt emotional about leaving Karla the way I did.

Now, I wanted to make things right one last time. When I went to the house, the door was in front of me, and it was almost like how I left—I went outside a lost man, and now I'd come back a lost man, but as a fugitive.

When I tried to decide whether or not to knock on the door, I felt like I was putting people's lives in danger—and worse, they happened to be my family. I didn't know what to say to Karla or even my father.

What should I say if they even recognized me? There was this struggle between going inside and telling them, "Hey, it's me, James," or just saying hello and leaving.

But I would soon learn that decision would come to me without me coming to them.

Out of nowhere, I saw the door open, and my heart started pounding. I closed my eyes until I heard a voice from inside say, "Hello."

It sounded like the voice of a woman, and when I got the chance to get a good look at her face, she was Black but had a very fair complexion with a ponytail and big, thick glasses. She was also wearing a pink shirt with white pants and sandals, holding a beer in her left hand.

In that moment, I knew who she was. "Ms. Truman."

"Actually, it's Dr. Truman. And you happen to be?"

In that moment, I could tell she didn't recognize me. I smiled and spoke, "Um, just a new person living around the neighborhood."

Then I noticed she looked at me like I was some kind of weirdo. She said with a kind voice, "Oh, well, it's nice meeting you, mister?"

In that moment, I had to make up a name, so I used the name of a lawyer I'd heard about—John Kolbe—and changed his last name to Kenyon.

"Um... Kenyon. John Kenyon."

"Well, it's nice to meet you, Mr. Kenyon."

She extended her hand for me to shake, and so I did. "I hope you have a good time living in Kansas."

"Same here, Dr. Truman."

In that moment, I really felt like I'd lost her forever, and I was finally ready to let go of my old life. But while I was about to let go of her hand, I noticed Karla was starting to hold on too tightly. Then she dropped her beer, and in that moment, I knew something was wrong.

"Um... Dr. Truman?" She wouldn't respond. Her face went from happy to shocked, and she stood there, looking at me with a surprised look on her face.

Because her nails were squeezing into my hand, I asked again, "Dr. Truman?" But she still wouldn't respond. "Dr. Truman, you're hurting my hand!"

She stood there in shock for about ten seconds until I slowly began to realize why she was squeezing my hand and why she had that terrified look on her face. She began to realize who I really was—who she was speaking to.

For the first time, I heard her say my name. "James?"

When she called my name, I was the one who was in shock. I didn't know what to say or do. I just stood there until I put my head down in shame, feeling like I'd ruined myself and my family by coming back here.

Then I raised my head and looked straight at her face. "Hi, Karla."

She looked at me again and became very emotional. Then her hand started to shake until she finally let go. She looked me straight in the eye, took a few steps back, and then rushed toward me.

In that moment, I thought she was going to kick my ass, and I tried to block her, but instead of attacking me, she hugged me and began to cry.

I then looked at her, breaking down in tears while she hugged me, and I slowly hugged her back. We held each other and just rotted together, and for the first time in my life, I knew that no matter how dark life gets and no matter how many people are in this world, the ones that are closest to you will always have your back no matter what.

And I learned in that special moment of embrace—you can be alone, you can be abandoned, but not with family, because family is forever.

# XIX

# HOMECOMING

It has been fifteen years since I left my family and five years as a fugitive. I couldn't understand why things like this happen, but I know that people say everything happens for a reason. As for my own reason, it was purely selfish, and I know that hard ugly truth is that once you're a fugitive, it's like putting a target not just on yourself but on everyone you care about. And it's even worse when you're actually innocent of the crime that you didn't commit.

So why did I even come back and let people come back into my life after all these years? Well, it's because the sad and pathetic truth is I can't stand another day alone, especially with the things I saw. So yeah, like I said, it's purely selfish, especially when I'm the one who's putting my own family in danger when I decided to let my own sister be part of my world.

When I returned home, I hugged her and we both wept like children. James began to slowly get a grip of ourselves. I got myself first to calm down, but my sister was struggling, so I began to help her calm down by trying to tell her, "It's alright, Karla."

She looked up to me and slapped me.

"Ow!" I yelled.

"You piece of crap!"

"What was that for?"

"Are you serious?"

"Yeah."

"I thought you were dead!"

"Well, consider this a resurrection."

She looked at me like I was stupid, but at the same time she gave me a hug, and I looked confused as ever and said, "Is it true?"

"Yes, it's me," I said.

"No, I mean, is it true what happened?"

I began to get confused and didn't quite understand what she meant, but I slowly realized what she really meant, and I let go of her. Then I looked around to see if anyone was hearing and said, "Oh... Well, let's just go inside and I'll tell you."

Karla looked at me with a suspicious look, but she let me in before I looked around outside, and she let me in. When I saw our home for the first time in fifteen years, I nearly felt somewhat nostalgic and glad, but at the same time I felt regret because what if Sarah and McNally find us and do something horrible to Karla? That would destroy me.

And while all my fears were consuming me at the idea that I may have made a great mistake and wanted to leave before something happened, suddenly Karla slowly came to me and touched my shoulder from behind my back, and I nearly freaked out.

"James, it's okay."

When I saw her, I told her, "Karla, I... I think I made a huge mistake."

"What?" she asked in shock.

"I shouldn't be here."

"What do you mean?"

"Just don't tell anyone that I was here, okay?"

Then she looked at me with disgust and anger and yelled, "No, I will not!"

I was shocked by the amount of anger from my own little sister, and I thought that D. was coming out, and in that moment, I was conflicted between my sister and my demons. In that moment, I knew that it would be foolish to stay.

I tried to explain to her and begged her to let me go, but she persisted like always.

"You left us fifteen years ago, and you're going to just abandon me again? No, I won't accept that again!"

"Karla, you don't understand."

"Oh really, so you're not the Osama Bin Laden of Smart City?"

At that moment I was shocked because I knew that she knew that I was a fugitive.

"You... you knew?" I asked.

"Of course I knew! It's all over the news. You killed those people and Barton's husband because of that drug!"

"NO!" I yelled.

She looked at me in shock, and when I realized what I'd done, I instantly said in a calmer voice, "I mean, no... I didn't kill them."

"Then who?"

"I don't know."

She looked at me with skepticism and asked, "James, tell me who."

"I don't know who... but I know it wasn't me."

"Then who do you think it was?"

"I don't know. It could be anybody, but it's not me."

Then Karla's skepticism slowly started to shrink, and she slowly realized that I was telling the truth. Then, out of a moment of weakness, I went down on my knees and covered my face with my hands.

"James... look at me," she said.

I did.

"I believe you. But you need to be strong and glad that you're home. We can fix this. We can help you get back to normal."

"There's no normal, Karla."

"But we can make one."

"How?"

"I'm a doctor too."

When she said that, I thought about the last time I had a doctor try to help me, and I told her, "I think that's not going to work out well, sis."

"Why not?"

"Because the last time I had a doctor try to help me, it did not end well."

"You would rather be with that lady and her underling?"

"No, but only the man who did this to me can reverse it."

Karla didn't believe that was possible.

"James, do you really think you can find that creep who did all this and he will willingly help you?"

"No, but I can try and make him confess for killing Barton's husband."

"That's never going to happen, James. You need help."

"Yeah... but not like this."

Then Karla got agitated and asked me, "Okay, bro, do you want to be alone?!"

"No," I said.

"Do you want to be lobotomized?"

"No!"

"Then let me help you!"

In that moment, I knew I wasn't conflicted between staying and running away again, because even though I will regret this whole thing, I knew I couldn't leave when I let myself get into another person's life, especially when that person happens to be my sister.

At first, I was going to say no, but I stopped myself for a few seconds and took a big sigh.

"Okay," I told Karla.

"Okay."

"Okay, sis, I'm just glad that I met you and not Dad."

"Well, you have to forgive him, James, like I forgave you."

"Yeah, I know, but... he's still alive, right?"

"Yeah."

"But where is he?" I asked.

"He's in a retirement home about ten minutes from here."

I smiled at her, and she smiled back. Then she gave me her hand, and I looked up and grabbed it and got up on my knees. We hugged each other, and in that moment, I knew that sometimes a little help can get us back on our knees.

# XX

# KARLA TRUMAN

Dr. Karla Truman, my own sister, she has been the closest person I had in life, even more than my father could have ever been, and out of all people, she was one of the many people who brought me up and helped me while we were too busy helping our father after our mother died.

The day I first left years ago, I would have had no idea that Karla would have ever been a doctor, let alone a doctor of medicine. It had been fifteen years since I abandoned her and left her to our father's misery and grief. At first, I would have thought that Karla would become just like our father, but I was grateful when she helped me and turned out to be a kind person and a kind doctor.

After I was done falling apart, Karla asked, "What did they do to you, James?" and I didn't really want to talk about it, so I said,

"I think it's better that you tell what they've done to you because the last time I saw you fifteen years ago, you were crying."

Karla paused for about five seconds and then she smiled while explaining everything that happened to her since I'd been gone.

She began to tell me that after I left, she and my father argued about the moment our father stopped her from trying to get me back home. So much so, Karla started screaming and physically slapping our father over and over. Then, about eight minutes of pure anger and hatred came from Karla. She told him that she would try to find me, but our father refused and had to use his own body to stop Karla from opening the door.

"If you want to leave, you have to get through me!" said our father, but Karla wasn't having it. She pushed him out of the way and went outside trying to search for me. To my shock, Karla had spent almost 24 hours searching everywhere but couldn't find me, as if I never existed.

The stress had Karla almost going mad with fear and grief until the next morning when all the hell she had to go through couldn't possibly get any worse. A group of men came to Karla and asked for money. Karla told them, "I don't have any." One of them grabbed her by the arm, and she turned and slapped the guy in the cheek. Another went to her and started holding her arms behind her while tying her with a rope. In that moment, Karla knew that things would be very ugly for her. Those animals tried to force themselves on her, had her clothes ripped, and started kissing her and touching her breasts. But then suddenly, a man came out of nowhere and started punching and kicking the living shit out of the men who were assaulting her. The man's hands were full of the blood of the pigs who tried to touch my sister.

When those scumbags got beaten up badly, they ran away crying. When Karla saw this, she was in complete horror. Then the man walked to Karla and said, "Are you alright?"

"James?" said Karla.

"Who?"

Then Karla understood that it wasn't me, a complete stranger.

"Let me give you a hand," said the man, and Karla raised her hand and got help.

Then the man asked Karla, "Are you alright?"

"Yeah."

"Do you have a place to go?" Karla started crying because she knew she didn't have a real home anymore.

"Hey, it's okay."

"No, it's not," said Karla.

"Yes, it is."

"Don't cry, miss. Hey, let's just call the police so they can help you."

Then Karla smiled and said, "Sure, I guess." Then the man called 911 and the police, and about thirty seconds later, they came.

"Stay still, I'll talk to him about everything," said the man.

"Okay." Karla stood still for about fifteen seconds while the man talked to the police. Karla didn't quite understand what they were saying because they were talking fast, but she did see the man giving a bribe to the officer. Then the man came to Karla and spoke.

"These nice policemen will take you to the police department to straighten things out and find the men who did this to you."

Then the officer came and gave her a coat to cover herself. Then Karla asked the man before leaving, "Who are you?" and the man turned and said to her, "Carlos... Carlos Moreno."

When Karla went to the cops, the officer who was bribed wasn't just an officer, and Carlos Moreno wasn't really a good and decent man, but instead, they both were connected to a crime organization that is responsible for drugs like fentanyl and human smuggling.

Karla, God bless her, was able to find out, after she discovered this horror show when she managed to go to the police department. She was told by the officer that he would call her family, but Karla refused and didn't want the officer to do so. The officer smiled and asked her, "You're a runaway?" Then Karla looked at the officer's eyes and spoke,

"I'm a runaway looking for a runaway."

The officer said he would be back and that it was best she could rest in a cell until they figured something out. She did go into a cell and slept for a few hours. While this was happening, she couldn't stop thinking about me and our father while wondering why, in God's green earth, she had to go through this.

While all of this was happening, she closed her eyes and opened them over and over every second because she was worried for my safety and, yes, even for our father because she felt somewhat saddened for how she reacted. Even though he's a miserable drunk, he was still our father.

When she started to see, little by little, some of the good memories we had together, they outweighed the bad moments in our lives. Then she smiled with a tear dropping from her face. She closed her eyes and fell asleep.

But then she heard a voice that was familiar, and the voice said, "Kid, you're awake?"

"Yeah." Then she realized it was the officer who was bribed and was with three other people. When she woke up, she saw them with ropes and a little towel.

"What are you doing?" Karla said, but the officers had a very sinister look in their eyes and she knew something was wrong. So she asked them again, "What are you doing?!" Then one of the officers grabbed her by the hair, another grabbed her by the arms and tied her up. Then one of them started punching her in the stomach over and over. But the most shocking was the officer that Karla knew had a towel filled with chloroform to knock her out.

Karla was in so much pain, even while telling me this story she nearly choked up because she went through one nightmare to another. When the officer was going to put her to sleep, Karla bit off his fingers while the officer struggled to drug her. Then, when blood started coming out of that corrupt bastard's fingers, some of the officers went to check on that asshole's hand.

While this was happening, Karla grabbed one of the officer's pockets to find a key and a gun to escape. There was a bit of a scuffle, but Karla shot that piece of shit in the crouch and managed to open the door and escape because many of the officers were either calling for help or were hurt.

When she began trying to escape, one of those pigs called the alarm, trying to find her, and many of the officers began to chase her left and right while trying to shoot her. But then, out of nowhere, one of the officers slapped one of the guys who was shooting and yelled, "We are supposed to keep that bitch alive!" and they stopped shooting. Instead, they just chased her. Then suddenly, after eighteen seconds of trying to catch her, she managed to escape.

When Karla knew that they were gone, she walked back home alone and half-naked for about ten minutes. It was one of the worst days she had ever experienced, but she managed to go inside her home after knocking on the door a few times. Then our father opened the door and said, "Karla?" She fell into our father's arms after nearly three days of hunger and fear.

The whole experience was so emotional even for me because I couldn't imagine what it was like for her. A few days later, Karla was able to tell her father everything that happened, and the F.B.I. came and arrested the officers for what they had done. But they never arrested Carlos Moreno for the bribe or the crime because of lack of evidence. In reality, it was likely because Carlos Moreno was a leader of the Mexican cartel.

XXI

# THE PATIENT

The hospital was called Candie's Hospital, and boy was it an interesting place to be in, because even though it was a hospital the healthcare was free and you didn't have to pay in any certain way. At first I thought it was a joke, but then I realized because of the great war many years ago every hospital is now nonprofit and free in an effort—or should I say an attempt—to reboot the entire system. But because of jackasses like Linda Smith and Snake Eyes that effort went down hard, and I know what you're thinking: how can a hospital run without any money? Little did I know it was run through donations from people in my state.

Besides that, when I first went into Candie's Hospital it had been a long time since I let a doctor help me with this type of sickness since Dr. Patrick Barton, and I never thought something like this would happen when my own doctor happens to be my sister. The last thing I wanted was to stay and let her into my life because I know the consequences of staying. At the same time I let my emotions get the better of me again, but I swore if this time when I leave it will just be between me and my sister, and I would never tell her where I would go, because I know she would be forced by people like Sarah Barton and Wilfred McNally to tell them where I am, and I don't want to put her in a box where she's forced to sell me out. However, if this treatment that Karla is saying could work—and I pray that it will—I can have a better chance of finding the Man in Black even more than I did when I was in Tibet.

When I went with Karla to the hospital, at first I was a bit worried because there were so many security guards, and every time I saw them I thought of my former rebel allies who were once great friends with me. Sometimes I have dreams that none of this ever happened and I was still a rebel for the resistance, but I know that will probably never happen, especially with my status as a fugitive. Even though I was innocent, many people back at Smart City still see me as a renegade.

Before we entered the hospital, we managed to create a fake identity with Karla's help: we glued an old photograph of me from my college years to a form and changed the name from James Truman to John Kenyon, which was one of my aliases. I never thought how she could do that, but I always knew Karla was very smart. It's just I never knew she could be so deceiving.

As John Kenyon, everybody let me in, and to my surprise it was so easy. I asked Karla, "Why they let us in like nothing?"

"It's because I'm the owner of this hospital," said Karla.

"You own your own hospital?" I yelled in shock. Karla told me to be quiet and I did, but I kept asking why she didn't tell me this earlier. Karla said, "Why didn't you ask?"

"Because I had no idea you'd become so big while I..." I began to almost be emotional because I'd seen how my little sister became successful while I was nothing more than a bum.

At that moment I almost cried, but then Karla came to me with her fingers on my chin and said, "Hey, hey, cheer up, bro. You're not alone, not anymore," and then she pointed to the laboratory where she works.

"And besides, we're here," said Karla.

At that moment I asked her, "Is this really going to work?"

"Yes... yes it will, because in this place you won't just control that demon inside of you, but you'll get rid of it completely." I smiled at her and we hugged.

"Now you ready?" said Karla.

"Yeah," I said, and then we entered the laboratory. As we entered we saw plenty of illnesses that had to do with drugs like fentanyl, cocaine, and yes, even Flakka. I said to her, "Interesting place," and as we kept walking Karla told me about the man who could help me with taking Flakka out of my system. When I heard this I was glad, but little did I know it was going to be a familiar face.

Karla then said to me, "J... John, I'd like you to meet your new doctor." I smiled and was about to shake hands until suddenly I saw his face, and to my shock it was somebody I never thought I'd see again.

"Kyle?"

"James?" said Kyle Jadiel. Karla began to look confused and said to me, "Wait, you know this man and he knows you?"

"Of course. Ms. Truman, your brother and I were old friends until..."

"Until Celia cheated on me with you!"

"That was a long time ago, James, and besides we met before also. It was when Smith came and brought you to my old job years ago."

"Oh, don't remind me," I said.

"Can somebody please tell me what's going on?" said Karla.

I said to her, "I'll tell you what's going on, sis. I don't want to have an antidote with this jerk as my doctor."

"And I don't want to work in a facility with this loser being my patient."

Then Karla yelled, "You want me to kick your ass again?!"

I yelled, "Bring it, bitch!"

"Hey, hey, hey, I suggest you two assholes both shut up and work together before I crack your skulls open!?!"

"But sis!" I yelled.

"No buts, James. You came so far."

"But he's a—"

"I know who he is, but he's still a professional doctor, and trust me he won't risk his job just to get even with you, okay?"

"Fine."

Then Karla turned to Kyle and said, "You owe him an apology."

"An apology? His girlfriend came to me!"

"Enough!" Karla yelled.

"Okay, I'm sorry." Then Karla looked at me and Kyle and asked if we were going to behave like grownups and work together as doctor and patient, and we both said, "Fine."

Then Karla went to Kyle and said, "How long can you make a drug that can treat Flakka?"

"Well, I believe we can make it in about a week."

"Good," said Karla.

Then Kyle asked her when I got sick with Flakka and Karla said to Kyle, "Since the last time he saw you."

Kyle wrote a note about when he'd be finished with the drug. It said March 8 at 12:00 PM, and in that moment I knew I had a chance to be free of D. for good, but at the same time I had my doubts if Kyle, of all people, could be the right man to do it.

"Let's go," said Karla, and we went out of the lab and drove back to the farm. Sometimes it's best to keep your friends close, but it's better to keep your enemies closer.

## XXII

# NIGHT AND DAY

We drove back to the farm to take a break while we waited for Kyle to make a possible antidote for me. Even though it was morning we took down the shades and looked left and right in case there was someone like Sarah or McNally spying on us.

Karla and I sat down in our chairs and looked face to face. I knew Karla didn't know what to do with herself or me, but I also read in her reaction that she wanted me to stay.

"James?"

"Yeah, Karla."

"After Dr. Jadiel gives you the antidote and it works, will you still stay with us so we can figure this out?" I smiled and sighed.

"Karla," I said.

"You know that if I stay you would be aiding a criminal, right?"

"Yeah, but you're not a criminal," said Karla.

"But they don't know that." Karla began to look sad and I began to feel horrible because I knew the last time she felt like this was when I abandoned her and our father.

"So you're not staying?" I bowed my head down and said to her in a soft but sad voice, "I'm sorry, sis."

She got up and spoke. "Well, it's already nighttime, so want to go to bed?"

"You have a second bed?"

"No, but I have a couch for myself."

"You don't have to do that, sis."

"Yeah, well I can tell it's been a while since you had a bed, right, bro?" I smiled and said, "Yeah." Then she asked me to follow her and I went to her room. It was filled with so much science stuff and a small lab with ants.

When I saw the ants, it reminded me of the time we picked ants together years ago for a school science project, because both Karla and I were in the same school but in different classes.

"I never thought you would still have these ants here, sis?"

"Yeah, I still keep those." We smiled and she said to me, "You want anything else?"

"Oh no, I'm okay, sis."

"Okay... good night."

"Yeah, good night." I looked around the room and saw many things and started thinking about the times we were children. It was a very loving and kind family; I could still feel the same love I had when I was still young. While lying down on the bed I felt the compassion that I hadn't felt in a long, long time since my mother died.

I almost choked up in tears at the thought of all this and wanted to die so badly because of the loss and pain I had to go through over the years. I prayed to God every day to just kill me because my pain was unbearable to live through.

I couldn't imagine having everything I ever wanted and throwing it all away to screw around with a few revolutionaries only for them to turn their backs on me for a crime I didn't even commit. Just the thought of it made me mad as ever, so much so that I couldn't bring myself to sleep.

While all of this was happening, I suddenly heard a tapping at the door. At first I thought it was just the sound of one of the animals on the farm, but it kept tapping louder and louder and it began to annoy me so much that I called for Karla to check what's going on, but she wouldn't respond and the tapping grew louder. My anger began to boil up.

"Karla, wake up!" but she wouldn't answer. "HEY SIS WAKE UP!!!"

Still nothing. I got up from the bed and started murmuring to myself in anger because I couldn't believe this was happening, but then I slowly began to calm myself down to avoid letting D. come out and do something stupid I would regret. I took a deep breath while the tapping was getting louder and I tried to ignore the sound.

Before I opened the door I still thought it was one of the animals that had escaped because of the loud sound that reminded me of a horse or a cow. When I began to open the door, to my shock it was none other than the faces of the people I tried to hide from: they were Sarah Barton and Wilfred McNally.

"You're under arrest," said Sarah. I shut the door in their faces. Then suddenly McNally knocked the door through and I fell with the door on me.

"Wait, you have to believe me, I didn't do it!" Then I turned my head and to my horror it was Karla seeing me on the floor crushed by a door while Sarah and McNally were going to arrest me.

When she saw and understood what was happening, she began screaming, "James, what's going on!"

"Karla, run!"

"James!" "Karla, for God's sake!"

"James, no!" Then suddenly out of nowhere I heard a gunshot. I turned and saw Karla on the ground with smoke coming from Sarah's gun. Karla was shot in the chest. Karla was killed by Sarah, and in that moment I nearly broke down because this happened again—first my mother, Dr. Barton, Wan Po, Li Mai, and Mai Ming.

"No," I said.

"Get his ass up!" When she said that, I snapped into D., but then McNally started kicking me in the face and I began to bleed. The more the blood came out, the more I began to feel tired and in pain.

McNally took me out through the door and handcuffed me. He then got me up along with Sarah and said, "It's a pleasure to see you again, Truman."

They walked me outside and Sarah started mocking me, saying, "Have fun getting the lobotomy, asshole."

"Karla!" I said, then louder, "Karla!!" I yelled the loudest, "KARLA!!!" and then I closed my eyes and opened them up and realized it was just a nightmare. I felt sweat pouring through me and I got up and went to the bathroom to wash water on my face. I washed once and felt nothing but sweaty, so I washed again, and again, until water began splashing across the floor. Then I heard a voice calling my name.

"James, I'm coming for you!"

"Who's there?" I yelled. I put my head up and looked at the mirror and saw my reflection, but then I went closer and all I saw was my face all wet. I got even closer and saw my face morph into something horrific. It was like the movie The Fly. My face began to fall apart in a disgusting, mutating way: my eyes were gone, my flesh was off, my jaw was gone revealing the face of the demon. In that moment I knew I was going to black out again. He grabbed me by the throat and slammed my head, knocking me down to the floor.

All I saw was darkness—complete and total darkness. Little did I know that was just the beginning. When it was day, and boy was it dark as night, the darkness slowly began to lift. A light slowly came toward me and I heard a voice again, but it was the voice of the demon, the voice of the light which had always been there. It was the voice of my mother. Then I woke up.

The moment I woke up I was outside the farm, somewhere far, far away in the woods, and I felt someone hugging me and saying, "Mom?"

"James?"

"Mom?!"

"It's me... Karla."

"Karla?" I said and I looked around. It was daylight. I asked her where I was and she said, "Don't you remember?" I shook my head.

"You were acting crazy and escaped through the house and acted like a wild animal. I drove to find you but you weren't you," she said. When she asked if it was Flakka, I said yes.

"James, we've got to have that antidote sooner than later."

"I know, sis."

Then a familiar voice came to me saying, "If you know, why aren't you willing to do something?"

"Who's there?" An elderly bald man with a goatee came to me, and seeing his face I knew who it was.

"Hello, son."

"Dad?" At that moment it was like déjà vu all over again. As a fugitive I never asked for any of this and I pray that no one else would. To be run from my past only to create more shit along the way just to get back to where I first started, but in an even worse position than before, is something no human being should ever go through.

When I saw my father for the first time in fifteen years since I ran away it was a bittersweet experience. When I first saw him I was shocked and at times resentful, but not as resentful as being wanted.

The moment I realized my father was with me and my sister I nearly broke down because I realized how low I'd sunk and wondered why I was still alive—tears came to my eyes.

Karla asked me to get on my feet so we could go to our dad's house to talk. I told her, "Do what you want, sis, but I'm not going to talk to him." My father didn't react to what I said; I believe he was stern and cold because he's not the only man who has a bit of demon inside him.

We drove back to our father's house. It was very similar to the farm, just a bit smaller; it almost reminded me of the barn. We went inside the house. I didn't talk to my father or even look at him, and neither did he.

The more we avoided eye contact and didn't say anything, Karla pulled the brakes on the car and yelled, "You two grow up and start talking like father and son."

"There's nothing to do, Karla," said Dad.

"Right, like there was nothing to do when Mom was dying," I said.

"You watch your filthy mouth, boy. What happened to your mother wasn't my fault."

"Bullshit!" I yelled.

"Hey, hey, hey, knock it off, both of you."

When Karla yelled that we both went silent but still hadn't spoken. A few minutes later we managed to get to Dad's house. When we went in, he came out with his cane. In that moment I wanted to push him out the door so a car could hit him, but I didn't—not for the goodness of my heart, but because Karla would call Sarah and McNally.

When Karla got out of the car she guided our father to his home and said, "Did you check with the doctor?"

"No, I haven't."

"Dad, you need to take better care of yourself."

"I know, I know." Then Karla turned to me and asked, "You're coming?"

"There's nothing for me here, sis."

"How can you say that?"

"How can you defend him after what he let happen to Mom?"

"I'm not defending him, James. I just wanted you both to calm down."

"Why?" I asked.

"Because things change since that day." I started laughing at what I heard because I felt how naive my sister was.

"Sis, people never change!"

"How do you know?" she asked.

"Look at him and look at me." At that moment Karla gave up trying to reason with me and said, "You're going to come in or what?" I looked at her eyes with those big glasses on and said, "Whatever," and I went inside.

# XXIII

# FAMILY IS FOREVER

yself, Karla, and our father went inside. One of the first things my sister asked was for us to calm down and to talk to each other eye to eye. At first, we kind of laughed and dismissed the whole thing, but Karla was persistent.

Karla told us that we are still family, and our father said to her, "No, we are family—he is not."

"Fine by me," I said. Karla began to get agitated about the whole thing and told me that I wasn't helping. I said, "Good."

"Oh, grow up, James!" Karla said.

"I don't need to grow up; I've already did."

"Yeah, and how did that work out for you?" said our father.

"Oh, shut up!" I yelled. Then Karla yelled for us to stop and told us, "If you two don't stop I'll call Barton on you, James, and I'll call the doctors to take you away, Dad."

Our father looked confused and asked Karla why Sarah Barton had to do with any of this. Karla had a look like she had really screwed up, and I did too, to the point that I yelled at her, asking why she even did that.

"What's going on, daughter?" asked our father. She tried to dismiss what she just said by saying, "Oh, it's nothing, Dad."

"It seems like something, alright!" said our father.

"No, it's nothing." Our father was getting even more persistent, to the point that he almost looked angry. It worried Karla so much that she actually spilled the beans on me.

"Because Barton wants him, okay!"

"Why did you say that?!" I yelled. Karla explained to me that our father actually has a heart problem, and due to his old age and poor health, she didn't want him to have a heart attack. I asked her, "Why didn't you tell me that in the first place?"

"Because you wanted nothing to do with him, James."

"Can someone explain what's going on?!" yelled our father.

"Shut up, you miserable old piece of shit!" I yelled.

"Hey! Hey!! Hey!!!" In that moment, the yelling and the snitching made me almost snap into D., but I closed my eyes and tried to calm down. Our father wouldn't shut up, but then Karla realized what I was trying to do and started to slowly relax, telling our father, "Dad, stop, please."

"Why? What's going on, Karla?" asked our father.

"It's a long story."

"Well, tell me right now." Karla looked at me and said to our father, "Just give him a minute." Our father looked at me and then at her and said, "Okay."

I was slowly given enough time to calm down and prevent the demon from taking over my mind and body again. I opened my eyes, and Karla asked me if I was okay. I told her that I was.

"Now tell me why Sarah Barton wants your brother." Our father asked.

Karla began to stutter, and I stood still, realizing how desperate she was not to tell him the truth.

I looked at her in the eye and told her, "Sis, you don't need to tell him anything... I'll tell him." Karla looked at me in shock.

"Are you sure, bro?"

"I'm sure, sis. This is all over; I'm leaving."

"You can't leave! What about the antidote?"

"Oh, screw the antidote. I bet that sack of shit is putting some bad ingredients just to get back at me."

"Do you really believe what you are saying, James?" I told her it doesn't matter because I was going to leave. Not because I wanted to keep the secret of me being a wanted fugitive, but because I didn't want Karla to see our father have a heart attack knowing that his own son was a criminal.

"I'm sorry, sis, but I'm leaving."

"Yeah, good riddance, you little bastard!" yelled our father.

"Dad?!" yelled Karla.

"What?!" yelled our father.

"Just let it go, sis."

"Where are you going, bro?"

"I'm going to Barton."

"WHAT!!!" she yelled.

"I'm going to turn myself in."

"Turn yourself in? What is this about, your daughter?" asked our father. In that moment, Karla used her body to block me from the door. She looked at me straight face to face and spoke,

"No, you aren't, bro!"

"Karla, out of my way, please!"

"No, I can't let you do that, James."

"I SAID MOVE!!!" I yelled. Even after I told her to move, she still wasn't showing any reaction; in fact, it was almost stoic. Then I realized that after I snapped at her, I saw her eyes almost beginning to water like she was about to cry, and it reminded me of the last time I abandoned her and our father.

So much emotion came over me and my sister. The more she looked at me in the eyes, the more my heart began to melt. In that moment, I almost had flashbacks of the times we were a family and remembered the good we had. For the first time in a long time, my whole life was flashing in front of me. I slowly couldn't feel any of the pain and misery at that moment, only the pure feeling of having a family in front of me. It was like having a second chance to prevent all of the nightmares that came afterward when I made the terrible mistake of abandoning my family.

She said to me, "Bro, you wouldn't hurt me, would you?" In that moment, Karla wept. My anger immediately collapsed, and I gasped as if I had been holding my breath the whole time. I began to think about the consequences of leaving my family, and I knew the last time didn't go as planned; in fact, it was one of the worst choices I had ever made.

I knew in that moment my life would suffer even worse. I could have been lobotomized or killed if I turned myself in, and I would have let the Man in Black get away with the whole thing. I wouldn't have been surprised if he laughed because he knows nobody can touch him with me gone forever—which means no more family, no more Celia, no more antidote, and no more freedom.

When I saw the consequences of abandoning them and saw Karla crying, I knew in that moment that I was in the same position that led me to become a wanted fugitive. I now had the chance to say "Never again." My fists began to soften and my vicious, bloodthirsty eyes became more peaceful.

When I saw Karla crying, I saw the sister who wanted me to stay with her, but instead I had abandoned her and, in fact, got her attacked by some thugs because she was trying to find me but I wasn't even there.

One of the first words I told her was, "K... Karla?"

"James?" My heart truly melted, like it collapsed into my stomach. Instead of attacking her, I hugged her. Instead of telling her to get out of my way, I got emotional and said, "I'm sorry, sis." I felt her body shaking and nearly choked up, telling her, "It's okay, Karla."

In that moment, it didn't matter if you have a friend or a girlfriend—they can come and go anytime the wind blows, but blood is forever. Family is forever.

# XXIV

# THE PILL

The day I decided to stay with my family, I thought about what could be worse than letting the Man in Black go free and living the rest of my life like this, with half a brain. Even though I felt bad at the idea of leaving my family again, I also knew I was playing with fire after what happened to Li Mai and Mai Ming back in Hong Kong.

But I felt it was best to not give up and to keep fighting, out of fear of regretting this for the rest of my life. Yes, Li Mai and Mai Ming were very close to me, but my own blood is just as much—even though one of them still hasn't forgiven me for blaming him for my mother's death. Still, a part of me wants to forgive him.

The next day, Karla and I decided to go back to Candie's hospital to pick up the possible antidote that Kyle created. Karla told me while going there that Kyle had created the antidote in the form of a pill.

We went inside to make an appointment, and Karla and I went to his office. Kyle was looking out the window. He turned to us and said, "At last," and started laughing. Karla and I looked confused. I asked Kyle,

"Why the Matrix reference, asshole?"

"Because I've got a red pill for you, loser."

"What did you call me?!" I yelled. Karla jumped in and told both of us to back off.

"I don't know why you two still hate each other, but you both need to get over it."

I stood up and said, "I'll tell you, sis—it's because he's the reason I left home years ago!"

"What?" Karla asked in shock.

"Yeah, don't you remember I was losing my freaking mind at home and left because this sack of shit made out with my girlfriend?"

Karla turned to Kyle with an angry look on her face.

"Is this true, Doctor?"

Kyle looked very pale. I had a grin on my face—now that Karla knew the whole story of why I left, the only person to blame wasn't me; it was the douchebag in front of her.

"Well... um, she told me James was out of control."

In that moment, I really wanted to kill the punk for saying that, so much so that I nearly let D. out and almost blacked out again. "I'LL KILL YA!!!" I yelled.

Karla had to restrain me while asking Kyle to give her the pill.

"Just give me the freaking pill, you miserable little twat!"

Kyle looked through his medicine cabinet, taking his time with a slight grin.

When I noticed that, I told Karla, "Get off me, Karla! I swear to God I'm going to kill this punk!"

Kyle was laughing as if he wouldn't even be touched. I wanted to break his jaw but didn't want to push Karla away.

"You better hurry up, Jadiel. I can't hold him for long!" Karla said. Kyle looked at me, noticing I was getting closer to getting out of my sister's grasp. In that moment, his smile disappeared.

"Okay, okay, here," he said, showing Karla a red pill. She snatched it from him while I continued cursing and yelling.

Karla tried to calm me down, repeating my name over and over."- James! James! It's okay, James, it's okay!"

I looked at Karla. Her eyes were full of compassion. She turned to Kyle with a very angry and vicious look and yelled,

"YOU'RE SO FIRED, JADEL!!!"

"What?!?!" yelled Kyle.

"You can't fire me; I just gave you the pill!"

"You insulted my brother. Your behavior was unacceptable, and by the way, you kept it a secret that you're the reason he suffered all these years. So yeah, you're fired!"

"So, you're firing me?" I jumped in and said,

"No, she's not firing you—she already fired you. So pack your bags and get the hell out!"

"I was… I was just… You can't do this to me! I worked hard for this!"

"Well, you should have worked harder," Karla said.

Then she turned to me. "Come on, James, let's go." Karla walked out, and so did I.

Before I fully left, I said to Kyle, "Thank you for the pill."

Kyle looked very angry. "SCREW YOU, TRUMAN!" he yelled.

I shut the door and started laughing.

We drove back to the farm. While Karla was driving, I held the pill in my hand and thought about what could have happened if I hadn't left. Even though it was satisfying to get a little even with Kyle, it was still Celia who cheated on me. Worse of all, it was my terrible attitude that had driven her to it. I began to wonder if all of this was actually my fault. I thought about the people I'd lost or who had turned against me, all because it started with me. Maybe, just maybe, I actually felt sorry for Kyle—we still could have been best friends if not for me.

While all of this was happening, I asked Karla, "Do you think Dad will forgive me someday?"

She turned to me and smiled. "If you can forgive yourself, you can forgive each other." I wondered if I could. After all that's happened, I wondered if my whole life had been a waste, if I had done more harm than good, even to my own sister who had forgiven me.

A few minutes later, we returned to the farm with the red pill in my hand. Karla told me the pill Kyle made has a few side effects, and she would check on me while asking if I felt anything weird. I told her I had doubts about trusting Kyle with this pill.

"What if this pill won't work? Trusting him was a mistake."

"Is that a medical analysis, big brother?" asked Karla.

"No, just a gut feeling." We smiled. I looked at the pill for a few seconds and went to my room. Karla had a strange look on her face, as if wondering what I was planning. I told her I was tired. She smiled and asked if I was going to take the pill.

"Yes," I said, sitting down on the couch. As she was about to leave so I could rest, I said, "Thank you."

"For what?" she asked.

"For helping and forgiving me." I lowered my head in shame, because I didn't deserve such kindness, especially from her. Karla came to me, noticed tears streaming down my face, and calmly told me to stop crying.

"You're my only brother, James, and I love you no matter what."

"I don't deserve your love," I said.

Karla explained why she forgave me for abandoning them. At first, she had been mad at me for years, but she realized I had a lot of issues going on in my life. Even if I had stayed, it would have made things worse, and I would either be dead or in a mental hospital. It took me a few minutes to accept that, but I slowly realized she had a point. Looking too much into the past wouldn't have helped, and I knew deep down that I probably would have killed myself or ended up locked away.

I took a breath and said, "You may be right." She smiled and patted me on the back.

"Now you're ready to let the demon die, right?"

I looked at her and smiled. "Yeah, I'm ready."

"Good... now take the pill." I put the pill in my mouth, drank a glass of water, and fell onto my bed.

Before I went to sleep, I said to Karla, "Thank you."

"You're welcome," she said, shutting the door and letting me rest, hoping the pill would finally free me of D. forever. In that moment, I truly believed everything would be fine. I closed my eyes and thought about my life and how far I'd come. Even though this pill might be an antidote, I still needed to find the Man in Black. Being free of D. could help me have an edge.

After a few minutes, I felt my personality changing, like I was coming out of darkness into the light. I realized I was dreaming. I saw a light coming from a very dark place—nothing and nobody around. The closer I walked to the light, the more my senses felt colorful and happy. For the first time in a long time, I truly felt free, so much so that I could see my hands coming out of the shadowy place.

I was ready to move forward, but suddenly the light started to dim. I didn't understand why. I tried to run to the light, but the darkness grew. Then I turned behind me in horror and noticed someone touching my shoulder. It was him—my enemy, the Demon.

I tried to run, but the more I ran, the darker it got. The more I tried to stay, the more he chased me. I finally had enough. I slapped his hand away from my shoulder. His eyes were dark, twisted, and evil, reflecting myself as if claiming me.

"You cannot escape me, James!"

"Get away from me, you bastard!"

He smiled with a ghoulish look, and I knew he was planning something awful. "I'm not scared of you!" I yelled.

He started laughing with a loud and thunderous voice and he said to me, "Yes, you are."

I tripped on the dark floor as he came closer. I dragged myself away, but it was too late. He put his foot on my chest, and I felt helpless. Then he landed on my face and I screamed and screamed and screamed. And I kept screaming until I realized that the whole thing was just a bad dream or just a bad acid trip from the pill. I wondered if there was some kind of side effect, or if Kyle really screwed with the pill. I began to feel somewhat unusual, like I wasn't myself—so much so that I could feel my hand shaking. When my heart slowly stopped beating, I began to feel like it was slowly turning into a heart of stone.

For the first time, I felt full of hatred and anger. I thought to myself that D. was coming out again, but to my surprise, he hadn't come out at all. Instead, it was just myself in bed, sweating.

However, I was still vigilant at the idea that D. could come out at any moment, just like he did with the mirror. I looked for any sign of evil that I felt, but nothing happened. For the first time, I began to feel more like myself than D., and for the first time, I felt like myself again.

I began to feel overjoyed and realized that it was already morning. I looked out the window and saw that everything was sunny. The farm never looked so wonderful, so much so that I ran to see Karla and tell her that I think the antidote really worked and that The Demon was finally gone.

When I managed to see Karla, she was resting. I tried to wake her up. "Karla! Karla!" I yelled, but she wouldn't answer.

"Karla, it worked!" I tried again, but still no answer.

"Karla?" I began to get nervous, but then I heard her snoring, and I began to laugh a little. She then woke up and looked at me, laughing and giggling with so much joy.

"I haven't seen that laugh in a long time," she said.

"Karla, it worked!"

"The antidote?" she said.

"Yeah!"

"The pill?!"

"Yeah!!"

She got up and hugged me, saying how great that was. She began to ask if I felt alright, and I told her something that I will never forget.

"Better... better than alright. I feel wonder..."

Then suddenly, I slipped my words like I was having a stutter, but I tried to keep speaking, repeating the answer.

"Won... wo... wooo."

I realized that something strange was going on, but I thought it was because of my excitement. Little did I know, I was in denial at the time.

"W. WA... Weh... fu.... of..."

Karla looked at me with concern, and I realized that something was wrong.

"James?" said Karla, but I couldn't answer. Instead, my voice slowly began to falter like a dying machine. I got very nervous, and to my horror, I finally realized the antidote might have some type of side effect—or Kyle had screwed around with the freaking thing.

"James, are you okay?"

Then I realized something was turning from bad to worse. I looked at my hand, which I could barely see. My vision was slowly becoming blurry. My head and body felt ill, so much so that I couldn't hear a single thing Karla was saying. It was like my ears were stuffed with plugs.

My head was spinning, and I began to feel sick to the point that I began spitting on the floor. Karla jumped out of the way.

"Dude!" yelled Karla.

Then we saw the floor with a red dot. Karla looked at me and said, "James?" I begged, with blood on my mouth while slurring my words.

"H. H. ello. H. ello... help. M. Me!"

Karla saw that I was going to fall and yelled, "James!" I fell to the floor and blacked out.

Sometimes I wondered if it was better to die or even just sleep. Sometimes I didn't even know the difference because a part of me had always been dead for quite a long time, even before I was infected with Flakka.

If there was one thing I would ask God, it would be: why, of all people, would I have to go through this struggle? Why couldn't I just be myself again? But a part of me didn't want to go back, instead wanting to kill everybody in my way and butcher every bit of flesh they had.

That was the struggle I lived with for years. When I woke up from my crisis, I realized that I wasn't at home anymore; I was at a hospital. It took a few seconds for me to realize that I was at Candie's Hospital.

I felt like a zombie. I couldn't move much, and even though I was conscious, it was extremely hard for me to get up. I wondered why until, to my surprise, I realized that one of the doctors had put a needle in my arm while I was sleeping.

I looked at my hand, where one of my fingers had been cut off by that pimp from Hong Kong, and I wondered what I'd gotten myself into. I wished I had died a long time ago. If reincarnation exists, I wished I had a better life.

After a few minutes of contemplating everything, I heard somebody knocking on the door. I said, "Come in." When the door opened, I saw my sister along with my father. She said to me,

"Hey, bro."

"Hey, Karla," I said while smiling, then turned to my father and said without any emotion, "Hey, Dad."

"Hello, son."

"What happened to me?" I asked both of them. Karla's smile slowly became more serious. She said that Kyle had been messing with my medicine, and I nearly had an overdose from sleeping pills—not an antidote. I closed my eyes, shook my head, and spoke.

"Of course he did."

"But now he's going to the authorities. I'm sure that Barton lady will have plenty of fun with him."

I looked at Karla in shock and asked, "Barton lady? You mean Sarah Barton?!"

"Yeah, but it's okay. She doesn't know you are here," she said.

"I need to get out of here."

"Wait, what?"

I got up and tried to find my clothes and get out of the hospital gown.

"Son, wait!" said Dad.

"No, Dad, I need to go!" I started rushing and searching like a lunatic for my clothes. I started sweating, and my heart was beating over and over again.

"James, listen to him!" Karla said.

I got mad and yelled at Karla, telling her that I wouldn't listen because I believed she may have unwittingly exposed me. Karla insisted that wasn't the case and that she didn't know.

"I'm sorry, sis, but this was a mistake."

"Look, James, I can make this right," said Karla.

"No, Karla, I don't think you can."

"What are you saying?" said Karla.

"I can't stay... I'm sorry, sis."

"I... but—" My dad jumped in and spoke,

"Son, please listen to y—"

I interrupted my dad and told him,

"Don't call me son. It's because of your bullshit of being a sloppy drunk that I'm in this mess in the first place."

Dad looked at me with the same look he gave when he kicked me out years ago. I yelled at him, screaming,

"WHAT ARE YOU GOING TO KICK ME OUT AGAIN?!?!"

I noticed his complexion slowly become red, like he was going to get angry. But I soon realized he was emotional—not with anger, but with sorrow. I saw tears coming down my old man's face, and he said to me,

"That's the last thing I ever wanted."

My anger turned to pity and guilt. I really felt like a douchebag for screaming at him and saying those things. Even though I blamed him for my mother's death, I had never had empathy for my father's problems.

"I loved your mother, James. As much as I did then, and still, deep down, I still love you."

My heart slowly melted with emotion, yet I didn't show it. I was prepared for anything—but nothing prepared me for the next thing he said:

"I know you've been through a lot, and yes, you may be right about what happened to your mother. It was my fault that you suffered those fifteen years. But I'm here now, son, and no matter what, I love you."

In that moment, I began to shake with so much emotion—love and hate mixed. I was conflicted about my duty to save myself or save my family. I slowly walked to my father, stared into his soft and elderly eyes, and cried. I hugged him instantly. He said,

"I'm sorry, son. I'm so sorry for everything."

Tears came to my eyes. Karla began to cry too and hugged us again.

"James, forgive me. Please forgive me for being a bad dad. I'm so sorry," he said.

"It's okay, Dad."

"I love you, son."

"I love you too, Dad."

Karla started crying, begging me to stay with her. I looked at her and said,

"Okay, but I need to hurry before Sarah finds out I was here."

"Okay, let's go," said Karla.

"You don't seem to have a record that I was here, right, sis?" I asked.

She thought for a few seconds and told me,

"I'll handle that, James. After all, I own this hospital."

I smiled. "Okay, let's go."

"But not like this," said Karla.

"What do you mean?"

"You need to wait for the dryer to finish."

"I beg your pardon?"

"Your clothes are in the dryer, James," said Dad.

"Oh, but can we wait at least until tomorrow? What if Barton finds me?"

Karla realized I was right and said, "Okay, let's go." I smiled, and we left back home with me wearing a hospital gown.

When we returned home, we came up with a plan to protect me from going to places where it was too risky. I needed to make sure that D. never came out, so Sarah would have no clue where I was. Karla promised she would still find a way to get rid of D. once and for all. This was the beginning of a long and tough road ahead for me, my sister, and even my father.

## TWO YEARS LATER

Wow. It had been so long since I lived together with my family, and things were going so well. Even though I couldn't get my life fully back, I hadn't blacked out or heard voices since, and everything was looking up.

Sometimes, when I went to bed, the nightmares got tense—but not as bad as they were two years ago. Sometimes, I got nervous about waking up one day and becoming the demon again.

What kept me from doing so was my family. They were my motivation to keep the demon inside, and I hoped it would stay that way. Ever since I decided to stay with my sister and father, I never left. Nothing bad happened for quite some time.

Maybe it was because I stopped getting close to other people—those who started trouble and then ran away like a bunch of cowards. Even though I warned them not to push me too far, they did it anyway. For me, I learned to keep going forward. Even if this whole thing collapsed, I knew and accepted that I couldn't calm the storm ahead of me. So I stopped trying, because what I could do was calm myself—the storm would pass.

At this time, I was still at my sister's farm, relaxing in my bed. Everything was going great. I got up and went to check on my sister. When I searched for her, I wondered what she was doing. Then I realized she was outside, playing with her new dog that we had found alone one time and raised. He was a Pekingese mixed with a poodle, and we called him Brownie.

When I saw her having fun with Brownie, I yelled, "Good morning, sis!" She smiled and waved.

"Good morning, James!"

"How's Brownie doing?"

"Great!"

I went outside and started to play with the little guy. My sister and I had a frisbee, and we had a lot of fun with Brownie, seeing him running and having fun like a wonderful dog.

While we played, Karla told me that Dad was going to the casino and wanted me to go with him. I looked confused because Dad usually asked Karla to go with him.

"Why me? Usually you go with Dad," I asked.

"I know, bro, but he says he wants to go with you this time," said Karla.

"But I have no money, sis."

"I'll give you some." She reached into her pocket with Brownie barking at her to play more. Karla told Brownie, "Okay, okay, fetch, boy," and she threw the frisbee again. Brownie ran after it. We both smiled, and she finally showed me the money—two hundred dollars. I looked surprised and asked,

"You sure, sis?"

"Yeah, we always play with two hundred dollars every week."

"Yikes."

"Oh, don't be sissy."

I slowly accepted the money with my hand but refused to grab it because I felt like Karla and Dad were having a gambling addiction.

"Just do it, bro," said Karla.

"Are you both getting addicted to gambling?"

"No, why would you say that?"

"I don't know, just wondering."

We looked at each other and smiled. I finally accepted the money. Karla later asked me to call Dad, and I spoke.

"Sure, sis."

I asked her what the casino was called, and she told me,

"The Golden Casino."

"Sounds nice," I said.

"Remember to call him later in the afternoon, okay? He's not much of an early bird, you know?"

"I know."

I was about to go back to my room, and Karla wanted me to still play with Brownie, but I smiled and said,

"Sorry, sis. I'm not much of an early bird either."

We both laughed, and I went back to my room to rest. After a few hours, I finally called Dad and spoke.

"Hey, Dad."

"Hello, James," said my dad.

"Want to go to the casino with me?"

"Sure, son."

What I thought was going to be the beginning of a great father-son relationship would turn into something far more sinister.

XXV

# THE GOLDEN CASINO

My father and I went to the casino that day. It seemed to me that everything, for the first time, really felt like life was going my way. Even though I couldn't find the man in black and force him to cure me, I still felt well enough to be a son of a man who had lost everything but was trying to get it back, even if it was only for a short time.

When I went into the casino, the place was crowded with people smoking. The entire building was golden—I mean really golden, like Trump Tower golden. For the first time, I thought to myself, what kind of casino is this anyway?

I gave my dad one hundred dollars and kept another hundred for myself. At first, I was nervous about coming in because I felt there could be many strangers and freaks looking for trouble. But the more I stayed, the more it seemed that the only trouble I had was the smoke coming from some dude's cigarette next to me.

We decided where we were going to play. I would play the slot machines while Dad played roulette. To make sure we didn't get lost, we both played in places close to each other.

I played the slot machine so much that I went from one hundred dollars to five hundred dollars. I was shocked that I did so well on my first try. But then I started betting like crazy because I wanted to gain more money. The more I did, my money was dropping. I was really getting annoyed—but not as annoyed as seeing my dad make a bet with some guy who looked and dressed like Al Capone, except with tan skin, a bushy mustache, and curly black hair.

When I saw Dad talking to him while losing at the slot machine, I almost got nervous. It looked like they started fine, but it slowly seemed like they were having an argument. I couldn't hear well, so I stopped playing the game and left my money in the slot machine to understand what was going on.

I assumed that Dad was gambling like crazy and had no money, so the man wanted him to make a bet on something else. Little did I know it was something else entirely. I came to Dad and asked,

"What's up?"

"Nothing, son," said Dad.

"You're okay?"

"Yes, I'm fine."

Then the man asked Dad if he was willing to bet on her. He started shaking, and his face looked angry. I was getting nervous.

"Are you going to bet, Carbon?" said the man.

"I didn't know we were going to bet on her."

"Well, I'm telling you now!"

The man kept yelling and cursing at my dad. I asked Dad,

"Just go, Dad."

"James, please!"

The man continued yelling and insulting my father repeatedly. I heard him make one of the biggest mistakes of his life: he said he wanted to bet on my sister. I got angry and disgusted that Dad was even considering this. I was furious at the man who wanted to use my sister.

"Hey! Don't talk to my dad like that, you bitch!" I yelled.

The man looked at me and said,

"Try saying that to someone else and see how that turns out."

I yelled, "Oh really?!" Then I saw a coffee cup next to one of the gamblers. I grabbed it and threw it on the man's clothes. Dad and I slammed the gambling table and threw coffee at the guy who wanted my sister. I heard people screaming.

"Whoa!" people yelled.

My dad shouted, "Hey! Hey! Hey!"

I started screaming, "NOBODY SCREWS WITH MY FAMILY, YOU PIECE OF SHIT!"

Then that same bastard ordered two big, muscular guys out of nowhere to come to him and said,

"That asshole threw coffee at me!"

They looked at me and Dad, but I was too busy staring at that sack of crap who wanted to hurt Karla. I was about to talk more, but my dad came out of nowhere and started yelling at me,

"Shut up, James! Do you want to go to prison?"

"Yeah! Go listen to daddy, asshole!"

"You're a—"

My dad stopped me and kept yelling, screaming at me to stop talking. "SHUT UP!"

The two big bastards came to us and said we had to leave. I saw the piece of shit waving at us, and the only word I could say was, "Dickhead."

We left on the spot. I really wanted to jump on the guy who treated my dad like trash and used my sister, but I was equally angry at Dad, who had almost made a bet on Karla.

We started arguing in the car while I was driving. He was yelling like a lunatic. Nothing annoyed me more than when he yelled,

"What's wrong with you, James?!"

"What's wrong with me? What's wrong with you? How can you bet on Karla?"

He stood there looking at me in shock and said, "James, that's not what happened."

"Don't lie to me!"

"James, that guy you just threw coffee at isn't just some punk you can beat."

"Oh really? Who is he, Al Capone?"

"Pretty much. And if you ever try a stunt like that again, I will personally call Barton!"

I looked at him in shock.

"You wouldn't dare!"

Dad and I stopped talking for almost the whole trip. Finally, I decided to park somewhere.

Dad looked confused. "What are you doing?"

I didn't say anything. I grabbed the phone Karla had given me and called her.

"What the hell are you doing, son?" Dad asked.

About five seconds later, I heard her say, "Hello?"

"Sis, come to Dad's house. We need to talk."

"No!" yelled Dad.

He lunged at me, trying to grab the phone. I didn't want to hurt him, but we were really struggling to get the phone. Karla was there hearing everything and yelling, "HELLO!"

I told him to sit down, but he wouldn't listen.

I yelled, "If you don't sit down, I'll knock you out and just get your gambling ass out, Karla!"

"Okay."

I drove to Dad's house. We hadn't talked for the whole trip. When all three of us sat at the dinner table, he heard Karla talking to us and had a quick argument about betting on my sister. We were probably yelling too loud, because Karla heard the whole thing outside. I heard her banging on the door, yelling, "JAMES, OPEN THE DOOR!"

I rushed to open it and saw her with a very pissed-off look in her eyes. She came to Dad and asked, "You bet me for some money?"

Dad looked at her and put his head down. He said something I never thought he would admit, but I knew he would with Karla.

"Yes."

Karla took a few steps back with a shocked look on her face. She turned to me, then back to Dad, and said, "After everything I've done for you, what kind of man sells his own daughter?"

Dad got mad and said, "Who are you to lecture me about gambling, you hypocrite!"

Karla stood there for a few seconds, shaking her head in disgust, and said, "Come on, James. Let's go."

"WAIT!" said Dad.

"Please don't leave."

"Why not?" I asked.

"Because..."

"Because what?" she asked.

Then Dad started to burst into tears and spoke, "Because I have cancer."

At first, we thought he was lying, so we laughed.

"Yeah, right!"

More tears started coming, and to our surprise, we realized he was serious. Our laughter slowly became more serious as well.

"So, you decided to sell your own daughter because you have cancer?" I said.

"I... but I'm sick," said Dad.

"James was right. You are an asshole."

We decided to go until we heard ringing at the door. We all wondered who it could be. I went to ask, but nobody answered. I asked again, and out of nowhere, there was a loud bang on the door. It was so loud that the door broke and fell on me. I didn't know who it was because the door was covering my face, and a bunch of shoes squished me.

Karla started yelling. I heard a struggle going on. It looked like Dad was fighting one of the burglars with his cane. Then I heard a loud slap on the face and Karla screaming "No!" over and over again. I started lifting the door away from me.

In that moment, I nearly snapped and was about to let D. come out, but I didn't want Karla and Dad to be hurt. With all my willpower, I stayed in control. I saw Dad on the floor and Karla being carried against her will.

I ran outside, trying to chase them, but two men tried to block me. I punched one of them. Another tried to grab me by the collar, and I scratched one of his eyes. Then I saw Karla being tied up inside a black van.

While all of this was happening, I noticed who the kidnapper was. Worse, I recognized him. It was the guy from the Golden Casino—the one I had thrown coffee at.

I tried to break the window open, but I soon realized it was unbreakable.

He started laughing at me for trying to save my sister. Then he said while I was chasing him, "Don't even call the authorities, because I own them!"

He drove off. I realized he was gone. I went to my knees and started screaming.

While I felt all hope was lost, I saw two of his thugs I had punched and scratched lying on the floor, knocked out cold. I saw one of them begging for my name and even crying. I nearly felt bad, but I wanted to know where they were hiding Karla.

I grabbed their bodies and rushed toward my dad. I looked at him and said, "Dad!"

He said, shaking like crazy, "You came back for me?"

"Don't think this changes anything... but yeah."

We both looked outside. Dad asked, "What are we going to do?"

I looked at the two guys on the floor with a very serious look on my face and said, "We're going to get her back!"

# XXVI

# SAVING KARLA TRUMAN

When Karla was kidnapped and one or two of the thugs were still on the floor, I already had an idea of what to do next. I helped Dad up from the floor and asked, "Who was that guy, Dad?"

"Someone very bad," he said.

"Do you know his name?"

Before he could answer, one of the goons started to get up. I rushed and grabbed him by the coat, dragging him away. Another was rising, so I knocked him out as well and grabbed the second thug.

I told Dad to yell for me if the thug got up. Then I looked around the house, searching for a way to interrogate him. I asked Dad, "Where's the basement again?"

"Turn right and go straight," Dad said.

I was about to head there when Dad, terrified, yelled, "James!"

"Yes?"

"Don't leave me with that guy on the floor."

"I told you, if he gets up, yell for help and I'll knock him out."

"But you can't just leave me with him."

"Well, you should have thought of that before you bet on my sister." I turned my back. If he wanted to act like a brat, I'd treat him like one.

I dragged the knocked-out thug to the basement and threw him down. I may have thrown him a little too hard, but if he died, so be it—I had another thug waiting for The Demon.

I searched for something to restrain him with and found an old wooden chair with cobwebs on it. Using metal objects, I fashioned makeshift shackles. After about nineteen minutes, I had a crude interrogation setup.

I had to wake the thug, hoping he wasn't brain damaged. I grabbed a bucket, poured sink water on his face, and yelled, "Where's my sister, asshole!"

He jumped, confused, then started laughing.

"What's so funny?" I asked.

"So, you're really going to torture me?" he mocked. "Look at you. I bet you've never skinned anyone, but someone skinned you with that missing finger."

I looked at my hand, remembering my finger being cut off years ago in Hong Kong. I slapped him.

"How about I cut off your tongue so we'll be even?"

"Ooh, scary," he said.

"You have no idea who you're messing with, do you?"

"Sure, I do—a little punk who doesn't know when to quit."

I realized he wasn't afraid of me, but I knew someone he would fear.

"You're right... but I know someone who can," I said.

"What, that old man?"

"No." I closed my eyes, focusing on all the pain and misery from my past. The more I did, the more he laughed—until he noticed things were darkening and began to panic.

"Okay, kid, whatever you're doing isn't funny anymore!"

I smirked. I could feel The Demon emerging. His laughter faded as fear crept in.

"FOR GOD'S SAKE, DO NOT DO ANYTHING CRAZY!"

I let out a terrifying, demonic voice: "You can stop me by telling me where she is and who your boss is."

"I CAN'T!" he screamed.

"Then enjoy your weeping and gnashing of teeth!"

He screamed until everything went black. I heard a heartbeat—or something worse—and flashes of light. In the flashes, I saw him bruised and bloody, my own hands covered in blood, and nails with flesh. Horrified, I snapped back to my body and realized what D. was doing.

The thug was a bloody, broken mess. I interrogated him until he finally whispered, "C...Ch... Carlos... Mono..."

I grabbed him by the hair. "What did you say?"

"I... please... kill me!"

"Who is your boss?"

"M... M... Moreno... Carlos Moreno!"

I recognized the name immediately—Karla had told me about him. I demanded, "Where is my sister?!"

"She's at the brothel at 317 West Main Street. They're planning to sell her at the border tomorrow."

"I hope you burn in hell!" I yelled, knocking him out.

I switched clothes—my own were bloody—into a coat, hat, and green tie to disguise myself as one of Moreno's men.

Dad screamed for me from upstairs. I rushed and saw a thug pointing a gun at him. I tackled the man and pummeled him until he was unconscious. Dad shouted, "Enough! You don't need to kill him!"

I looked at the thug—his teeth were broken or gone, and his face bruised.

I said to Dad, "Did you know about Carlos Moreno?"

"Know what?"

"That guy is the reason my sister is being sold."

"I was never going to take that bet," Dad said.

"Then why all of this?"

Dad explained. He had been a boxer managed by Moreno. When he couldn't make money, Moreno forced him to become a hitman for the cartel. When Dad discovered Moreno sold women and drugs to children, he wanted out. Moreno threatened that if he left, Karla would become a prostitute and he would kill Dad.

Dad begged for understanding. "I would never have bet on Karla. I just wanted you to love me as your father."

"I understand, Dad, but I need to go," I said.

"Go where? The authorities are owned by Moreno!"

"No, I'm going to get her."

Dad looked shocked at my disguise.

"I've been through worse. I'll find her."

"You're crazy. Moreno is a psychopath; he and his men will kill you."

"Well, these guys were tough, but now Moreno's men are clowns," I said.

"You want your daughter or not?"

"Yes, but I don't want to lose you too."

"You won't lose me."

I wrote down a phone number for backup—Sarah Barton—and gave it to Dad.

"If I don't make it within 24 hours, call this number," I said.

He looked nervous. "But Barton is trying to find you, right?"

"Yes, but I need backup, that's why."

"She'll arrest you, James!"

"I'll find a way out. I always have."

I drove to 317 West Main Street. My disguise and the smell of blood were my only hope of not being noticed. The area was chaotic, like Vegas—full of casinos, gangsters, and prostitutes.

I approached a security man. "Where's Don Moreno?" I asked, dressed as a gangster.

"La Jefa, east arriba," he replied.

I turned left and right, speaking Spanish with a tense accent. "Gracias."

"De nada."

Thanks to Celia, I could speak Spanish convincingly. I went inside, where music blared and the party was wild. Half-naked women and local celebrities were everywhere. I showed one woman a photo of Karla.

"Oh honey, I think she's one of the new girls," she said.

"New girls?"

"Yes, baby. She's upstairs, but have fun with me instead."

"Thanks, babe, but I already have a girlfriend," I said, leaving to go upstairs.

Moreno's men were guarding the door to where I believed he was. I asked them in Spanish, "¿Está el jefe allí?"

"Yes," they replied.

I asked if I could speak with him, but they said he was busy.

"¿Quién es ella?" I asked, and they responded, mocking, "Esa perra Karla Truman."

I was shaking with rage. One thug approached, and I grabbed a pistol from his pocket.

"WHO'S THE BITCH NOW, EH?!" I yelled.

They looked at each other and spoke in English. "You're not one of us, are you, hermano?"

I panicked. "Oh shit," I muttered.

They grabbed me by the neck and started beating me. The door opened, and the last thing I saw was Carlos Moreno.

"Well, well, look what we have here," he said. I begged him to let Karla go, but he laughed.

"Boo hoo, Truman. At least if you had stayed home, your ass wouldn't have died!"

"Why are you doing this?" I asked.

"You know why, you miserable wretch." His voice sounded eerily like the Man in Black. Memories from Hong Kong flashed through my mind. I realized my quest may have finally led me to him.

Moreno put his foot on my chest and said, "Lights out, Carbon!"

He stomped my head, knocking me out.

# XXVII

# FATHER AND SON

Moreno left me unconscious, and all I can think of before all of this happened was the feeling of being so helpless and so powerless that I really felt that this could be the end of my life.

While I was knocked out, I could hear the voice that sounded like that of a woman—one that I hadn't heard in a long time—and she was calling my name over and over. But the voice later went from feminine to masculine, and when that voice changed from someone I knew and even may have loved, it morphed into someone else, and it was that of Carlos Moreno. He started laughing at me because he finally got me.

After experiencing that nightmare, I was awakened to realize that I was tied up in that basement, bleeding, with my nose feeling like it was fractured. It was very confusing for only a couple of minutes until I realized that I was actually caught by Moreno while I was trying to save my sister.

When I saw the ropes on me, I started having flashbacks to the time The Man In Black—or Carlos Moreno, or whatever his name is—when he injected flakka into my body. That was the beginning of how my life went to hell, and I really believed that I was going to be injected with something worse. I then struggled to get out of the ropes that were on me, hoping I could do the same thing I did before.

After about nineteen seconds of struggling to get free, I heard a thundering sound, like someone was knocking at the door twice, and I realized that someone was coming.

When the door opened, I realized that it was Moreno. I looked at him straight in the eye, and I never felt so much hatred and anger coming out because the man I saw right now could very well be the man I'd been searching for seven years. But I realized that he wasn't the only person there—someone else was there, and to my horror, it was my father.

He was all bruised up, and I nearly got up from my chair, but then suddenly one of Moreno's men punched me in the gut. I started coughing blood from my lungs, and Moreno came to me and asked the guy who punched me to tie me up. He then came close to me, slapped me on the right cheek, and told me face to face:

"Look at me, Cabron. The only reason you're alive is so I can torture and kill your father in front of you. After that, I'll torture and kill you too, and I'll make money selling your sister's pussy."

When he said that, I spat on his face. He then looked at me while asking another one of his men for a handkerchief and started laughing at first while wiping his face, but then he grabbed me by the throat, and I could hear my dad begging Moreno.

"Stop! Please!"

"Why should I?" asked Moreno.

"Please, I'll pay everything. Just let him go."

"You should have thought of that before screwing with me."

"Please don't."

The same guy who punched me in the gut also punched my dad in the jaw, and I yelled:

"YOU SAVAGE BASTARD!!!"

"What are you going to do about it, asshole, eh? Get up and kill me?!"

Then he looked at me with my finger, which was cut open years ago in Hong Kong, and he said:

"Did you fingerbang your sister? You rednecks always screw with families, right?"

In that moment, I was freaking out. He started laughing, as did his goons, both inside this room and outside. The next thing Moreno said to me was:

"My advice to you two is to enjoy your last days on this earth because it's going to be very painful... Oh, and James, say hi to Patrick Barton for me."

In that moment, I had no doubt who Carlos Moreno was and that he was The Man In Black. He then took one last look at me with a very sinister grin and left. My dad and I looked at each other face to face. At first, we didn't say anything, but later on, we would finally speak—not in the way most people would like to see.

"This is all your fault!" I yelled.

"My fault?"

"Yes. If you had been a grown-ass man instead of being crippled by your alcohol and grief, I wouldn't be... hell, if you even knew how to fight, I wouldn't be stuck here with a loser for a father!"

When I said those things, my dad started to boil up with anger, so much so that I could see his complexion turning redder and redder.

"SCREW YOU, YA LITTLE BASTARD!"

"Oh, really? I'm the little bastard who let the woman you love die!"

"I'M GOING TO KILL YOU!" yelled my dad.

"Oh, you're going to kill me?!"

In that moment, my anger nearly boiled up to the point that I couldn't take it anymore. I could hear the voice of D. daring me to take out my own father, and I didn't know what to do because I was conflicted—seeing him as my father, but D. only sees him as just a man.

When my own father said that he was going to kill me, I let D. come out of my body. To my surprise, it was only his voice that boiled up and came out yelling with a very demonic-sounding voice and rage:

"I'LL KILL YOU! YOU'RE NOT MY FATHER! YOU'RE JUST SOME MAN!!"

When I said those words as The Demon, my dad's anger stopped. For the first time, he got to see a very darker side of me that I was trying both to control and avoid.

He then asked me something that I never thought dad would say. Not only did he hear the voice of a demon, but in his mind, he even saw The Demon.

"What was that... James?"

When I saw him calm down, he realized that something was truly wrong with me, more than he thought. He knew in that moment that I wasn't just a fugitive with problems, but something much more dangerous. It was like he saw my whole life in front of him.

"James... Speak to me."

I stayed silent.

"James... Please speak to me."

I didn't say a word.

"James... What did they do to you, my son?"

I finally replied:

"Everything."

A tear came to my father's eye, and he said,

"I'm so sorry."

I finally told him what happened to me all these years. I did as much as I could—the raping when I met Celia, the time I became a rebel for Mark Talbot, and losing myself to Flakka. Every single detail, including what happened in Hong Kong.

At first, when he asked what happened there, I didn't want to speak, but he was persistent, and I told him that there was a woman I used to work with who was a good friend. People destroyed her life, and she became a prostitute. She had a daughter, but many enemies as well. One of them cut off the tip of my finger, and the last time I saw her was when she and her daughter were killed when Sarah Barton tried to arrest me. The man who killed them was someone who was my friend, but he felt that I destroyed his life. In the end, I don't know what exactly happened to him; all I knew was that he was in the ocean along with myself.

When I finally finished telling my dad my story and my own struggle for seventeen years, I asked him:

"I'm tired, Dad. I'm so tired of running or being alone. I just want to die. So what's the point?"

"Don't say that, James."

"Why not?" I asked.

"Because you're not alone in this."

"I am alone in this."

"What would happen if that Man In Black got away?"

"I don't care."

"I do, and I know that your mother would say the same thing. She would never want you to give up, just like I'm never going to give up on fighting cancer."

"I'm just tired. I can't fight it anymore."

"If you need strength, get some of mine by remembering me, your mother, Karla, and Celia. We don't want you to die, James, and deep down, I know you would regret everything if you let yourself die. Don't give up, James. Remember us always when you feel down."

"But how can I get out of this? I'm trapped. It's too late."

"No, it's not too late, son."

When he said that, it took me a couple of minutes to realize what he meant.

"You called?" I asked.

"Yes."

"When?"

"Very soon."

We both smiled and looked at each other. I said to Dad:

"I'm sorry for what I said."

He smiled and spoke:

"It's okay, son."

Then, about nine seconds later, Moreno opened the door and started clapping slowly. He was accompanied by a few of his thugs and said,

"Nice talk. Too bad it won't mean anything."

Moreno then grabbed a gun and said,

"Goodbye."

I glanced at my dad, and he looked at me with a smile and a wink in his eyes. In that moment, I knew Sarah was coming. I looked straight into Moreno's eyes and smiled.

"What's so funny?" he asked.

"You... You're dead!"

Then, out of nowhere, the door broke, and a bunch of people came barging into the building. Both sides started spraying bullets. So many of Moreno's men were shot that Moreno had to drop his gun and hide until one of Sarah's men shot him in the leg. He started screaming.

While the shooting was happening, I knew I had to escape, so I decided to dislocate my own hand to break free. I did this while the shooting was happening so nobody could pay attention to me and my father.

The shooting lasted for a few minutes, outside and inside the building. When it was all finished, Moreno was on the floor with five bullet holes—in the leg, arms, ear, and cheek.

While all of this was happening, Sarah came to Moreno and said,

"You're little human-trafficking operation is gone. We got all the girls free. A little old man tipped us off!"

When I heard that, I knew Karla would be safe.

When Moreno heard this, he saw my dad looking at him with a smile. In that moment, I knew it was my dad who did this. Moreno started cursing and screaming while trying to grab his gun. With one of his arms bleeding, he was able to reach for it, but then Sarah stepped on his hand and said,

"Go on, try it. But in a few months, you'll be hanged!"

"Okay, okay, I give up!"

"Really? How very kind of you."

"It's better than dying."

"No shit... Take 'me."

Sarah's men took him while my father and I were hiding in a closet. I could see a glimpse, while opening the door a little bit, that one of the men who carried that broken piece of crap was McNally. I could tell it was him because of the clown's lovable smile when he made a bad joke to Moreno, who was in complete agony:

"Don't worry, Moreno. We'll clean you. Might even have a bath... a bloodbath."

Moreno rolled his eyes, and Sarah said,

"Can we go now?"

"Sure, boss."

Then they were all going away, until suddenly one of Moreno's shoes fell on me in the closet. In that moment, Sarah turned and said,

"Did you hear something?"

Her men all looked around and shook their heads, but Sarah was doubtful. In that moment, I heard her say:

"Check the closet."

"What?"

"Check the damn closet."

In that moment, I knew we were screwed.

"But boss," said McNally.

"Just do it, Wilfred."

"Okay, okay."

McNally told one of Sarah's men to take Moreno outside along with another guy. In that moment, I knew if he opened the closet, I was screwed. I never felt so much fear in my life.

McNally walked in and was in front of the closet, holding the doorknob. He began opening the door. I closed my eyes, ready for the worst. When I opened them, I heard screaming from outside the closet. I could hear Sarah screaming and even the sound of gunfire. To my horror, I realized it was McNally—he was shot by Moreno.

In that moment, I could hear Moreno laughing. Sarah tried to wrestle the gun from Moreno. She knocked him down to the floor, pointed the gun at him, and was ready to pull the trigger. I knew if she shot him, my chances of being free would be over, so I did something on pure instinct. I got out of the closet. My dad tried to stop me, but I couldn't help myself.

"SARAH, NO!"

She turned to me, shocked.

"You!"

She decided to point the gun at me as well as her men. At first, I felt like I had screwed myself over. I didn't know what to do. All I saw was my father, Sarah and her men, and McNally on the floor with blood coming from his head. I didn't know what to do, so I tried to reason with her by having her make a choice.

"Sarah, stop. It's either McNally or me. You can't do both."

"And why the hell not?"

"Because you can't do this alone. So please, just drop the gun and call 911."

When I said that, Sarah asked me why I cared for McNally.

"Because I'm innocent of your husband's death, but he isn't."

She looked at McNally, twitching with blood coming from both his head and ears. She looked at me and Moreno. She realized I was being honest with her and that Moreno could be The Man In Black.

"Stand down, men... Just to let you know, I will not stop. If you are innocent, you have every chance to prove it in a court of law."

She called on her men to help pick up McNally. She even called 911. Then she turned to Moreno and handcuffed him.

About a few seconds later, shots were fired and the sound of broken glass shattered. Sarah yelled,

"Who's shooting?!"

"Boss, they've escaped!"

In that moment, she saw both my father and me escaping through a glass window. She began yelling loudly and furiously:

"JAMES!!!"

My father and I ran, and I asked him:

"Why did he do that?"

"Because he can, that's why," said my dad.

We both ran for our lives, trying to get back to the house. We even called for a ride as drifters until someone came to help us. When they did, we managed to go back to our house while waiting for Karla.

## THE NEXT DAY

About 24 hours of waiting, we were both so nervous about what had happened, but then there was a knock on the door. My dad told me to hide in the backyard, and I did.

While I waited outside, I tried to hear the whole conversation. I realized it was the voice of Sarah and a few other men. I didn't hear the words very clearly, but I could tell it was a serious conversation.

In that moment, I wondered if something had happened to Karla. After a few minutes of talking, I came inside with a very sad look on my face and asked,

"Dad?"

He turned to me, and so did Karla along with her dog, Brownie.

"Sis!" I ran toward her. She spoke:

"Hey, bro."

Dad came, and we all held each other and started crying together. Even Brownie had tears and started licking all three of us for about three minutes. Hugging me, I then asked my dad,

"Was Sarah here?"

He said yes.

"What about McNally?" I asked.

He was silent, so I asked him again:

"Is he okay?"

He had his head down and wouldn't answer. I turned to Karla and walked back little by little in shock. While all this was happening, I realized why my dad wouldn't say anything.

"He died, didn't he?"

"James... I'm so sorry," said Karla.

I broke down in tears because, even though he and Sarah tried to hunt me for all these years, and whether he knew it or not, he was still my friend. I may have my sister back, but my life would never be the same. McNally would never know the truth about who really killed Sarah's husband, The Man In Black.

It was one of the scariest moments in my life to see another person I cared about shot. To know that gangster was now in police custody, in a hospital, breathing, and might even bribe a judge to be acquitted for the death of someone I knew and cared about, made me pissed off.

What's worse, that moment was very likely the same bastard who killed Sarah's husband. That was the straw that broke the camel's back for me to such an extent that I told both Karla and my dad:

"I'm sorry."

"For what?" said Dad.

"I'm going back to Smart City."

"What? Why?!"

"I'm going after Moreno."

"The hell you are!" yelled Dad.

"Dad, listen."

"NO!"

"Dad, please!"

"I almost lost both of you once, and I won't lose you again."

"Dad, I'm not a kid. I'm 37 years old."

"But..."

"BUT WHAT!" I yelled. Karla asked me to calm down and begged me not to go to the hospital because Sarah could find me there.

"You don't understand, sis."

"What don't I understand?"

"He..."

"He what?" asked Dad.

"He killed Barton's husband and framed me."

"WHAT!" They both yelled.

"Okay, I just came back from a long day of hell, so can we take a step back and STOP YELLING!!!"

They stood there in shock. A few seconds later, Karla came to me and spoke:

"If you do this and he's the one you've been looking for, how do you know he's going to help you go back to normal?"

"I'll make him."

"But, son, you could die."

"Which is worse, Dad? To die innocent or to be found guilty and cut open?"

My dad put his head down and took a deep breath. Karla came to him and said:

"Dad, this is your chance to be free. If he believes he can do this, then he should."

"I can't lose your brother again; I can't lose my son again."

At that moment, my dad wept and nearly fell to the floor. We both rushed to pick him up so he wouldn't fall, and I told him:

"I'm going to die, Dad, and you're going to lose me. You told me if I needed strength, to get some of yours by remembering everyone I love, right?"

"Yes."

"So, tell me, where's your strength?"

He turned to me, looked me in the eyes, and said:

"If you do this and he's the one who did all this, go get the son of a bitch!"

Karla and I smiled. I spoke:

"Thank you."

In that moment, I gave them both a family hug and drove off to get The Man In Black, to force him to make me an antidote and confess his crimes so I could be free.

# XXVIII

# CARLOS MORENO

When I drove away to Smart City to confront Moreno, at first I thought to myself, what the hell am I even thinking? What if I get caught and get sent back to Smart City and cut open for doing something I didn't even do?

So, I had to come up with a plan while driving on the road, which is probably the dumbest thing I have ever done, or at least the second dumbest thing I have ever done. But besides that, it really makes breaking into a hospital worth it if Carlos Moreno is The Man in Black.

This could be a chance to get closer to The Man in Black, and nothing was going to stand in my way. No matter what happened, I had decided to spend seven years of my life finding one man who could free me from this nightmare.

The drive was painfully long; it must have taken me about three to four hours. Sometimes I had to use a bottle to piss because I didn't want anyone to notice me. I knew there were probably wanted posters of me, and even though it showed me with a fauxhawk and chin goatee, I still had the same face.

When I finally made it to Smart City, I had a smile on my face, believing I had finally found this guy. But to my shock, I realized that Smart City was no longer the freedom-loving place I had known seven years ago. In fact, it looked a lot like Linda Smith's Smart City, but worse.

"What the hell is this?" I muttered.

There were multiple cameras, and Sarah's men looked like the U.S. military had come to town. What's worse, they had bigger and more advanced weapons. But nothing shocked me more than seeing one of Sarah's men beating a young kid because he refused to listen and tried to walk past him.

I got out of my car and confronted the officer. "Hey, he's just a kid!"

"Get back, or you'll go to jail next!" one of the brutes yelled, pushing me to the floor. Then, seeing me face to face, he told his partner, "Hey dude, that punk looks like James Truman."

The other man turned to me and said, "Bruh, that is James Truman!"

When I realized what was happening, I got up and ran for my life. Like an idiot, I left my car, but out of pure instinct and fear, I didn't think about the fact that cars are faster than people. I was too afraid and full of adrenaline to realize that.

They started shooting at me as I ran, and I covered my head with my arms, afraid they would shoot me in the head.

After about fifteen seconds of running for my life, I saw a trash can and tried to hide behind it, damn near in a back alley, hoping they wouldn't notice me. I started shaking in fear and outrage, nearly letting The Demon come out of me, but I kept breathing while shaking in and out.

The more I did, the more I saw flashes and voices of my past haunting me. Miraculously, I slowly managed to overcome it by thinking of my family and the faces I loved now. That gave me the strength to move forward, and I calmed myself and kept The Demon in check.

When I came out of my flashbacks, I slowly looked around from the back alley and finally saw where Moreno was hiding. He was at what was once called The Resistance, but because we had taken down Linda Smith seven years ago, it had been renamed and rebuilt as The Base.

Seeing that place again gave me pure nostalgia, mixed with a little sadness after everything that had happened. I knew there were armed guards and snipers in that building, and I didn't know how to get in. I thought my chance was over until I saw a handful of doctors in lab coats coming in, clearly for Moreno. I realized I needed to knock one of them out and avoid being noticed.

I slowly walked, hiding like a shadow or a ninja, trying not to be seen. If I did all hope will be lost but when I saw that whole line of people, they reminded me of that ridley Scott's 1984 Apple commercial. I thought to myself, what has happened to my Smart City?

I went back and forth, in and out of the alley, hoping to not be seen by anyone, even the two morons who are searching for me. Then I saw one of those who was all the way in the back the first time, having to tie his shoes. Because the poor bastard was limping a lot I knew I had found my disguise, so I knocked him out and grabbed him by the coat hoping he didn't fall and get too hurt

I used his clothes—he had nothing on except his underwear and socks. About nineteen minutes later, I had dressed like a doctor: lab coat, scrub pants, and even an N94 mask.

when I got in with the rest of the doctors I was afraid I could be noticed But, to my surprise, I managed to convince many people in the building that I was a doctor because those morons didn't notice that I had an I.D. with another face.

When I followed the doctors my assumption was they we're going to where Carlos Moreno was. I had my doubts and yet I followed the doctors. After about seven seconds I saw him but I realized the doctors weren't there for Moreno but for McNally. I needed to get out of that line and thankfully, because I was in the back on the line, I managed to get out and sneak in to Moreno's room.

His room looked more like a jail cell than a hospital room. It was completely nasty looking to the point that I wondered what Sarah is doing to Smart City. And yes, I hate this guy with a passion, but what about the rest of the men and women who did nothing as bad as this guy and yet they are subjected to suffer in a terrible place like this?

When I confronted Moreno face to face, he didn't seem to recognize me.He asked me "Are you my doctor?"

"Yes," I said.

"Am I going to walk again?"

In that moment I looked him straight in the eyes and all I could see was the blood of the people whose lives were completely destroyed because of this bastard, and he has the nerve to think only about himself.

I knew that the only way to know If he's really The Man in Black was to play along until he slipped up. I decided to tell him that he will walk again and then I've began to ask him a couple of questions.

"Did you ever come to Smart City before?"

"Yeah, seven years ago," said Moreno.

"Why did you go there?"

"Business, only business."

"What Kind of business?" He looked at me with a dismissive look in his eyes and said, "I can't tell you."

"Why not?"

"Are you going to help me or not, I'm in pain." I wanted to say that I really wanted to watch him suffer and force him to bleed even harder but I knew If I did, I would probably snap back into D. and be exposed so I said to him. "Sure, just let me get some medicine. "

I decided to go to the cabinet and give him an antibiotic to make him calm down and when I did, I started telling him that he's going to be okay and even though it sickened me I realized I had to play nice to this piece of shit.

So, I started asking him things like what is his favorite hobby, and if he has any family, he then told me that his favorite hobby was gambling and that's one of the reasons why he built The Golden Casino when he was just 27 years old with his father Salvador Orlando Moreno.

They worked as father and son as part of a casino business but in reality their real business was being leaders of the Mexican cartel at the border of Texas. They did plenty of terrible things—they killed people and even sold people and they always saw it as a way to make money. Moreno had no thoughts in his mind of what is right and wrong because he told me that he had no feelings while doing any of this.

When he was telling me his story, I thought this guy is a sociopath and it surprised me that a human being could act like this. He has no humanity in his actions, none what's so ever, and when I saw his eyes, those black eyes as dark as a gorilla's, I thought, " what kind of man is this?"

At first, I wanted to puke because of what he did but the thing that shocked me was when he said, If It weren't for my father I probably would have turned out differently but I have no regrets."

When he said that it was like a guy who knows what he's doing is wrong and doesn't take responsibility, with no remorse or regret. His story was so twisted that I nearly got sick but I knew I need a confession so I decided to ask him about what kind of business he did in Smart City.

"Well, I met with other leaders to sell my drug."

"What kind of drug?"

"Are you serious?"

"Yes, I'm serious."

"Okay man, no need to get stern...It was flakka."

In that moment I realized I'm almost getting a confession out of him so I decided to get closer to him and asked, "Did you ever meet a man named Truman?"

"Yeah, I knew his father and I made his son and daughter suffer." In that moment I clenched my fist because I wanted to punch his ass so freaking hard but I realized I had to keep my cool so I asked him one final question.

"Did you drug him?"

"Yes, along with Linda Smith and..." and before he was about to finish, I grabbed him by the throat and he started fighting me. He began choking and after about nine seconds I realized that I was blacking out again and started hearing The Demon's voice again.

"Kill Him!" Said D.

When I realized what happened I let go and he started coughing. He then looked at me with anger and yelled, "What the hell is your problem!"

So, then I lift up the mask I had on and revealed to him who I was. He then looked at me with shock and spoke, "You!"

"Damn right It's me."

"How did you get in here?"

"I used to work here before you destroyed my life."

"I don't know what you're talking about."

I was about to grab him by the throat and before I did, I yelled, "DON'T LIE TO ME!!!"

"I'm serious!"

"Are you him?"

"Who?"

"Don't play stupid. I'm asking are you the one who killed Patrick Barton?"

Then he started laughing at me and I started yelling at him to stop laughing but he wouldn't listen so I threaten to choke him again and said "Don't make me kill you."

"So, you're telling me you didn't kill Sarah Barton's own husband?"

I was confused and started asking him to not play dumb but then he said to me that the only one who's playing dumb is me.

I started to laugh and said "You want me to kill you?"

"If you're so innocent, why are you threatening to kill me?" said Moreno.

"Because you did this to me, your drug destroyed me and my life."

"Look, I seriously don't know what you're talking about." He looked at me face to face and to my shock I realized he may have been telling the truth.

"But If you're not the man in black..."

"Man In black...Oh you mean that doctor."

"Doctor?" Moreno explained to me that he knew a doctor who he gave Flakka and many other drugs to, hoping to make a profit. He had a ski mask and a fedora hat because he wanted to remain anonymous.

"So, you don't know who he Is?"

"Of course, I know who he is."

"Then tell me who is he?"

"If I tell you I'll be a dead man."

I smiled and spoke.

"What? You're afraid of a little old doctor?"

"He's not just a doctor, he's a billionaire who has connections with a lot of people. This guy Is a sicko."

"Keep going."

"Look, I can only say so much. Now go before I scream or call for help."

"I'm not going anywhere."

"Okay, then HE..." And then I grabbed him by the throat and told him to shut up and I looked at him face to face and told him, "I'm not some bitch you can pimp around, now tell me WHO IS HE?!?!"

He shook his head, so I told him, "You're going to die asshole and the amount of time you want to talk is up to you!"

He still wouldn't answer so I squeezed him even harder. He still wouldn't talk so I raised my left fist and I started hearing the voice of The Demon again.

He told me, "What are you waiting for? Kill the bastard."

When I realized what I was doing I let both hands go and Moreno started shooting. He even had my handprint on his throat while all of this was happening, I Looked at him while breathing heavily and it took a minute to relax completely. It took Moreno a while too.

Moreno tells me are you going to talk or are you going to die?!"

"Okay I'll talk...This doctor, or Man in Black, he...He's from New York his name is..." and then Moreno died but not by me or by The Demon but by a gunshot wound. I turned and notice that the window had a bullet hole and I saw who shot him and It no one other than The Man in Black, and I saw him trying to escape.

"No, you freaking don't."

I was about to open the door to run when Sarah and her men came and said, "You!"

"Sarah?!"

"I should have known Moreno didn't kill my husband, that's why you had to kill him too."

"Sarah, Please, Patrick's killer is right there."

She refused to listen and believe me and while all this was happening, I knew if I stay The Man in Black will escape, so I had no choice but to push Sarah and a few of my old colleagues out of the way and jumped through the glass window.

I rushed outside hoping to find The Man in Black but he already gone.

# XXIX

# GOODBYE AND GOOD LUCK

D ammit. To think that I had him in the first place and to realize that the man who I thought ruined my whole life was actually nothing more than an accomplice—someone who knew everything that happened to me—and that The Man in Black was really someone else.

I couldn't believe it at all. What's worse, I had to run for my life again without The Man in Black. I had no idea who he was, but thanks to Moreno, I finally had a clue: he happens to be a doctor, and he had connections with Linda Smith.

But that raised another question: why would a doctor betray his oath and kill a bunch of people just to get to me? And the second question, which I think is more important—who gives a shit? Because now I was still a wanted fugitive, and I had no choice but to leave my family again. I had come back to Smart City for nothing, and their lives would be at risk, just like Patrick Barton, Wan Po, Li Mai, and Mai Ming.

Out of all people, I couldn't let that happen to my family. I couldn't let my past doom my father and sister. I refused to let that be their fate. Every time I was with someone, bad shit happened to the people I cared about. I understood why—it was because of the freaking drug injected into me seven years ago. I couldn't have a normal life when I was a freak.

It took me a few hours of outrunning and hiding from Sarah and her men. Sweat and tears later, I realized I had to go home and tell my family that I had to leave alone.

When I returned home, my head was down. I didn't show any emotion because I didn't want to break down in front of them. It would only make it harder for them to let me go if they saw me crying.

At my father's house, I knocked on the door over and over. I heard a voice—my father's voice. When he opened the door, he said, "Son?"

"Hi, Dad."

We hugged tightly. He asked if I had found out who The Man in Black was. I said I hadn't, but I had another clue: his last name starts with M, and he is a doctor. I then asked if Karla was there. He said,

"She's here, and she's with Brownie."

"That's good to hear," I said.

My dad slowly realized what was going on. He asked me what was wrong, and I told him I had no choice.

"What do you mean, son?"

I knew this was going to be hard for both myself and my family, but I also knew I had to be ready to travel again. I couldn't risk their lives. Sarah would know I was here, and I didn't want to endanger them like I had Li Mai and Mai Ming.

I finally said, "I'm sorry, Dad."

"Sorry about what?"

"I have to go."

"What?!"

"I can't stay."

He realized that my attempt to capture The Man in Black had failed and that Sarah would come after me wherever I traveled. My dad knew his and my sister's lives would be endangered.

"So, you have to leave... again."

"I'm sorry, Dad, but I have to go."

"I understand. It's just like when you left us the first time."

"It's not like that, Dad. When I left, I was selfish. Now I'm doing the most selfless thing I could do—I'm protecting you all."

My dad looked at me, tears in his eyes.

I said, "I'm trying to protect you and Karla."

"I know."

"But someday we'll meet again."

"I don't know, son. Without you in my life, I'm already dead."

I realized what he meant. His cancer was spreading, and he believed if I left, his heart would break, his will to live gone, and the cancer would worsen.

"Dad, please, we will meet again. Don't say that."

He looked at me, tears in his eyes, and hugged me again. I cried too, seeing this little old man in agony and sorrow.

When we stopped hugging, I told him, "When I find The Man in Black, make me an antidote, and get a confession for the murders, remember I will come back here. We'll have the biggest party ever, okay?"

My dad smiled. "Okay."

"How about we put some music on that day, like hardcore gangster rap?"

"I'm more of a James Brown kind of guy."

"I like James Brown too, so we'll put on James Brown," I said.

We smiled and hugged again. I told my dad not to tell Karla until tomorrow, and he agreed. She would be very emotional and try to convince me to stay, but this was for their own good.

I then asked my dad to close his eyes and imagine the party we'd have together, playing James Brown's *I Feel Good*. He did, even though he knew this was the second time I'd leave him and Karla. At least for him, it was a better goodbye than last time, and I knew it made him smile. Then I was gone.

Two hours later, I decided to take a bus to New York, where Moreno said The Man in Black was. Knowing some hints about him, I hoped I could someday find this guy.

When the bus arrived, I sighed deeply, realizing how lonely things would be again without Dad and Karla. I wished I could hold her and let her know I was going to New York, but I couldn't. If I did, she might tell someone, and I couldn't risk putting them in danger.

As I was about to board, I heard a loud voice screaming my name.

"James! James!"

I turned and saw Karla. I skipped the bus and rushed to her.

"What are you doing here?"

"I convinced Dad to tell me where you were going. Why, James?"

Her big eyes behind those glasses made me realize I was in real trouble. The bus driver was asking if I was coming.

I screamed, "Just drive!"

We started talking.

"Why, James?" she asked.

"I have no choice. I have to protect you two," I said.

"But why abandon us like you did years ago?"

"It's not like that, sis. Back then I didn't think about you two, but I do now."

"We can fix this," she said.

I shook my head. There was no fixing this here. I had to do it on my own.

"But where are you going? When are you coming back?"

I couldn't tell her. If I did, Sarah could find out and force her to betray me. I had to be honest without giving details. She started crying.

"Look at me," I said. She wouldn't, so I raised my voice. "Look at me, sis!"

She finally looked at me, her eyes wide behind her glasses.

I said, "When you were young, you were always the happiest part of my life. You're also the strongest woman I know."

"That's not true," she said.

"Yes, it is. You've strengthened me and forgiven both me and Dad for everything we did. I may have physical strength, but you, a doctor and a forgiver, have shown me how to be strong and happy. These past two years were everything I ever wanted—a normal, happy life with a family. It was one of the best years I've had, even as a wanted fugitive."

We smiled and hugged.

"Be good to Dad, okay?"

"I will."

"I love you, sis."

"I love you too, bro."

Tears filled my eyes.

"Remember, this isn't the end. I'll be back. When I do, you'll see me at the door a new man. But I can't do that if you won't let me go for now. Always remember, I'll come back, sis. That I promise!"

"Okay."

"Okay?" We smiled again, wiped our tears, and knew she understood. We stayed and waited for the next bus, sharing stories of our childhood, laughing, and enjoying the brief reunion.

When the bus came, I looked at Karla and held her hand as if she were going to force me to stay. She smiled and let me go.

"Goodbye," I said.

"Good luck," she replied. I waved one last time as the bus pulled away.

Three hours later, I arrived in New York. I saw homeless people and hookers asking for money or offering services. I ignored them. Walking the streets all night, I got hungry but had no money. I couldn't break in to get food, so I scavenged from a dumpster.

Among the garbage, I found a New York Times newspaper. I read the front page, hoping for clues.

I was shocked. The headline read:

"Wilfred McNally Survived Assassination Attempt"

At the bottom:

"Father of Wanted Fugitive Dies at 82"

McNally survived, but my own father had lost his fight with cancer. I broke.

## THREE YEARS LATER

Three years had passed since I left. Things couldn't have been worse. I was alone again, seemingly forever. I had left my sister and father behind. My father was dead, and my sister and I were orphans.

I had also lost a former friend, who believed I killed another former friend's husband and died thinking I was a murderer. Sometimes I questioned everything, even the existence of The Man in Black. I knew the killer was never me.

Life in New York was brutal. I let my hair grow into an afro and a stubble. I suffered all day in the heat and froze all night on the streets. I just wanted to end this nightmare sooner rather than later.

Weeks passed of begging for food and water. I was just another bum, with no name, no future, no identity. Every time I closed my eyes, all I saw was The Man in Black. I didn't want this to be my end: sitting and begging for coins or dollars. I decided to do the one thing I could—make a call from a phone booth.

At first, I wanted to call Karla to apologize, but I realized Sarah could tap the call and put both of us in danger. I had already told them I wouldn't put them at risk. I decided to call someone I hadn't seen or heard from in a very long time, even longer than Dad or Karla.

The phone booth had a phone book. I looked at multiple names, contemplating my choices. I didn't want to hurt anyone else I loved. But after ten or fifteen minutes, I decided to call.

The phone rang. I was afraid of losing another loved one. Almost, I was about to hang up, but then I heard a familiar voice:

"Hello?"

"Is this Buck Meyer?"

"Who is this?"

"It's me... cuz."

"James?"

I smiled. He asked where I was and how I was. I told him it had been a long, hard fight. He promised he was coming and asked where I was. I told him Manhattan.

"I'm coming to get you!" said Buck.

"Okay, but don't tell anyone else, man."

"I know you're in deep trouble, aren't you?"

"Yeah, but it's not what they're telling you."

"What does that mean?"

"I didn't do it. I'm innocent."

Buck paused. I asked if he was okay.

"Don't worry, man. I'm coming."

He hung up the phone. That was the beginning of my next journey in New York.

XXX

# WELCOME BACK JIMMY!

W e all make mistakes, and we all have to learn from our mistakes, and I question at times if calling for my cousin was a good choice or was it another mistake that will lead to heartbreak and potentially death, and that's what's been keeping me up at night.

And even if I can be with my cousin and hope that I can get closer to confront The Man in Black, all I can do now is wait. But at the same time, I have to be vigilant because that bastard could be anyone or even anywhere. And Christ, sometimes I wish that I didn't have to struggle in life, and most of all I wish that I was forgotten and died a long time ago because I'm afraid of my own future.

But sometimes I realize that even though I struggle now for years, it's my belief that it's only a temporary curse that has a way out. But for people who are like my cousin, William Moshe "Buck" Meyer, it's a curse forever.

A long time ago when I was a kid, me and my family were camping in the forest. Almost everyone I knew was there with me—my dad, my sister, and even my mother—but I also had other relatives too joining the camp. One of them was my Uncle Walter, and of course, my cousin Buck.

One time when it was midnight, I heard some noises that woke me up, and I thought at first that it was a bear. I was afraid and hid behind my parents to protect me from whatever was there. But when the noise stopped, I went to check for myself, and there was nothing there. But I noticed that Buck was missing.

I woke up my parents and my uncle that Buck was gone, and the whole family began trying to find him around the woods. We screamed and called for Buck, but it didn't seem like we were getting any closer to finding him at all. It was too dark to see anything, and even though we had a flashlight, the power was having some issues, so we were following blind.

After about eight minutes of searching for Buck, my uncle almost had a panic attack, but my parents tried to calm him down, and so did I, until I heard something in the woods that sounded like Buck crying. I tried to tell my parents, but they told me it was just a bear. But I refused to believe them and ran to find out who it was. My parents tried to stop me, and they almost did, but I got out because the flashlight's power was gone, and they lost me while trying to run after me.

When I began trying to find out where those cries were coming from, it was very hard to see, and sometimes I tripped, but I got back up. After about four minutes of searching for that voice, I finally found Buck. When I saw him, I tried to tell the other family members, but Buck stopped me and told me to stay.

"Cuz."

"Cuz, you know I can't do that?" I said.

"Please, Jimmy, don't leave me, okay."

"But why?" I asked.

"Just please hear me out. I don't want my dad to find out why I ran away."

I was confused and wondered what his plan was, but it took me a few seconds, and I decided, "Alright, I'll sit, but make it quick." And I sat down and heard him, and he slowly told me in great detail why he ran and why he was crying. I wanted to know why he ran away, but the real kicker was why he wanted me not to tell his father.

"Why don't you want to tell him what's going on?"

"Because he wouldn't understand," said Buck.

"Why?"

"He believes too much in God and how gay people are bad."

When he said that, I realized what he meant, so I asked him if he was gay, and he looked at me and said that he thinks so, but he's not too sure.

"Just don't tell my father, okay, Jimmy? Tell him and your Uncle George and Aunt Wanda that I was sleepwalking, okay?"

I had plenty of sympathy for Buck because I believed he was confused and lost, because he didn't want to be alone, and he didn't want his overly religious father to reject him. As a four-year-old boy, I felt the weight of what it was like for a child to go through something like that.

It was my first taste of understanding the real world and how it works. We hugged each other, and I told him, "Don't worry, Cuz." About a few minutes later, our family saw me hugging Buck, and my uncle came to Buck and started crying. My parents looked at me with anger to the point my father yelled, "How can you do this to us, Son?!"

"But Daddy, I thought you and Mommy knew where to find me. Cuz was sleepwalking and—"

"I don't want to hear excuses, boy!" yelled Dad.

Then Uncle Walter looked up into the stars and said, "Thank you, God," and he hugged his son, while my mom was trying to tell my dad to leave me alone because all I did was tell them that I heard Buck crying, and I was right.

"Let it go, George. He did the right thing. We should have listened to our son," said Mom.

"But Wanda—"

"Let it go."

"Alright."

After my mother chewed on my father, she turned to me with a kind face and a wonderful smile and said to me, "Come on, Son, let's go back."

"Okay, Mommy."

We all went back to the tents and rested, and after all these years later, even while meeting Uncle Walter again in Hong Kong, I kept my promise to Buck that I would never tell his father about why he really ran away, and I made sure that he never does.

Sometimes I wish things could have been better for my cousin, and sometimes I wish I told my family the truth about Buck and why he really ran away that night—not because I wanted to embarrass him, but because I sometimes believed that they would accept him either way.

But I knew if I did, he would be hated by his father, and I didn't want Buck to have that kind of life of his dad knowing the truth. But at the same time, nobody has to suffer for life because of who he is or that he wants to tell the truth but can't.

That night changed everything I knew growing up about how the world works and how unfair life can be. Because now not only do I have to suffer the burden of keeping a huge secret from his father and never telling the truth to my family for decades starting from a very young age, but my burden is nothing compared to Buck's own burden, and I respect him as much as I feel sorry for him, even while I'm freezing my ass on the streets waiting for him to come.

And when Buck did come to pick me up, I was expecting a regular car or minivan. But to my own shock, I would find two things that were completely different. One was that the man who was driving was *not* Buck, and the other was that the car was actually a limo.

When the man came out of the limo, he walked toward me and said, "Mr. Truman."

"What?" I asked.

"Is your name James David Truman?"

"Yes."

"Master William wants to speak to you."

And I knew in that moment that it was Buck, because his real name was William Meyer. But the fact that the poor child who I hadn't seen in years now had the money to afford a limo and a butler was unbelievable. But then again, I knew his father had some stuff in his background that was completely different than before, so I had a lot on my mind already that was too much to take in.

When the butler asked me if I was coming, I said, "Uh... yes." As soon as he was going to go back to the driver's seat, I said, "Wait!"

"Yes, Mr. Truman?"

"Who are you?"

"My name is Franklin Osiris. I am both Master William's and Master Walter's butler."

"Walter... as in Walter Meyer?!"

"Correct."

"Where is he? Is he okay?"

"Master Walter is at the mansion, and so is Master William. Now shall we go, sir?"

I had a confused look on my face, and Osiris noticed and said, "Are you alright, Mr. Truman?"

"But my uncle Walter Meyer was arrested in Hong Kong!"

"Yes, that's true, but he was released on bail, and due to lack of evidence, he was set free. So now can we go, sir?"

And I smiled because I knew that Uncle Walter was okay and that he made it home. I was so happy to see that because over the years I wondered whether he made it or not, and now I know that he's safe.

So I decided to go inside the limo and hope for the best. We drove to wherever Buck and Uncle Walter were living. I was curious where my uncle and cousin lived now, because if they could afford a limo and a butler, they surely could afford a mansion.

Even though things seemed a lot different compared to before, I never thought a middle-class family like the Meyers would one day have so much money and power. I wanted to know how that was even possible, so I asked Osiris, "Um... Mr. Osiris?"

"Yes, Mr. Truman?"

"How did my cousin and his father become wealthy?"

And Osiris explained to me that Uncle Walter became a billionaire because, in his early years as a psychologist, he later decided that he was tired of staying in his middle-class status. He chose to switch careers and decided to work as a doctor of medicine. Later on, he grew tired of just treating people and wanted to expand his career into finding cures for other types of illnesses such as Alzheimer's, schizophrenia, and autism.

It took Uncle Walter some time to find some type of antidote for mental problems—so much so that it nearly took half of his time and money because nobody believed he could achieve such a thing. When he finally found a company to sell his inventions, he received a hundred million dollars from a pharmaceutical company, and the owner of the company was Bradley Lieber.

At first, Uncle Walter wasn't part of the board of that company. In fact, Mr. Lieber blocked any chance of Uncle Walter becoming a member, if not the boss of the company, because Mr. Lieber hated his middle-class roots and only saw Uncle Walter as a geek with no future other than creating cures. But when Mr. Lieber was indicted and convicted because it was revealed that he was a drug addict and was removed from the board effective immediately—and that drug was none other than Flakka, the same drug that was both inside and expanded into my system—when the board needed a replacement, they decided that because of Mr. Lieber's history of blocking Uncle Walter and because of Uncle Walter's creations and his fresh and kind approach to others, they decided that he should not just become a new member of the board but also the new CEO of the pharmaceutical company. That was the beginning of how he made billions of dollars curing every mental illness with his injections, which he called *Neuroma*.

After all that, when I went with Osiris, I saw through the window everything looking so gross and miserable in New York City. Boy, it was one of the biggest stench assaults for both my eyes and my nose. I knew that New York is called Fear City for a reason, but I never thought it would be such a disgusting pile of piss. I saw everything that was so disgusting it's almost hard to imagine. I hoped that I would never get to see anything like this ever again, because all I saw in that city was fights, drugs, and rats—lots and lots of rats. To be honest, I wanted nothing to do with this crap, and I even told Osiris to hurry the hell up because of all that crap going on in the streets. And he did.

When I finally got out of that rat-infested, piss-smelling nightmare of a city, Osiris drove me to a place that looked as if nobody lived there. There was plenty of grass with a road that led to a giant gate. When Osiris stopped, there was a man in uniform who asked,

"Can I see some identification?"

"Certainly," said Osiris, and he gave him his ID.

The man looked at me and turned to Osiris and said, "Who's the bum?" And in that moment, Osiris and I were both annoyed about how that guy treated me.

Osiris said, "This bum, as you called him, happens to be the cousin of Master William."

The guy's face started to fall, and he realized what he said could get him in trouble.

"Oh my God, I am so sorry, Mr.... um... Mr.—" While he struggled on what to say, I knew that I couldn't use my real name for him to call me by, so I made one up. I remembered a few streets I knew—one of them was Nelson Street, and the other was Dale Street—so I used both names and said,

"My name is Nelson... Dale Nelson."

"Okay, Mr. Nelson, welcome to the mansion," and he opened the gates. I was sent in and saw one of the biggest mansions I have ever seen, with one of the longest stairs and gardens in my wildest dreams. I couldn't believe that a bum like me could actually visit a mansion, let alone one that belongs to my cousin.

I asked Osiris, "Is this really my cousin's mansion?"

"Yes, Mr. Truman—or should I say Nelson," smiled Osiris.

"You don't be a smart ass."

"Okay, okay, but yeah, this is both Master Walter and Master William's mansion."

"Wow," I said in shock.

When we finally parked, I was about to open the door, but Osiris stopped me and said,

"I'll take care of that."

Then I stood back, and he got out. He opened the door for me, and I couldn't believe how beautiful the mansion looked and how quiet it seemed. It was almost a peaceful place to live, to the point that I was glad to see it and wanted to stay. But at the same time, my peace later went to sadness because I knew I could never really be part of all this while I'm still a wanted fugitive.

When I went upstairs in the mansion, I still couldn't believe that all of this was actually made and came from my uncle and my cousin. I couldn't believe they let me be part of that family, even though I never thought I'd have a family again.

When Osiris and I managed to go to the door, it had one of those lion door knockers. I was hesitant to knock on the door because the place seemed so much bigger than me, and I still couldn't believe all of this came from my blood. When I asked Osiris to knock on the door, he saw that I was nervous and said to me,

"Don't be humble, Mr. Truman. You are family."

And I smiled and knocked on the door.

About one or two minutes later, I heard someone coming closer. He opened the door, and I realized, to my shock, it was someone I never thought I would see in a long time—it was my own cousin.

"Jimmy!" said Buck.

"Hello, Cuz, long time no see."

"Osiris, take my cousin to rest, and tomorrow we'll give him a tour, show him where he can take a shower, and give him the best clothes. I want a banquet for myself and my cousin. We have a lot of things to talk about."

"Yes, Master William."

Me and Buck smiled, and he said to me,

"Welcome back, Jimmy!"

And that was the beginning of my new journey in New York. I rested on this huge bed, all dirty with my boots on me, and just started thinking about what I've got myself into. In fact, I was wondering if I had just endangered my cousin the same way I've endangered many other people in my life, so much so that I was thinking about escaping from the mansion. I saw a window, and it gave me the idea of trying to jump out and kill myself. But obviously, I didn't, though I wanted to so badly because I didn't want Buck's life to be destroyed just like with Patrick and Sarah, with Li Mai and Mai Ming, and with my dad and Karla.

Sometimes I couldn't believe how far I've come, but at the same time, every moment and every second I wake up with the feeling of just wanting to die because I didn't want everyone I cared about to suffer. I really believed that this could get worse if I stay too long.

While I was in bed thinking about everything that had happened over many years, I started remembering my time at Smart City when I was at Blackstone. I saw nothing but complete darkness when Celia left after everything that happened, and I still wonder what happened to her to this day, and I couldn't let it go for so many years.

Just like I missed Celia and felt bad about how many times I wished I could say sorry for everything that happened, it's hard to realize how long you've been down and how low you've sunk, especially when you see two people you've also known get shot and killed by your former best friend.

At times, I questioned if Mike from Hong Kong was still alive, and I still wondered what happened to everyone else I came across and wondered if I would ever see them again. But nothing matches that question more than wondering about The Man in Black, and even if I find him, the question that really haunts me is how exactly I will force him to give me an antidote to The Demon.

So yeah, many things happened to me over the years, and many of them are some of the strangest and most horrible events of my life. Sometimes I wondered if my life is doomed to suffer and die a horrible death with no wife, no children, no family. No matter how many times I close my eyes, all I see is blood of everyone I cared about on my hands. I wished this on nobody, and I hope I never see anyone innocent suffer for this monstrosity of a life I am living right now.

While I was on the bed thinking about my whole life and what's next, I heard a knock on the door, and I asked,

"Who is it?"

"It's time to take a shower, Mr. Truman."

"Okay, I'm coming."

While I opened the door, I was given almost a mini tour around the mansion until I finally went to the bathroom, and it was huge. Even though I knew this belonged to my cousin, I still couldn't believe he and his father could afford something like this.

After I was in the bathroom, Osiris said he would bring new clothes for me in about ten minutes, and he asked me what size I am. I told him that I'm 1XL, and he smiled and said, "So is Master William." Then he told me that he would come back in about ten minutes, after which I would receive high-class clothing. When he said that, I thought it was a joke and started to laugh. But I soon realized that Osiris was serious about me dressing up like a billionaire, because for many people, an ugly and dirty-looking guy doesn't look like a billionaire.

Osiris explained that he had come prepared for that and wanted me to look as clean as possible. In that moment, I agreed to everything he was preparing for me and decided to take a shower. Exactly ten minutes later, I received both a black top as well as black pants, an orange tie, black dress socks, and brown dress shoes.

After I finished taking a shower, I dressed and was given a tour around the whole mansion. Until I sat down at a banquet in front of me, where I sat face to face with my cousin, and he said to me,

"It's good to see you again, Jimmy."

"Cuz, you didn't have to do all this for me."

"But I knew that you were in trouble, and I wanted to help you, just like you helped me years ago."

"Yeah, you're right. I'm grateful; I just never thought you guys would have such a beautiful life while I... I... um... I—"

In that moment, I nearly cried, and Buck saw me looking misty and said to me,

"Hey man, it's okay. You're safe, and I could never imagine what you've been through, but we are going to get through this."

"How? I'm a wanted fugitive."

"You helped me years ago and never gave up on me when I was down, and I swear I won't give up on you either. So stop doubting yourself, because many people believe in you, Jimmy."

"Thanks, man."

Then Buck looked at me strangely, and I was wondering what was going on with him because he seemed quite confused. Then he looked at me with a surprised look on his face and said,

"JIMMY, YOUR FINGER!!"

"What?"

"What happened to your finger?"

"Oh, this? Well... um... it's a long story."

# XXXI

# THE PARTY

Sometimes I wondered what if I stayed home instead of running away from my family. And sometimes I wondered if I was doing the right thing right now. But none shook me more than the thought of losing everything every time I closed my eyes.

But make no mistake, I'm glad that I've seen my family again. I regret that I didn't leave sooner to prevent them from getting hurt, because bad things happened to those I care about, and sometimes I feel like I'm cursed to live with that guilt.

While being with my family may help me in the short term, I knew if I stayed too long, it would destroy me and my family in the long term. But while I was at my cousin's mansion, eating at his banquet, I really felt a strange feeling of a bit of sadness.

But that sadness would later come with joy through a knock on the door while Buck and I were talking. When Buck asked Osiris to open the door for him, he said one word.

"Yes."

"Hello, Osiris."

"Master Walter, come in, sir."

When Osiris said Master Walter, I nearly jumped out of my chair as if I was electrocuted, because I couldn't believe after all these years, I finally got to see him again. But when he came in, he didn't recognize me and instead said to Buck, "Hello, son."

"Hello, father. Say hello to our guest."

He turned to me, and I waved at him. He just stood there frozen, and his face went from having a smile to a very shocked expression. He looked at me straight in the eye and said, "James."

"Hi, Uncle Walter."

"You made it out?!" said Uncle Walter.

"I was about to say the same thing."

Then Uncle Walter rushed toward me and hugged me. At first, I just stood there in shock, but I slowly hugged him back. He told me, "Oh my god, I thought they got to you."

"Not a chance," I said.

Then Buck looked at both of us with a confused look on his face, wondering what was going on. Uncle Walter explained to him that seven years ago, he found James in Hong Kong during one of his secret businesses.

"Wait a minute. You found Jimmy alone in Hong Kong seven years ago and you didn't tell me?"

"I thought he was dead or worse."

"Dead by whom?"

Then Uncle Walter looked at Buck like he was acting stupid, and after a few seconds, Buck finally realized that it was Sarah Barton that I was running away from.

"Oh... yeah."

Then Uncle Walter said to me that we should have a party celebrating my return, because after seven years, he thought I was dead and now I'm alive. But I explained to him that would be impossible because that could risk exposing myself and others to Sarah, and who knows who would tell Barton that I'm hiding at this place.

"But nephew—"

"I'm sorry, Uncle Walter, but that's too much of a risk. If you want to do a party, I cannot join it."

Then Buck looked at me and said that he already called a party tonight. I told him to cancel it.

"Jimmy, you know I can't do that. So many people are already coming soon, and they traveled from places like Smart City to come to New York."

"Wait a minute, Smart City?" I asked.

"Yeah, and you know I can't just cancel a party while they're driving."

"Buck, what have you done?!"

"What did I do?"

"Bruh, many people know who I am in Smart City. It is ground zero for me being public enemy number one."

"Oh no," said Buck.

"Oh yeah."

"Jesus Christ, what now?!" said Uncle Walter.

"I have to go."

"Go where?"

"Anywhere but here."

"But you just came back, nephew."

"I'm sorry, Uncle Walter."

Then Uncle Walter finally snapped and told me that I'm not going anywhere because he's not going to lose me again. I told him what would he prefer—me getting caught and sent back to Smart City to have my brains cut open?

"Of course not, but you leaving us—over my dead body."

And just like many times before, I knew I should leave, but because of my own bleeding heart, I didn't have the strength to abandon the people I cared about again. I began to shiver inside, torn between wanting to stay and needing to leave.

But it wasn't until I saw my Uncle Walter's face—it reminded me of Karla's face when I abandoned her and Dad years ago, and how much of a huge mistake that was. And again, because of my bleeding heart, I listened to my uncle and gave in to my emotions.

"Alright... alright. But how can I stay without being recognized? It isn't safe for me or for you. How can I stay without someone recognizing me?"

We stood there wondering what we should do, because they would come, and the party would have people from Smart City. We stood there thinking about what plan could work. Some of us thought I should stay outside until the party was over, and some believed I should just hide upstairs with the doors locked.

But Buck suddenly had an idea.

"What is it?"

"It's from one of my oldest parties years ago, but I think it could help."

"Like what?"

He told us that he would tell his friends to wear domino masks over all our faces so they wouldn't recognize me or anyone else.

Uncle Walter said, "Good idea." Then he looked at me and asked if I would agree. I stood there for about five seconds and said, "Alright." I agreed to stay.

## TWO HOURS LATER

While I stayed, I decided to keep myself from going downstairs instead of joining them with a mask on, because even though I'd be wearing something to cover my face, I still wouldn't go. I was afraid of being recognized anyway.

While the party was happening, I even locked myself in Buck's room and waited there until the party was over. Sometimes I started thinking about Celia upstairs, wondering where she was, while Uncle Walter and some of my cousin's rich friends—including Buck's secret boyfriend Carl Miller—were having fun downstairs, dancing, and secretly making love either outside or in a bathroom.

When I was upstairs with a domino mask in my hands, I heard something that sounded like a knock on the door. I was afraid it could be someone who would recognize me, so I put on the domino mask and said, "Who is it?"

"Um... it's Buck."

"Okay, I'm coming."

I got up from the bed and unlocked the door with the mask on.

"Did everybody leave?" I asked.

"Not yet, but I just wanted to make sure you're okay."

"I'm fine."

Then Buck looked at me straight in the eye, and I could tell he knew I was lying because I seemed a bit sad. But he didn't say anything for a few seconds.

"Well, I just wanted to make sure."

"Okay, thanks, cuz."

I was about to close the door, but he held it with his hand and spoke.

"Hey, wait. You haven't heard what else I wanted to say to you."

"Okay, cuz, but give it a few seconds because I don't want anyone to come up and see me."

"Okay, okay. Um... how about I give you a job as one of my limo drivers?"

"You're serious?"

"I'm just saying, because I don't want you to get too bored in this mansion all the time."

I stood there thinking for a few seconds, and to be honest, I wanted to get out of this place and do something. But I didn't want to be noticed, and I asked him, "What if somebody recognizes me?"

"Don't worry, I've got an idea," said Buck.

"Okay, what's the idea?"

"I can give you a hat and sunglasses so that people won't recognize you."

I was a little worried about his plan because I believed people aren't too stupid not to recognize me with a hat and glasses.

"I don't know, man."

"Come on, cuz, give it a try."

"Okay, I'll think about it."

"Okay, that's good."

"Yeah, but where am I going to drive you to?"

"You're not going to drive me—you're going to drive some of my friends."

"What!"

"Come on, Jimmy."

"Cuz, I'm literally hiding upstairs so that your friends won't recognize me."

"They won't recognize you, trust me. These morons aren't too bright."

"Yikes, that's how you treat your friends, Buck? By calling them morons behind their backs?"

"But they are."

I stood there surprised that Buck would call people who were friends with him morons while they were downstairs. Even though I didn't know these people, I knew and grew up with my cousin, and I never thought he would call people close to him names.

"Like your boyfriend?" I said.

"Hey, hey, hey! That's different."

"Oh, how's it different?"

Then he looked at me in shock, and I sighed and said, "Okay, sorry about that, cuz. It's just I was thinking a lot lately. But don't worry, I'll accept your offer."

"You sure?"

"I'm sure."

I smiled, and he looked at me with a small grin on his face because this time, he knew I was telling the truth.

"Who am I going to pick up?" I asked.

"Some strippers," said Buck.

"I beg your pardon."

"Come on, Jimmy, you're not going to punk out on me, are you?"

"No, I'm just surprised."

"Don't worry, cuz, you might have a girl give you a lap dance."

"That would be great."

We both laughed, and I accepted the offer to become a limo driver.

After the conversation with Buck, I locked the door and went back to bed, hoping for the best. But the sad truth was that the decision to work as a limo driver would soon create a series of events that would change my life—and the lives of the people I love—forever.

# XXXII

# CELIA MENDOZA

The next day after I took the job, I was given a hat and sunglasses in the hope that nobody would know that I am James David Truman, and hopefully it would stay that way for as long as it takes. But who knows what could happen.

I was told by Buck to go to a strip club to pick up some strippers who were leaving to go home and needed a ride. He gave me the address to somewhere called *The Wild Cougar*, a quote-unquote gentlemen's club, by nine o'clock.

It took me about eleven to fifteen minutes to drive from the mansion to the strip club, and when I arrived, I had to wait a while until at least midnight for the club to close. I did, but it wasn't easy. In fact, I got pretty bored just waiting from nine o'clock to twelve o'clock.

When it was finally midnight, I saw the girls coming out, and they came into the limo half-naked. They asked me, "You, are you like the driver?"

"Yeah."

"Thanks, honey. The name's Kelly."

"Dale Nelson."

They all came in, and I was about to leave, but one of them told me that I had to wait for another girl because she was dealing with some things. I asked her, "What things?"

"I don't really know, honey. She's new in town."

"What's her name?"

"Sofie."

In that moment, I realized that I had to wait a little while longer, and I said to myself, "Okay, James, just remember you're getting paid to do this."

So I waited for a few minutes, but when things went from a few minutes to more than thirty minutes and then an hour, I said to myself, "How long is this going to take, for God's sake!"

"Chill, babe, she's coming," said one of the strippers.

But I was getting very sick and tired of waiting for hours doing nothing, so I decided to say, "Screw this!"

I was about to turn on the gas when suddenly I saw a fight between some jerk and a stripper, and one of the girls said, "That's her! That's Sofie!"

Then I saw the guy punching her with his fist in one hand and a broken glass of whiskey in the other. I saw the girls yelling, "Let's get him, girls!"

"No, I'll do it!" I yelled.

Then I got out of the car and went up to the drunken bastard and yelled, "Leave her alone!"

That drunken moron started laughing, so I grabbed him by the collar. He looked at me and saw my eyes. I didn't blink or even look another way, but stared straight at him like I was taking his soul—so much so, in fact, that I almost let D. chew him up into pieces. And I almost did.

Then suddenly, I saw my arm throw the bastard to the floor, and I smashed his head open with blood coming out. But the strangest thing was, I felt like I didn't do it, as if someone else came and pushed my arm to the side.

In that moment, I knew it was the Demon trying to control me, and I began to shiver at the thought of the whole thing. I almost fainted when I saw the guy on the ground. He was still alive but in serious pain. He then ran off, all wobbly and confused.

In that moment, I didn't know what to feel, but I knew what to do—and it was to help the girl on the floor, the same one that guy had been beating up.

"Are you okay?" I asked.

She turned to me, and I saw her face. To my shock, it reminded me of someone I hadn't seen in a long, long time. But a few seconds later, I realized she wasn't a reminder—she was the real deal.

To my surprise, I said with a chill down my spine, "I... you... no. It can't be. It can't be!"

"James?"

"Celia?"

In that moment, I couldn't believe it. After ten years, I finally got to see her again—my own girlfriend who left Smart City years ago after everything that happened—and now she was in New York working as a stripper.

I just couldn't believe it. For the first time ever, I finally realized just how low we'd sunk.

While all of this was happening, the guy I took down yelled, saying that he'd call 911 to arrest us both. I started laughing and said to the little punk, "Go ahead! You're the one who started it, so go ahead, call 911, moron!"

He stood there, did nothing, wobbled around, and vanished.

"What are you doing here, babe?" I asked.

"I was about to say the same thing about you."

When I was about to respond, I saw some of the strippers honking the horn and yelling, "You! Driver! Sophia! Can we go now?"

"Um... sure, girls. We'll talk about this later," said Celia.

We both entered the limo, Celia in the back with the other girls, me driving in the front, and we went on our way.

ONE HOUR LATER

After I was done sending all the strippers home, I saved Celia for last. While parking next to her apartment, I hadn't spoken a single word to her and refused to even look at her, because I was thinking a lot—like why she abandoned me when I needed her.

Sure, she was struggling with the thought of me getting my brain cut open, but I never thought she would abandon me in the last moment. Sometimes it's hard to live, but quitting on the people you love is even harder. Celia knew this, so I thought she would be with me until the end. But now I realized that wasn't true.

What's worse, I bet she now thinks of me as the American Osama Bin Laden or something, after that damn fire that happened years ago.

After I was done bringing home the other strippers, Celia finally spoke to me and asked how I found her, but I wouldn't answer. Then she asked if it was true about me killing Dr. Patrick Barton, and I still wouldn't answer. Lastly, she asked why I wasn't speaking to her, and I replied, "Why did you leave me alone to get my brain cut open?"

"You're still mad about that?" said Celia.

"Of course I'm mad! I want to know why you left me."

"James, you have to understand, I... I wasn't strong enough to see what they were going to do to you."

"But you were strong enough to abandon me?"

"Oh, like you've abandoned me years ago!"

I stood in shock when she said that and asked her the same question she asked me—was she still mad about that? She said, "Not as much as seeing you kill Sarah's husband. How could you do this?"

"I didn't do it!"

"Oh yeah, of course, it was the Man in Black that killed him, right?"

"Yes!" I yelled.

She stood in shock, and after a few seconds, she asked if I was serious. I explained to her the truth of what happened that night—that the Man in Black, the one who injected me with Flakka years ago, killed Sarah's husband.

When she heard me say this, she began to laugh at first. My head was down, but after about seven seconds of laughing, she looked at me again. Her laughter stopped, and when she saw my face—the sad, powerless look on it—she knew in that moment I was telling the truth.

"Oh my god, you're telling the truth. I... I'm sorry, James."

"It doesn't matter."

"Of course it matters."

"No, it doesn't. I'm never going to find that guy, so sometimes I just feel like killing myself."

"No, don't say that, James. Why don't you let me help you?"

"Oh, now you want to help me?"

"James... please."

"Why did you leave me alone after all these years? I thought you loved me."

"I do, babe, you know I do."

She tried to touch my face, but I pulled her hand away. Celia then put her face down for a few seconds, only to lift it again and explain to me why she did what she did.

It wasn't because she stopped loving me, but because she was having a crisis—between helping me and keeping her sanity through all the pain and misery going on in Smart City. She also explained that she did her best to stay, and it wasn't her intention to abandon me, but she felt a complete struggle between what she wanted and what she needed to do.

That's why she left Smart City and went back home. What's more, she tried to go back to her old life and house again, but her house was gone. She decided to move to New York and tried to find different jobs, but nobody wanted her, so she found work as a stripper as a way to survive.

After she explained to me everything that happened over the years, I felt bad for her and wished that I had stopped thinking less about myself and more about her. What's more, she began to have tears in her eyes, and I felt bad about all the things I'd said to her.

She said, "It doesn't matter."

"Sure it does."

She looked at me and smiled. She had a napkin in her hand and wrote on it with a pen she had in her purse, then gave it to me. It was her new phone number: (212) 158-9132.

I said to her that I couldn't, but she insisted. I explained to her that because I'm a fugitive, it could risk Sarah tapping it and put her life, as well as mine, in danger.

So she wrote on the other side and gave me her address. She explained to me the times when she leaves and comes back—that she stays home from 12:50 a.m. to 3:30 p.m. and leaves at 4:00 p.m. to go back to work.

In that moment, I wanted to stay and be together with her, but I knew that would be impossible and could risk her for aiding and abetting a wanted fugitive. When I explained that to Celia, she told me she didn't care.

I told her that I do care, but I also explained that I could still visit from time to time, but not for too long—at least not until I find the Man in Black.

"You really think you're going to find the creep in black, James, on your own?"

"It's a long shot, and I know it's a long shot, but it's all I've got."

Then she gave me a kiss on the cheek and said, "It's not all you've got."

Then Celia got out of the car and said to me, "If you're in any trouble, babe, just remember—you're not alone."

"Thanks, babe."

"And remember, if you're in any trouble, I'll be there."

I smiled at her, and she smiled back and left for her apartment.

Sometimes being happy is one thing, but being free is another. And until I find the Man in Black, I can never truly be happy or free. But I will never give up, because I have a lot to lose—and everything to prove.

# XXXIII

# THE NEEDLES

Well, that was one of both the most intense and best days of my life. I never thought I'd see Celia, and what's more, I never thought I would see family members after all these years. After being alone for so long, I wish that none of this would have happened.

However, nobody can change the past, but they can change what they do with it. Sometimes grief can either be a sign of despair or a sign of growth, but what I'm afraid of is that my despair is nothing but despair and not growth.

Sure, I'm back with my family, but only for the short term, because long term I have no choice but to go back being alone and find the Man in Black. I still don't know who he is or where he is; what's more, I'm afraid I'll never find him or be cured. But that's a journey for another day.

When I returned to the mansion after bringing Celia and those girls back home, I was both happy and sad at the idea of meeting her, knowing that it's only for a short while because of the life I live. I don't know if I'm strong enough to accept that.

And what's more is when I returned to the mansion and went up those stairs, it was one of the strangest experiences of my life. Sometimes I wondered if I could go forward after meeting Celia and knowing that it won't be easy to say goodbye again.

What's worse is the more I doubted that I would ever be with her again, the more it drove me tense at the idea—to the point of anxiety—so much so that I could hear D.'s devilish voice coming back to haunt me, saying, "You'll never see her again, fool. You will be with me now and forever."

He started laughing and insulting me, calling me a fool every single moment. I heard nothing but his voice, and it was driving me insane. When I went upstairs I saw a picture frame of Buck with his father and mother, who passed away when Buck was born. I imagined my old life—me, my father, mother, and sister—along with Celia in the picture, and a tear dropped to my eye. I screamed with a loud voice and smashed the photo. When I realized what I did, I gasped in shock and started to break down to the floor.

What's more was after I did that, Buck yelled, "What's wrong?"

He rushed upstairs and saw me crying on the floor in pain. He came to me and asked if I was okay, but I wouldn't answer. I just lay there with tears in my eyes.

"What happened, Jimmy?" said Buck. I looked at him with tears and anguish on my face, but I still hadn't spoken. Buck looked at me with an empathetic face and said, "What did they do to you, Cuz?"

Then I finally spoke and said to him, "Everything." Buck came to me and started to hold me with a hug and spoke.

"I'm right here. We're going to figure this out."

"I don't want to go back. I don't want to lose you guys," I said.

"It's all right. We're a team, Jimmy. I'm never going to let you go."

"I can't do this anymore."

"Yes, you can, Cuz."

"I'm drowning, Buck."

"It's okay, Jimmy. Let yourself go. I'll pick up the pieces."

"What's the point, Cuz?" And then Buck said something that I will never forget—his words resonated big time with me: "I thought the same thing too, but you didn't give up on me and I'm not giving up on you."

"That was many years ago, Cuz."

"But your words still helped me and you saved me when I was done living."

After hearing that I wiped my tears and slowly got up from the floor. He said to me that he may not know all the answers, but he knew that I am loved and that he and many in my family don't want me to give up but want me to live.

"For what, so I can suffer forever?" I asked.

"No—so you can stop suffering, so you can be free."

"But it's too painful, Buck."

"Pain is a moment, an hour, a day, or even a year or a decade. If you quit, it's forever."

He then explained to me that if I die, then we'll be the ones who will suffer forever as well. So I shouldn't give up, not for my sake alone but for all the people I care about. No matter if I'm alone or with somebody, I need to remember there are people who love me.

"So live. Don't give up, Jimmy. You're almost there," said Buck.

Then I smiled and said, "Thanks for helping me, man."

"Always, Cuz. Always," said Buck.

A few seconds later I heard footsteps upstairs and Uncle Walter asking if everything was okay.

Buck told him, "Everything's okay, Dad."

"Well, tell James that I've got work for him tomorrow."

"But Dad, he just came from work."

I looked at Buck and said, "It's okay, Cuz. I can handle myself," and I told Uncle Walter that I would accept. Buck and I smiled, got back on our feet, and went back to my bed.

"Thanks for giving me strength, Buck."

"You gave me strength, Jimmy, and because of that you gave me wealth. I owe you everything."

"I owe you for giving me strength."

We both smiled and said good night to each other, and that was something that seemed like a sign that things would get better. For myself, even a short-term moment can motivate me to go on when things get tough. I owe Buck for that, even if I win or lose this fight to gain my freedom.

The Next Day

I wonder what could happen if I let my pain consume me and let it twist me up. Sometimes I wonder if it's possible to have a peaceful life or even a peaceful death, but now I'm questioning everything that I went through.

But I have something to prove in this world, and even if it's all for nothing and I'm never going to find the Man in Black—or I'll find him and he'll destroy my chance to be free—at least I'm back with the people I love, and I never thought I'd come back.

When I decided to come back to my family after living five years in the East, I never thought I could survive. I was wrong, and I went back home with my family, which is even more than I could hope for.

Even though I returned to my family and they brought me back some good memories, I knew if I stayed they'd risk gambling with their lives just to save my ass, only to see me leave again. So what's the point other than going back to the nightmare of living as a wanted fugitive, all alone and with no future?

I know living with my cousin won't last forever and it could risk bad things happening to him and many in my family if I stay—just like when I met Uncle Walter at a restaurant in Manhattan. I had a suit on at the time and Osiris drove both of us to that place, saying he had a new job for me and he didn't want to say anything except to me.

At first I was wondering what was going on, but I knew when to keep my mouth shut because I knew it was important. I wondered what it could be; my guess was it had something to do with business, but little did I know.

When we finally went to the restaurant, Uncle Walter told me to keep my voice down because he was afraid someone would hear us. When I heard this I was thinking, What have I got myself into?

A few minutes later Uncle Walter paid about a thousand dollars so we could get upstairs and have the best seats and the best food they had—so much so that we also saw a huge banquet and were given some of the biggest and classiest foods I have ever seen and some of the cleanest windows and shiniest plates I have ever seen. I couldn't believe that this was for me and my uncle, as if I shouldn't even be there.

After we received our food, I saw Uncle Walter's face go from kind and soft-looking to something more serious and tense.

"Are you okay?" I said.

"I'm fine. Just keep your voice down."

"Okay, okay."

Uncle Walter looked left and right to see if anybody was hearing or watching us. When he didn't see anyone, Uncle Walter explained to me what was going on.

"Nephew, you know that we helped you and we know that you used to be a freedom fighter, right?"

"Yeah."

"And you've fought against Linda Smith, right?"

"Where are you going with this?"

"Just hear me out."

"Okay."

"I need you for a job."

"What kind of job?" Uncle Walter explained to me that he needed me and only me because he said that I have what he called special skills on how to take down a handful of people. He wants me to meet them.

"What do you mean?" I asked.

"I mean I need you to meet up with a few people."

"Who are they?"

"A couple of crooks."

"WHAT?!"

"Shh... Look, I need you to be quiet."

"Why are you asking me to meet up with criminals?"

"Because you're one of them, right?"

"I'm not one of them and you know that."

"Yeah, but they don't know."

"But why even meet with them?"

"Because they're trying to blackmail my son."

"Blackmail for what?"

"They know he's a little... um... different."

"What do you mean different?"

"Well... um... they... um... they want me to be part of their criminal organization by making illegal drugs, but I refused, so they want to embarrass my son in front of the whole world to see."

"What could that possibly be?"

"I think you know, James."

"Know what?"

"That he's gay."

"What!"

"I said be quiet!"

"How?"

"One, it's because I'm his father, and two, I'm not stupid."

"But when did you know?"

"Since he ran away to the woods when he was just a kid."

"Then why didn't you tell him that you knew?"

"I didn't want him to feel bad and I felt I should wait for him to tell me."

"But why didn't you tell me this before he told me?"

"Wait—he told you before he told me?!"

"Hey now, who needs to be quiet?"

"Don't get cute with me, nephew."

"So... you want me to go after a bunch of criminals to protect your son's name?"

"Well, yeah."

"I'm not no hitman, Uncle Walter."

"But you are family, right?"

"Yeah."

"And you would protect your family, right?"

"Yeah."

"Good. Now I need you to take this." He had a huge briefcase and when he opened it he gave me a medium-size bat and asked me to use it to go after one of the members who is blackmailing Buck. He said he would do the rest when he takes that punk to him. When I saw that bat I wondered what I was getting myself into, but if this is the only way to help my cousin I would do anything.

Uncle Walter explained to me that one of those guys who are black-mailing Buck is a member of a gang called the Needles and his name is Vincent Casper Valentini, but he goes by Vinny. He's at a flea market in Long Island, he has a tattoo on his cheek, and he usually smokes a joint with his right hand.

"Okay."

"Are you sure you can do this, nephew?"

"I've survived worse."

"That's good to hear." Then he asked me to shake his hand and I did. To be honest, I never wanted to go back and fight a bunch of criminals again, and I never thought I would ever meet up with more criminals since I took down Linda Smith with the Rebels years ago.

When I decided to be part of my uncle's world I thought it would be a place of privilege and peace, but instead I found myself in a dark world filled with gangsters—and to think that peace for me would ever happen in this world.

After we were finished discussing our plan for me to get one of the members of the Needles, we paid for our food and left the restaurant. Little did I know Uncle Walter already had a car for me to drive to Long Island—not a limo, but a minivan that I would use so I could blend in with the crowd as another customer or something.

I knew that this was going to be a big task, but little did I know that this would unwittingly let me get closer and closer to finding out who the Man in Black really is.

One Hour Later

After my meeting with Uncle Walter I drove to the flea market and looked everywhere for this guy. I focused on his description so much that I almost had a car accident while driving around searching for this punk, but luckily nobody was injured and the car drove off.

When I finally parked and entered the flea market I looked for this guy to see if he had a tattoo on his cheek or if he was smoking with his right hand, or even the fact that he looked pretty scary and tough, but the crowd prevented me from seeing clearly.

About twenty minutes of looking around, it seemed like things were getting hopeless to the point that I decided to leave and return to the car. But when I was walking away I suddenly had the feeling to turn back and see one last time if he was there—and to my surprise, he was.

I saw a guy exactly how Uncle Walter described him: he had the tattoo of a needle on his cheek, smoked with his right hand, wore a muscle shirt and dark blue jeans, and reminded me almost of Snake Eyes.

When I saw the guy I went back to confront him and said, "Mr. Valentini?"

"What's it to ya?" he said.

"Walter Meyer says hello."

"Shit—stay away from me!" Then he slapped me on the face and started running away like a bitch. I started chasing him, and boy, it was one of the most dangerous risks because the more my heart started beating trying to get this guy, the more I felt the Demon trying to get out and wanting to tear this slippery bastard apart.

He started pushing other people out of the way and sometimes using them as human shields so I could bump into them while he tried to escape. I managed to get closer and closer because of my training as a revolutionary back at Smart City.

While the chase was going on I started feeling myself getting dizzy after running and jumping for a handful of minutes. I couldn't believe this guy could run that fast without breaking his lungs, but who am I to judge his running.

When I finally got close enough to grab him by his shirt, I used all my body weight to jump on him and pushed him down to the floor. He turned and started kicking the living shit out of me while trying to get me off of him, but I managed to subdue him by knocking his head on the cement.

At first I thought it was maybe D. who used my anger against me to crack this dude's skull, but either way I was worried because I saw blood coming from his head and it started squirting on my hands. At first I thought I killed him, but I checked his pulse to see if he was still alive—thank God he was. He was still a mess physically and who knows how long that was going to last.

When the chase was over a bunch of security guards started chasing me. I realized that I needed to leave with this guy fast, so I grabbed him, held his body on my back, and started running while tired but scared shitless.

It was one of the most dangerous risks I almost had to go through, so much so that I nearly decided to drop this guy off me so I could run for my life. But if I did, who knows what he would do next with a bunch of criminals like him after knowing it was Uncle Walter who sent me. So I kept running faster and faster with him on my back while the guards ran even faster after us.

Then I thought it was over for me until I suddenly saw a limo, and to my surprise it was Osiris. At first I thought I was seeing things, but when he yelled, "Get in!" I then realized that he was really there and I also knew that this was going to be tough but I had no choice. I looked at the window and used all my strength and speed to squeeze through and broke into the limo by breaking through the window.

"Jesus Christ, Mr. Truman."

"Just drive, dammit!" I yelled.

And then we finally drove away from the flea market and never saw those guards again. Thankfully, nobody surprisingly called the authorities.

Thirty Minutes Later

After I escaped from the flea market, Osiris drove us to the mansion and blood was squirting all over my suit. I was worried if I could even let my uncle see me with blood on me and wondered if Valentini was even alive.

I asked Osiris if he had a napkin and he looked around and gave me a handkerchief instead. I covered his head while applying pressure to stop the bleeding, and after a few minutes the bleeding stopped and we managed to get into the mansion. Osiris and I yelled for help.

Then Uncle Walter came and we both carried this guy and checked for his pulse to see if he was still okay. He told us that he was still alive and if he kept bleeding he would die. After he told me that we grabbed a chair and tied him up. Then Uncle Walter asked Osiris for a bucket and filled it with water and he did. Uncle Walter splashed water at Valentini and he woke up.

"What the hell is going on!" yelled Valentini.

"Hey asshole, look at me," said Uncle Walter. "Did you kidnap me? Wasn't there security at the flea market?!"

"Yeah, but I managed to outrun them," I said.

"Quiet, James. Now listen, Valentini, if you ever go after my son again, I'll kill you."

"Ha—when I get out I'll kill you." And then Uncle Walter slapped the guy in the face and told him to shut up. At that moment I was shocked to see him become so aggressive and I wondered what he had become—so much so it was almost like he was another person.

He kept slapping him and I was afraid that he was going to kill him, so much so that I grabbed him by the arm and yelled at him, "What is wrong with you?"

"Let go of me!"

"Uncle Walter, stop—you're killing him!"

"I won't stop until he stops."

Then Valentini started to laugh with blood coming from both his head and his mouth and he told us something that I never thought was going to happen: "Wow. You don't know, do you?"

"Know what?!" I yelled. "We're already coming after him, morons."

"Who?!" yelled Uncle Walter, but Valentini still wouldn't answer. Uncle Walter asked him again.

He said something that brought chills down our spine: "Your son."

"What?!"

"While you three clowns came after me, we're already planning on going after him!"

"You miserable piece of shit—I'll kill you!" yelled Uncle Walter. He then slapped him so hard that the chair fell down along with Valentini, and Uncle Walter asked Osiris for a pistol. I asked Uncle Walter what he was doing but he still wouldn't answer, so I asked him again and he looked at me with a bloodthirsty look in his eyes and told me to go find my cousin.

"So you want me to look around for Buck while you kill this guy? Are you out of your mind, Uncle?"

"Number one, he's at his boyfriend's mansion and number two, it's either this sack of crap or your cousin!"

"Uncle Walter, please don't do this."

"Tick tock, James. Tick tock!" I looked at Valentini and Uncle Walter for a few seconds and I just threw my hands up and said, "Okay, I'm going."

"He lives around midtown. You'll see his mansion there; it's the only mansion there."

"I understand." And then Uncle Walter asked Osiris to give me a gun. It was a .38 revolver and he gave it to me and spoke, "Okay. Now go!" At that moment I wondered what I had got myself into, but then Valentini started screaming and begging me to not let Uncle Walter kill him and he said to me, "You can't do this. If you kill me my friends will find you three. Don't do this, please don't do this!"

"You should have thought of that before you screwed with our family."

"You can't do this!"

"Oh yeah? Why not?"

"Because...because..."

"Because what!" For a few seconds he wouldn't answer and Uncle Walter kept pressing me to go. I decided to leave.

"Screw you, heartless maniacs!" yelled Valentini.

I went outside and while I was going to drive the limo, I heard a gunshot and I turned and knew that Uncle Walter killed him. I wondered at that moment what I'd got myself into, but all I knew in that moment was to save my cousin Buck Meyer.

# XXXIV

# THE TRUTH

After my uncle killed Valentini, I rushed inside the limo that Osiris picked me up with and drove like a complete nutjob, hitting everywhere and everything while honking to get people out over and over again.

The more I started thinking about Buck and what those thugs were going to do to him, the more I could feel The Demon coming out. The more I drove while thinking about Buck, I could hear him calling my name while trying to control me, and while I was sweating with the fear that Buck might be dead already, I blacked out.

The next thing I knew, I opened my eyes and realized that I was suddenly close to a huge mansion, and the limo was completely useless after getting all bumped and broken, with smoke coming from the engine.

When I smelled the smoke, I freaked out and admittedly jumped out of the vehicle and hit my chin on the solid ground. Then I turned and saw the limo burning. In that moment, I had flashes of the day my life was completely destroyed when The Man In Black killed all those people and framed me for it, but after a few seconds of staring at the limo, I managed to shake it off and tried to run my way into finding Buck. When I looked around, I couldn't find a single mansion and wondered where D. sent me, only to realize that I was lost.

At that moment, I put my knees down and wondered what he did to me because I was now lost and didn't know any way to find the mansion. Without the limo, I was completely lost.

To my shock, I realized where I was and couldn't believe it because I thought D. put me somewhere far away randomly, but it turns out that I was in midtown. I couldn't believe it at first and asked myself how he knew, only to hear his voice again telling me that he never left me. At that moment, I covered my ears, and when I finally put them down, I got up and ran to try to find the mansion.

About three minutes of searching and running to find a single mansion, I managed to see one far away and wondered what I had gotten myself into. I rushed towards it with all my strength and speed.

When I caught up to the mansion, it took me about five minutes to get there. When I touched the door, I started slamming it and yelled for Buck's name.

"BUCK, ARE YOU OKAY?!?!" I yelled.

Yet nobody answered. I tried again and yelled,

"BUCK, IT'S JIMMY! PLEASE OPEN UP!!!"

Nobody answered, and my whole body was so freaking stressed out that I started hitting the door with all my strength. When that didn't work, I started to kick it, hoping that it could create a hole so I could dig and get inside.

"BUCK, OPEN THE DOOR!!!" I yelled with no answer.

After seconds of trying to enter the door with no avail, I almost gave up, but thinking of Buck being hurt, I started hitting the damn thing with all my strength and weight. After about four hits, I managed to create a crack in the door, and I started hitting that crack over and over until finally the door broke, with pieces flying inside the mansion.

I then got my hand inside and tried to open the door, and I managed to do so. When I got in, I saw that the mansion was having a party, the music was still on, but the people inside were all dead.

I said to myself, "Oh my god, I'm too late."

I rushed inside hoping to see anyone alive and went everywhere, but the whole room was filled with blood. I knew that I was too late to prevent this because I had blacked out and let my demon take over me.

But I didn't give up and tried to find any survivors, even though it seemed hopeless. Then I went upstairs, and all I saw was blood. In that moment, I thought to myself that it was too late, and there was nobody alive.

After failing to see anyone who survived, to my surprise, I heard the sound of someone crying. I searched for that sound and asked,

"Who's there?!"

"Stay away from me!" said the survivor.

"Buck?"

"Please don't hurt me!" In that moment, I heard the person hiding in a closet, crying.

Then I said to the person, "It's okay, I'm not going to hurt you."

"They took him, they took my boyfriend!" said the stranger.

"Who?"

"Buck... Buck Meyer."

"You're Carl Miller."

"How do you know me?"

I opened the closet and told him that it was because I'm his cousin and I'm trying to find him. I then asked Carl where they took him, if he knew, and Carl said that they were taking him to the docks so they could drown him in the ocean.

"You know where this place is?" I asked.

"Yeah," said Carl.

"Drive me there, please."

"Are you crazy?"

"What? You love him."

"Yeah, but I can't do anything. Even the authorities are bought and owned by those gangsters."

"But I can."

"Yeah, right. How?"

"I...I'm trained for this."

"You're an officer?"

"Something like this."

"And your Buck's cousin?"

"Yeah."

"Wait a minute. You're James David Truman. You're a wanted fugitive."

"Yeah, and I'm trying to save your boyfriend and my cousin."

"You really think you can take those guys out?"

"Trust me, I've seen worse and I'm still standing."

Carl looked at the bodies and may have wondered about Buck and if he could even survive. Out of complete desperation, he decided, "The hell with it," and said,

"Okay, but how are you going to save Buck?"

"I used to be a freedom fighter. I know how to fight back, but first, do you have a car?"

"Yeah, but why?"

"I need a ride."

"I... Um... I—"

"You're a miserable coward. Do you even care or realize what is happening?!"

"Okay, okay, but I'm not going to get shot."

"You're not going to get shot. You're going to drive."

"Okay."

"And don't even think about calling the authorities because I'll know."

"Okay, okay."

"Ready?"

"Yeah."

"Let's go save Buck."

We both rushed downstairs and went outside for Carl to drive me to the docks. I still had the gun in my hand, cold as ice but waiting to be hot like fire to see those thugs get what was coming to them.

FIFTEEN MINUTES LATER

After Carl and I agreed to go to the docks to save Buck from those blackmailing kidnappers, we slowly started to speak to each other while

I drove to the docks to get Buck back. One of the first things I asked was how he met Buck. At first he wouldn't respond, but after a minute of convincing him to talk, he opened his mouth and said, "In college."

"Pardon me?" I asked.

"We met at college. At first I didn't really like Buck, but I slowly grew to know him better."

"How did that happen?"

"I was a bit of a jerk and felt nobody could understand me."

"What made you think that?" Carl looked at me like I was an idiot and then I realized his reasons were exactly like Buck's. I responded, "Oh... sorry."

"But he helped me so much," Carl said.

"So you like yourself now, right?"

"Yeah."

"That's nice."

"So what about you?"

"What about me?"

"You know, besides being a..." I couldn't finish.

"A wanted fugitive, public enemy number one, the American Osama Bin Laden?"

"I was going to say, do you have someone you love?"

In that moment I nearly choked up, crying, but I managed to get the strength to answer without breaking. "Yeah. She's... um... her name is Celia."

"You sound like she's not your girlfriend anymore."

"Maybe she's not."

"I'm sorry, man."

"Yeah, but it's better this way. Still, I would prefer none of this had happened."

"You sound less like Osama Bin Laden and more like Saint Francis. Are you really the guy?"

"Yeah, but I didn't kill those people."

"Then who?"

"A man whose chances of me finding him are beyond my reach."

"What's his name?"

"I... I don't know, and maybe I will never know."

While we were talking, Carl pointed and said, "There—that's the docks."

"Well, let's go," I said.

"Are you sure?"

"Are you serious?"

"Damn right I'm serious. I have no shooting skills."

"Okay. So stay in the car. I'll take these suckers out."

"With that tiny gun?"

"I had experience with multiple guns and shots and killed multiple thugs. I'll find a way."

Carl looked at me with concern and said, "Good luck." I nodded and got out of the car to confront those bastards.

When I went to the docks and searched around looking for them, it took a long walk to find anything resembling Sicilian gangsters. If I saw a guy in a suit, I would shoot him without hesitation because I wasn't going to risk my life just to save a potential gangster.

After a minute or two of looking, I started to get nervous about not finding Buck and wondered if this was the actual place where they were holding him. Then I saw a black van and thought, If Buck is inside that van... I rushed to check while trying not to be noticed.

When I finally put my ear to the van, I heard screams from inside.

"Buck?!" I asked.

"Help me please, someone help me."

"Buck, is that you?!" he said.

In that moment I tried to open the truck, but it was locked. I told Buck I'd be back, but he started begging me to stay. I told him again that I was coming back, then I went to the front of the truck and found nobody and the keys were gone. I didn't know what to do.

I found a crowbar inside, but the window was closed, so I needed to break it. I used all my strength to smash the glass to reach in and grab the crowbar. Glass cut my hands and blood poured out, and pieces of glass embedded in my skin. I almost let D. out, but my will to save Buck kept him at bay—at least for that moment.

I grabbed the crowbar and started trying to pry open the back door while telling Buck, "It's okay, cuz, it's okay!"

"Please just let me out," Buck pleaded.

"Don't worry, man... I'm so sorry for letting this happen."

"It's not your fault, Jimmy. Just help out and we can talk about this later."

While I worked to open the lock, I finally did, and joy overwhelmed me. I thought I might save my cousin even though these barbarians were around. Suddenly I heard a gunshot that nearly hit me, tearing through the van. It was one of the Needles.

"That was just a warning. One more move and you're a dead man."

They told me to drop the crowbar. I put my hands behind my head and went down on my knees. A man hit me in the head with his gun and I fell to the floor. One of them told me that because I'd come trying to save Buck, I had to watch him die. Another gangster opened the door, and I yelled, "Run Buck!"

"I suggest you shut it, bitch!" said one of the Needles. "Please don't hurt him. Kill me, not him!"

"We are going to kill you—just not yet. You both will see each other in the next world."

They started laughing at me and Buck. One of them grabbed Buck out of the van and he struggled.

"Take your hands off me!" Buck yelled.

The man who had his hands on Buck got annoyed. Buck bit him on the hand and started to run. I yelled for Buck to keep running. The guy who was bitten turned, pointed a shotgun at Buck and shouted, "You asked for this, yak cocksucker!"

Buck was shot in the leg and blood poured out. They started laughing and mocking him for being gay. In that moment I was enraged and started to let the demon take over. I began to scream and scream and everything went dark. The last thing I heard was the chorus of multiple men screaming all at once.

## Ten Minutes Later

Some things are better left unknown, especially to my family. What's worse is for them to see a side of me that nobody in my family has seen and to realize they might reject you if they know what kind of person you are. That's exactly what came next.

When I regained consciousness I heard my heart beating louder and louder and only remembered bits and pieces. I did know the aftermath of what happened when I came back.

To my horror, I saw what D. did to those guys. They were all killed and their bodies were tortured, turned into some kind of sick experiment I'd never seen before: skulls exposed, skin ripped open, severed heads and arms tied up with belts, eyes cut and shoved into mouths—belts covered with skin like a blanket. Some bodies twitched although they weren't breathing. I nearly vomited at the sight and wondered what D. had done.

Even though I was shocked, with blood and guts all over me and my hands dripping with human blood, I turned and saw Buck and Carl looking at me. They stared as if frozen, like statues. I tried to talk to them, but as I got closer I saw tears on their faces and sweat pouring down. Buck started to gag and vomit.

"Buck!" I yelled.

Carl grabbed my arm and started crushing it with all his strength. "Don't you dare touch him, you freak," he snarled.

"Hey, easy, man—you're crushing my arm."

"Don't come near us, you sick maniac!" Carl shoved my arm away and I fell to the floor. Carl tried to calm Buck while Buck continued vomiting.

"I've just saved you two," I said. "Saved you from throwing your lives away with this freaking shit."

"What would you have us do?" Carl demanded.

"Get Buck and leave."

"You told me to save Buck," Carl said.

"Yeah, while not turning these gangsters into some sick, twisted science experiment."

"It wasn't me," I said.

"What?" Buck demanded.

"It wasn't me!"

"Of course it was you, maniac!"

"IT WASN'T ME!!!"

I started to shake. When Buck finally stopped vomiting, he asked, "Then who was it?"

I was too ashamed to answer at first. "Jimmy, then who was it? Because there's only one person here who did that crap!"

"Buck... I... um..."

"You better answer because now the rest of them are coming for us and it's all your fault."

"Buck, you have to understand—"

"Understand what? What did they do to you, Jimmy?"

Buck started to get sick again and vomited. Carl looked at me with fear and anger and Buck terrified me. I realized they were right to be terrified. I put my head down and told them everything: how ten years ago I was infected by a drug called flakka, how a man in black injected me and how that drug created a dual personality—one that I recognized as James Truman and the other that was The Demon.

I explained that the Man in Black framed me so the world believed I'd killed many people in that fire he sabotaged years ago and that he'd killed Patrick Barton, making it appear I was the killer. I told Buck about the endless nights of fire, the nightmares, and that the Man in Black was the only person who knew how to help me get rid of the Demon. I'd spent ten years hunting him down and had finally had some clues.

When I finished, Buck said, "Why are you telling me this now?"

"You wanted to know, right?" I asked.

"So you're after this Man in Black for what he did to you ten years ago so you can find peace. Right?"

"Yes."

"And you don't care whose life you've ruined in the way, right?"

"No!"

"Then what?"

"I... I just... I wanted to go back to who I was before."

"Right now, Jimmy, there's no going back to what you were before."

"Maybe... but we need to go."

"Like this?" Carl asked, looking at my clothes. I realized I couldn't go out covered in blood, so I needed a plan to dispose of the remains and change. "I'll take off my clothes after I put the remains in the river," I said.

"You won't be wearing any clothes at all in the van, so don't expect to get my clothes," Carl said bluntly.

"I know. So can I take out the remains?"

"Knock yourself out," he said. They grabbed the bodies, drove away, and dumped them into the river. I kicked the remains and threw them down, then stripped and threw my bloody clothes into the water. Buck went with Carl to the mansion while I took the van and followed because they were still afraid of me, even though I'd told them everything and they had seen I was sincere.

We drove about twenty minutes and finally arrived back at the mansion. I was naked and tried to hide like Austin Powers.

When we got upstairs, I was the first to knock on the door. Osiris opened and saw me with no clothes and said, "Good lord, Mr. Truman!"

"Can I take a shower?" I asked.

"Um... y-yes. Is Master William safe?"

"I'm okay, Osiris," Buck answered.

"Okay... now let us go inside."

Carl, Buck, and I all went inside  and I went to take a shower.

# XXXV

# THE HOTEL

For the past ten years, I've lost friends and family, but I never thought, and never wanted, to see them see me in such a blind rage that would slaughter people regardless of being good or bad. To see my cousin and his boyfriend see me as some kind of maniac demonstrated exactly why a flakka-infected fugitive shouldn't be too close to the people I love—or anyone—and why The Demon inside me must be destroyed after I capture the Man in Black. But the question is when.

Sometimes I honestly question if I could ever find him, but also at times I wondered if he's even real. Maybe if I had run away when I was 20 years old, none of this would have happened. I wouldn't have been raped, and I wouldn't have had to join the resistance. But most of all, I wouldn't have had to spend ten years of hell searching for the Man in Black.

But those questions and what-ifs would have to wait, because after all that had happened, and after I tortured and slaughtered the members of the Needles, Buck, Carl, and I went back to the mansion. I tried my best not to be seen and rushed inside so I could take a shower. When I did, I was freaking out almost to the point of anxiety about the whole thing. When the water sprinklers were on my face, I started having strange visions of what happened at the docks. These flashes were from

D's memories, as if he was trying to tell me something, and I almost fainted while covering my face, laying on the tub.

After a few minutes, I slowly gained the strength to get up and get out of my fetal position. When I was done taking a shower, I grabbed the largest towel I had ever seen and thought to myself, *This is ridiculous.* While I was about to dry myself, I heard a loud knock on the door. I covered myself, opened it, and saw Uncle Walter.

"Hi, Uncle Walter... Um, what did you do with Valentini's body, anyway?"

Instead of answering, I was shocked by a flash of light and a brutal pain on my left cheek. I realized the feeling was from my uncle, who punched me so hard and fast that I couldn't see it coming.

"Why did you hit me?!" I asked.

"No. What happened? And what did you do?"

"What are you talking about?"

He punched me again. I wanted to hit back but couldn't because he was still my uncle. I had never seen him this way before. When I saw his eyes and remembered what happened at the docks, I soon realized what he meant and why he was punching me. But I didn't know what to do—if I told him every detail, he would never let me come anywhere near his son or me again because he would see even worse than what had happened when he and I were in Hong Kong.

"My son has been vomiting for nearly an hour. What happened?"

"I can't tell you."

"Tell me, or I'll call the authorities."

"NO."

"I'm sorry, what?!"

"Please don't call them!"

"Then tell me what happened back there, nephew."

"I... I... I... Um... I... some of the Needles got gutted like fish."

"What are you talking about?"

"I killed them."

"You killed them?"

"But I may have tortured them too."

Uncle Walter's face turned pale, like he had seen a ghost. He looked terrified and asked, "You tortured and killed members of the Needles?"

"Yes."

"Get out."

"What?"

"I SAID GET OUT!!!"

"Uncle Walter..."

"Don't come back. You've just risked us all, and now these gangsters are going to kill us if we stay."

"You're... you're leaving New York?"

"Because of you. Now get out."

"Uncle Walter, please understand."

"Dress up and get out."

Listening to my uncle talk the way he did, and knowing he meant every single word, I knew I couldn't stay anymore. Because of D's actions, I had no choice but to go alone again and watch my uncle and my cousin disappear from my life forever. A minute or two later, I knew I couldn't stay and that Uncle Walter had made up his mind.

I still tried to reason with him. Even after I came out of the bathroom and dressed, we started to argue about me staying or leaving. Buck, who was still sick and traumatized, saw the whole thing.

While he watched, I begged my uncle not to let me leave, and Buck tried to defend me, but Uncle Walter told him to stay out of it. I told Buck not to raise his voice.

"What do you know about having a son?"

"Nothing, but I know how to have a cousin."

"I don't need to hear this."

"Uncle Walter, please."

"Why did you do it? We were just supposed to save Buck and escape. That's it."

"You really think they wouldn't kill us if I didn't kill them?"

"Yes, I do!"

"Wrong. If I didn't kill those guys, it would have gotten even worse."

"Well, we may never know, do we?!"

"Yes, I do, because I'm not a coward who lets his nephew do his dirty work."

Out of nowhere, Uncle Walter hit me again. In that moment, I finally said screw it and punched him in the cheek and nose. We started to wrestle. I bit him in the hand, and Buck jumped up, trying to tell us to break it up. Uncle Walter yelled, "Get out now, you miserable w—"

"Miserable what? Miserable what, you freaking piece of—"

"HEY, ENOUGH!!!" yelled Buck. "Buck, I... I..."

"Calm the hell down, just go..."

"What, you too?"

"Please, Jimmy. We'll talk about this tomorrow."

"Where can I go?"

"To hell, that's what!"

"Dad, enough!"

"Look, Jimmy, me and Carl will take care of this. Just... just go."

Thanks to the way he said it, I slowly began to calm down. I worried about making things worse and didn't want Buck to get too involved. I told him, "Okay... see you soon, cuz."

"Just go to one of the closest hotels here. I'll find you."

"Okay."

Buck gave me a couple hundred dollars from his pocket so I could get a hotel. In that moment, I decided to leave and hoped things could get better, but I seriously doubted it.

## Fifteen Minutes Later

When I paid for the hotel and went upstairs to room 101, I decided to rest on the bed. However, I felt terrible about the whole thing. The more I thought about what happened, the more I began daydreaming about the fight with my uncle.

The more I thought about it, the more guilty I felt, like I had done something wrong. Even though it wasn't completely my fault—I had no control and couldn't even remember what happened—it was still my anger that led to all of this. What's worse, I hadn't blacked out when I confronted my uncle, which really got to me. I nearly choked up because I felt like I didn't belong anywhere and was losing my own identity.

The more time I spent in the hotel, the more I knew things would get worse because now I was alone and didn't know what to do with myself. I felt like I shouldn't be too close to anyone—not even my family.

While all of this was happening, I heard thumping sounds coming from somewhere. At first, I thought it was just a couple having sex or something, but then I heard a voice that sounded like a woman screaming for help. I went to the door to check, like a dumbass, not knowing if I could get killed by some thug.

To my shock, the scream sounded very familiar. I didn't know exactly who the woman was until I finally saw her face. It was Celia, dragged by her hair by some thug while screaming for help, the thug threatening to rape and skin her alive.

When I realized it was Celia, I ran toward the guy, jumped him, and started kicking and punching him repeatedly with all my speed and strength. I could feel The Demon coming out again; my hands were shaking from the thrill and smell of blood.

While I was beating him, I heard Celia trying to stop me.

"James, stop! It's over!" she yelled.

But I wouldn't answer. I kept punching and kicking. For about three seconds, I was about to black out and let D. rip him apart. Celia came closer and yelled in my ear, "STOP!"

I turned and almost slapped her but stopped at the last second, remembering what I had done to her years ago. Instead, I lowered my hand and saw the blood on me; my hands were shaking from the whole experience.

Seeing my hands covered in thick red blood, smelling it, and remembering the experience with the Needles freaked me out. I was about to leave, perhaps even try to kill myself, but I couldn't take any more of this nightmare. Celia stopped me and tried to convince me to stay.

"I'm sorry, babe. I can't," I said.

"James, it's okay."

"It's not okay. None of this is okay."

"What are you planning to do?"

"I'm going to end this."

"What?"

"It's better that I die."

"Like hell you are."

"Get out of my way, Celia."

"I SAID GET OUT!!!" I yelled. "No, I won't let you kill yourself."

"What do you want me to do, babe?"

"I want you to stay."

"What about this piece of shit on the floor?"

"I'll call 911."

"What?"

"Just hide, and I'll call the authorities to bring this sack of crap to jail."

Then out of nowhere the piece of garbage who attacked Celia opened his fat mouth and said, "Hey, hey, hey, I'll pay, just don't call the authorities."

Then the moron reached for his pocket and had a few hundred dollar bills. Celia snapped and grabbed the money from his hands and shredded it into pieces and threw it in his face. "Get out!" yelled Celia.

"Why? I was about to pay instead."

"I don't want your money, you piece of shit."

"No, you listen here, bitch," he said.

"No, you listen here, bitch—go jump in a lake, or I'll call the authorities."

"Do you know who I am, you slut?"

"I don't give a shit, tu hijo de gran puta!"

"Really, bitch? I'm one of the freaking Needles. We own the authorities."

I was shocked to realize one of the Needles was here after D. had just slaughtered some of the associates. I nearly freaked out, hoping this piece of shit wouldn't call the rest of the Needles after Celia and me. I didn't know whether to kill him or let D. take over and slaughter him in front of Celia.

Three seconds later, I yelled, "GO!"

I started acting like a wild man, kicking him repeatedly while screaming "GO!" over and over. He ran downstairs, limping, and I yelled, "NEVER COME BACK."

I turned and went to check on Celia to see if she was ok. She looked at me with so much emotion in her eyes. We realized how low we had sunk and how our lives had been turned upside down.

We went inside my room, held hands, and stood there together. We began a romantic dance, and slowly we began to smile, and we began to laugh then when we both we're finished dancing we both looked at each other then we kissed and the rest was history.

Sometimes I question my life, but I never questioned my love for Celia. Despite everything, I never lost my soul with her, and I never will. When love is real, love is forever and I will keep that in mind for the rest of my life.

There were times that I felt alone and abandoned. What's worse, I even felt forgotten, but not just by my family—by all the people that I left or left me. Do I have regret? Of course I do. Hell yeah, I have regrets, but not in meeting others, but in myself and the thought of losing someone, becoming another memory.

But after Celia and I had sex in the hotel bed, we held on together with our hands, and the first thing I noticed was I heard a voice. I didn't know who or where it was coming from. At first, I thought it was that Needles thug, but I slowly realized it was the voice of a female.

"Who's there?" I asked.

"James!"

"Who's there?"

But no answer came except her calling my name. I got out of the bed and slowly walked, little by little, to where the voice was.

"James! Help me!" said the woman.

"Who's calling me? Who are you?"

When the voice got louder, I got closer, until I hit my head against the door and realized it was coming from outside the room. I unlocked the door and went outside, only to suddenly find myself back on the farm many years ago. I looked around and thought, *What the hell is going on?*

Suddenly, I heard the voice again. It was clearer and louder than before. I rushed toward it, and when I heard the woman again, I realized her voice sounded familiar. As I ran faster and faster toward the voice, I could feel the walls closing in more and more, and everything was getting slower and slower.

While all of this was happening, I thought to myself that this couldn't be happening—or maybe it was another hallucination created by D. As I wondered what was going on, I suddenly heard the voice again. In my heart, I knew who she was, but in my mind, I couldn't believe it. It was the voice of someone I hadn't heard since I was a kid. To my shock, it sounded a lot like my mother.

"James, help me."

"Mother?"

"James, he's going to kill me!"

"Who?"

But no answer came. I started to slowly speed up from this nightmare—or hallucination—and the walls began to push back. I finally managed to push through this hell I was in and went to her room. I finally saw her. What's more, I realized my body had somehow turned into that of a child while I saw my mother again. I couldn't understand how this was even possible, but I didn't care. I even broke down in tears.

"James?"

"Mom?"

"Oh, my teddy bear."

I rushed toward her and hugged her. "How is this even possible?" I asked.

"What do you mean, baby?"

"I... I thought y..."

Suddenly, my joy turned to horror when I saw The Man in Black coming up behind her. I was about to tell my mother to get out, but to my horror, my mouth was gone. I realized I couldn't speak.

The Man in Black got closer and closer. I tried to warn her, but I was helpless. While she smiled, the man was there, and I kept pointing at him, but she didn't notice. Each time I begged her to turn, she just smiled and said nothing, while tears filled my eyes and my voice remained muffled.

Suddenly, she turned, and The Man in Black tapped her on the shoulder and stabbed her in the head. With a muffled and mouthless voice, I screamed and screamed. One of the last things I heard from her was, "He killed me because of your grandparents."

Then I woke up back in the hotel with Celia and realized the whole thing was just a nightmare. I was confused. Why would I dream of my mother telling me The Man in Black killed her, and why because of my grandparents? To be honest, I thought it was just another stupid nightmare, but it felt more real than previous nightmares. I couldn't help but feel that it really was my mother's ghost. Worse, I felt too scared even to think about that horrific experience of reliving her death at the hands of someone I'd been chasing for ten years. I asked myself how I could even dream of something so horrible unless it was D. screwing with me again.

Whatever the case, I went to the bathroom and splashed water on my face. When I finished, I got a towel and washed my face to slowly take all the anxiety from my body. Suddenly, I noticed something strange about the mirror. It was kind of blurry, and I didn't understand why or what was causing it.

Then, suddenly, the water went from cold to hot, but there was nothing steamy in the bathroom or its surroundings. When I went to dry my face, I suddenly jumped as if I were electrocuted when I saw the demon looking straight at me, jumping out of the mirror. He grabbed me by the throat, pushed me back toward the mirror, and slammed my head.

I was so scared and felt like I was really losing my mind. There was nothing I could do. After I got slammed, I started cursing obscenities and began to sweat heavily. Then I felt someone tapping me on the arm. I raised my arm to punch whoever was tapping me, but I realized the person I was about to punch was Celia. The whole thing was just another nightmare.

I was in shock to realize she was there. When I saw her face, I knew she looked scared, like I was some kind of monster. I backed off from punching her. She saw me sweating with bloodshot eyes and asked, "What happened, babe?"

"I... It's nothing, babe. I... I just had a bad dream."

"Are you okay?"

"Yeah, sure, babe. I'm fine... let's just go back to sleep."

After that, Celia and I laid our heads down on the pillow, but then we heard a phone call and wondered what was going on tonight. I reached for the phone and said, with a rude tone, "What do you want?"

"Jimmy, please help!"

"Buck?"

"Jimmy, I think the Needles are in the mansion!"

"What?!"

"They're coming for both me and Dad. Help!"

"Okay, I'm coming!"

Celia asked what was wrong, and I told her that the Needles were coming for my uncle and my cousin, Uncle Walter.

"What happened?"

"Someone screwed with the Needles."

"What kind of dibshit screws with those gangsters?"

"I'm the dibshit."

"WHAT!"

"We need to get them away. We need to go somewhere and disappear."

"Where?"

"I don't know, but we need to get out of New York fast."

"Okay."

"Do you trust me, babe?"

"You know I do, babe, but I don't know about this, James."

"They're my family, Celia. I owe them everything."

"Okay."

"What time is it?"

"5:50 a.m."

"You got a car?"

"Yeah."

"Okay, let's go."

Then Celia and I dressed up and drove to the mansion.

Fifteen Minutes Later

Celia and I drove to the mansion. When we finally got there, we rushed to the door and started knocking over and over, hoping Osiris would help. I even yelled for him to come out and let us in, but he wouldn't answer.

The more I tried to get in, the more hopeless and scared I became, because I really thought it was over. Then Celia told me to get out of the way. She took a paperclip from her pocket.

I asked her, "Why didn't you tell me?"

"I didn't know it was going to be locked," said Celia.

"Are you serious?"

"Just let me open it, James."

About a minute or two later, the door was open. We went in, and the mansion was dark. Celia and I tripped over something, only to realize it was Osiris. When I realized he was on the ground, I checked his pulse and saw he was still alive.

I kept looking around for anything or anyone, only to see Celia suddenly on the floor again. This time I knew something was very, very wrong. I checked her neck and saw a tranquilizer dart embedded in it.

"What the hell?!" I said in shock.

Suddenly, I was hit by something that felt like a bullet, only to realize it was another tranquilizer dart. My vision slowly went dim and blurry. About a second or two later, I fell to the floor and lost consciousness.

# XXXVI

# GLASNOST

Wow, that was a painful fall. I've felt many things in my life that were both weird and agonizing, but that dose of tranquilizer was completely strong, so much so that I couldn't feel anything. When I hit my head, I felt both the shaking in my legs and the agony of having knocked my head.

The day I woke up, I had no idea where I was or what even happened. About a minute or two later, I slowly remembered what had happened and jumped up, only to feel something preventing me from getting up—my hands were completely tied behind my back. What was worse, I saw Celia, Uncle Walter, Osiris, Buck, and Carl all tied up with me, both tied to metal chairs.

I realized that we were all tied up in a place that looked like an office. Nothing shocked me more than when I saw a man sitting in a chair, and I yelled, "Oh my god, it's the Needles!"

When I yelled the word *Needles*, everyone next to me awakened and realized what had happened. We tried to scream for the man to get away from us, but slowly I realized the man looked somewhat familiar. It turned out he was someone I hadn't seen in years—my long-lost friend Ivan Kovalenko.

"Ivan?" I asked.

"Hey, buddy," said Ivan.

"How... why... what happened?!"

"Take it easy. It's been a long story."

Celia jumped in and asked, "You better tell us now?"

"Okay, okay. You're here for protection."

"We've got enough protection already," said Uncle Walter.

"Tell that to the Needles."

"You got a reason why you've taken us here, sir, or whatever this is?" said Osiris.

"It's been a crazy story, Mr. Osiris," said Ivan.

"What do you mean?" I asked.

"After I found out who killed the Needles, my agency tried to find you."

"Uh... agency?" I said.

"Yes, old friend."

"Jimmy, you know this guy?" said Buck.

"He's a long-lost friend of my cousin."

"No, I mean, can we trust him?"

"I made friends with this man many years ago."

"Since when?"

"Since I met Uncle Walter in Hong Kong."

"You're serious?"

"Yep." Then Ivan interrupted and spoke.

"Now that we got that out of the way, can I finally answer your questions?"

"Yes. First of all, why are we here?" said Carl.

"And what kind of U.S. agency is this anyway?" said Celia.

"U.S. agency?"

"Yes."

"Ms. Mendoza, this isn't the United States. This is Europe."

"Europe?!" we all yelled.

"Yes," said Ivan.

"Which part of Europe? Romania or Italy?"

"Ukraine."

"WHAT?!?"

"Please understand, I only did this because it was the only way to protect you from the Needles."

"But why Ukraine? Why not somewhere in the United States? And how long have we been here?" I asked.

"Please relax, all of you. I'll explain, but I have good reasons."

"Then start talking, because we are not staying in some war zone!" said Uncle Walter.

"I am the owner of a secret agency called Glasnost."

"Okay, so?"

"With our intelligence, we were able to find James and save you all from the Needles."

"But we can't stay here, Ivan."

"Would you rather get killed by a group of gangsters?"

"I'd rather not get killed by a group of Russians."

"But James..."

"We're done here, Ivan. It's been nice to see you. I just wish you hadn't done this."

"I understand."

"Now, can you let us go?"

"Of course."

"LEE!"

When he said Lee, I realized the man was Lee Chen, another person I thought I would never see in a long time. When I saw him, he looked at me and said, "Hi, James."

"Lee?" Then he untied us all and spoke:

"You are all free to go, but Ivan would like to speak to James."

"The hell he would."

"Uncle Walter, please."

"No, James. This man kidnapped us."

"He didn't kidnap us. He was just trying to save us from those gangsters."

"But he didn't have to send us to Ukraine! It's a bloody war zone here, nephew, come on!"

I was about to walk away, but Ivan said something that would soon change my life—and his.

"I know how to get the Man in Black."

"Excuse me?"

"I know how to get the man who injected James with flakka and framed him for murder."

"What do you mean, you know how to—"

"Mr. Meyer, this isn't a criminal organization. It's a secret agency."

"I don't care what it is."

"Uncle Walter, please... What do you mean you know how to get the Man in Black?"

"If you help us, we'll help you. After all, you're a former freedom fighter, right?"

"Yes."

"And we are fighting for our freedom as well, and we need someone like you."

"You want my nephew to go fight in that war?"

"The government needs someone with his skills, Mr. Meyer."

"What are you planning, Kovalenko?"

"If James helps us, we would help him find the Man in Black at the same time."

"You can't possibly be serious," Uncle Walter interrupted.

"Dad, please just hear him out."

"Quiet."

"But Dad, if James wants us to find him, it's better than being alone."

"He's not alone."

"Yes... yes, I am alone," I said.

"But, nephew—"

"I can't stay with you all and endanger Uncle Walter. I can't do this on my own."

Uncle Walter said, "James, he's just using you for his government."

"No, he's a freedom fighter, just like I was, and a friend."

"But nephew, you don't know he can really do this."

"Come on, Uncle Walter. You let me confront the Needles before."

Everyone looked at Uncle Walter.

Buck said, "Are you serious?"

"Son, you must understand—"

"Dad, don't tell me you actually sent Jimmy to take on those gangsters!"

"I... I..."

"Dad, what were you thinking? He could have been killed!"

I jumped in the conversation and said, "I know how to defend myself, cuz."

"Jimmy, please."

"No, cut it. I'm not the same child that helped you years ago, okay? I was a freedom fighter."

"But Jimmy—"

"But nothing. Look, I know you're all trying to help, but none of you can help me find the Man in Black."

"But babe, you can't do this. You'll get yourself killed," said Celia.

"Celia, you were with me when I joined the resistance and fought that Linda Smith, right?"

"Yes, but..."

"And you were with me when I felt blue, right?"

"Yes."

"So, what's the difference between joining freedom fighters in a smart city and freedom fighters in Kyiv?"

"I... um... I..."

"Please, I know you're all trying to help, but I need to do this."

"I... I understand."

"I understand too," said Carl. "

I understand," said Osiris.

"I understand, cuz," said Buck.

Then Uncle Walter took a few steps, looked at both me and Ivan, and said, "I... I... I'll go along with whatever you think is right."

"Thank you all."

Ivan stepped closer and spoke, "Now that we have an agreement, anyone who wants to leave, my men will help escort you to Canada."

We all looked at each other. Uncle Walter said, "No thank you, Mr. Kovalenko. If my nephew stays and we leave, that will be unacceptable."

"So, which would you prefer?"

"We'll do our part and stay for his sake."

"Alright, Mr. Meyer. You will all be sent to one of Ukraine's best mansions under our protection."

"We understand."

"Now, James, I promise you I will never stop until we find the Man in Black."

"Thanks, Ivan."

"And remember, this war is about fighting for freedom, just like you've fought for freedom."

"I haven't fought for others for a long, long time."

"But now you will again, my friend, and it will be just like old times."

I smiled, giving him a hug. He said, "It's been good to see you again... Now, Lee, come here."

Lee came to us. We all hugged each other like brothers. I then asked Ivan a question.

"Yes, James?" said Ivan.

"How did you build all this?"

"Actually, James, since I regained all of my memories, I remembered that I was the head of Glasnost."

"What does Glasnost mean?" I asked.

"Well, Glasnost was inspired by Mikhail Gorbachev. It means openness."

"Okay, so why use it?"

"We use it as an insult because the Russian Federation today hates Gorbachev for his democratic views."

"You're joking?"

"Nope."

"So, you used Glasnost as a way to remind Russians how anti-democratic they are?"

"Well, yes."

When I heard that, I started laughing. Slowly, Lee and Ivan started laughing along with us too. Uncle Walter, Celia, Osiris, and Carl all smiled because they saw me happy and didn't want to erase my joy.

Little did we know, nothing lasts forever, and that includes joy. Now, after we all agreed on staying in Ukraine so I could find the Man in Black, I had also stayed to become a soldier against the Russian army. It seemed just like old times—only this time, instead of another revolution, I was a foreign volunteer joining the Ukrainian army. It felt like ten years ago.

# XXXVII

# FOG OF WAR

Myself and everyone else went to a giant nuclear bomb shelter funded by the Ukrainian government for their protection, and what's more, it could withstand any bombing that the Russians could hit us with—bulletproof glass so that the bullets wouldn't hit us.

The building that I was in, along with the rest of my family and friends, was huge, and it seemed like it was made by a billionaire, with tables, chairs, beds, food, and even a television set with a radio as well.

Everything was going well, and it seemed like nothing bad was going to happen at all, but to my surprise, that all changed when Celia kindly asked my family that she wanted to speak with me alone. They said, "Where?"

"Outside," said Celia.

"What?"

"Outside, please?"

"We can't go outside; there's a war out there!"

"I SAID GO!" Then I was shocked when Celia yelled at my family, and I asked her what her problem was. She responded with, "I can't do this, babe. I just can't do this!"

"What are you saying, Celia?"

"I'm sorry, babe. Can I live a life with you being chased by Sarah? But I can't do this."

"Are you breaking up with me?"

"Babe... I... I..."

Then my head went down, and I said to Celia something that I would later come to regret.

"So what, you wanna go back to being a stripper?"

Then she slapped me in the face and spoke,

"How can you say that to me?"

"How can you yell at my family?"

Then Uncle Walter came out of nowhere and asked Celia and me to knock it off, but I told Uncle Walter to keep out of this. Celia raised her voice again and told him to back off, and when she raised her voice again, I got mad and yelled at Celia to knock it off for yelling at my family twice.

"Don't you get it? I'm sick of living like this, Babe! I can't do this anymore!" yelled Celia.

"You're not the only one who is sick of living like this."

"Well, don't act like this is normal!"

"I never said that."

"But you think that you really believe that this is normal!"

And then I snapped and yelled with a loud voice, "HOW DO YOU KNOW?!?!"

She looked at me with a shocked look and said, "Babe, calm down, I know that..."

"KNOW WHAT IT'S LIKE? YOU DON'T KNOW WHAT THIS IS LIKE!!!"

"Babe, please."

"I'VE LOST EVERYTHING! I CAN NEVER HAVE A NOR-MAL LIFE!!!"

Then I turned my head and closed my eyes, trying to stop myself from breaking down with tears in my eyes.

"Babe... Look at me... Look at me, babe."

But I wouldn't let her look at me or even touch me.

"If you want to leave, just go."

"Babe... I..."

"Get out."

"James."

"Get out!"

Then Celia went towards the door and turned to see me along with Uncle Walter, Buck, Carl, and Osiris, and the last thing she said before leaving, which got me pissed off but, looking back, made me truly regret my decision to let her leave and not keep trying to convince her to stay, "I'm sorry, everyone... I'm so sorry."

"I SAID GET OUT!!!"

The last thing I saw was her face looking at me with emotion as if she was going to cry, and she shut the door. While all of that was happening, my own family looked at me like I was some kind of asshole, and Uncle Walter said to me, "What were you thinking, nephew?"

"What?!"

"You didn't have to go that far. Just, what were you thinking?"

Then Buck came to me and said, "Jimmy, that was really messed up."

"But she yelled at y'all, Cuz."

"Two wrongs don't make a right, Jimmy. She loves you. She was just stressed out."

"But..."

"But nothing. Have you ever considered what she's been going through after ten years?"

"I... I..."

"Now she's in a war zone alone, with bombs and bullets outside."

"Oh my God. You're right."

Then I rushed towards the door and went outside, trying to find Celia, and tried and tried while rain was pouring on me and the bombs were being thrown in the night.

"Celia, don't be afraid, I'm back."

But to my horror, I still couldn't find her. I kept searching over and over, but I still couldn't find her at all.

"Celia."

After five minutes of searching with bombs being thrown and no way of finding her in this warzone, I realized how low I'd truly sunk. I knew in that moment that the last time I would see Celia was with her leaving with tears in her eyes, and I only had myself to blame. Then I yelled with a loud voice in complete agony,

"WHERE ARE YOU, CELIA?!?!"

Then I looked at my reflection in a puddle of water on the floor and started to cry, screaming and screaming.

## THREE MONTHS LATER

Buck, Carl, Osiris, and Uncle Walter were trying to still live somewhat of a normal life during a time of war, even while living in a bomb shelter monitored by the Ukrainian government. As for myself, I hadn't really moved on since I kicked out Celia and said those regretful things to her.

I still have lots of regrets in my life, but I never thought I would sink this low, and every day I wish that I wasn't even born. In fact, if I had the strength, I would have killed myself and done it right this time.

As for the family, they were having the time of their life, maybe because of their wealth, which gave them great protection and peace during a war—just like Uncle Walter, who was now making business in Ukraine, while Buck lived very well with Carl, and they brought some of their friends to Ukraine. But before they could go, Buck asked them two questions: one about handling living in a war zone, and the other was whether they knew who James David Truman was.

Osiris was still living his life as the butler, showing tremendous bravery and loyalty to the Meyer family. In fact, he had been a good and faithful servant, but most of all, a great friend.

As for myself, I spent these three months as a foreign volunteer in the Ukrainian army. I still went by the alias Dale Nelson so I wouldn't be recognized as a wanted fugitive who had been on the run from Sarah Barton.

The first days in Ukraine were dreadful and scary because we struggled to go through the city of Bakhmut. I managed to handle it by seeing the war as another fight for freedom, just like I did when I joined the resistance—only this time, instead of Mark Talbot, it was Ivan Kovalenko, and instead of Smart City, it was Bakhmut.

We struggled to get through Russian forces, and some of us got killed. At times, we had to retreat to cities like the Donbass region and occupied Crimea. When we couldn't fight for days, the Ukrainian government told us we'd take a break for a few days and that another group of soldiers would come to battle in the war.

At first, I wondered why they did this in such a fight for survival, but little did I know, Glasnost told the Ukrainian generals that Ivan didn't want me to die. They allowed me to take a break for a few days along with the other soldiers to create the illusion of fairness. When I found out, I was furious because I felt like I was being babysat in the war and not really being a soldier.

When I returned to my family, I was still in my uniform and was surprised to meet some of Buck's friends: Daniel Davis, Billy Hopkins, and Wolf Trumbo. The rest didn't come because they were afraid of getting shot or bombed and knew who I was.

When they came, they all referred to Buck as "The King."

At first, I asked Buck, "Why do they call you the King?"

"Because I'm rich," he said with a smile.

"Oh," I said. And we both smiled and laughed.

Later, Buck and his friends were eating at a banquet inside the bomb shelter. He asked me if I would join, and I said, "Sure."

So, me, Buck, Carl, and the rest of Buck's pals were sitting and eating at the banquet. Everything seemed peaceful. I started to make jokes and talk about our time as a family. I even had the pleasure of learning more about Buck's friends' sense of humor—and boy, they were just as funny as ever.

One of them told everyone there was a time when Buck was at a party, drinking heavily. He noticed a dude he thought was Carl and touched the dude's chest. It felt soft and squishy, only to realize it was a woman who was just as drunk and horny as him. When Buck realized what he did, he started to sober up and tried to run away from the lady chasing him, screaming, "I'm Gay! I'm Gay!"

And everybody laughed, including me.

But while at the banquet, I started to have strange thoughts in my head. I could feel them but didn't know where they came from or where they were going. Eventually, I realized the thoughts were coming from D., and I began to hear his voice, strongly mocking me about losing Celia.

At first, I thought I could handle it because this wasn't the first time I'd heard voices from that evil bastard, but he kept saying her name, and I felt frustrated and terrified. I began to put my hands over my ears to stop the voices. Everyone at the banquet stared at me, concerned and embarrassed.

When Buck saw me gnashing my teeth and weeping, he became concerned for my wellbeing. He got up from his chair to check on me, and when he put his arm around me, I slapped his hand away and yelled, "Don't touch me."

Realizing what I had done, I started to break down, reminded of the time I slapped Celia many years ago. I wondered what kind of life I was living. When I saw Buck's face, not with anger or hate but with love and sadness, I started to break down further, saying, "I'm so sorry."

Buck realized what was going on. He slowly hugged me tightly, and all of Buck's friends came and hugged me out of compassion and sadness. Buck whispered in my ear with a tear on his face, "It's okay, Jimmy. Everything is going to be okay."

## FIVE DAYS LATER

Some things in life are a struggle, but for me, even when I thought it was impossible, there is no such thing. I suffered a lot in my life, but even though my flesh may fail, my God will never fail, and I know I can do this, even in times of grief and suffering.

Just like when I went to war in Bakhmut. When I first joined the Ukrainian army, I felt like nothing could scare or break me, because I had seen many things that once terrified me. I've seen many things that once terrified me. You can't break a man who's already been broken, so I thought this war would be a piece of cake.

But little did I know. When I entered Bakhmut and saw the woods and trees, everything seemed quiet. I wondered what I was even doing there, but how naïve I was. Five or ten minutes later, I was walking with my combat uniform and gun with tons and tons of ammo. Suddenly, one of my fellow soldiers, who was also the commander of the group, Nico Olek, was next to me along with the rest.

A few minutes later, I heard something. At first, I thought it was Russians, but it turned out to be just a few black birds. I turned and kept walking, but one soldier heard something and went closer. We saw a small ledge we had to jump from to get closer to the sound. A few seconds later, I realized what the sound was and yelled at the soldier, "No! Don't get your ass back here!"

He refused to listen. When he jumped off the ledge, he lost his legs and his life. Out of nowhere, shots were fired. The Russians were everywhere, with tanks displaying a Z logo, shooting and throwing bombs at us. I didn't know what to do. I thought this would be like the revolution Mark Talbot started with me, but it turned out to be a complete struggle, if not impossible to move forward.

Commander Olek told us to retreat. He grabbed me by the collar and told me to run. I did. While all this madness was happening, my heart was racing, and I was freaking out. I felt D. coming out and was afraid of letting him do something stupid and crazy again, so I decided to hide somewhere. I started to calm down and found a boulder to hide behind. It was tough and scary because I slowly began to hear D.'s voice laughing and mocking the hell out of me with so much hate and evil. I started to have visions of my past, and got so sick, I dropped my gun, went down on my knees, and screamed in a fit of rage.

When I screamed, I realized I made a big mistake. The Russians could easily hear me. The last thing I heard was D. laughing at me before vanishing from my mind. I began to freak out, hearing footsteps approaching faster and faster. Out of fear, I closed my eyes, believing I was going to die. Suddenly, someone was next to me. Instinct kicked in.

"Stay back!" I yelled, grabbing my gun and pulling the trigger. I killed the soldier. At first, I thought it was a Russian and it turned out to be the exact opposite. Little did I know it was Commander Nico Olek.

## TWO WEEKS LATER

Two weeks after I killed Commander Olek, Ivan told me this would be my last time as a Ukrainian soldier. He would suspend me from joining the army and return me to the United States. However, he would return me in a month to have enough time to find the Man in Black. I was emotionally devastated about killing Commander Olek and hadn't left my room in five days.

Buck, Carl, Osiris, and Uncle Walter were worried I might commit suicide. They wanted to so badly to help, but each time I pushed them away. They did the one thing that could prevent me from giving up my own life and that was to call Celia.

At first, she refused to come back to Ukraine, but Buck told her everything that had happened over the past three months: the time I searched for her, my breakdown at the banquet, Commander Olek, and every single detail. Celia teared up when he told her and agreed to finally come check on me.

When she arrived, I was drinking heavily with a gun next to me. In fact if my family knew the amount of alcohol I had in me, they would have called the hospital. I told them to go away, but they kept pushing for days. Each time I opened my room, I nearly pointed a gun at them to scare them away.

They knew I would never have shot them, but they realized in that moment that I was having a serious—and I mean freaking serious—problem. When Celia did come, I heard her knock on the door, and I said, "Leave me alone."

But with a sad and drunken voice, she knocked on the door again. I started to get pissed and yelled, "I SAID LEAVE!"

Then Celia began to speak, and she said, "Babe, it's me."

When I found out it was Celia, I couldn't believe it. In fact, I thought it was D. manipulating me again, but I felt like she was really there. I saw my gun and bottle and put them underneath my pillow. When I was in front of the door, I nearly choked up while opening it.

When I saw Celia, we both rushed toward each other and hugged, and I began crying, and so did she.

"I'm sorry, Celia," I said.

"It's okay."

"I looked everywhere for you, and I couldn't find you."

She looked at me with a kind and beautiful look in her eyes and told me that she would be there for me, and that everything was going to be okay. Then we kissed and went to the bed together.

Celia and I slept together. We kept looking at each other and even kissed each other while we slowly began to fall asleep. I realized that I hadn't had that kind of life for a very long time—pure happiness, even while bombs were being thrown in the air.

Sometimes I forget where and who I am, but I never forget her and how much I love her, even to this day. While I am here for the sake of my own love and the promise of going forward, I will never give up until I find The Man in Black, make him confess, and I'll be free at last.

After a few minutes, I slept and began dreaming about many things in my life—some made sense and others didn't. One thing that stood out was that I had another dream, or should I say nightmare, about the death of my mother and what happened after she died.

At a very young and sad age, I lost my mother. I was the one who had to bury her the day she passed away. In the dream, I suffered a lot, just as I did in real life, on my knees, after I saw her casket going down slowly, crying just like I did when I was a child. But one thing was different from my memories—The Man in Black was hiding next to a tree.

When I saw him, he waved his hand in a way that made it look like he was trying to tell me to catch him. I was furious and began to chase him as he ran away in the woods. I was absolutely furious. I ran toward him and began chasing him, and the more I did, somehow my body slowly began to morph back from a child to a teenager to a man every time a tree passed me.

Nothing shocked me more than when I finally caught him. I began beating him over and over, but he seemed to like it. The harder I hit, the harder he laughed. The more this psychopath laughed at me, the more I began to flip the hell out. I decided to grab his hat and throw it off him, as well as his mask.

Before I did, I heard a voice coming from his mouth that sounded very familiar. It wasn't the voice of a stranger but someone familiar. I never realized who it was until I realized he was faking his voice the whole time. He sounded a lot like Uncle Walter.

Then, after I heard his voice change from sinister and dark to southern and kind, I woke up from my bed sweating. I was getting nervous about the whole thing. Many questions about that dream came to my head: Who was The Man in Black? Did he really kill my mother? Could it really be someone like my uncle, or was I just having a bad dream and nothing else?

I then looked at Celia. The question about The Man in Black slowly turned my hopelessness to hope. I got up and washed my face while thinking about what I was going to do now and whether Ivan would really find me The Man in Black.

# XXXVIII

# Ivan Kovalenko

After Celia came back, she and I decided never to leave again and that we would fight this regardless of where we were or what we faced because we always knew who we were, and that's all that mattered. So we stayed together in Ukraine until Ivan found The Man in Black.

We came up with a plan: when he finally captured The Man in Black, we would call Sarah and tell her that her husband's killer was in Ukraine and that we would cooperate fully on how, where, and when we found him. And now that day was today.

With the help of my own friend, who runs Ukraine's biggest organization during the war against Russia, I went back to Glasnost after receiving a phone call from Ivan. He said to me, "Good news, James."

"What's the good news?" I asked.

"We got him."

"What?!"

"We found The Man in Black."

"You actually caught the vermin?!"

"Yeah, come inside."

I woke Celia and told her that Ivan finally got him, and she asked me, "Who?"

"The Man in Black!"

"What?"

"Patrick's killer."

"WHAT?!"

"Yeah, they've finally got him. I need to go!"

"But it's too early."

"I don't care. I need to do this."

Then I gave her a kiss and said, "Wish me luck, babe!"

After the kiss, I ran to meet with Ivan. It took me about twenty minutes to get there, and I needed to catch my breath from time to time. When I finally entered the building, it was huge and remarkably untouched by the war, almost reminding me of the building The Resistance used.

When I entered the building, I was having trouble finding Ivan because the building was so freaking huge, and I had trouble knowing where I was going. Then I saw a soldier who was guarding the place, and I told him that I was a member of Glasnost and that I worked for Ivan Kovalenko. The soldier didn't understand what I was saying, and things were getting heated. I thought there was going to be a huge and ugly fight, but then Ivan came and said in Ukrainian that I was with him, and he told me to walk with him.

After things cooled, I asked Ivan if he really found The Man in Black, because I still had my doubts after 10 years of trying to find him. He looked at me and said that he was sure it was The Man in Black. He reassured me that The Man in Black was there. In fact, he told me that he was in a cage underneath the building with two armed Ukrainian soldiers keeping an eye on him so he wouldn't escape.

Even though I was reassured, I asked him if I could see him face to face. Then he asked me,

"Are you sure, man?"

"Yes."

"Okay, but trust me, that psychopath has a big mouth."

"I know."

Ivan took me to an elevator, and we went down to the basement. When we got out, I saw two Ukrainian soldiers in uniform with guns, one on the left and another on the right. Nothing shocked me more than when I saw their prisoner.

I came closer to see for myself and confirmed that he was really The Man in Black, now in a cage. He had a truly miserable look in his eyes, but he was still wearing a ski mask and that damn stupid hat on his head.

When I saw him looking at me, I started to laugh and mock him over the irony of him being caught and caged like an animal.

"Look at you now! You took everything from me, you miserable son of a bitch!"

I kept mocking him over and over, saying things like,

"You took my soul; you took my life!"

Then he looked at me with the same cold-blooded look in his eyes, and it slowly turned to rage, as if his eyes went from black to red. He started to grab me by the throat, and I began to choke while struggling to get out.

The two soldiers, along with Ivan, started punching The Man in Black's hands, but nothing worked. One of the soldiers shot him in the hand without orders, and Ivan slapped the gun away from him.

"HEY!" I yelled.

"James, it's okay."

"It's not okay! I need him alive!"

"I know, I know."

Even though he got shot, he somehow found the strength to laugh. I yelled back at him to shut up, but he still laughed.

"It's not worth it, James. Let's go up."

"But what if he dies from the bullet?"

Ivan turned to the Ukrainian soldier and spoke to him in Ukrainian. Then he said to me,

"Let's go upstairs."

"What did you tell them?"

"I told them to send in a medic to patch him up."

"Thank you, Ivan."

"Of course, James."

After Ivan and I went upstairs, we went to his office. I was so happy and thankful for Ivan's help, but I was confused and shocked at how he found The Man in Black so fast. I asked him, and he spoke.

"He was here, in Ukraine."

"Are you serious?"

"I wouldn't lie to you, James. It's as if he was living here or following you."

"What a stalker, that lunatic."

Then Ivan told me that he was going to make a call to Sarah Barton to tell her that they'd found The Man in Black but didn't want to tell her that it wasn't me, because she wouldn't believe I was innocent. He said it in a way to make her believe it was me without mentioning me. When Sarah answered the phone, she said,

"Hello?"

"Mrs. Barton?" said Ivan.

"Who's asking?"

"Mrs. Barton, this is Ivan Kovalenko. I had friends who were interrogated by you over Mr. Truman."

"So, what? You want payback?"

"No, I want to help you."

"Oh really?"

"Yes, I have captured your husband's killer."

"What?"

"You heard me. He's in Ukraine. I have him in my basement."

"WHAT?!"

"Yes. I suggest you hurry, and I promise we will be cooperating on every level."

"Why should I trust you?"

"Because if you don't come, he will kill me."

"Okay... okay. I will send a few of my men to arrest him. Don't tell anyone else but me."

"I understand."

"And thank you."

"You are very welcome, Mrs. Barton, but please hurry. I don't know how much longer I can last."

"We are coming, Mr. Kovalenko."

"Okay, thank you, ma'am. Goodbye."

"Goodbye, sir."

Ivan hung up, and we did a high five, celebrating that we had finally got the bastard. We both hoped and prayed that we would make him confess and force him to make an antidote to get flakka out of my system once and for all.

We were really so happy about the whole thing, and I was so grateful for Ivan. While we waited for Sarah's men to come to Ukraine to finally arrest The Man who killed Dr. Patrick Barton, we talked about many things, including the days before we met, the day we met, and when we became friends. The part that got us interested was what happened to both of us over the years, but neither of us had the stomach to talk about that until Ivan said,

"So, what happened since the last time I saw you?"

"Are we really doing this, man?"

"What? It's okay."

"Okay, so tell me what happened to you?"

"I... I... Um... maybe we should talk about something else."

"I know the feeling."

"Okay, wise guy, I'll tell you. But after I finish telling you my story, you'll tell me yours."

"Okay. No problem, man."

"Good!"

Before we were going to speak, there was a knock on the door. Ivan said, "Come in," and it was Lee.

"Why is a medic here? Did something happen?"

"Something like that."

We both started laughing.

"No, seriously. What happened?"

"The dumbass in black got shot."

"What? How?" I jumped in the conversation and told Lee that The Man in Black was choking me, and one of Ivan's soldiers shot him to back off.

"Oh…" said Lee.

"Yeah. So… um… Lee?"

"Yeah, James?"

"Me and Ivan wanted to know what happened to us over the years. How about you?"

Lee turned pale and, with a nervous smile, said that he thought the medic was here and that he needed to go. And he did.

"Why is everyone so terrified to talk about what happened over the years?" I asked.

Ivan told me it's because it's not a happy story.

"Catch me up."

"Okay, James, but you're not going to like it."

"It's about the war, isn't it?"

Ivan put his head down, took a deep breath in and out, looked slowly into my eyes, and spoke.

"Yes."

Ivan then told me stories about what happened after Wan Po sacrificed himself to save Mike. He left, becoming a monk, went home to Ukraine, and worked in the war, only to back off for a time, but the Russians tortured and killed his friends and family—not his, but many of Lee's and many soldiers who lost loved ones. He said that he created Glasnost because he wanted revenge against the Russians. He spent years trying to work for the Ukrainian government to get revenge, and every single member of Glasnost lost a loved one to the Russians. In that moment, I understood and respected him even more for having the strength to keep going and honor those he lost.

After Ivan finished telling me his past, he asked me to tell him about mine. I was going to tell him everything, but Ivan told me to be quiet because he heard something inside the building that sounded strange.

"What's wrong?" I asked.

"I think there are shots being fired."

"There's a war going on, Ivan. Of course there are shots being fired."

"No, I mean close to us."

"Russians?"

We thought for a few seconds but stopped when we heard screams coming from inside the building. We realized it was coming from the basement and both yelled, "Oh God, no!"

After we heard the shots, Ivan and I rushed downstairs, sweating like crazy because we were so nervous and so close to capturing The Man in Black. We refused to accept that something could happen to change that.

When we got downstairs, instead of the elevator, we rushed so fast that we nearly slipped multiple times. When we finally reached the basement, to our shock, we discovered that the medic had been stabbed and that the two soldiers guarding The Man in Black had been shot. Nothing made things worse until we saw that The Man in Black was out of his cage. I couldn't believe this was happening.

Ivan went to one of the soldiers. He was dead. The other was bleeding to death and nearly unconscious, but Ivan shook him to wake him up so he could explain what happened. Suddenly, something that looked like a black hat moved. Then I realized it belonged to The Man in Black. But the hat began to move, and I realized it wasn't just a hat—it was The Man in Black, hiding with a gun in his hand.

I yelled, "Ivan! Get down!"

The Man in Black got up and shot Ivan, killing him. When I saw him dead, I went down on my knees and asked The Man in Black, "Why?"

He started laughing and said, "You'll see."

I charged him, but he knocked me out with his gun, and I fell to the floor.

# XXXIX

# ESCAPE TO NEW YORK

I was so close—so freaking close—to getting my life back. When the moment came when he knocked me out, I knew I was screwed, but I had no idea how screwed I could get. In fact, I wondered what could get worse. And it truly did get worse. Sometimes I wished I had been successful at taking my own life, but I couldn't, either because I was too weak to kill myself or because I was strong enough to keep going, even if it was all in vain. Whatever the reason, it didn't matter now.

The only thing that mattered was that when I got up and checked on Ivan, I realized he was dead. I wept over his body. I thought things couldn't get worse—but of course they could. And, in fact, they already did.

Next, a bunch of Ukrainian soldiers came downstairs after hearing gunshots. When they saw me with Ivan's body, they all accused me of killing him. I slowly begged them not to shoot me and explained it wasn't me, but they didn't listen or care. I kept pushing for them to understand, but they all pointed their guns at me. I knew I was screwed. Sarah was coming to Ukraine, and Glasnost believed I had killed Ivan.

They screamed at me to get on my knees or they would blow me up. I slowly lowered myself but didn't go fully down. I couldn't let my life end like this. Instead, I grabbed my shoe and threw it at them. They started spraying bullets at it as it flew overhead. I began to run upstairs, dodging obstacles, trying to escape. One of the soldiers noticed me getting away and told the others to chase me. I ran as fast as I could, bullets flying from all sides.

The experience was traumatizing. I had flashes of what happened to Ivan, which reminded me of what happened to Dr. Patrick Barton. The two experiences seemed to merge together. The more I remembered, the more pain I felt, as if I were losing both limbs. My heart was racing. In that moment, I knew something was going to happen, but I didn't know what to do. I felt like I was losing my mind.

The stress was awakening The Demon inside me. I screamed, "NO!"

About nine seconds later, I blacked out. The last thing I heard was myself screaming while bullets sprayed everywhere.

When I woke up, I was in a pile of rubble filled with guns, half-naked, and covered in blood. I truly believed I may have killed some of Ivan's soldiers. If I had, as The Demon, it was too late to fix anything. Whether it was a misunderstanding or not didn't matter. Sarah knew where I was, and The Man in Black had escaped again.

I knew that if I stayed to find him, I could very well be killed or, worse, continue searching in vain, only to have Sarah capture me and take me back to Smart City. I didn't know which was worse. Instead of choosing the lesser of two evils, I decided to wash myself of the blood stains, then return to the bunker and tell my family and friends that we needed to leave.

After about twenty minutes of searching for water in this godforsaken nightmare, I finally found a river. I washed my hands and clothes. Even though the blood was gone from my clothes, the smell remained thick.

I then had to navigate through bombs and shootings to survive. It took about fifteen minutes to finally see the bunker. It was far away, but I made it. I knocked on the door three times because nobody answered. Each knock grew louder. Finally, Uncle Walter came and said, "What's wrong with you, nephew?!"

He saw the sad and terrified look on my face, smelled the blood on my clothes, and his anger and confusion turned into fear and compassion as I started sniffling.

"James?" he asked.

"Help me," I whispered.

I shook and fell, but Uncle Walter caught me and began calling for help.

## FORTY MINUTES LATER

Buck, Osiris, Carl, Celia, and Uncle Walter were all there, mumbling about why I came back terrified, half-naked, and smelling of blood. They all stared at me as I lay on a bed with food and water in the building.

Celia asked Uncle Walter, "Why would James come back like this?"

I got up. "Because we need to get out of Ukraine. Now!"

"Easy, Jimmy, what do you mean?" said Uncle Walter.

"I... um... I..."

His concern slowly turned to fear. He stepped back, saying with a terrified look, "You've killed them?"

"No. The Man in Black did."

"That creep in black you told me about?"

"Yes."

"I don't know what happened, but Ivan tried to help, and The Man in Black escaped and killed him."

"But why do you smell like blood?"

"Because I blacked out while they all thought I killed Ivan."

"Jimmy, are you sure you didn't kill them?" asked Buck.

"Of course not, cuz. But I know who killed Ivan."

"Jimmy, this is bad."

"I know, I know, but you have to believe me."

"Look, babe, we believe you, but..." said Celia.

"But what?"

"We need you to explain more."

"Okay... Okay. After they started chasing me, I was in a place that looked like a bomb went off."

"You think it was the Russians?" said Carl.

"I don't know, but it could be."

"But if that's the case, Mr. Truman, how are you still alive?"

"I don't know... But I do know it's not just Glasnost coming for me."

"What do you mean?"

"Sarah Barton is coming to Ukraine."

"WHAT?!?!" yelled everyone.

"How?!" said Uncle Walter.

"Ivan came up with a plan to call Sarah so he could get The Man in Black."

"And you didn't say it was The Man in Black so she would believe you two?" said Uncle Walter.

"Yeah."

"Okay... oh shit... holy shit." Uncle Walter thought about the next steps. After a few minutes, he said, "We have to go back to New York."

"Are you serious about The Needles?"

"Who cares? We can't stay here. The Russians, the Needles, Barton—we need to leave now!"

I asked Celia if she would stay with me when we got back home. She smiled. "For you. Forever and ever, babe."

"Okay, let's go."

Everyone agreed we had to go back to New York. We knew it would be hard, with soldiers searching for us and Barton coming to Ukraine it would be very ugly and very hard to not get screwed either way. While trying to escape, we planned to take a train. Before we made it, some of Ivan's men tried to chase us, but we miraculously managed to get on and headed to the airport.

To our surprise, Sarah hadn't arrived yet, but we continued without anyone chasing us. At the airport, we saw the suffering in Ukraine, both inside and out. Everyone began crying as we looked out the windows. We held hands, saying, "Slava Ukraine," which means "Glory to Ukraine."

TEN HOURS LATER

We came back and walked around Manhattan. We looked at the buildings and saw some of the homeless people pissing around the streets close to Madison Square Garden. I looked around and said to myself, "God bless this shithole."

Then we all laughed. While we were in New York, we didn't have a car with us, so we had no choice but to walk from the airport to the mansion. We knew it was going to suck, but we needed to go along just to get over it. So we decided to suck it up and walk back. We began to walk together and had a lot of fun, talking about how we were feeling older and saying stupid things like how we had enough money to get a plane but not a car.

While we were having a good time, our feet were killing us, and we needed to take a break for a while. So we went to the restaurant where Uncle Walter told me to get Vinny Valentini. We decided that we needed to eat and drink, then go back to walking so we could get back to the mansion, and we did.

After about fifty minutes of eating, talking, and laughing, we went back to walking outside and talked about how much fun we had and so many other things. I'm a little emotional even talking about this now while writing because it was such a nice time. For the first time in a long while, it almost felt like I'd forgotten I was a wanted fugitive and instead felt like a normal human being.

But while we had a great time walking and talking, nothing was ever meant to last forever—not in this world. About an hour or two later, we managed to get to the mansion, but to our horror, we noticed that there were two men there. They looked suspicious, if not familiar.

In that moment, I went to check what was going on, but I stopped when I saw the mansion—only to see it burn.

"No! What have you done?!"

The two assholes started laughing. I wanted to beat them up so badly, but I didn't want to see my family's home burned to the ground. Buck, Celia, Osiris, Carl, and Celia all looked in shock, and they were all screaming for help. Then Buck came to me and said,

"Jimmy, who did this?!"

"They did!" I yelled.

Then Buck grabbed one of the thugs by the collar, and the other one was going to escape, but I grabbed him by the throat. We began yelling at them to tell us who they were.

"Who are you? Who sent you?" we spoke.

But they wouldn't answer. Then I saw pieces of the mansion coming apart. Buck looked at me and grabbed his phone while holding one of the thugs.

"Jimmy, get Celia, hide, and call 911. Let the four of us take care of these chumps."

"Sure, cuz," I said, and I went to hide somewhere along with Celia, next to the garden somewhere close to the house. There was a fence, so we could hide. Then I looked at the phone and called 911. I was shaking, and Celia knew I was too tense to talk, so she came to me and spoke.

"It's okay, James. It's okay."

Then she looked at me with a smile and looked into my eyes. She spoke again, saying, "Yes, I'm calling because there's a fire coming from—"

Then Celia flinched while standing there, and I got even more nervous.

"Celia... Are you okay, babe?" I asked.

Then she dropped the phone and fell face-first. I noticed a tranquilizer dart on her back, and she fell off me.

"BABE!" I yelled. I looked around while holding her, filled with so much anger, and said to myself, "Who's the miserable son of a bitch who did this?!"

Out of nowhere, I felt a stinging pain like I was kicked by a horse and went down as well. Before I did, I saw four men coming closer. I saw that one of them was Uncle Walter, but my vision was so blurry that I couldn't make out who the rest of the men were. All I could make out were Buck, Osiris, and Carl.

Before I was knocked out, I saw Uncle Walter bending down, looking at me. I tried to reach my hand to him, but I was too weak because of the tranquilizer in my system. I begged him with the little strength I had and said,

"Help me!"

But instead of helping me, he looked at me with his head turned to the side and said,

"Why should I help a miserable wretch like you?"

After he said that, I fell to the floor and was knocked out.

# XL

# THE TURNING POINT

When I woke up, I was dazed and confused. I had these voices coming from my head again, but it wasn't from The Demon; it was from my own mother, saying to me that she hadn't given up on me and that I should stay strong. When I heard her voice, I stood up in shock, only to realize I was chained like a damn slave.

But not only was I in a cage. To my shock, I was held along with Celia, Carl, and Buck, who were all knocked out. At first, I tried to wake them up, but they were too far asleep. I tried to break out of my chains, but I couldn't without feeling the pressure on my bones. I began to scream,

"HELP! SOMEONE HELP US!"

And nobody could hear us. I wondered where I was, only to realize that the place smelled burned, as if there was a fire. I realized I was in the mansion. Hours later, I began to wonder who could have done this, but then I realized the only explanation was The Man In Black. But The Man In Black was gone, so there's no way he could have done this.

A few seconds later, I realized that The Man In Black may not have shown himself, but his voice did—and it was through the mouth of my own uncle. Then I realized something: before I was knocked out, I saw a man coming after me, and I realized it was Uncle Walter. His voice sounded strange, dark, and sinister, the type that reminded me of The Man In Black. When he called me a miserable wretch, I realized something I should have known years ago: The Man In Black was Dr. Walter Philip Meyer—my uncle.

When I found out who he was, I knew who trapped us here. I stopped begging for help and started calling him out,

"FIGHT ME, YOU BASTARD! I KNOW WHO YOU ARE!"

Then, out of nowhere, I heard the sounds of clapping and footsteps coming down. At first, I thought it was him, but it turned out to be none other than Osiris.

"You?!" I yelled.

"Hello, Mr. Truman."

"Where's your boss?"

"The boss of me is me!"

"Don't give me that crap. Where's Walter?"

"Oh, you're not going to call him Uncle, sir?"

"He's no uncle of mine."

Then I heard another person laughing, and I was shocked to see someone I believed to be dead. There were two of them: one was Vinny Valentini, and to my shock, it was my former friend-turned-enemy Mike De Veny, whose face was scarred like it had been clawed.

"Hello, Robert Dent," said Mike De Veny.

"Or would you prefer Dale Nelson?" said Vinny Valentini.

"This can't be real. Both of you are dead!"

"Are we?" they said.

"I killed your mouthy ass in the ocean... and you, Walter, shot you."

They both started laughing. I got pissed and yelled, "STOP LAUGHING!"

"MAKE US," said both of them.

"How are you still alive, and why are you working with Walter?"

"Are you serious?"

Then they started to explain to me why they were working with him. They explained that Walter saved them after I tried to kill them, when De Veny had his face scarred and Valentini almost got shot.

"But how did he find you guys?" I asked.

They both smiled and said, "He didn't. He found you first."

"What do you mean?"

"You think you were finding him. He was actually finding you so he could break you."

"But why?!"

Then, out of nowhere, Celia, Carl, and Buck all woke up and began yelling, "HELP! WHAT'S GOING ON? HELP!!!"

Then a man came out of nowhere. There was the sound of gunfire, and a loud voice yelled, "SHUT UP!!"

"Why are you doing this?" said Buck.

"I said shut up."

"Why?"

Then I heard footsteps coming down, and I saw The Man In Black with his ski mask, along with his hat and black jumpsuit. For the first time, I saw him removing his mask. He revealed himself to Buck, everyone else, and me, and said, "Because I'm your father!"

"Dad?"

"Sorry I tell you this, son, but I'm only here for revenge."

"Revenge for what?!" I yelled.

"You really wanna know, your miserable wretch?"

"Get us off these chains, and I'll answer your question."

"Funny, but that's not going to happen, nephew!"

"Don't call me nephew, you son of a bitch."

"Would you rather be called a miserable wretch?"

"Shut your filthy mouth! You destroyed me and our lives! Why?"

"DESTROYED YOUR LIVES... WHAT ABOUT MY LIFE, NEPHEW?!?!"

"What are you even talking about?"

"You really wanna know."

"Yeah, I'm curious, Walter. What made you turn into a clown in black?"

"Okay, nephew, I'll tell you."

Walter then explained everything: how, where, and when he started doing this. He told me he wanted to destroy my life while pretending to be good. He told me his life was destroyed a long time ago, and that he wanted revenge because, for many years, he was raised in an abusive relationship by his parents—my own grandparents. They beat and molested him when he was just a child and treated my mother, her own sister, with respect and kindness. That made Walter feel both jealous and alone, so much so that one day he snapped, killing both his parents with poison, leaving him and his sister as orphans, and he began to live and grow up in an orphanage.

But Uncle Walter didn't just poison his parents. One day at the orphanage, he even poisoned a bully who had pushed him and turned his back on him. Walter yelled, "Don't turn your back on me!"

They fought, and Walter had a rock and slammed it on the boy's head, killing him. In that moment, Walter's hatred and darkness became a turning point in his life. He didn't just want to kill those who bullied him; he wanted to kill everyone he hated. Walter was slowly growing psychotic. He began killing little animals like dogs and pigeons, and he wanted to kill everyone in his family.

None of this shocked me more than when he revealed that he didn't just kill my grandparents, the kid, and those animals, but also the people burning in that building and Dr. Barton. To my shock, I realized why I was having those nightmares about my mother. I slowly realized that he may have killed her.

I then asked Walter, "Did you kill my mother?"

"Let me finish, nephew!"

"DID YOU KILL HER?"

Then he smiled and said, "Yes... Yes, I killed her."

"Why? She did nothing to you."

"Exactly. Where was she when I needed her?"

"She was just a child."

"She was complacent."

"All those murders just to get back at the few you're mad at."

"SHUT UP!!!"

"NO, YOU SHUT UP!!!"

I slowly began to struggle to get out of the chains to escape and jump on Uncle Walter, but then he asked Osiris for a gun and pointed it at Buck, his only son.

"If you try to escape, I'll shoot him dead."

"You wouldn't hurt your own son. You love your son."

"I do what I must, even if killing his gay ass."

"You... You knew?"

"Of course, I knew, son. Why would I think that Carl Miller of all people was just your friend?"

"Did you tell him, Jimmy?"

"No, I didn't, Buck... Just... Just put the gun down! You put the gun down!"

"Only if you back the hell off, nephew!"

"NEVER!"

To my shock, Walter then shot Buck in the stomach. I heard a blood-curdling scream from everyone—Carl, Celia, Buck, and even myself—screaming to the top of our lungs. I realized how far Walter was willing to go. He didn't care about anyone, not even his son. He always knew that Buck was gay and mocked him. I looked at Walter's dark and evil eyes and said, "Oh my God, you don't care about anyone, do you? Not even your flesh and blood?"

"I'm entirely capable of killing my own flesh and blood," he said.

"You've killed my mother, your own sister!" I yelled.

"I can't believe someone you could have trusted me so blindly! SHUT UP!"

"I had fun killing your mother. NOT as much as I had fun ruining your life."

"YOU SON OF A BITCH!!!"

Walter, along with Osiris, De Venny, and even Valentini, started to laugh maniacally. I tried to escape, but the more I tried, the louder their laughter became. I could feel The Demon coming out.

If there was ever a better chance to let him out, it was now. But I knew that if he came out, Walter could die. If I didn't let him out, I could die. Out of pure instinct, I decided whatever happens, I needed to get out and save my friends and family. I began to try to break the bones in my wrist. When Walter noticed, his laugh slowly went away, and his face started to get nervous.

"W... What are you doing?" asked Walter.

"I'm going to send you to hell, you miserable wretch!" I yelled.

I broke my wrist, slipped out of one of the chains, and tried to go after the others.

"STOP HIM! KILL HIM NOW!!!"

Within seconds, I was free of my chains and lunged, but I was blocked by Mike De Veny, Vinny Valentini, and Osiris. We started fighting with fists and kicks. I managed to subdue Valentini, grabbed a gun from his pocket, shot Mike in the knee, and killed Osiris. Mike and I struggled over the gun, bullets flying everywhere, while Carl and Celia screamed.

I knocked De Veny to the floor and was about to untie Buck, Carl, and Celia when Walter aimed the gun at me and yelled,

"Nobody move!"

I looked him in the eye and yelled, "You think I'm afraid of you!"

I snatched the gun from his hand and pointed it at my own arm. Everyone looked at me like I was insane. I said, "You think I'm afraid of you! I can take a bullet, do you seriously think I can't punch?!"

I could feel D. coming out of me. I was going to black out, but I didn't care anymore. I aimed the gun at Walter. He started shaking.

"This is for my mother... for everyone you've killed!" I yelled.

Then Uncle Walter showed me something I thought I would never see. He yelled, "WAIT!"

To my shock, he had a tube. He said it was something I had been trying to find for ten years. I slowly began to calm down and pointed the gun down.

Walter yelled, "Drop the gun, or I'll break this."

"The antidote."

"Drop the freaking gun, or I swear to God I'll break this shit!"

I pointed the gun back at him, believing he had more than one antidote.

"Why should I? You can just make another one."

"It will take 100 years to replicate something like this, nephew." He explained that this antidote was rare, made by flowers and other ingredients that no longer exist. He yelled, "Now, nephew, drop the damn gun!"

I didn't know what to do. If it was true, this could be my only chance.

"I said drop the damn gun now!"

"Okay... okay..." I said.

"Do it now!"

I was shaking with fear and anxiety. If I shot him, the tube would break. If I didn't, he could break it himself. I dropped the gun to the floor and said, "Okay."

Walter smiled and yelled, "Fool!"

"No! No!! NO!!!" I yelled as he smashed the antidote against the wall. I went down on my knees, crying, touching pieces of the glass.

Walter said to me, "See you in hell, you miserable wretch."

I got up and began to attack him, but he slapped me. I fell to the floor. Walter tried to escape, and I began to chase him, but then I heard Celia.

"James! Come here!"

I saw Buck was seriously injured, and Celia and Carl were tied up. I freed all three of them and held Buck slumping face down.

"You're going to be alright, cuz," I said.

"Thanks, Jimmy, but I'm too far gone."

"Don't say that. You're going to be alright."

"Jimmy..."

"Yeah, cuz?"

"Why does my father hate me?"

I couldn't respond. Buck started crying and bleeding out.

"Stay with me, cuz," Carl said. Celia began to break down in tears. Buck's final words were, "Does God hate me?"

He died. I was in shock. After ten years of trying to find The Man In Black, force him to make me an antidote, and make him confess, I failed. I knew that once I moved forward, there was no turning back. Celia slowly began to hug me, and Carl held onto Buck's body. I wept, and the more I wept, the more Celia held onto me, because now my own cousin was gone... gone forever.

## ONE WEEK LATER

Weeks later, Buck had a funeral, and it was revealed that Buck had written a will: a million dollars went to me. I was both shocked and saddened that he never told me. Things got worse when members of Glasnost came from Ukraine to the funeral to arrest me. Worse than that, Sarah—of all people—came as well, along with McNally and the rest of her thugs. I knew I had to hide somewhere fast, but I didn't know where, and I didn't know what was going to happen to everyone I knew and cared about.

I allowed my instincts to kick in and went upstairs to the top of the building to hide. Sarah began talking to some of the people, including Carl, about where I was. I was completely in conflict about letting Carl be arrested or turning myself in. Either way, I was screwed, personally or physically.

Sarah accused members of the funeral, including Buck's friends, of aiding and abetting a criminal from Smart City. I knew she was coming after me. She told the people, "A dangerous man is here, and I know you're hiding him!"

At first, everyone was terrified and disgusted, but no one was more disgusted than Carl. He came to Sarah and slapped her in the face.

"Don't you have any respect?!" yelled Carl.

"Carl, what are you doing?!" said Celia.

"Telling this red-haired bitch to get out of my sight, that's what I'm doing!"

Then Sarah started laughing, but she got really pissed and yelled, "GET HIM!"

The funeral erupted into violence. Many people were arrested, including Carl. Celia ran upstairs and told me it was a freaking mess downstairs and that they were arresting everyone, even Carl. She asked me to go with her and try to escape together, maybe even have a child with her, but I told her, "It's over. I don't want to keep running."

"James, we can go somewhere peaceful," said Celia.

"Peaceful? What's peaceful? Some candy-ass monk? Some candy-ass shrink?"

"James, don't get mad."

"Yeah, well it's the truth. Do you really think you can try to talk me out of this?"

"But you can't kill yourself. It's not going to bring Buck back."

"So, I'll join him. But hey, why do you care? For years, I was raped, injected, and tortured with no friends or family to help me, but then you came and abandoned me. You gave up on me and walked away!"

Celia put her head down for a few seconds, then lifted it and said with tears in her eyes, "You have to understand, I was going to lose you forever. I thought those doctors were going to cut you open. I couldn't handle that. I still have nightmares about it."

"SO, AM I!!!" I yelled. I refused to look at her.

She came to me and touched my cheek, trying to make me look at her.

"James… I… I'm sorry. I'm so sorry. Look at me, babe. Look at me. You have me, and I'm never going to leave you again."

"You don't know that," I said.

"Yes, I do… Give me a chance to make things right."

"Even if it was possible, it's only a matter of time before Barton finds me."

"She'll give up eventually."

"Oh, you don't know Barton then, because she'll never quit. I can't bear to lose anyone else to her."

"But I can't bear to lose you too, James."

"Why?"

"Why?!"

"Yeah, why?!"

"Because we're family."

"I have no family."

Celia smiled at me, a kind and beautiful look in her eyes.

"Yes, you do. I'm your family, and even though Sarah doesn't realize it, she's still your friend. If you kill yourself, she would keep thinking of you as her enemy forever. And who's going to get Walter? Do you really want him to win?"

"I want nothing more than to beat a confession out of him and make him cure me."

"Then fight, James. Don't give up, and start fighting. I'll be there to help you."

"That's impossible."

"Why?"

"Because I need to do this alone."

"James, what are you doing?"

She noticed me walking backward. She tried to help me stay, but I knew it would be both dangerous and impossible. I had no choice; I had to leave. The last words I said to her were, "Goodbye, Celia."

She ran toward me, yelling, "NO, JAMES! NO!"

Then I jumped off the building backward. She started crying because she believed I had killed myself, but little did she know, I never died. When she looked down, my body was gone. At first, I contemplated suicide at her home by threatening to jump off the building, but I stopped myself. I only wanted to really end my life when I saw Celia. Even though she wouldn't know for now that I didn't really hurt myself, I believed it was best to go alone again.

There was probably no way I could get my life back, but at least I now knew who The Man In Black was. After I jumped off, she continued crying and weeping, saying one word:

"No!"

Little did she know, I was actually holding onto the ledge, moving slowly down so I could run away and find Walter. The more she screamed and called for me, the more I could hear her cry, again and again, no matter how far I tried to go. I turned one last time and said, "I'll always love you."

And I went off to walk alone again.

## ONE YEAR LATER

It had been a long life since I abandoned everyone I knew and cared for. It made me believe that I should never have been close to anyone, and maybe I never would be again. What happens next would be a mystery, because I honestly had no idea what to do. All I knew was I had to find Walter Meyer, who I now knew was The Man In Black.

To protect myself from being recognized, I let my hair grow into long dreads and even grew a beard so that Sarah and McNally couldn't find me. Most importantly, I gave up on finding an antidote and instead focused on finding Walter. I realized that with the antidote destroyed, all hope was lost to get rid of The Demon—but hope was not lost to find The Man In Black.

After receiving one million dollars from Buck, I now went by the name Billy Davis, named after some of Buck's friends who were arrested the last time I saw them during the funeral. I decided to spend the rest of my life alone, accepting my fate and hoping I could do some good with the money. Maybe I could just keep going until the end, even with such evil inside me, and still do some good while I had the time.

My name is James David Truman, and whatever happens next, *Odyssey* will be the last Odyssey.

# ABOUT THE AUTHOR

Miguel Olmedo was born in Providence, Rhode Island, where he began his early life struggling with mental illness, and he has used his experience with it in the process of writing *City of Anarchy*. Since the year 2012, he is now living a happy and healthy life with his family and has now learned to let go of his past, and he gives thanks to God for giving him a blessed life, and he also thanks his family for believing in him in order to write this book. He also gives his biggest thanks to his grandfather, who believed very much in him, and he would love to dedicate this book to him.

www.ingramcontent.com/pod-product-compliance
Lightning Source LLC
Chambersburg PA
CBHW060949030726
47503CB00003B/789